MW00415876

I MIGHT
BE IN
TROUBLE

ALSO BY DANIEL ALEMAN

Brighter Than the Sun

Indivisible

I MIGHT BE IN TROUBLE

DANIEL ALEMAN

GRAND
CENTRAL

NEW YORK BOSTON

Copyright © 2024 by Daniel Aleman

Jacket design by Anna Morrison. Jacket illustration by Danielle Del Plato. Jacket photo of book by Adobe Stock. Jacket copyright © 2024 by Hachette Book Group, Inc.

Grand Central Publishing
Hachette Book Group
1290 Avenue of the Americas, New York, NY 10104
grandcentralpublishing.com
@grandcentralpub

First Edition: December 2024

Grand Central Publishing is a division of Hachette Book Group, Inc. The Grand Central Publishing name and logo is a registered trademark of Hachette Book Group, Inc.

The publisher is not responsible for websites (or their content) that are not owned by the publisher.

The Hachette Speakers Bureau provides a wide range of authors for speaking events. To find out more, go to hachettespeakersbureau.com or email HachetteSpeakers@hbgusa.com.

Grand Central Publishing books may be purchased in bulk for business, educational, or promotional use. For information, please contact your local bookseller or the Hachette Book Group Special Markets Department at special.markets@hbgusa.com.

Library of Congress Cataloging-in-Publication Data

Names: Aleman, Daniel, author.
Title: I might be in trouble / Daniel Aleman.
Description: First edition. | New York : Grand Central Publishing, 2024.
Identifiers: LCCN 2023054965 | ISBN 9781538766347 (hardcover) | ISBN 9781538766361 (ebook)
Subjects: LCGFT: Black humor. | Thrillers (Fiction) | Novels.
Classification: LCC PR9199.4.A398 I33 2024 | DDC 813/.6—dc23/eng/20240112
LC record available at https://lccn.loc.gov/2023054965

ISBNs: 9781538766347 (hardcover), 9781538766361 (ebook)

Printed in the United States of America

LSC-C

Printing 1, 2024

*This book is dedicated to you, if you are familiar
with one or more of these experiences:*

*1. Feeling alone in a crowded room
2. Getting something you really wanted, and then losing it
3. Waking up to find that the person you went out
with the night before is lying dead next to you*

A SLIGHT COMPLICATION

It's 6:47 a.m.

Staring at the numbers flashing on the clock brings an odd sense of comfort to my chest. The time is one of the few things I can be certain of—an undeniable fact, something to hold on to even in this moment, when I'm not sure I can trust myself or my own memory.

I'm foggy with exhaustion. Every inch of my body is protesting all the alcohol I drank last night. Nothing feels real, except for those tiny numbers shining in green. But then, unexpectedly, a million questions flood my mind: *What exactly happened? What have I done? How did I end up here?* It's this last question that grabs hold of me, that makes everything else take a back seat.

How did I end up here?

I never thought of myself as capable of killing someone, not even accidentally. I find it hard to believe I'm actually responsible for doing this, but I wonder how surprised other people would be if they could catch a glimpse of me right now. They might say they were able to see something in me all along—some sort of sign that told them David Alvarez was deranged. Some indication that he might just have the gall to end a man's life so unexpectedly, so callously.

Although, I realize with a small glimmer of hope, there's also the possibility that it's not callousness I've shown, but stupidity.

Yes, that seems a lot more likely. I've been stupid. Going out to meet this handsome stranger, agreeing to keep the drinks coming even when we were both wasted, bringing him back to my apartment—it was all just a matter of making one bad choice after another, wasn't it?

I wish I could take it all back. I wish I could return to twelve hours ago and stop myself from going through with any of it—but perhaps the string of poor decision-making that led to this moment began much earlier than yesterday. It may have begun in Stacey's office, during the last meeting I had with her. Or maybe even before that, when I started making all the mistakes that led to my career imploding.

How did I end up here?

I try to push the question away, all too aware that I'll drive myself mad if I keep attempting to answer it. For now, there are more important things to consider, much more urgent matters to occupy myself with, two critical facts I need to focus on.

It's 6:47 a.m., and there's a dead body on my bed.

PART I

CHAPTER ONE

An author much younger and wiser than I am now once wrote, *My legs are my favorite part of my body, because they take me anywhere I want to go.*

That's how it all began—with that one sentence scribbled across the back of a receipt for a BLT and a Diet Coke. Those eighteen words turned into eighty thousand, which turned into a book deal, which turned into the start of what should've been an incredible career. The writer in question was...well, me, except I no longer feel like him. I'm no longer the kid who had big dreams of becoming a published author, being on bestseller lists, and seeing the cover of his book staring back at him through bookstore windows all over the city.

Every single one of those things *did* become a reality, but I've learned the hard way that sometimes dreams aren't everything you'd made them out to be. Now, all I have is the memory of the words that got me further than I ever thought I would go, and these same old legs, which cramp up a lot more than they used to.

As I stare down at my thighs, I don't feel the strength I once did. I don't feel the urge to get out there, and chase after my dreams, and make things happen. I see nothing but a faded stain on my khakis that survived the wash—ketchup, most likely—and a slight trembling motion that only gets worse when I sneak a glance at the time on the dashboard and realize it's almost seven.

"Uh...isn't there a faster route we could take?" I ask the Uber driver.

"Sorry, buddy," he replies. "Map says we're already on the fastest one."

I lean my head back, letting out a long breath as I stare out the window at the red lights of cars braking all around us. I hate first dates. *Hate* them. I hate the back-and-forth on the apps; hate the first encounter when you don't know if you should go for a hug, or a hand-shake, or a polite nod; hate the boring questions of where you're from, and what you do for a living, and what you enjoy doing in your free time. Tonight, though, I mostly hate the anxiety of being late.

"Don't worry," the driver says to me. "We just gotta get through the next couple intersections. I'll get you there in no time."

Trying to keep busy, I open the camera app on my phone so I can take one more look at my hair. I swear, it always refuses to behave right before important events. If only anyone had seen me yesterday—I spent the entire day inside my apartment and my hair looked glorious, but tonight it's awfully poofy, as if I'd blow-dried it to add volume in all the wrong places.

I'm doing my best to flatten it, not shying away from using a bit of spit where needed, when the driver clears his throat.

"We're here."

"Damn," I say, my eyes still glued to my phone screen. I'm pretty sure I've only made my hair worse, and now I desperately need to look at myself in an actual mirror.

"Are you...getting out? I have another ride waiting."

"Sorry." I lower my phone. "Could you just...move the rearview mirror a tiny bit?"

"What?"

"The mirror. I need it real quick."

Staring at the driver from behind, I can tell he's frowning, but there's hardly any point in explaining what I mean—this will only take a second. I lean forward, sneaking into the gap between the front seats so I can get closer.

"Whoa, buddy, what are you doing?" he says, cowering back against the side of the car.

"I just gotta—"

"Get out!"

Flinching, I move back. I open the car door, and I've barely had a chance to step onto the sidewalk before he starts pulling away, the tires screeching as he drives off.

"I'll give you five stars!" I shout after him, but it's probably too late. I don't think he heard me.

With no time to waste, I turn around and walk straight toward a cloud of smoke that's coming from a group of women wearing high heels and expensive coats. I hold my breath briefly to inhale as little of the smoke as possible, and then I make my way through a set of glass doors.

I didn't know what to expect, but it certainly wasn't this. For a place called *the glory hole* (all lowercase), this is a lot classier than I thought. Golden candlelight everywhere, sleek high-top tables, and a fancy bar covered in crystal, behind which two obscenely good-looking servers are standing.

I spot my date sitting right in the middle of the room. Making one final attempt to flatten my hair, I approach him with as much confidence as I can muster.

"Shane?"

He looks up, and my first thought is *yes*. He's hot. Too hot for my own good, really. Caramel brown eyes, strong jaw, shiny blond hair—the kind you could run a brush through *once* and would end up looking absolutely perfect. As if I wasn't feeling self-conscious enough already.

7

"Hey," he says, smiling at me from the corner of his mouth. "Dave, right?"

"David," I correct him. "I've never thought of myself as cool enough to be able to pull off 'Dave.'"

I let out a small laugh, but he frowns in response. Noted—no more jokes. At least not until I've figured out his sense of humor.

"Sorry I'm late," I say as I take a seat across the table from him. "Traffic was horrible."

"Nah, don't worry about it. I barely just walked in the door myself."

"I gotta say, you *actually* look like your photos—which is honestly a relief these days." Damn it. There goes another joke—a half joke, though. Maybe this one will work better.

"Yeah, thanks, man."

He looks over my shoulder, probably trying to see where our server's gone, but the brief silence that falls between us is too much for me to bear.

"Well...do *I* look like my photos?" I blurt out, smiling at him in what I hope will come across as a playful way.

He narrows his eyes, searching my face. "Yeah," he says, nodding slightly. "For the most part."

For the most part. Fuck, I need a drink.

I reach for the menu. "What are we having?"

When the server comes, we order overpriced cocktails, which makes me hope that Shane is planning to get the bill at the end of the night. It was he who picked this place, and twenty-dollar cocktails are exactly the type of thing I promised myself I would cut back on. Still, when we look down to find that we've gone through our first round a little too fast, I'm quick to flag down our waiter and order another. Sometimes I just need a little alcohol to get me feeling more chatty.

"So," I say once we're halfway through our second drink. Or

maybe it's the third—they're strong enough that I'm starting to lose count. "You're in tech, right?"

"Tech sales."

"What's the difference?"

Shane leans forward, setting his elbows on the table. "Well... tech people *create* the technology. I just sell it."

"Yeah. That makes sense."

"How about you?" he asks me. "What do you do?"

I take a sip of my cocktail. "I'm a writer."

"But, like...what's your actual job?"

"I...write books."

Shane frowns. "Oh."

"Yeah."

"So, what, you wake up in the morning and...write?"

"That's...kinda what full-time writers are meant to do, yeah. But I'm between projects at the moment."

"Interesting," Shane says in a way that tells me he doesn't think it's interesting at all. "Have you written anything I might've heard of?"

Only one of the top-selling debut novels of 2021, I almost reply. Instead, I shrug a little and say, "Maybe. You might recognize my first book if you saw it. We got pretty good coverage for it—big displays in bookstores and everything."

"Oh, I don't spend much time in bookstores," he replies. "I'm more of a gym type of guy."

"Hmm. I figured you would be."

"Well, thank you."

When I meet his eyes, he's smiling. He has taken my comment as a compliment, which is probably a good thing. And, I mean, he *does* have a great body. While he tells me about how he wakes up at five every morning to hit the gym before work, I notice that the top buttons of his shirt are undone, revealing a smooth, golden chest.

I should be trying harder. I should be focusing on being nice, and listening to him, and making a solid attempt at finding some common ground. God knows I've been on more than one bad first date lately, so I could really use a meaningful connection for once. But while Shane continues his monologue, and I keep drinking sips of my cocktail, feeling the alcohol rush to my head, I simply can't help it: my mind starts to wander.

Not now, I say to myself. *Leave me alone.*

The thought of Jeremy always has a way of sneaking into my head—especially when I least want it to. It lingers somewhere in the background during every single date I go on. It rushes through my veins when I walk past some corners in the city or get off at certain subway stops. It's with me in the shower, while I'm sitting on the couch by myself watching television, and when I wake up every morning.

With Jeremy, there were no awkward silences, no misunderstood jokes, no need for defensiveness. I guess it's only natural I would compare every guy to him (but, actually, Jeremy can go fuck himself). He was the best sex I've ever had (seriously—he can go straight to hell). But with him, it wasn't only about the physical connection. It was about the way he looked at me on our first date, the way he held my hand over the table while we were sitting inside that hole-in-the-wall restaurant in the East Village he loved so much, and the way he said, "You're exactly who I hoped you would be."

I frowned. "What do you mean?"

"You're the kind of person I've been looking for."

It was the way he kept ordering one round of vodka sodas with a slice of orange after the other, even as the hours went by and the restaurant emptied around us. It was the way a deep sadness flooded my chest when I realized the date was coming to an end, and the fact that he made it vanish altogether when he asked if I wanted to go to a different bar so we could keep talking. It was the way I leaned over in my stool and undid the top button of his shirt just because I could, and the way he touched me as if he'd known me for years and not hours—a squeeze of my thigh, a graze of my arm, a gentle brush of my face.

And then, at the end of the night, the way he kissed me softly and asked the most heart-stopping question I have ever heard. *Can I see you again tomorrow?*

Maybe no one else stands a chance. Maybe, no matter how many first dates I go on, it's all pointless, because no one will ever come close to Jeremy. But I still sit here, drinking cocktails I can't afford and listening to details about a weight-lifting routine I couldn't possibly care less about, hoping to sense a spark between me and Shane. Hoping to feel something—anything.

"Anyway," he says after a while, readjusting the collar of his shirt. He must've become aware that he went on a bit longer than he should have, because he sets his elbows back down over the table and asks, "Why don't you tell me more about your books?"

I give him a small smile. "Well, I guess...the first one did really well." Saying that *The Millers* did "really well" might be an understatement, but sometimes it's hard for me to talk about it without feeling like I'm bragging.

"What's it about?"

"It's about this family. At the beginning of the book, the characters seem like your average, all-American, next-door-neighbor kind of people. But then you start to see the ways in which each of them is broken—and the ways in which they're all complicit in the others' brokenness. You could say it's an exploration of how family shapes us, for better or for worse." *A raw, unfiltered glimpse into the psyche of the modern American family*, the *New York Times* called it. But I don't say that.

"Wow," Shane says. His eyes are glazed over, which is probably an effect of the alcohol. Then again, I could just be boring him to death.

"My second book came out last year," I add.

"Oh. A sequel?"

"No, no. It's a standalone novel."

"Another big success, I bet."

I let out a laugh. "Yeah," I say, staring down at my near-empty glass. "It sure is."

There isn't much more to say about it. It's not like I'm gonna sit here and explain what a major flop *Walking Home* was. I'm not about to tell Shane about the awful reviews, or the disappointing sales numbers, or the lack of media coverage. I'm here because I need to have a fun night for a change, because I want to get to know this ridiculously good-looking guy, and because I want to feel a connection. The last thing I should be doing is turning this into a pity party. I'm meant to be fun, and likeable, and easygoing. I'm meant to be the kind of guy you'd want to go out with again, the kind you might just see yourself settling down with.

When I meet his eyes again, there's still that same glossiness to them, but there are other things, too—curiosity, wonder, eagerness. His bottom lip trembles slightly, and I just know he's dying to say something. *That's so impressive*, perhaps. Or, *You're incredible. I want to know everything about you.* All of them things Jeremy once said to me, all of them things I've been aching to hear again since we broke up last year.

I lean toward Shane, watching as he draws in a deep breath—watching as he licks his lips, preparing to speak the words he's itching to get off his chest.

And then he says, "You wanna get out of here?"

"Uh...where do you want to go?"

"We could go somewhere private and fuck?"

I can't help myself—I roll my eyes. I just want to make sure he knows for one second that I find his proposition ridiculous, that I'm not as easy as that, that I do possess at least an ounce of self-respect. I reach for my glass, take a big gulp to finish my drink, and set it back down with a bang that's louder than I'd intended.

I lift my eyebrows at him. "Your place or mine?"

It takes me about two seconds to know this isn't going to be good sex—the two seconds after he slides into me, which is when I realize he's not gonna give me any time to adjust, not gonna offer me any courtesy. He's just gonna go for it.

"Oh, God," he yells out. "I'm inside you!"

I guess he's one of those. And I don't just mean a screamer—he's one of those dominant guys who thinks he's *the man* simply because he's a top, and who would never, *ever* let anyone near his own ass.

"You're mine! I'm inside you!"

"Yeah, you are," I yell back, because what else am I meant to do? Lie here quietly while he rails me? "You're inside me!"

"I am, baby," he says. "Fuck, yes, I am."

My apartment is tiny. I can see all of it from here—the kitchenette, the couch, the desk where I do most of my writing. When I lived with Jeremy, we had a two-bedroom on the Upper East Side, but now I live in a studio—not that you would know it's a studio from the amount of money I pay every month. I should've probably looked for a better deal, but when I found the listing for this second-floor unit in a brownstone, I was desperate to sign a lease—any lease. I don't think I could've spent a second longer than I did inside our old apartment. I needed to get away from the memories, from the heartbreak, from the silence.

Leave me alone! I tell my intrusive thoughts for the second time tonight. *I'm busy.*

Shane lets out a loud grunt as he bangs his body against mine.

"Do you like that big cock?"

"Oh, I love it," I say. "It's so big."

It's actually not. But again, what else am I meant to say?

He picks up the pace, which makes the bed creak dangerously underneath us. He'd better not break the frame, because if he does, I'm going to be in the very awkward position of having to ask him to transfer me money. This date has already turned out to be expensive enough as it is. Shane conveniently went to the bathroom just as our waiter brought out the check, which left me with no option but to hand over my credit card and pray it would go through. Breaking my bed and making me buy a new one on top of that would be going a bit too far, though.

"Flip over."

"What?"

Shane wipes sweat off his forehead. "I wanna fuck you doggy style."

Ugh, I hate doggy style. Couldn't even tell you why—I just do. Still, I flip over and get on all fours so he can do his thing.

I'm totally okay with this, by the way. I'd be lying if I said I wasn't into it, at least a little bit. And, honestly, it's probably better this way—now that I'm not facing Shane, he could be anyone. I might even be able to fool myself into imagining he's Jere—*no.* We're not going there. But he could certainly be one of the other guys I've dated in the past year. One of the nice ones. One of the ones I actually liked, and hoped to go on a second date with, and felt heartbroken over when they stopped answering texts.

"Oh, baby, you feel amazing!"

Okay, never mind. It's gonna be hard to imagine he's someone else.

"Yeah?" I answer. "Give it to me!"

By the time he finishes, we're both exhausted. We lie side by side on the bed, breathing heavily and staring up at the ceiling. I don't think either of us even says anything. I don't remember discussing whether he should sleep here or go home, don't remember telling him I need to be up early tomorrow.

All I know is that the feeling of someone lying next to me is comforting, so I cozy up to him and hold on tight to my pillow. The alcohol is swirling inside my head, making me tired and foggy. Right here and now, everything feels okay—everything feels exactly as it should, and for that I am grateful. It isn't until the moments right before I drift off to sleep that I start to remember.

I remember that I'd promised myself I wouldn't do this anymore. No more sleeping around, no more wasting my time with men who aren't right for me. I promised I would stop pursuing people and things and situations that led to me feeling like shit in the end. I said I would focus on what actually matters—writing, getting another book deal, and finding someone who loves me and who I can love back. Someone good. Someone like Jeremy.

The thing is, this is not the first time I've said these things to myself, not the first time I've given myself an ultimatum.

It certainly won't be the last.

CHAPTER TWO

Emptiness. That's all I feel in the morning when I wake up.

It's blissful, really. The soft sunlight filtering through the curtains, the feeling of the silky sheets against my skin, the warmth of a body beside me.

Wait a second.

Fuck.

I roll over to find Shane lying there. He looks unnaturally beautiful while he's sleeping. His chest is smooth, his muscles strong and defined. Even his hair is perfect—only slightly windswept, as if a gentle breeze and not a full night had gone by.

"Good morning," I say softly.

Nothing. He keeps sleeping peacefully.

"Shane?" I ask, a little louder this time, but he still doesn't react.

Perhaps I should let him sleep. I should start getting ready and try again in a bit.

I throw the covers off me, but my attempt at getting out of bed is thwarted the second I lift my head from the pillow. There's a pounding that seems to have come out of nowhere, making every inch of my brain ache. Those cocktails were definitely strong.

There's gotta be a bottle of Advil around here—except I have no idea where I last put it. It's not on the bedside table, but at least there's my phone. I reach for it, lift the screen up to my face, and—

"Oh, shit."

It's almost eight thirty, and I'm supposed to be in Midtown by nine.

"Shane!" I yell. "Shane, you gotta wake up!"

Slowly, he opens his eyes, letting out a low groan. "What time is it?"

"Eight thirty."

"Oh, shit." He shoots into a sitting position, rubbing his forehead. "I was supposed to go to the gym this morning. Did my alarm go off?"

"I didn't hear it," I say as I sort through the clothes that are scattered around the bed, trying to figure out what is mine and what is his.

"Well..." Shane leans across the bed, stretching out an arm to grab hold of my wrist. "Since we've slept in already, do you wanna..."

"What?"

"Go again?"

"No!" I answer, slapping his hand away. "I really do have to go. I have a meeting I can't miss."

When my literary agent asks to see me in person, it's always because she has either very good or very bad news. The thing I've learned, however, is that she always likes to tease the good news when she has some. *I just heard from Wagner, and I'd love to walk you through some exciting updates*, she'll write. Or, *Do you think you'll be able to make it down to the office tomorrow? You'll want to hear what I have to say!* This time, there was no use of the words *love* or *exciting*, no exclamation marks. There was only an email asking if I was free for a meeting, so I already know what type of news I'll be getting today.

"All right, all right," Shane says. He gets up and reaches for the shirt he was wearing last night.

While I get ready, throwing on the nicest clothes I can find, I can't help but feel guilty for snapping at him. I've been on the receiving end of this situation plenty of times before, so I'm all too familiar with the hurt of being woken up and thrown out in the morning.

As we're making our way out of the apartment and down the stairs, there's no sign that Shane has felt any sort of sting. There's no resentment, no sadness on his face—only a bit of redness in his eyes and what appears to be an incontrollable need to yawn every two seconds.

"Last night was fun," he says once we've walked out the front door of my building.

"It was."

"Sex was great," he adds, giving me a flirty smile.

"It…was?" I clear my throat. "I mean—it was, yeah."

"So, I guess…I'll see you soon?"

"Sure. Listen, I'm sorry. I just really have to—"

"Make it to your meeting. No worries. Go."

I pull at the building door once to make sure it's locked, and then I turn around and start running down 90th Street without even stopping to wonder whether Shane is watching me or whether I look stupid from behind as I sprint in the direction of Central Park West.

Into the subway station, toward the Downtown platform, and onto the B train I go. My legs shake the entire ride. It's as if they're impatient, eager to keep moving, even though I'm already making my way to Stacey's office as fast as I can.

I get off at 47th Street and rush down Sixth Avenue until I reach the right building. By the time I've made it across the brightly lit lobby and into an elevator, it's fifteen minutes past nine.

"You're late, darling" is the first thing Stacey says to me.

Her office is so pristine that just standing on the white carpet wearing the same shoes I wore out on the street feels wrong. The tall windows face north, overlooking the skyscrapers along Sixth Avenue, and there's a shelf covering an entire wall filled with books Stacey has sold throughout her decades-long career as a literary agent, including everything from memoir, to thriller, to commercial and literary fiction—a collection every bit as eclectic as she is.

Other things worth noting: vases filled with white peonies, which are always fresh and blossoming regardless of the time of year, a strong smell of perfume—Chanel No. 5—and Stacey Hixon-Jones herself. She must be in her late fifties or early sixties, but you wouldn't know it from looking at her. In the four years we've worked together, she hasn't changed one bit: same blond hair, same sharp cheekbones, same piercing blue eyes. The only thing that's different is her glasses, which used to be round but are now cat-eye shaped.

"I'm sorry," I say to her. "I was—"

"And you're covered in sweat."

"I ran all the way from the station. I'm so—"

"Well, there was no need to run. If you were going to be late as it was, you may as well have showed up late and composed. Not late and sweaty."

I hold her gaze for an instant, not knowing what to say. But then she smiles at me from the corner of her mouth, and I smile back. Stacey may have a peculiar sense of humor, but she is one of the few people I trust with my life—the only person who hasn't given up on me, and never, ever would.

"Don't just stand there," she says. "Take a seat."

I step forward and do as she says. Somewhere below, a car beeps, and the faint sound of a siren goes by.

"Can I offer you some water?" Stacey asks.

"I'm okay."

"Coffee?"

"No, thanks."

"Whiskey?"

I narrow my eyes at her. "Why? Will I need it?"

"I'm not following," she answers with a small shake of her head.

"You only offer me alcohol when you have bad news."

"I'm not sure that's true. I'm just trying to make sure you're comfortable," she replies. "But, since you mentioned it...I do have bad news."

"Tell me. What is it?"

Stacey lets out a long sigh. "Wagner rejected the option."

She's talking about the book I submitted to my publisher barely last week. The one they were supposed to fall head over heels for. The one that was meant to be a shoo-in.

I think I'm gonna throw up. I can almost feel the cocktails from last night burning my throat. The pounding headache returns, and I lean forward in my seat, staring down at the shiny surface of the desk while I take deep breaths.

"How about that whiskey now?" Stacey asks.

I shake my head. "Water," I manage to say. My mouth feels very dry all of a sudden. "I—I need water."

I'm not sure exactly how it happens, but one second Stacey is making a gesture with her hand, and the next her assistant is inside the office, holding out a glass for me.

"Thank you." I chug the water in a few big gulps and hand the glass back to him. "Can I get some more?"

It isn't until I've finished my second glass that I'm able to think more clearly. I set it down gently on the desk and look up to meet Stacey's watchful gaze.

"Why?" I ask. "Why did they reject it?"

"Jackie said it felt like too much of the same."

"That's exactly what she wanted," I say, moving toward the edge of my seat. "You were there. You—you heard her say it. When we got the low sales numbers for *Walking Home,* she said the issue was that I'd strayed too far from my debut. She said I should've—"

"I know what she said."

"So...I write the perfect companion to *The Millers,* and now she doesn't want it?"

"You know how these things are," Stacey says, hunching her shoulders slightly. "The market changes. Contemporary drama isn't the hot thing it was when *The Millers* came out. This third manuscript may have worked if we had tried to sell it even a year ago, but family sagas are not what they're looking for anymore."

There's something in her voice that sounds a lot like masked disappointment. She would never admit it—not in plain words, at least—but I know all too well that she'd also been placing her hopes in this book. She'd been counting on the boost that a new deal with Wagner would give to both of our careers. This past year can't have been easy for her, either—not with all the big-name authors who have dropped her for seemingly unknown and unrelated reasons.

"What else did Jackie say?"

"There wasn't much else to say, unfortunately."

I turn toward the window, staring out at the surrounding buildings and thinking about the people in them. Wondering about what's happening behind all that glass and steel. Telling myself that somewhere out there, someone is also having a bad day, and the thought makes me feel a bit better somehow—a little less alone.

"It's over, isn't it?" I say in a half whisper. "My writing career."

Stacey rolls her eyes. "It's not *over.*"

"Well...reviewers hate me. My readers resent me. My publisher doesn't want me. It sounds like it's over to me."

"Reviewers don't hate you. Need I remind you how many starred reviews *The Millers* received?"

"Are you saying 'the main character is as flat as the paper the book is printed on' isn't hate?"

"I mean…we both know some trade reviewers are tougher than others. It's nothing personal, darling. Perhaps it's true that *Walking Home* wasn't your best work. It may have been quieter and more internal than some people would've liked, but you're capable of a lot more—I know that much."

"The option book is some of my best work."

"It's certainly—"

"Nearly as good as *The Millers*."

"It may be so, but—"

"Can we sell it to a different publisher?"

"We can try," Stacey says. "Although we have to be strategic here. Look at the facts, dear: Book one was a big success. Book two…not so much. So book three is the real test now. Is David Alvarez a one-hit wonder, or is he someone who can learn from his mistakes? Someone who can get readers excited about his work again? It may be tempting to go ahead and find a new publisher… but is this really the book you want to put out there? Are you convinced it's the one that will help you redeem yourself?"

I press my lips together, trying to find the answer. I've been working on this manuscript for so long. It has taken everything out of me—every last bit of will, and patience, and creativity. I've tried so hard to come up with something good, something that's a worthy follow-up to *The Millers*…but I can't say I'd be willing to bet my entire future on it. I can't say whether it will find its audience, or disappoint in the way *Walking Home* did.

"What I think," Stacey says, "is that if we want to make money— real money—you'll need to branch out."

"Branch out?"

"Write something entirely new. Something irresistible—maybe

even in a different genre. You'll have to come up with a story that inspires editors to bet on you again."

I push my chair back to get on my feet. Stacey is one of the founding partners of Coles & Hixon-Jones Literary and Media, so her office is more than big enough to pace around. While I move from one end of the room to the other, however, I can't help but feel claustrophobic. I wish there was just a little more space in here—a little more oxygen.

"I don't have any other stories," I say. "This was supposed to be the one."

"Something brilliant will come to you," Stacey replies. "Just take some time to—"

"I don't *have* time."

The money I got for *The Millers* and *Walking Home* was good. Very good. Promise half a million dollars to a twenty-four-year-old, and he'll think he's set for life. But then there were the taxes and the agency fees. There were big student loans to repay, and expenses to cover over the past four years—health insurance, and New York rent, and everyday life. Add to that some investments that didn't pay off the way they should have, and all of a sudden there's nothing but a few thousand dollars in a bank account and the hope that other book deals will come.

I was so certain this third manuscript was going to be the answer to everything. Stacey walked me through it when I signed the two-book contract with Wagner—she said publishers like to include option clauses because they want to have first-look rights over an author's future work. She said that as long as I didn't mess up in a big way, and as long as the relationship with my publisher was good, there was no reason they would reject it. "Option books are typically a shoo-in," she assured me.

I guess I *did* mess up. In a big way. Right around the time when

I started working on *Walking Home*, I may have listened to the wrong people—a few older authors who warned me against repeating myself with my second novel. "You have to switch things up," they said. "Your readers will *hate* you if you give them a recycled story."

How was I supposed to know that what my readers actually wanted in that moment was more of the same? How was I meant to come up with another masterpiece when we were on such a tight editorial schedule? How could I have known the reviews were going to be terrible when Jackie and Stacey both assured me the book was good enough to go to print? How would I have ever predicted that I'd find myself here, pacing around Stacey's office, with no money, no boyfriend, no offers of publication, and no more stories to tell?

"How badly do you need cash?" Stacey asks, lifting her chin slightly.

"Pretty badly, I'd say."

I haven't looked at my bank account in a while. Checking my balance has caused me one or two panic attacks in the past few months, so I've figured it's best to stay away from it. Out of sight, out of mind, and in the meantime, I told myself I'd put all my energy into my third book.

Stacey folds her hands neatly over the desk. "Here's what we'll do: I will call Jackie and tell her you're working on something new—something great."

"Why would—"

"Meanwhile," Stacey adds pointedly, "you will write a proposal—three chapters and an outline. It will be intelligent, and provocative, and entirely irresistible."

I stop pacing and look straight into her eyes. This is why I love her. She always has a plan, always knows exactly what to do in a moment of crisis. The thing about today, though, is that her ability to help me can only go so far. She can't make brilliant book ideas magically appear, can't write the proposal for me, can't promise that Wagner will buy my next book even if I come up with something amazing.

"I don't know if I can do it," I say, looking down at my feet.

"*I* know you can. You're capable of wonderful things, darling."

"What will I even write about? How will I—"

"Live a little," Stacey says. "Go out there, meet new people, try new things. The right story will find you."

"Yeah." What she didn't mention is that "living a little" requires the one thing I do not have right now: money. I can't afford to travel, or eat out, or even join a gym. I can't afford to go to any of the places where I could meet interesting people, or where stories would be most likely to find me. "You're probably right."

"I know it's all less than ideal. It's a tough industry, but you're tough, too. Don't forget that."

I don't respond. I shift my gaze back toward the window, staring out at the city again.

"I can ask Josh to move some meetings if you want us to go grab a drink," Stacey adds after what feels like a long silence. "You can commiserate all you want. How does that sound?"

I swear, sometimes it feels like Stacey's mission in life is to put a drink in my hand. Maybe I'm more fun to be around when I'm not sober—or maybe she just misses the good old days, when it felt like we were constantly being handed reasons to toast with each other.

"No, no," I answer. "I should head out."

Stacey stares at me through her glasses for a moment. It's as if I were a book and she was reading me, trying to understand what's actually going through my mind.

"Very well," she says. "Go live your life. I'll be expecting your pages soon."

I step out of her office thinking of those better times—days when I left this building feeling like I was walking on air. Thinking of the phone call where Stacey told me Wagner—a renowned imprint at a Big Five publisher—was making a half-a-million-dollar, two-book preemptive offer. Thinking of how Jeremy took the rest of the day off work so we could go out and celebrate. Thinking of the glowing reviews for *The Millers*, the packed bookstore where I had my launch party, and that feeling I used to get deep down—a certainty that I had *made it*.

I'm crossing the lobby of the building, approaching the revolving doors, when I stop suddenly. It's as if my legs have stopped working, refusing to carry me even one step further.

"Sorry," I say to a couple of suited men who were walking right behind me. "I'm sorry."

I move aside, retreating to a corner of the lobby as I pull my phone out of my pocket. With shaking fingers, I open my banking app, scroll down to look at the balance, and—

Shit. Three thousand five hundred and seventy-eight dollars left.

Twenty-nine hundred dollars for next month's rent, five hundred for my phone bill and health insurance, another hundred for the minimum payment on my credit card, and that leaves me with...a total of seventy-eight dollars for food and other expenses for the rest of the month.

Live a little. Stacey's voice seems to ring in my ears while I make my way back toward the exit. I push past the revolving doors, and as soon as I step outside, I stop to look up and down Sixth Avenue.

I should go somewhere—a touristy spot, maybe, where I'd be more likely to see something a bit out of the ordinary. Times Square is not far, so maybe I could start there. Or perhaps I could hop on the subway and explore a part of the city I don't know very well. Or strike up a conversation with a stranger or two and see if that helps.

This is New York City, for crying out loud. There should be millions of stories waiting to find me, millions of possibilities waiting to be discovered.

But it's also true that I'm tired. And hungover. And a little heartbroken after hearing the news about the option. I could just head home, recharge, and go out looking for a story tomorrow.

So I make my way toward the subway station and hop on an Uptown train. It's pretty busy, but I manage to find a seat beside a mother and her toddler. While we speed toward the Upper West Side, the train creaking and racketing as the dark tunnel flashes past the windows, I become aware that the toddler is staring at me.

She has a cute button nose and a big bow in her hair, and she seems to find me deeply fascinating, because she just won't look away.

"Why are you sad?" she asks suddenly.

"Having a rough day," I answer, throwing her a sideways glance.

The corners of her mouth twist downward. "Me too."

"Excuse me, could you please not talk to my child?"

I look up to find the mother staring at me with a mean frown on her face.

"She talked to me fir—you know what? Fine. I'm sorry."

I cross my arms and slide to the far edge of my seat, trying to put as much distance as possible between me and them.

But even as stations come and go and the train doors keep opening and closing, the toddler won't take her eyes off me. She continues staring as if I were a circus animal—something to be amazed by, something that may have once possessed the ability to dazzle an entire crowd. Something to be regarded for entertainment.

CHAPTER THREE

New Jersey used to be one of my favorite places in the world. It used to be home, the state where I was born, a place where I belonged. Now, I avoid it as much as I can. If it were up to me, I'd pretend it had been erased from the map, hold on to the good memories, and never return.

Unfortunately, there are at least two days a year when it's absolutely nonnegotiable for me to visit—Christmas and Father's Day. Two days that I used to fret and that I've learned to tolerate.

Today is neither, but still, I'm here, getting off the train at Morristown station. It's been nearly five months since my last visit, four weeks before I was meant to be back here again, and three days since Stacey gave me the news about the option. Three days I've spent trying to convince myself not to do what I'm about to do—of trying to come up with a story worth telling, and of wondering how it was that someone as unimaginative as me ever became a published author in the first place.

I grab a taxi outside the station and stare out the window during the ride to the neighborhood where I grew up. Sometimes I find it hard to believe that this is where I'm actually from. There's something so familiar about the streets of Manhattan—something that makes me feel as though I've lived there forever, even though the first eighteen years of my life were spent here, in this pretty little town where nothing ever changes. Well...*almost* nothing, I should say.

My old home is among the few things that *have* changed. Back when my parents first bought it, it was cute and tiny, tucked between two fancier-looking houses. It has since been renovated—painted, expanded, made to look a lot more like its bigger and better neighbors. It's almost appropriate, truly, the way its exterior has evolved to match its interior, because the people inside it have also evolved in wholly unexpected and unusual ways.

"There you go, buddy," the taxi driver says to me as he pulls over.

"Thanks."

I swipe my credit card and wait breathlessly for the authorization to go through. I only leave a one-dollar tip, which may seem cheap to the driver but is entirely painful to me. The train ride and the taxi fare have set me back quite a bit already, and every single dollar counts at this point.

As I walk up the front lawn of the house, I'm reminded of last Christmas. There was an argument, as usual. I was faulted for everything that's wrong with the family, as usual. *The Millers* was at the center of the argument...which has also started to become the usual.

My legs are my favorite part of my body, because they take me anywhere I want to go, I wrote as the opening sentence of the book. As for the second line...let's just say, it sort of shifts the tone a little bit: *When it comes to my family, where I want to go is far, far away.*

If anyone asks—and a lot of people have over the past couple years—I'd say my family is *very* different from the one in my novel. "God, can you imagine?" I'll tell them. "No, no. My family is nowhere near as awful as that."

I never set out to write about Pa, or Sheila, or Billy, or even myself. But I guess I *did* write about an emotionally distant father, an evil stepmother, a bratty child, and a trainwreck of an older son. It makes you wonder, doesn't it? How much an author chooses the story they want to tell, and how much the story chooses them. In this case, I can confidently say *The Millers* chose me. I wrote that book on weekends and evenings, whenever I had time off work. I would sit at my laptop every single day, typing into the late hours of the night, because I had a dream of becoming an author and because I was desperate to escape the shitty marketing job I got right out of college.

The words came pouring out of me as if I'd memorized them in a past life and was only just remembering them. It was the same with the characters—I felt as though I had met them before. I knew their minds, their hearts, their deepest secrets, and the way they wished to be perceived by the world—which was very different from the people they really were behind closed doors.

I just wish my family hadn't taken the book so personally. I mean, the characters could really be *anybody*. When Sheila read it, however, shortly after it was published, she called me in a panic.

"You've turned our entire lives into a product for people to consume, and criticize, and deride!" she said to me.

I'm not sure how much my dad agrees with any of that. He hasn't even read the whole book, as far as I know, but he's still resentful—particularly because *The Millers* upset Sheila, and Sheila should never, ever be made to feel upset.

I walk up the front steps of the house and stare fixedly at the door, which is painted dark blue and has a fancy bronze knocker that is entirely pointless because they have a doorbell anyway. Here is my last chance to turn around, call an Uber back to the train station, and pretend I was never in Morristown. I could text Pa saying something came up and I couldn't make it out after all. But then, trying my best to swallow my pride, I ring the bell.

There's no answer. I wait patiently on the stoop, but even after several minutes and a couple more tries with the bell, there's no sign anyone's home.

I'm starting to worry, wondering if I should give my father a call, when—all too suddenly—the door opens, and Sheila appears.

"David!" she says. "We were expecting you much earlier. We'd almost assumed you had changed your mind about coming."

I smile out of the corners of my mouth. I texted Pa last night, specifically saying I was hoping to stop by around noon, so I suppose the message got lost somewhere between the moment he received my text and the moment he spoke to Sheila about my visit. It wouldn't be the first time the three of us have had communication issues.

"I thought we'd agreed on noon," I say. "Must've slipped my dad's mind."

Sheila returns my smile, but there's no affection in her eyes. She is everything my mom was not: blond, curvy, and short, but the differences don't end there. Where my mom was soft, Sheila is harsh. Where my mom was kind, and caring, and attentive, Sheila can be cruel, and indifferent, and hurtful. Not to everyone, of course, but I seem to have a way of bringing out the worst in her.

"Come on in. Your dad's just upstairs."

She moves aside so I can step into the house, and I follow her to the living room.

My dad and Sheila got married when I was sixteen, which was right around the time when all the renovations started—mostly small things here and there that Sheila wanted fixed, modernized, and replaced. Then she started insisting she wanted to paint the walls a brighter shade of white, and change the carpet in the bedrooms, and update the backsplash in the kitchen. The changes added up over time, until the house became nearly unrecognizable from the one I grew up in—the one that used to be filled with warmth, and color, and the smell of Mexican food cooking on the stove.

The living room is one of the areas that has seen the most updates. It's no longer the cozy space that might've inspired you to sit around with the whole family or read a good book with your feet up on the coffee table. If Sheila had her way—and she has, for the most part—the room would be just like a museum, all the carefully selected decorations and furniture meant to be seen but not touched...and *definitely* not sat on.

Still, I lower myself onto the couch, leaning back as comfortably as I can despite the cushions being hard from lack of use.

"I'll go grab your father," Sheila says before disappearing down the hall.

While I sit alone, I can't help but think about my mother. Some people are loud in their absence. When they die, they leave behind a hole that can be felt and never filled, but my mom is not one of those people. There is no trace of her around the house, no sign that she was ever even here.

She was perfectly young, perfectly healthy, and perfectly happy the day her car turned over on the New Jersey Turnpike, which meant her death came with no warning and no time to prepare. There was nothing but a few desperate phone calls and a grim-looking doctor who explained to Pa and a twelve-year-old me that he had tried his best to save her, but there wasn't anything he could've done.

I don't remember much from the years after she passed away. I guess grief can do that to you—it erases your memory, erases parts of you that you never even knew you were losing until one day you look back and realize that they're gone. Young David must've found a way to cope, though. He must've found a way to press a Fast-Forward button after Ma's death, because the next thing I knew, Pa was spending a lot of time with Sheila, who had been my math tutor when I was in the eighth grade, and I was being asked to start calling her by her first name instead of Miss Cockwell.

My eyes fall on the mantelpiece, which is filled with photographs. There used to be pictures of my mom there—pictures of the family we used to be. As the years have gone by, the old frames have been taken off to make space for the new, and now the mantelpiece is mostly a timeline of Billy's life—from the pink ball he was in the weeks after he was born, to the bright-eyed kid he became as a toddler, to the blond, skinny boy with a big tooth gap that he is today. Pa and Sheila feature prominently, too—cheesy photos of them on their wedding day, pictures of the vacations they've taken over the years (mostly to all-inclusive resorts in Mexico), and plenty of images of them standing proudly next to Billy, looking like a happy family of three. I'm sure there must be other photos of me on there, but from this angle, the only one I can see is from graduation day, wearing my cap and purple gown in front of Madison Square Garden.

I don't fault Billy for anything, by the way—not at all. He didn't choose to put all those photos up there, didn't choose to be a son to his father and mother. He also certainly didn't choose to be born on the day that he was—the exact day I moved into my dorm at NYU. It was never his intention to cause Sheila's water to break just as Pa and I were getting into the city, which forced my dad to dump me on the sidewalk with all my things and turn right back around to go to the hospital, all thoughts of helping me get settled in and taking me out to dinner that night left forgotten.

I couldn't not think about how symbolic it all was while I unpacked, with my new roommate—a kid from Kansas who wore heavy eye makeup and called himself a goth—observing me unblinkingly, following every move I made. One son out, one son in. A perfect replacement, really.

I hear my father before I see him. Calm, heavy footsteps coming down the stairs, a brief pause once he reaches the bottom, and then—

"David!"

My father doesn't call me *Day-vid*, as everyone else does. He's always pronounced my name the Mexican way: *Dah-veed*, even though we don't typically speak Spanish to each other—mostly because speaking Spanish would make Sheila feel left out, and Sheila should never, ever be made to feel left out.

"Hi, Pa," I say, taking a long look at him as he stands by the entrance of the living room. He's been on a strict diet over the past few months—the doctor said it would be good for his heart—so he's lost weight since I saw him at Christmas. That's not to say he doesn't still have a decent belly, because he does, but his pants and polo shirt fit much more loosely than they once did. Beyond that, he looks pretty much the same, except for his thick black hair, which has a bit more gray than it used to; his mustache, which appears to be in need of a trim; and his skin, which looks sun-kissed, surely from spending time gardening in the front and back yards.

"This is quite a surprise," he says. "To what do we owe this visit?"

The truth bubbles inside my chest, but I choke on my own words. I'll have to tell Pa the real reason I'm here, and I'll have to do it soon, but perhaps I could buy myself a little time before I do.

"I just...figured I'd stop by."

He steps forward to join me on the couch. There's another empty two-seater and an armchair, but he insists on sitting beside me—his idea of closeness, I think. A great substitute for a hug or a warm greeting.

"How are you?" he asks, narrowing his eyes at me as if searching for the answer on my face.

"I'm all right."

"How's New York?"

"Great."

"Your writing?"

"Good."

"Jeremy?"

"Still taking time apart."

Taking time apart. That's how I phrased it when I told my dad things had ended between me and Jeremy. Because saying something like, "He broke me. He left when I needed him the most. He took a piece of me, ran away with it, and never looked back" would've had a *slightly* dramatic ring to it, and my father has never been much for drama.

He nods slowly. "That's a shame."

My dad liked Jeremy. He liked the way he centered me, liked the way he was a stabilizing force in my life. Jeremy, on the other hand, wasn't a big fan of my dad. He didn't like the way he threw me off balance, the way he managed to destabilize me even when everything else was going well.

"How about you?" I ask. "How's everything around here?"

"Good, good," Pa answers. "Sheila took up sculpting recently. You know how she is—always looking for ways to fill her time. She's been rearranging a few things around the house to make room for her art." He nods toward one of the side tables in the living room, where there's a shapeless, gray blob made out of what looks an awful lot like Play-Doh. I'm not even sure what it's meant to be—a pigeon, maybe?

"Oh, nice. It, uh...really brightens the space," I say. "And Billy?"

"Better than ever. He's looking forward to the start of summer break."

"That's good to hear."

There's a moment of silence, during which all we can hear are the sounds of Sheila scraping and banging something upstairs. One of her sculptures, probably. Then, almost at the same time, Pa and I draw in deep breaths to speak.

"Are you—"

"Why are you here, David? Really?"

I frown at him. "What do you mean?"

"I can't remember the last time you were here on a day that wasn't Christmas or Father's Day."

"I mean...it's not like I keep track of the exact days I come over."

I do.

"I'm sure I must've been here other times in the past couple of years."

I haven't.

"Just tell me," Pa says. "Why today?"

I swear, for an instant, I almost abandon my plan. I almost allow my pride to get the best of me and stick to a version of the story where I really did come here just to visit, with no ulterior motives.

But then I say, "I need help."

"Say that again? I didn't hear you."

I clear my throat and repeat, in a louder voice, "I need help."

"Help?" Pa asks, his eyes widening. "As in, rehab?"

I love that he would assume the worst of me right away, but I never do drugs, and I don't even drink that much...most of the time.

"No, it's not that."

"Are you sick?"

I shake my head, trying my best to keep my face straight. "No, it's, uh..."

"What, then?"

"It's the book."

"*The Millers*? Is someone trying to sue you for defamation?"

36

Again, it's lovely that he would assume the worst, but I keep shaking my head vigorously.

"It's the third book," I manage to say. "My publisher doesn't want it."

"Oh." Pa stops moving, stops breathing, but judging by the way his eye twitches, I'm guessing he heard what I said, and now he's only waiting for me to give him an explanation.

"I was so sure they were going to acquire it. I thought they were going to promise me another good amount of money and publish it, but...they won't."

"So, what now?"

"That's the thing. My agent told me to write something new—something different, so that hopefully they'll like it and sign me again. But I need to come up with a new idea. It's gonna take a while to write the proposal, and polish it, and...I just need *time*."

Pa's frown deepens. "So you're asking for money."

"No! I—I mean, yes! But I'll pay back every penny. With interest, if you want. All I need is to be able to cover the bills for a few months while I work on the new book."

"What happened to the money you got for the first two?"

"It's gone."

"And the rainy-day fund I told you to have?"

"Used it."

"What about royalties? Shouldn't you be getting a check twice a year?"

"The books haven't earned out their advances just yet."

"Well, David..." My father lets out a sigh of his own, filling the air around us with all the disappointment that's been building inside his chest. "How much money do you need?"

"Ten thousand dollars," I say, but it comes out as a question: *Ten thousand dollars?*

Another sigh, longer and heavier than the first. "I warned you about this, you know?" he says, his tone becoming stern all of a sudden. "I told you how unstable a writing career would be."

"I know."

"That's why I advised you to get a business degree."

"I know." More so *forced* than *advised*, actually. I wanted to major in creative writing. I wanted to study the craft, and meet other people who were as passionate about it as I was, and spend my college days reading, writing, and working toward my dreams, but Pa wouldn't hear of it. He didn't think I could do it, didn't think I'd be able to make a living out of telling stories, and I listened to him. I applied to the Stern School of Business at NYU, did a concentration in marketing, and got a job at an advertising firm right after college.

For the longest time, I resented him. I felt as though he had pushed me away from my dream, but looking back, perhaps it became true *because* of my father. There's nothing quite like having someone tell you that you can't have the things you want to make you work even harder to get them. Nothing like the idea of one day being able to say "You were wrong about me" to give you drive, and focus, and inspiration to keep going.

"Well, at least you have your degree to fall back on," Pa says. "Why not get a real job? Something in marketing—a stable position to help you get back on your feet?"

No, a voice says inside my head. I hated my marketing job. Hated it, hated it, hated it. The people were nice, but I spent every single day in the office feeling like I was in the wrong place. Wanting to escape the routine. Fantasizing about making something happen for myself.

Going back to a nine-to-five now would be like accepting that I've failed—that I was never meant to do what I love most in the world—and I have not failed. Not completely. Not yet.

"Why not?" Pa asks, and that's when I realize I spoke the word *no* out loud.

"I haven't worked in marketing in four years."

"So?"

"So my only relevant experience is that shitty assistant position I had," I reply. "Who's gonna hire a twenty-eight-year-old with a four-year gap on his CV and mediocre qualifications?"

"It's a matter of looking," Pa says, raising his eyebrows. "You'll find something eventually."

"It's not as simple as that," I tell him in a small voice. "I need the money now. By the time I find something, it'll be too late. I'll lose my apartment. I won't be able to keep up with the debt, and—"

"Then you should've started looking sooner! You're old enough to know better by now, David."

"You don't understand," I mumble through the knot forming in my throat.

"I think I do," Pa says. "You've come here asking for help, but you won't even help yourself. It's about time you started taking responsibility for your own life."

But I have. I *did* take responsibility. I did everything my father wanted me to do—I got a practical degree, and a stable job, and a decent lifestyle. And then I went and did all the things he thought I *couldn't* do—I made a name for myself in publishing, was in a loving relationship, and achieved more than I ever believed I would.

What I find funny, though, is that people talk about dreams coming true as if it were a point of arrival—a final destination, and once you've reached it, there should be no going back. Once you've found the love of your life, you're not meant to go on living without them. Once you've become a successful author, you're not meant to return to being a struggling writer. Once you've reached a certain level of fame, you're not meant to go back to being unknown, uninteresting, undesirable.

Nobody talks about what it's like to get everything you ever wanted…and then lose it. There's no rulebook for what to do when that happens. At best, people will show you pity. At worst, they'll deem you unworthy of the things you had achieved—or even blame you for losing them. Anything to hold on to their idea that realized dreams should be static, and that anyone who finds themself in my position was simply too stupid or too reckless to maintain their success.

"You're too reckless, David."

"Maybe I am," I reply. I have nothing else to say. I don't have the energy to explain that things simply have not worked out the way they were supposed to—that I never wanted to end up here. That having to ask for his help is the worst possible situation I could've ever imagined for myself. And I've been in some pretty shitty situations before.

"I can't give you money," he says. There is an air of finality to his tone—something that makes this sound like the end of the conversation.

"You—you can't?"

He shakes his head firmly. "I'm saving for my retirement. I don't want to be an insurance salesman until the day I die."

"You'll get the money back. If—"

"I can't just pull ten thousand dollars out of my pocket. The money's put away, and I need to be smart with it. I can't afford to take risks—not if I want to retire before I'm too old to enjoy life."

I lean back against the couch. My whole body feels strangely weak. It's as if every ounce of adrenaline has left me, and now all I can do is sit here motionlessly.

"Perhaps these are lessons you need to learn for yourself, mijo. Prudence. Caution. Planning for the future." Pa smacks his lips, nodding wisely. "I daresay you may just thank me one day."

"Yeah," I say with the only shred of strength I'm able to find within me. "I'm sure I will."

"How about I treat you to lunch, though?"

I let out a snort, but quickly try to pass it off as a cough. So he'll leave me to fend for myself and comfortably watch from the sidelines as my dreams fade away into nothing. But at least he'll treat me to lunch.

"It's fine," I answer. "I should head back to the city."

"Are you sure? It's Saturday, so you know what that means."

"Uh... do I?"

"We go to Red Lobster on Saturdays," Pa says. "Me, Sheila, Billy. And you, if you'd like to join us today."

I look into his eyes, which are the same shade of deep brown as mine. There's something that lights up in his gaze when he speaks Sheila's and Billy's names. Something so gentle in the way he talks about their Saturday tradition.

"I'm... I'm pretty sure, yeah." The knot in my throat comes back, and I swallow hard, trying to make it go away. "I'm not really in the mood for seafood. You guys have fun, though."

By the time I step outside, I feel like there's a force pulling me toward Manhattan. I need to get out of here. Out of this house, out of this town, out of this state. I need to go back to New York and get lost among its streets, people, and buildings. I need to get myself to my apartment, sit at my desk, and come up with a brilliant concept for my next book. But first, I may need to think of other ways to cover the bills and pay the rent, because I don't think I'll be able to focus on much else until I do.

I'm walking across the lush green front lawn, pulling my phone out of my pocket to figure out when the next train to Penn Station leaves, when someone calls after me.

"David?"

I stop in my tracks. A defensive instinct kicks in every time my name comes out of Sheila's mouth—probably from all the times she's said it in anger, or judgment, or disappointment over the years.

Slowly, I turn around, pressing my lips together into a small smile and using a hand to shield my eyes from the sun.

"Hey, Sheila!" I call back. She's standing in the doorway, staring blankly at me. I didn't give much thought to her clothes earlier, but I see now that she's wearing a light pink blouse and white, flowery pants.

"You're leaving so soon?" she asks as she descends the front steps of the house. She walks briskly to meet me in the middle of the yard, still staring at me with an indecipherable look on her face.

"Yeah. The plan was just to stop by for a quick visit."

She nods, her blond hair swaying gently.

"Listen," she says, lowering her voice, "I overheard the conversation you had with your father."

She pauses dramatically, as if expecting me to respond. But what does she expect me to do—say, *Oh, wonderful*? Or, *Thanks for* not *minding your own business*?

"I know you and I have had our ups and downs," she says after a long moment. "More downs than ups, really."

I let out an awkward laugh, thinking she's going to try to pass that comment off as a joke, but her expression remains dead serious.

"I want to help you, though," she adds. "Maybe put the past behind us. Start fresh." That's when I notice she's holding something in her hands.

A checkbook.

"Oh, Sheila," I cry out, my chest swelling with relief. I could kiss her right now. I could sink to my knees, hug her legs, and say, *Thank you, thank you, thank you*.

Of all the people I hoped might save me, I never thought it would be her. Maybe I've been wrong about Sheila all along—maybe

I resented her as a teenager simply because she wasn't my mom, and I haven't always accepted my share of the blame for the tension that's permeated our relationship since I was young. Or perhaps she's changed—perhaps she's no longer the harsh person she used to be, and she genuinely wants to make things right between us. Whatever the reason, I don't think I've ever been as grateful to anyone as I am now.

"I—I don't know what to say. I'm so—"

"You can say you'll pay me back."

"Every penny," I say. "I promise. You have no idea how much this mea—"

"I can't give you the amount you asked for from your father. But I can give you something considerable."

"I understand." My whole body is shaking. I take little side-to-side steps on the spot, because there is simply too much joy in my heart to remain still. "Whatever you can offer will make a huge difference. It's—"

"I'm glad to help."

She sets the checkbook over the palm of her left hand. Fishing out a pen from her pocket with her right, she scribbles something, signs swiftly, and rips off the check.

"Use it well," she says as she hands it to me.

"Thank you, Sheila. Thank you so—" I sneak a glance down and choke when I see the amount. One hundred and twenty-five dollars.

"Are you all right?" she asks.

"Yeah," I answer with a small cough. "Yeah, I just—I have something in my throat."

Disappointment. And shock. And heartbreak, because for one brief moment, I really did think everything was going to be okay. I really did think Sheila was going to offer the helping hand I so desperately need, but she won't. No one will.

I keep coughing, covering my mouth with my elbow, until I'm able to breathe normally again.

"I do appreciate your willingness to help, Sheila," I say finally. "I really do."

She smiles—a full smile, showing teeth and all, which she almost never does. She's genuinely proud of herself, proud of her generosity.

"I'm just happy to be able to make a difference," she says.

At least the hundred and twenty-five dollars will cover my train and taxi rides, and perhaps even a few meals, which means the trip home won't have been a complete waste after all.

"Take care of yourself, David," Sheila says, turning back toward the house. "We'll see you soon."

"Yes. See you soon."

Father's Day is a little over a month away. And with that thought comes a bit of hope, because wouldn't it be nice to return as a new person? To sit at the table across from Pa and Sheila and tell them all about the new book idea I came up with, and how much my agent and editor love it, and how everything is back on track? To repay Sheila her one hundred and twenty-five dollars, and offer to buy everyone lunch for a change?

There might've been some truth to what Pa said after all—perhaps I just need a little pressure to make something great happen. My next book could be the one that defines my career, the one that reestablishes me as an author to watch. The struggle I'm facing now may just be what pushes me toward greatness.

That's what I keep telling myself during the Uber ride to the station. By the time I'm on the train, watching the city skyline flash past the window, I've managed to convince myself that I'll find a way. Everything will be all right—it's just a matter of time.

We're approaching Secaucus, the last station before New York Penn, when my phone pings with a new message.

My heart jumps when I see Shane's name on the screen. I haven't heard from him since we woke up next to each other on Wednesday, but here he is, willingly reaching out again: Hey, handsome.

I open the chat to see a gray bubble with three dots below his first message. He's typing something else.

Thanks again for the other night. It was lots of fun, reads his second text. Aw. That's nice of him.

I'm about to reply, but then I realize he's typing once more— except the gray bubble goes away after a few seconds. Two or three times it happens: he starts typing, only to delete what he'd written, and then he starts again.

Poor thing. He's probably trying to figure out what to say, try-ing to seem cool, changing his mind over and over again. I must've made quite an impression on him, if he's this nervous about reach-ing out. Maybe we should give things another shot—go on a second date and see if we click better than we did on the first.

The train is speeding past Secaucus. We're on our way to the final stop, and the skyline is coming closer and closer, but it isn't until right before the train enters the tunnel, about to plunge into darkness, that Shane's message finally pops up.

I hate having to share bad news, but I did a routine STI screen-ing a couple days ago, and it came back positive for gonorrhea. Thought you should know so you can get yourself checked. Sorry, handsome.

I read the text once. Twice. It isn't until the third time that it finally sinks in.

"This station stop is New York Penn," the recording overhead says. "When leaving the train, please watch the gap."

Fuck.

CHAPTER FOUR

Gonorrhea, I type into my laptop.

I lean back in my chair and stare at the Word document on the screen, the cursor blinking expectantly. There's got to be a story here. I just have to think of the right angle.

It's been nearly a week since Shane texted me. An awful week of waiting for the infection window period to pass so I could get tested, of stressing over every single penny I spent, and of not getting any closer to writing my proposal or finding another way to make money. In a moment of desperation, I followed my father's advice and sent out more than two dozen applications for marketing jobs, but I haven't heard from any of them so far, which was one more thing that made the week awful.

But this afternoon, forty-eight hours after getting pricked, and swabbed, and having to pee in a cup—and several hundred dollars in additional credit card debt later—I finally received my test results: *negative*. It's probably too soon to laugh about it, but it's also the most interesting thing that has happened to me lately, and Stacey said the right story would find me...so this has *got* to be it.

All the lights in the apartment are off, except for my desk lamp. This is my favorite way to write—when 90th Street is quiet, but I can feel the city pulsing somewhere outside my windows, flowing with the kind of energy that a Thursday night in early summer can bring.

The inspiration just won't come, though. Not tonight, not lately. I've thought of over a hundred different premises in the past week alone: A queer story where the romance builds slowly and beautifully, only to have the protagonists *not* end up together. A fantasy where the main character discovers magic he never imagined he would have, and then has to grapple with the privilege and responsibility of his new powers. A thriller with an unreliable narrator where, in the end, we learn it was he who committed the crime.

The thing is, premises are easy enough to come up with, but it's not just about finding a story—it's about finding *the* story.

It will be intelligent, and provocative, and entirely irresistible, Stacey said, and none of the ideas I've had so far feel that way. None of them excite me the way that they should.

I shift my gaze away from the window and back to my laptop. My Word document is still blank other than the word *gonorrhea*, and the cursor is still blinking, daring me to type something else.

A modern version of Sex and the City, *starring queer Latino characters*, I write. There could be something there. I could make it fresh and relatable. I mean, what sexually active gay guy hasn't received that *Sorry, handsome* text at one point or another? That could happen near the start of the story—I could use it as the inciting incident, perhaps. It's also true that I could look to myself for inspiration for the main character, since back in the day, my college friends used to tell me I was *such* a Carrie. I would take the compliment gladly, because Carrie Bradshaw was exactly who I wanted to become. I wanted to be as free as she was—as glamorous. I wanted to be liked, to have friends who supported me no matter what, to be chased after by men. The thing is, I didn't know then what I know now: that bitch was lying. Heartbreak is not fun, making a living as a writer is hard, and there is no sex worth having in this city.

I hit the Delete button, watching all the words disappear until the document is blank again. It was a stupid idea, anyway. I can do much better than that—I *know* I can, but I'm getting tired. I could use a little break.

Instinctively, I reach for my phone to open Grindr—the worst app ever known to mankind—and dozens of small squares pop up. Some are faces, others are torsos, others are nothing but a gray logo, which means people are browsing anonymously. Many of them have headlines underneath: Looking. Blow me. Visiting. Can host NOW.

It occurred to me earlier today that this would be a good place to find stories—much better than any of the other dating sites I'm on—so I redownloaded the app after being off it for a few months. I may not be able to do anything that will require spending money, but I *can* chat up random strangers and see if anything comes of it.

I scroll down, seeing if any of the faces or torsos or headlines catch my attention. Here's one, for example—a silver fox with a straight nose and a perfectly groomed beard. I click into his profile to find out that he's forty-two. Native New Yorker, avid foodie. Into fit. Not typically looking for now.

I don't really work out, but I am pretty slim. Call it genetics, because I can't seem to put on weight, even if I try (and I have). That should be good enough to meet his "fit" requirement...right? Either way, I type a message: Hey.

I don't have to wait too long for his response. You're 28?

Yeah, I write back.

Too young. Not here to fix your daddy issues.

A second later, the conversation disappears. He's blocked me.

I roll my eyes, setting my phone down on the desk. I'll never understand why everyone is so quick to judge people with daddy issues, but not the fathers who are responsible for causing those issues in the first place.

I should probably give up for the night—not just on Grindr, but on writing. It's only nine, yet I feel like I've been here for hours, typing sentences into my laptop and then deleting them. Coming up with new ideas and then beating myself up for being so unoriginal.

I've nearly made the decision to close my laptop and go brush my teeth when my phone pings suddenly with the sound of a new Grindr message. I reach for it immediately.

Hello, there. How's your evening so far?

The profile is empty except for his age—thirty-six—and two simple words: Just ask. Before I can respond to his first message or think of any questions, however, a photo pops up in the chat: A man with dark hair that is neatly pulled back, standing on what seems to be a pier. He has a deep gaze and a sharp jaw, and behind him is a lake surrounded by luscious green mountains. A drink in his hand, an expensive tie around his neck, a confident smirk on his face—he's gorgeous.

Evening's going well, I write. How about yours?

It's not too bad. A little lonely, though, he replies, along with a sad face emoji.

Oh?

His response comes almost immediately. I went and got myself a big hotel room. It was bound to get a bit solitary, I suppose.

My fingers move fast over the keyboard as I type. Maybe I could come keep you company.

I can't help but cringe as I hit Send. I swear I'm not usually like this.

Do you have any other pics? he asks.

I have a few on my public profile, but I still send him a couple more: a selfie I took in Central Park last month, as well as a cute photo that was taken on the beach in Montauk, which I had to strategically crop Jeremy out of, since it was originally a coupley pic, but I just look too good not to use it for online dating.

You're adorable, the dark-haired stranger responds. But I meant sexier pics.

When it comes to nudes, I don't send them. I just get them.

Haha. Fair enough.

A brief pause. And then…oh wow. A dick pic. He's big. Holy shit.

I'm staying at the Plaza, he says. Is that far from you?

I bite my lip. A big room at the Plaza, huh? Who the hell is this guy?

Not too far, I reply.

Why don't you stop by?

I should really say no. I need to get up early tomorrow and try sitting in front of my laptop again. I also literally just had that STI scare, which I am so glad to be over with and not at all in a rush to repeat, regardless of being on PrEP and any other precautions this stranger and I may take. And didn't I tell myself after hooking up with Shane that that would be the last time? That I'd only go on quality dates from now on, so I can find someone special?

Then again, this guy is really good-looking. And he's staying at the Plaza. *And* he has a big penis.

I'm going.

I push my chair back and head into the bathroom so quickly I nearly forget to respond to him. I run back to the desk, pick up my phone with shaking hands, and write: Text you when I'm five minutes away?

Sounds good, he says. I'll meet you just inside the front doors of the hotel.

A rush of energy courses through my veins as I return to the bathroom. I guess this is really happening.

While I shower, a little voice of wisdom tells me to stay home— that I may regret this later, just as I regretted Shane, just as I've regretted so many others before. Although...isn't there also a possibility that I won't?

There's something about this guy that intrigues me, beyond the fancy hotel room and...you know, the size of his dick. He sounds so *polite*, even in his messages. British, maybe? Or perhaps he's simply a nice guy—one of the good ones.

I'll find out soon enough, but I have a feeling that this time will be different. That this time, it'll all be worth it.

I find him waiting near the lobby, just as he said he would be, with his hands in his pockets and his hair slicked back exactly like it was in his photo.

He doesn't seem expectant, doesn't seem nervous. He's simply standing there looking at ease, as if he's absolutely certain that he belongs, projecting the confidence of a model or a Roman statue.

"Hey," I say, my tone way too high. Now that I'm standing right next to him, I can't help but notice he's slightly shorter than I'd anticipated, but it doesn't really matter—the way he carries himself more than makes up for the height deficit.

"Hey," he replies. He does *not* have a British accent, to my disappointment, but his voice is most certainly deep and sexy. "Nice to see you."

Classy. Making it seem like this isn't a first encounter, just in case anyone is watching or listening. There are well-dressed people passing by, but they all seem more interested in the sparkling chandelier that's hanging overhead, the round table with dramatic flowers that's directly underneath it, or getting through to the bar in the back, which is busy with the sound of dozens of voices.

"Shall we?" he asks, gesturing toward a set of French doors

to the left. There are golden letters right above it that say HOTEL LOBBY, and a sign to the side indicates that only hotel guests can enter beyond that point.

"Sure."

I am mesmerized as I follow him—not by the beauty of the hotel, which I've seen a few times before, but by this gorgeous stranger. The way he steps lightly over the carpeted floors, walking with his shoulders arched back. The way he gives knowing nods to the staff, as if he shared a language with them that only they understood. The way his suit is built so precisely for his body, so that his pants and jacket stay perfectly in place regardless of the movements he makes.

When we step into an elevator, I can't help but sneak a glance down at what I'm wearing: a button-down shirt, a pair of khakis—which are thankfully not the ones that have the old ketchup stain on them—and a sleek gold bracelet that Jeremy gifted me last year. Cute yet formal—good enough to not look out of place at the Plaza, I told myself before leaving home, but now I feel incredibly underdressed.

"Can I offer you something to drink?" he asks me once we're inside his room. He wasn't lying when he said it was big—he's got a suite all to himself, with a bar, a living room that is entirely separate from the bedroom, and furniture that makes me think of *The Great Gatsby*.

"Uh…whatever you're having," I say, putting my hands in my back pockets as I look around. I'm trying not to seem too impressed by it all, but it's hard. This place looks like a fucking palace.

"You should take a peek out the window," he says while he moves around the bar area, making clinking noises.

"Why?"

He presses his lips into a sly smile. "It's quite a view."

I do as he says and go closer to the window. When I pull back the thick golden curtains, I can't help but let out a sigh. He was right. Even in the darkness, the view of Central Park is spectacular. Beyond it, the Upper East Side glitters with the light of a million tiny windows.

"Thoughts?" he asks.

"It's amazing."

He sneaks up behind me and plants a kiss on the side of my neck. I lean into him, taking in the smell of his cologne. There's something about his touch, about the feeling of his lips against my skin that's just so... *right*. When I turn toward him, I realize he's holding two glasses of champagne.

"Cheers," he says as he hands me one, staring deep into my eyes. That's when I know for sure that he's feeling it, too—this longing. He wants me every bit as much as I want him.

I clink my glass against his. "Cheers."

It's hard to tell exactly how it happens. One second we're admiring the view, sipping champagne, and suddenly his lips are on my neck again, and a moment later we're kissing.

He's unbuttoning my shirt.

I'm removing his jacket.

He's grabbing the back of my hair.

I'm undoing his pants.

Our half-empty champagne glasses are abandoned on a little side table, and he's holding my hand, guiding me toward the bedroom.

And then we're on the bed, making out and playing with each other's bodies. After what feels like forever—or all too soon, maybe—we're having sex, and it's the most incredible thing I've ever experienced in my life. The way he moves, the way he makes decisions for the both of us as to what will feel best. There is an assuredness to him—he knows what he likes, and he also seems to know what I'll like before I've even figured it out myself.

I'm gonna go ahead and call it right now: This is the best sex

I've ever had. Better than Jeremy. Oh, so much better, but I can't be bothered with the thought of Jeremy right now. All that matters is the feeling of this handsome man breathing into my neck, and the shape of his muscles, and the taste of his lips.

The bed doesn't squeak, doesn't move an inch, even when he's fucking me hard. Quality stuff, I'm telling you. But he doesn't always fuck me hard. He switches up the pace, so at times it's fast and thrilling, and at others it's slow and romantic.

That is, until he speeds up again, and this time we both know there's no going back, no more slowing down. He's getting closer. I'm getting closer. We're both nearly there, and it's gonna happen at the same time, and—

"I'll get you a towel."

I once read somewhere that half of a bottom's life consists of waiting for tops to get towels, and I can confirm it's one hundred percent true. The seconds stretch on while he heads off to the bathroom, and by the time he returns, I may as well have aged a few years.

"Here you go," he says, handing the towel to me.

It's soft and fluffy, but I hardly notice, because something more important is happening beside me. He has lain back down and is staring right at me, one hand beneath his head and the other on my chest. I have no idea where any of this is coming from, but there seems to be such marvel in his eyes—almost as if he were seeing me for the very first time.

"You're really something, aren't you?" he says, his breathing still heavy.

"Something good, I hope." I've been called *something* before, and it's not typically intended as a compliment. It's meant to mean I'm difficult, tough to deal with. A real piece of work.

"Something *very* good," he replies in a soft whisper. "I'm Robert, by the way."

I can't believe I forgot to ask for his name earlier. It wouldn't be the first time I've had sex with someone without knowing anything about them, but this time is different. He's someone whose name feels important to know.

"You look like a Robert," I whisper back.

"Really? How so?"

"I don't know. You just do." He's not a Rob. *Definitely* not a Robbie. He's strong, sophisticated, confident. A Robert, most certainly.

He narrows his eyes at me. "You look like a...like a Daniel, perhaps."

"Wow. Close. David, actually."

"David." He speaks my name as if it were exquisite, music to his ears.

Every time I end up in bed with someone new, I wish for it to be the way it is now. I wish to be looked at the way Robert is looking at me—to feel special, to feel wanted, to feel like I could stay there forever. I wish to find someone I can love and who can love me back, build a relationship from the ground up, and live the happily-ever-after that eluded me when Jeremy decided to leave. But I know better than that, even tonight. Nothing good or lasting ever comes from Grindr. This was always meant to be a one-time thing, and now it must come to an end.

I roll over to get out of bed. Setting my feet over the soft carpet, I start retracing our steps—a sock here, a shirt there. Moving as silently as a shadow, Robert follows me, picking up his own clothes and putting them on.

"Thank you," I say as I sit on the couch in the living room, putting on my shoes. "This was great."

"Thank *you*," he answers. He's right by the window, slipping on his suit jacket. "Listen..."

Words hang from his lips. For someone who is able to move through life with as much certainty as he does, he seems quite apprehensive all of a sudden. Frowning slightly, he turns toward me and says, "I don't mean to be too forward, but...would you want to go out for a drink?"

I just love being gay. It's perfectly okay to have sex with someone whose name you don't know. Ask that same person out for a drink, and well...you run the risk of being too forward.

"I'd like that," I say, rising from the couch. Deep down, a glimmer of light has appeared within me—one that feels a lot like relief, and excitement, and hope. "Really like that, actually."

"Great. Because I'd really like to as well."

He does one final check to make sure his shirt is properly tucked in, and just like that, he looks perfect again, as if I hadn't torn off all his clothes a short while ago. I only hope I look half as composed as he does.

"Where should we go?" I ask.

Robert's mouth twists into a thoughtful grimace. It only lasts a second, though, before he presses the palms of his hands together, becoming very serious.

"Grab those glasses," he says.

"These ones?" I ask, picking up the champagne flutes we left on a side table when we started undressing.

"Thank you." He reaches for one of them and downs its contents in one big gulp. He hands the empty glass back to me and then gives a small nod, as if indicating I should do the same.

And so I do. I drink the champagne that's left in the second glass all at once, trying hard not to make a face as I swallow.

"Beautiful," Robert says. "Hold on to those."

He rushes behind the bar and picks up the open bottle of champagne from the bucket of ice where he'd left it. Holding it by the neck, he loosely covers it with a towel and turns toward me.

"Ready to go?"

I'm not sure who this is anymore. I thought I had him figured out, but standing in front of me is not the collected, confident man from earlier. There is something playful in his eyes as he awaits my response—something almost childlike.

I smile at him. "Let's do it."

We head out of the room, down the elevator, and across the lobby. I'm all too aware of the champagne glasses in my hands the whole time, but I don't care if anyone sees them. There's an instinct inside my chest telling me that as long as I'm next to Robert, I can get away with anything.

As we approach the main entrance to the hotel, he throws a quick nod at a sharply dressed doorman.

"Could we get a car, please?"

"Of course, sir."

We walk out into the warm night air and wait on the front steps of the hotel. An instant later, a black sedan pulls up in front of us.

"After you," Robert says while the doorman holds the back door open for us.

I hop in, trying to keep the champagne glasses from clanging against each other, and slide across the plush leather seat to make space for Robert.

I'm not sure when or how he gave instructions on where to go, because not a word is spoken inside the car before the driver hits the pedal, turning onto Fifth Avenue. The slight possibility that this is all too good to be true and I'm actually being kidnapped crosses my mind. How stupid would that make me? It would be like getting in the back of an ice cream truck, except it's a Town Car. And instead of ice cream, there's champagne and a good-looking man.

"May I?" Robert asks, lifting the champagne bottle.

I hold up the glasses so he can fill them up, and then he takes one for himself.

"Do you do this a lot?" I ask as Fifth Avenue flashes past us.

"What?"

"Drink champagne with strangers in the back of Town Cars?"

He lets out a smile from the corner of his mouth. "First time, actually," he says. "You?"

"Also my first time."

"Here's to new adventures, then." He raises his glass slightly.

"To new adventures."

"And, I mean..." he adds, placing a hand on my thigh, "we're hardly strangers by now, wouldn't you say?"

I lean into his touch, and his lips find mine. He must've shaved yesterday or this morning, because his face is hairless, but I can feel gentle stubble brushing against my skin. He kisses me hungrily, passionately, as if he can't get enough of me even though we had sex no more than twenty minutes ago. And if I'm being honest, I can't get enough of him, either.

Champagne spilling on the floor of the car. Blurred lights outside the tinted windows. Strong hands holding me. None of this feels real. It's hard to understand how earlier tonight, I was sitting inside my apartment all alone, searching for a story to tell, but I suppose Stacey was right: a story has found me, and it's much better than anything I could've come up with myself.

CHAPTER FIVE

By the time the car comes to a full stop, the champagne bottle is empty, our glasses are discarded on the leather seats, and I feel entirely intoxicated—not from the alcohol, but from Robert himself. I wish we could stay here forever, being driven around Manhattan, refilling our glasses and breathing into each other's mouths, but the door opens suddenly, and Robert and I have no choice but to step out. With a hand on my shoulder, he leads the way across the sidewalk and into a busy bar.

Here's what I am able to register, despite my level of intoxication: We are being led to a booth for two in a cozy corner of the bar. There are red lights, crystal chandeliers, and gold panels covering the walls, and soft music is playing in the background.

"What do you want to drink?" Robert asks me as he picks up a menu.

"Hmm..." Now that I've had champagne, I really shouldn't switch to cocktails—and *definitely* not to beer—or I'll be hungover tomorrow, regretting every single sip of alcohol I drank.

Somehow, he reads my mind. "Did you enjoy the champagne earlier?"

"I did."

"Why not get another bottle, then?"

When the waiter comes to take our order, Robert subtly whispers into his ear what we want, and a few minutes later, we have an ice bucket holding a bottle and two fresh glasses of champagne in front of us.

"I hope you'll like this," he says, reaching for one of them. "It's different from what we had at the hotel."

"It's perfect." I haven't even tried it, but I just know.

He unbuttons his suit jacket, staring at me without blinking. "How are you feeling?"

"Great. I just...want to know more about you."

"I'll tell you everything," he replies. "But first...I have a confession to make."

Oh God. Here we go. He's about to tell me he tested positive for gonorrhea recently. Or he's not looking for anything serious—this is only and exclusively for fun. Or he's married with two kids and lives in a beautiful house in Massachusetts.

"You seemed familiar in your photos," he begins, "and...I realized a while ago why that was."

It's worse than I thought. He knows about me—he knows I'm a failure, a fraud. He has read the reviews for *Walking Home* and is aware of every scathing comment that has ever been made about my inability to write a good book.

I swallow hard. "You did?"

He nods. "It wasn't until you told me your name that it clicked. I...actually own one of your books. *The Millers*, is it?"

"Yeah, that's the one."

"I must've bought it a couple of years ago. I mean, I remember seeing it everywhere back then." It's hard to tell in the reddish light, but I'm almost sure his eyes just sparkled with something that looked a lot like wonder. "I've read it. And...I loved it."

"You...did?"

"Mm-hmm. I hope that's not weird to you."

At some point, back when Jeremy and I broke up and I started dating again, this was something I thought about a lot—how my life wasn't entirely private anymore. I was someone you could google, someone whose interviews you could read online, whose most intimate thoughts you could easily purchase from any bookstore. Someone you could make up your mind about before you ever even met him.

That thought used to intimidate me, but not this time. Because if Robert has read *The Millers* and enjoyed it, it must mean he knows me. He knows how I think, how I view myself, how I interact with the world. And that is all I want—to be known by him, to be understood, to be desired.

"It's not weird at all," I say in a whisper. "Thank you."

"In that case, you'll have to sign my copy sometime." His lips twist into a smile. "I still have it at home."

"Where is home?" It's another thing I can't believe I hadn't thought to ask. It seems like an important detail.

"I live in L.A.," he answers, raising his eyebrows. "But it's New York that feels like home. I went to college here."

"NYU?"

"Columbia."

Damn. I should have known. There's an Ivy League air about him.

"I lived in the city for several years after, and now I come here for work all the time."

"Really?" I ask, managing to remain composed even though my chest is swelling with hope. Because maybe we could make this work. Maybe, if he comes to New York regularly, we could truly get to know each other and fall in love. And one day, he could move back here for good—or I could go to L.A. Not that I want to get ahead of myself or anything.

"What kind of work do you do?" I ask.

"Finance."

"Oh." Jeremy was also a finance guy. I've always gone for logical, numerical men—they tend to be a good complement to my uncertain, creative chaos. "Tell me more."

"I manage a hedge fund. Boring stuff, really," he says. "What I want is to hear more about you. What's the author life like?"

Normally, I would say that it's great. A dream come true. But, deep down, I know Robert wants to hear the real answer. I know I can be honest.

"It's hard," I say. "One minute, you can be on top of the world, and the next..."

He finishes my sentence for me. "The whole world is crushing you."

"Exactly."

"Well," he says, "it is my job to assess risk. To place bets on people and things that will come out on top. For what it's worth...I would bet on you."

Something inside me melts. Where did this man come from? Seriously. How is it that I've spent an entire year heartbroken, going on shitty dates and being cast aside by guys I didn't even like that much, and all of a sudden he's here? The person I've been looking for? The one I've been so desperate to find?

"How did you start writing?" he asks, leaning slightly closer to me.

"I don't really remember," I reply. When I realize he's still staring at me fixedly, seeming unsatisfied with my answer, I clear my throat. "I mean...it's something I've always done. It was tough sometimes, you know? Being a closeted gay kid at school. I never felt like I belonged anywhere, so books were the place I escaped to. But I guess I started writing more seriously after my mom died. That's when telling stories became...a necessity, almost."

I remain frozen in my seat for a moment. I'm shocked—shocked that I told Robert all of this, shocked at my own honesty. Mostly, I'm shocked at the way he's staring at me, because he doesn't look at all uncomfortable, doesn't appear to be giving me any indication that I've overshared.

"What do you mean?" he asks.

"Huh?"

"How can telling stories be a necessity?"

I look down at the table, unable to hold his gaze any longer. "It's just…when I'm writing, I can be anyone I want to be. I can say all the things that sometimes I don't dare to speak out loud."

"Like what?"

"Well, that's the whole point of my books, isn't it? To answer that question so I don't have to."

He lets out a small smile, and I take this as an opportunity to change the subject. We'll have plenty of time further down the line to talk about all this. For tonight, I'd rather focus on less serious things, like the taste of the champagne, or the sound of Robert's voice, or the feeling of his hand on my thigh.

I'm not sure how long we've been here when he announces he's going to the bathroom, and I'm left waiting impatiently for him to come back. Time seems to move more slowly when he's not around, but the instant I see him returning, looking as chiseled as ever in his suit, everything feels all right again.

"Let's get out of here," he says, coming to a stop beside the table instead of sitting down.

"Shouldn't we pay the bill first?"

"Already did," he answers. "Come on."

"Where are we going?"

He grimaces thoughtfully, the same way he did back at the hotel. "I haven't decided yet."

I don't need to be asked again. I slide out of the booth and

63

follow Robert out of the bar. While he moves toward the edge of the sidewalk, trying to flag down a cab, I take a look around. We're in SoHo, from what I can tell. There is a closed boutique next door to the place where we just were, and a group of drunk girls is stumbling nearby, moving toward the entrance of the bar.

Before I can take in any other details about our surroundings, a yellow taxi stops in front of us, and we get in.

"Ninth Avenue and Fourteenth," Robert says to the driver. I have no idea what awaits us there, but I don't ask. I'd almost rather not know.

There's no champagne to entertain us this time around, but we do have each other's lips. That's how we keep busy during the ride, until the driver clears his throat to announce that we've arrived. Robert pulls a few bills out of his wallet without even looking at how much money he's handing over, and then we get out of the taxi and run across the street together.

Through an unassuming door, down a long set of steps, past a velvet curtain, and we find ourselves standing by a wide dance floor. Sweaty bodies move to loud music while green and blue strobe lights travel back and forth across the room.

"What do you want?" Robert shouts into my ear, gesturing toward the bar.

"Surprise me!" I shout back, because that seems to be what he does best. This is the last place I imagined he would bring us to, yet here we are, accepting pink cocktails from the bartender. Pressing our bodies together on the dance floor. Breathing heavily into each other's necks and kissing as if there's no one else around.

I'm not sure how many rounds of drinks he buys. It could be two—maybe three—and then we're on the move again.

The next bar is on the rooftop of a hotel, and it has a direct view of the Empire State Building. My ears are still ringing from the loud music and energy of the club, but there's something almost blissful about this place—about the soft piano playing in the background, the warm breeze hitting us from the side, and the feeling of Robert sitting right next to me on a low couch.

He orders us drinks and a couple of appetizers to share, and while we pick at them, exchanging long glances and flirty smiles, an unwelcome thought takes over my mind—*Jeremy*.

Maybe I'm getting so tired I can't think clearly anymore, because the last thing I want is to be reminiscing about my ex while I'm sitting next to a man who seems to have been handmade just for me. But now that the thought of Jeremy is here to stay, I can't help but admit to myself that there are plenty of similarities between him and Robert.

If I relax my vision, Robert's face almost blurs into Jeremy's. They look alike, really, save for a few important details. Robert is older than Jeremy, obviously. Jeremy's hair was black, the color of coal, whereas Robert's is more of a deep brown, streaked with gray here and there. Jeremy's eyes were like swimming in a lake—still, calm, liquid blue. Robert's are dark green, and they're more like a river—hypnotizing, fast, ever-changing. The kind of eyes I could get lost in forever.

Robert is who Jeremy might become in a few years—classier, more mature, more sure of himself. Not that Jeremy isn't all of those things, but he's still in the process of fully becoming them, whereas Robert is there. He is all that and more.

"What are you thinking about?" he asks, studying my face.

"Me?" I reply, as if it weren't already obvious who he's talking to. "Oh. Um...nothing."

He smiles from the corner of his mouth. "You ready to go somewhere else?"

I sneak a glance down at the half-eaten appetizers on the table. I'm not sure I'm ready to give them up just yet—I could use a little more fuel if we're gonna keep going at this pace—but I don't say it out loud.

"Sure," I reply instead. The word comes out slightly slurred, even though I don't feel that drunk—or at least not as drunk as I should feel, given the amount of alcohol we've consumed. "Do you have somewhere in mind?"

"Maybe we could walk around for a bit, see if any other places catch our eye?"

When we step out of the building, the night air feels much cooler than it did earlier. Spring has not fully given way to summer yet, even though Memorial Day is only a few days away.

As we walk the first couple of blocks, I keep waiting for Robert to speak up, until I realize that maybe he won't. He must've been right earlier when he said we're no longer strangers, because there's actually something comforting about the silence. Walking beside him through near-empty city streets has a way of feeling familiar and safe.

"Can you hear that?" he asks suddenly, reaching for my hand.

We come to a stop in the middle of the sidewalk. I hold his gaze while I try to listen for the sound he's talking about, and once the distant noise of traffic and sirens fades into the background, I'm able to make it out—a waterfall.

He pulls on my hand, and we've only gone a few more steps further when we find ourselves at the entrance of a narrow park—one of Manhattan's privately owned green spaces. It's beautiful, with twinkling lights hanging from the trees, potted flowers all over, and a grand waterfall covering the back wall.

"I'd forgotten this was here," he says as we move deeper into the park. With the sound of water hitting rocks becoming louder and louder, we may as well have been transported out of the city. "I used to eat lunch here all the time—my old office was just around the corner."

I'd say something in response, if only I wasn't so mesmerized by this place. It's not my first time here, either, but it looks entirely different tonight. Maybe I'm just wasted. Or maybe it's an effect of being here with Robert.

We sit down, extremely close but not touching, and for a while, we just stare straight ahead at the waterfall. Then, without warning, Robert turns to look at me.

"Can I ask you something?"

Slowly, I nod. "Anything."

"Does it ever get lonely? Being a writer?"

"It does, yeah."

"How do you deal with that? How do you—?"

"I...don't. I mean, writing helps, in and of itself. I never feel lonely when I'm lost in my own stories. As for the rest of the time...I've gotten used to it, I guess. In some ways, it's been me against the world for a long time—even before I started writing for a living."

"I also feel lonely sometimes."

I raise my eyebrows at him. When he told me earlier that he was feeling lonely in his hotel room, I thought it was a line—a way to get me into his bed, but now there is a deep, undeniable honesty on his face.

"How is that possible? You're so..." *magnetic, handsome, charming*, I almost say. It makes absolutely no sense for someone like him to feel alone.

"It's all smoke and mirrors," he replies, as if he'd somehow heard the words I stopped myself from speaking. "There's something about what you said before that resonated with me—how you couldn't be yourself while growing up. I felt that, too—and still do, at times. Finance isn't necessarily the easiest industry to be in as a gay man. There are days when I feel like the only way to deal with it all is to become someone else. In fact...my grandmother used to go so far as to say that there are two versions to each of us: who we are in public, and who we are in private, when no one is watching."

"Which one do you feel like now?"

"Neither," Robert answers, the twinkling lights reflecting in his eyes. "There must be a third version of me I didn't know about: who I am when I'm with you."

I could swear, for a few seconds, my heart stops beating, because I feel the same way—I'm not the old David. I am not the lonely, desperate writer I become when I'm by myself in my apartment; not the fun, engaging author I manage to be during book events; not the messy, irresponsible person my family makes me out to be. Tonight, I'm someone entirely new. Someone better.

"I'm sorry," he says, looking down at his lap. "I didn't mean for the conversation to take such a serious turn. We can..."

"It's okay. You can talk to me about anything."

I mean it. I hope he knows he's safe with me, that there's nothing he could possibly say that would make me judge him.

"What do you wanna do?" he asks. "If you're tired, we can call it a night."

"I don't want this to end yet."

He smiles. "That's what I hoped you would say."

"What are our options, then?"

"We could hit up a few more bars. Start making our way Uptown and circle back to the hotel later, if you want?"

"I do want."

"Excellent."

And so we head out of the park, back into taxis and bright lights. Another bar, more kissing. Another bar, more drinking. The feeling of his hands on my back, the brush of his beard on my skin, the smell of his cologne. It's like a cycle I never want to break.

There comes a point when I don't know where we are anymore,

don't know what time it is, or even where my body ends and his begins. The only thing I know for sure is that his touch has become familiar. It's like I've been waiting for him my whole life, and now that he's here, everything finally makes sense. All the things I've been looking for, all the things that have slipped out of my hands: love, safety, even money—he's here to give me all of that and more. Goodbye to the loneliness, goodbye to the stress about paying bills, goodbye to asking myself what's to become of my life, because here is my answer. My confident, attractive, wonderful answer.

Suddenly, I turn a key and we're crossing the threshold of my apartment. I don't remember when or how we decided to come here. He has a room at the fucking Plaza, for crying out loud. Why would we want to sleep in my shitty studio?

We stumble through the darkness, starting to tear off each other's clothes, but then he pulls away from me.

"Hold on, hold on," he says, sounding just as drunk as I feel. "I really do need to pee."

Oh, right, *that's* the reason we came here. A few images come to me: We were at a bar on Columbus, I think. Then we were sitting in a taxi. The windows were cracked open, our heads resting back against the seat, and Robert was mumbling that he should've used the bathroom at the bar.

"My apartment's just here," I said, signaling loosely out the window as if I actually knew what street we were driving past.

"Quick pit stop before heading back to my hotel?"

I let out a giggly laugh that was unlike my own. I don't remember telling the driver my address, but we made it here, so I must've managed to explain where to go.

God, I'm so drunk. But so happy. *Drappy*. Is that even a word?

Let me google it to find out. Or, better yet, I should type it into my notes app so I can use it in my next book. It's a brilliant word.

I pull my phone out of my pocket, but the battery is dead. It doesn't matter, anyway. I just heard the toilet flushing. Robert's coming back any minute, and I want him next to me so badly. I want him to hurry up already so he can keep kissing me.

The door opens and Robert's shadow appears, backlit against the bathroom light. His shirt is off and the outline of his muscles is a sight to behold. Fuck, he's hot.

When he speaks, though, he doesn't say anything sensual. Instead, he mumbles, "I have a bit of a headache."

Oh no! I don't want him to have a headache! I want him to feel good, to feel as good as I do.

But I think he'll be okay. If he wasn't okay, he wouldn't be kissing me. He wouldn't be taking off my clothes. He wouldn't be pushing me into the bed, holding me tight as we fall on top of the mattress.

We shouldn't be doing this here. We should call a taxi so we can head back to his hotel—but I suppose the Plaza will still be there in the morning. For tonight, we have this: our hands, our lips, our bodies, and this magnetic force that keeps pulling us toward each other.

And so I let go. I empty my mind of any thought, any resistance, and allow myself to sink into him.

CHAPTER SIX

He was not a dream.

That is my first thought when I wake up. Robert is lying next to me, still as a statue, looking perfect and peaceful.

Last night really happened—that is my second thought. We really did have amazing sex, and sipped champagne in the back of a Town Car, and made our way through the city together, spinning from one bar to the next, drinking, laughing, and becoming new versions of the people we used to be.

I know that there's a hangover lingering somewhere in the back of my head, waiting for the right moment to strike, but I try my best to ignore it. I can't remember the last time I drank as much as I did last night. I'm not even sure when or how we made it back to my apartment, but I'll ask Robert once he wakes up—maybe he'll be able to fill in some of the gaps.

For now, I'm just happy to be here, because I feel so damn lucky. Lucky to have met him, lucky to be lying next to him, lucky to witness how beautiful he looks as he breathes slowly.

Except... *is* he breathing? He is awfully still, now that I think of it. His chest doesn't seem to be rising or falling at all.

"Robert?" I ask.

He doesn't move.

"Robert, wake up," I say, squeezing his arm. There is something desperate in my voice, as if an instinct deep inside me knew something my mind hasn't fully realized yet—something I *don't want* to realize.

He's going to open his eyes any second. He's going to draw in a deep inhale, and slowly remember where he is and why he slept here, and he's going to smile as soon as he sees me beside him.

The seconds stretch on as I wait for all of those things to happen, but none of them do, so I sit up on the bed, placing my hands on his shoulders. I lift him up slightly, but his neck just bends backward like a rag doll, his head hanging heavily over the pillow.

He's dead.

The scream doesn't quite leave my mouth. It comes out like a high, desperate howl from the lowest part of my throat. I roll over in bed, trying to untangle my legs from the sheets, and once my feet are firmly planted on the hardwood floors, I turn to look at him again.

Holy fuck, he's dead!

What the hell happened last night? Did I kill him? Oh my God, I must have killed him.

Memories flash in my mind—champagne flutes, green and blue strobe lights, kissing in taxis. Then...nothing. The last part of the night is a complete blur, and it doesn't help that my heart is beating so fast that it's about to break a hole through my chest, because I can't think clearly or even slow down long enough to make a decent attempt at remembering what went down once we got back to my apartment.

We must've had sex before falling asleep. Yes, I'm pretty sure we did. Maybe something went wrong while we were doing it...maybe he asked me to choke him and I went too far. But no, that doesn't make sense. I think I'd remember, because it would be so unlike me to choke someone in the first place. Or maybe...wait, no. That is impossible. There's no way I sat on his face for so long that he suffocated...is there?

I take a few clumsy steps forward, my eyes searching the apartment for any evidence that could tell me what happened, and that's when my gaze falls on the desk. My closed laptop is sitting on top of it, right next to a pen and a pad with a note written in a drunk, messy scrawl: *Important to remember—drappy.*

What the fuck is *drappy*? Is it code for something? A key piece of the puzzle I left for myself to find once I woke up? I'll need to come back to it, try to remember the significance of that word, but first I should figure out what to do about the body on my bed.

I need to call 911. That is definitely the right move—if only I could find my phone. I take another look at the desk, check the bedside table and the kitchen counter, but it's nowhere to be seen. It isn't until I pick up the pants I was wearing last night that I feel its weight inside one of the pockets. I pull it out, but when I touch the screen, nothing happens. It's dead.

I stumble back toward the bed, reaching for the cord that's plugged into the wall, and I stick the end of it into my phone. A charging symbol appears, but the screen remains black otherwise. I'll have to give it a few minutes.

While I wait, pacing anxiously by the bed, my eyes fall on the microwave clock, where the numbers 6:47 are flashing in green. I focus on them for a moment, trying to push away the million questions that are spinning inside my mind, and when the time changes to 6:48, a few words come back to me. *I have a bit of a headache.*

Which one of us said that? I think it was me. I must've not been feeling well toward the end of the night, which might explain why Robert brought me home. When I close my eyes, I see something: an open palm holding three tiny, blue pills. The thing is...it's not my own hand I see. It's Robert's.

I have a bit of a headache.

Oh no! Do you want to take something for it?

You know what, I think I will. Something strong, preferably. It's a pretty awful one.

A couple of years ago, I started getting bad migraines. They got so bad, in fact, that my doctor gave me some pills that were supposed to help. But...as far as I recall, the pills were white and not blue.

My feet carry me to the bathroom before I've even made up my mind about going to check. The mirrored cabinet is half open, which doesn't feel to me like a good sign. Inside, there's all my hair and facial products, as well as two pill bottles I've barely touched in the past year.

The first would be the migraine medication. The second contains my "rainy-day pills," as Jeremy used to call them. Antidepressants, which I hated taking because they made my mind foggy, but which my doctor prescribed anyway. I only ever took them on my worst days, so the bottle is still more than half full.

Here you go—these should help.

Thanks. How many should I take?

Two, I think. Three at most.

Oh my God. I definitely killed him.

I must've given him the wrong bottle. We were so fucking drunk that neither of us made sure it was the correct one—hell, we were so drunk that it felt like a good idea for him to take my prescription pills.

I don't want you to have a headache! I want you to feel good, to feel as good as I do.

I don't think you're meant to take more than one of the antidepressants, let alone three—especially not with the amount of alcohol we consumed last night.

Fuck, fuck, fuck. What do I do? I'm going to be blamed for this. It's all over, isn't it? Not just my writing career, but my entire life. I just never thought it would end this way, never thought of myself as capable of killing someone, not even accidentally.

A soft ping comes from outside the bathroom, which tells me my phone has turned on. I run toward it, pick it up with shaking hands, and scroll through my contacts. Who do I call? I don't think I can dial 911 anymore. I won't be strong enough to do it. I need someone to come help me, someone I can talk to about all this before I turn myself in.

My family is out of the question. Oh, can you imagine? *You did this to yourself, David*, my dad will say. *You're too reckless.* Sheila will be smirking in the background, having already entered the numbers 911 into her phone, her finger hovering over the button so she can place the call at any second.

Jeremy is my next best option. I miss him more than ever right at this moment—I miss the safety he used to make me feel. If only we'd stayed together, none of this would be happening. But what am I meant to do—call after not speaking to him in nearly a year and say, *Uh…I know this is kinda weird, but I think I just killed the guy I hooked up with last night?*

In terms of friends…I have no friends. I never really formed strong bonds as a teen, even though I tried. I guess there were too many things that got in the way—the grief of losing my mom, the stress over my dad and Sheila's sudden decision to get married, my inability to be myself at school because I wasn't out yet and was terrified anyone would see me for who I truly was.

I was so certain it would all change once I moved to the city. I once dreamed of having the kind of friends you live across the hall from in your twenties, the kind you meet up with for brunch every single Sunday and who will always be there for you. I dreamed of having friends that I would find myself eating dinner with twenty years down the line, reminiscing about the good old days after having spent decades by each other's side.

For a while, I thought that was who my college friends would eventually become, but they didn't. They started off as the kind of people I sat next to in class and grew into buddies I would party with on weekends. I'm sure we could've become more than that, if any of them had stayed in New York. Some of them did, for a year or two after graduation, until they found job opportunities in San Francisco. Or moved to Vancouver to be with their boyfriends. Or went to grad school in Boston. One by one, my friends disappeared, making empty promises to stay in touch and to come visit. Now, they're the kind of people you text every year to wish them a happy birthday, or message on Instagram to say "Looks amazing!" when they're at a nice restaurant or on vacation. None of them are the kind of friends you call to help you figure out what to do with a dead body.

No one ever warned me this could happen. No one ever told me friendships could fade so easily, or that the older you get, the harder it is to form new connections. No one ever said I might find myself here, with absolutely nobody to call in an emergency and nobody to come to my rescue. I don't understand how I ended up so alone, don't get why it is that every single person I've ever known has either left or given up on me.

Except for one. Someone who has been there for the good and the bad over the past four years, someone who would never, ever turn her back on me.

"Stacey," I pant into the phone as soon as she picks up. "Stacey, I need you."

"Who is this?"

"It's me. It's—it's David," I say, but she responds with nothing but silence. "David Alvarez, your client?"

"Darling, it's early. What could you possibly need at this ungodly hour?"

Sneaking a glance at the microwave, I see the time has inched just a few minutes closer to seven.

"I might be in trouble. I need you to come to my apartment."

"Why would I—"

"Please. I wouldn't ask if it wasn't really important—a life-and-death situation. I'm serious."

Stacey lets out a loud sigh into the phone. "It'll take me a while to get all the way up there from Brooklyn."

"It doesn't matter. Please just...just come."

A brief pause. "Should I be worried, David?"

"I, uh..." Unable to find an answer to her question, I clear my throat. "It'll all be better once you get here."

The instant we hang up, my legs start feeling weak. I lower myself to sit on the edge of the bed, still clutching my cell phone tightly, but when I catch a glimpse of Robert out of the corner of my eye, I jump back to my feet as if I'd been electrocuted.

I try sitting at the desk chair instead, and when that doesn't work, I lock myself in the bathroom, but none of it is enough. I can't seem to find a way to put sufficient distance between me and Robert's lifeless body.

In the end, I opt for waiting right outside my building. I take a seat on the front steps and stare out at 90th Street, hugging my legs. This would be a beautiful morning, if there wasn't...you know, a dead body waiting for me upstairs. The sunlight is trickling softly through the leaves of trees, and people are starting to step out of their homes, either to head off to work early or take their dogs out for a morning walk. I can feel the city coming to life all around me, even as a heavy darkness spreads within my chest.

After a while, the hangover starts to settle in. I should drink some water, get some food in me, but I can't bring myself to stand up, can't wrap my mind around the idea of stepping back inside the apartment—not until Stacey arrives, at least. My head gets heavier, my mouth gets drier, and all I can do is sit here motionless, feeling more hungover than I've ever felt in my life—as if this day wasn't already terrible enough as it is.

———

"There's a dead body on your bed, darling," Stacey says the moment we walk into my apartment.

"There—there is, yeah." The front door swings shut behind us, letting out a faint squeak before clicking softly into place.

Stacey doesn't seem angry, doesn't seem the least bit outraged or surprised, which makes me wonder two things. The first is whether she had been expecting to find something like this all along— whether she has always thought me capable of murder, so that when I called earlier, she automatically assumed that's what had happened. The second is whether this is the first dead body she's ever seen—and something is telling me it isn't.

"Why is there a dead body on your bed, again?" she asks.

"I...I think I killed him."

"Is that why you called me? To make me an accessory to murder?" The most subtle of frowns appears on her face. "I can't say I appreciate that, dear. I don't think I'd do well in prison. A few decades ago, maybe, but not now. I'm getting old, you see, and I've become accustomed to a certain lifestyle."

"That's not why I called you," I reply. Now that she mentions it, why *did* I call her? It hadn't crossed my mind that asking her to come over might implicate her in this whole mess. I guess I just wanted someone else to be here. I wanted to not feel so fucking alone, at least for a little while, before the cops come to take me away.

"Are you going to explain what happened, then?"

I look down at the floor. I feel like a child all of a sudden, about to justify his actions after doing something wrong. Deep down, I wish I actually *was* a child, because then I might be entitled to the comfort, the protection, and the understanding I so desperately want in this moment.

"Last night, I was...just home, really, sitting at my desk," I begin. "I was trying to come up with a story, like you told me to."

"Well, David, I don't recall saying that you should kill someone for the sake of getting a book deal. That might've been taking things a bit too far."

"I never set out to kill anybody!" I say, my voice coming out as a shriek. "I was...I was simply trying to write, but the inspiration wouldn't come, so I went on Grindr."

"What *is* Grindr, exactly?"

"You don't want to know," I answer firmly. "Anyway...I started chatting with this guy, and he invited me over to his hotel. He was staying at the Plaza, so...so I went over, and we fooled around, and then he asked me if I wanted to go out for a drink."

"He had a room at the Plaza, yet you chose to spend the night *here*?" Stacey asks, her eyes traveling around the apartment in a way that feels a tad judgmental.

"Stacey, that's not the point!"

"What is the point, then?"

"The point is...we went out. We had such a fun time, going around the city, hopping from one bar to the next, and..."

Stacey peeks at me from above her glasses. "And?"

"We had the most amazing night," I answer, swallowing hard. I can't believe it's over just like that. I can't believe I killed one of the few men I've ever truly liked—that I'll never get to lie beside him again, or taste his lips, or get to know him well enough for us to fall in love.

"Darling, you can just jump straight to the part where you committed murder," Stacey says, and that's when I explain everything to her—how drunk we got, how we made the decision to come back here, how Robert complained about a bad headache, how he took the wrong pills.

"What happened after you gave him the pills?" she asks once I'm done telling the story.

"We had sex one last time, and then we fell asleep."

"At least he went out with a bang."

"Stacey!"

"What? I meant you two had a banging night out on the town, by the sound of it. Get your mind out of the gutter, David!"

I shake my head, bringing a hand up to cover my mouth. "I'm going down for this, aren't I?"

Stacey shrugs. "Well..."

"*Stacey!*"

"What did I do this time?"

"You're supposed to tell me it's gonna be okay," I reply, sounding like I'm begging. "You're meant to say I'm gonna be fine, even if it's not true."

"First things first, my dear," Stacey says. "Have you made sure he's *actually* dead?"

"How would I do that?"

"Check for a pulse, of course. What other way is there?"

Stacey takes a few steps toward the bed. With the assuredness of a paramedic or a detective, she lifts Robert's arm and places two fingers on his wrist. Then, she tries the side of his neck, just beneath his jaw, and finally, she lifts his left eyelid with one hand, turns on the flashlight on her phone with the other, and shines a light into his eye.

"He's dead," she announces, turning back toward me.

"Are you sure?" My lungs deflate like a balloon. For a moment, I'd allowed myself to hope that Stacey would find a pulse—that not all was lost yet.

"Very dead. Can't have been too long, though, because he's still warm."

How does Stacey know all of this? I suppose she may have picked up a few things about dealing with dead bodies from all the books she's worked on throughout the years, but she's never told me much about her past. All I truly know about Stacey is that she's passionate about publishing and she's been married several times... and didn't I hear a rumor once that a couple of those husbands died under somewhat mysterious circumstances?

Before I can ask any questions, she starts rubbing her chin thoughtfully, which makes me feel like we're back in her office, sitting across from each other at her desk trying to find the answer to a complicated industry-related issue. She's even wearing work clothes—a bright yellow pantsuit I've seen her in once or twice before—which make her look all the more businesslike.

"Where are the pills?" she asks suddenly.

"In the bathroom."

"Show them to me."

I don't question her. I trust that she knows what she's doing, so I rush into the bathroom, grab the bottle from the cabinet, and return a second later, holding it up for her to see.

"These are one milligram each," she says, looking at the tiny pills through the translucent plastic.

"Yeah. So?"

"You said he took three?"

"He—he did."

"He had three milligrams in total, then."

"What are you getting at?"

"I'm trying to figure out whether that'd be enough Xanax to kill anyone," she says. "I'm just not sure."

"How could you not be sure?" I ask shrilly.

"Well, three milligrams sounds like a decently high dose. One of my ex-husbands used to take half a milligram a day, and it worked just fine for him. And everybody knows the first and most important rule of antidepressants, darling: they should never be mixed with alcohol. If you two drank as much as you made it sound, then..."

"Then what?"

"We're in hazy territory. There's no way for us to know whether or not the pills killed him."

There's a long pause, during which I wait for Stacey to make a final declaration: that I'm probably guilty. That I should turn myself in, pretend she was never here, and never contact her again.

A second later, though, she draws in a long breath and says, "Then again...it might not have been your fault."

"Really?" A small glimmer of hope returns to my chest, but I know better than to let it overpower me.

"He was complaining about a headache, wasn't he? It's entirely possible that he suffered a stroke. Or even a heart attack. Coincidences *do* happen, David. Perhaps he just passed away in the wrong place at the wrong time. But..."

"Why does there have to be a *but*? Can't we just leave it at 'I didn't kill him, let's carry on with our lives'?"

"But," Stacey continues as if she hadn't heard me, "given the very real possibility that you *did* play a role in his death, it might be best to cover your tracks."

"Cover my tracks?"

"Think about it, dear—police all over this tiny apartment. Your entire home wrecked. The coroner examining this body for hours—no, days—while you languish in custody. Even if they came to the conclusion that you had nothing to do with it, you'll be all over the news by then, won't you? One can only imagine the headlines: *Struggling Author Murders Lover. David Alvarez Named a Person of Interest in the Death of Powerful Businessman.* You'll be the talk of the industry, love, and *no one* wants to be the talk of the industry. Editors at every publishing house will read about this, influencers will have a field day with it, and before you know it, your very own readers will be telling their neighbors and book clubs about it. Getting a deal for your third book has proven to be challenging enough as it is, and if all this happens, well... I daresay it'll be near impossible. Remember, the court of public opinion won't be kind to you— even if you're innocent."

My face starts feeling very hot as I think about this "best-case scenario"—one in which Robert died of natural causes, but my reputation and career would still be ruined forever. As for the worst-case scenario... well, it would probably involve a manslaughter charge and prison time. It'll involve a disappointed look in my father's eyes as I stare at him from across a packed courtroom, an online mob that will follow me for years to come, and a permanent stain on my criminal record and romantic prospects.

I can just picture myself a few years from now, fresh out of prison and sitting in a dimly lit bar in front of a good-looking guy who stares back at me with some sort of sick fascination. *So you're that author who murdered a man you slept with, aren't you?*

No, no, I didn't murder him, I'll be forced to say. *He was just found dead in my bed. Totally different thing.*

I'm never going to find another boyfriend again, am I? Never going to escape from the shadow this will cast upon my life, never going to recover from the consequences of what happened last night.

"What do we do?" All hope has quickly left my body, leaving

behind nothing but a faint feeling of nausea that makes me worry I might throw up. "How do we stop all that from happening?"

"I can think of one thing." I could swear, for the briefest moment, Stacey's eyes light up with the same kind of eagerness she shows whenever she's trying to prove that there are no lengths she won't go to for her clients—that she's still one of the best agents in the industry.

"Tell me." I take a step closer to her, desperate to hear the solution, desperate to find a way to fix this mess. "What is it?"

"You said he has a hotel room in the city, didn't you? What if we simply...transported him there? Laid him to rest in his own bed for housekeeping to find once they come to clean the room?"

"That's crazy."

"Crazier than sitting back and watching your entire life crumble?" Stacey asks, grimacing a little. "I don't know about that, dear. It's a tough one."

I almost want to laugh. The feeling doesn't belong in this moment—it would be psychopathic to let out a chuckle when there's a dead man *right there*, but there's something about Stacey's tone that seems equally out of place. She may as well be talking about moving a sack of potatoes.

"What's in it for you?"

"Excuse me?"

"Why are you helping me?"

"I take no pleasure in any of this, David, believe me. But what kind of agent would I be if I didn't advocate for my clients' interests, no matter what?" Stacey replies, lifting her chin proudly. "If I can keep you out of prison and off the headlines, my job here will be done. Granted, of course, that once we've gotten rid of the body, you'll write that book we talked about. Nothing would make me happier than to watch your writing career take off once again, unhindered by any of what's happened here."

"I can't do this," I mumble in a whisper. "It would be so wrong. We can't—"

"It's your decision, really," she replies slowly. "I will support you either way. But you know what I would do if it was my future at risk. If we do nothing, there is a one hundred percent probability that you'll get in trouble. If we move him . . . you'd be giving yourself a solid chance to get away with it and put this behind you."

I have no idea where she's finding the strength to remain calm, no idea how she's able to make decisions under this kind of pressure, because I'm about to start hyperventilating.

"People will see us," I say, breathing heavily. "There'll be security cameras, and—"

"Then it's a good thing there are credit card records from all the bars you went to yesterday. He had a big night out—that's what we'll tell people. He is still extremely drunk, and we desperately need to put him to bed. If anyone were to come asking questions later, we'd tell them he was alive the last time we saw him, and that he must have passed away in his hotel room. The end."

"Someone will find out the truth."

"They'll do an autopsy, yes," Stacey says, nodding to herself. "If it turns out he died of natural causes, no one will ask more questions. And if he didn't, there'll be no way to trace the pills he took back to you. They'll find drugs in his system, call it an overdose, and perhaps contact us to ask some clarifying questions about what happened before we dropped him off at his hotel. Whereas if his lifeless body is found in your apartment, well . . . that'll open up every last detail of your life to scrutiny. The press will be tipped off the minute the police get here, the entire investigation will revolve around you, and you already know how the rest of that story will play out."

I can't believe Stacey is starting to make sense. I can't believe

I'm actually considering this, can't believe either of us would be as unhinged as to actually go through with this plan.

Could it really be as simple as that—taking him to his hotel and laying him to rest peacefully on his bed? I mean, we were meant to sleep at the Plaza anyway. We could've easily woken up there instead, and I could've snuck out of the room this morning, and then it would all be the same. What Stacey is saying is that we should just make a tiny correction to a mistake Robert and I made last night, which was falling asleep in my apartment rather than at his hotel. There's hardly anything morally wrong with that…right?

"Where's his wallet?" I ask.

"What?"

"His wallet. The hotel room key must be in it."

"Try his pants," Stacey says, nodding toward the ground beside the bed.

I bend down to pick them up, but just as I'm about to stick a hand into one of the pockets, Stacey grabs hold of my arm to stop me.

"Just a second."

She reaches into her purse and pulls out a set of fancy leather gloves I've only ever seen her wear during winter.

"We wouldn't want our fingerprints all over his wallet, would we?" she asks as she slips them on.

"Why are you carrying gloves? It's summer."

"I had to come prepared, darling."

I swallow hard. So she *was* expecting to find something criminal when she agreed to come to my apartment.

"Is there anything else in there I should know about?" I ask, staring at the big purse hanging over her shoulder, but she doesn't seem to hear me.

She sticks a few leather-gloved fingers into the pocket of Robert's pants and pulls out a sleek black wallet. Allowing the pants to fall back to the floor, she flips the wallet open and bites the inside of her cheek while she looks through it.

"Robert Wallace," she reads out loud, looking down at his driver's license. "Forty-six years old. Good for him! I wouldn't have guessed—wouldn't have guessed that at all."

"That's because he's thirty-six." I clear my throat. "*Was* thirty-six."

"Says forty-six right here."

I reach out to grab the license from Stacey, all thought of not leaving fingerprints on his stuff forgotten. There it is—Robert Edward Wallace. Height: 5'7". Weight: 145 pounds. An address in Malibu, California, postal code 90265. Date of birth...January 7, 1978.

He lied to me. With that realization comes a cold, dark feeling that begins in my chest and slowly travels downward until it settles in the pit of my stomach. He managed to fool me into thinking he was ten years younger than he really was, and it didn't even cross my mind to doubt him. Then again...I never actually asked about his age, did I? I only got it from his Grindr profile, and everyone lies on Grindr (I mean, *I* don't, but everyone else does). There's also the slight possibility that he entered the wrong year by accident when he created his account, which would make it an honest mistake.

So...it's not like he actually *lied*. And what difference would it make, anyway? Age is just a number, and Robert was everything I've been looking for in a man. I would've wanted him even if he was fifty-six, or sixty-six. His age doesn't change what happened last night, doesn't change any of the things I felt.

"What else is there?" I ask, handing the license back to Stacey.

"Credit cards, business cards, and...I thought he had a room at the Plaza?"

"He did."

"Why is there a key card for the Hilton in here?"

"Must be old. Look again."

Stacey keeps pulling cards out of the wallet, and sure enough, when she finds the one for the Plaza, she holds it up for me to see.

"We're actually doing this, then?" she asks.

"Yeah," I say, nodding slowly. "Seems like we are."

First thing to do is dress him. Stacey looks away while I take the covers off and slip his heavy legs through the holes of his pants. Then, she helps me lift him so we can put his shirt and suit jacket on. Once I've done his buttons and tucked in the shirt, I take a step back from the bed to take a good look at him.

"He looks wrong."

"Wrong how?"

"He looked so composed in his suit yesterday. Now he's all… wrinkled."

"He had a long night, remember?" Stacey says. "You can't forget, dear. That's the story."

"I just hope people will believe he's actually drunk."

"They'll have no reason not to. That's what's brilliant about our plan—we'll be hiding in plain sight. Now, let's get going. We need to get him back to his hotel before housekeeping goes in to clean the room."

"How do we do this?" I ask. "Do we just…"

"Carry him? Well, of course. How else are we meant to do it?"

A dark thought crosses my mind. There's a big suitcase under the bed—the one I use when I'm going on longer trips. But we *definitely* cannot do that. Putting a body in a suitcase is a little too fucked up, even by the standards of what we're planning to do. Besides, I don't think it would be big enough to fit Robert anyway.

And so, left with no other choice, Stacey and I drag him out of bed. She puts one of his arms over her shoulders, and I do the same with the other arm. He's every bit as heavy as I thought he would be, but we still manage to carry him toward the front door of the apartment, his limp feet dragging along the wooden floors with every step we take.

We're about to open the door when I remember something.

"Wait, wait, wait," I say. "I need to get my phone."

"Couldn't have thought of that sooner, could you?" Stacey grunts as we lower Robert to the ground and lean him back against a wall, his legs stretched out on the floor in front of him.

I run around the bed to go unplug my phone, which is now at seventy-four percent battery, and shove it into my pocket. I'm half-way back toward Stacey when I touch my other pocket and realize something else is missing.

"Oh! Wallet."

I reach for the pants I was wearing last night. The instant I wrap a hand around my wallet, another thought comes to me, and so I skip back to the bedside table.

"Maybe a pair of sunglasses, for his eyes," I say, reaching into one of the drawers.

"Are you sure you have everything now?" Stacey says sharply once I finally return to her side. "We can't keep doing this all day."

"I'm sure," I say, leaning down to grab Robert's arm. "Let's go."

Out of the apartment and down the hallway we go. Robert's head hangs heavily from his neck, rolling from one side to the other, which makes me worry that he doesn't look drunk at all. He looks dead—*very* dead, but at least there's no one around to witness it. This will be a problem for later, when we're out in public, but for now, we just have to worry about getting him out of the building.

The instant we reach the top of the stairs, Stacey and I stop and meet each other's eyes.

"I hope you haven't been skipping out on the gym," she says, raising her eyebrows slightly.

"Of course I've been skipping out on the gym!" I snap back. "You know full well I don't have money for the membership."

"At least one of us is fit, then. You should be grateful for all the Pilates I do."

I draw in a deep breath, trying to find some sort of extraordinary strength within me, and then we start going down the stairs.

Bang, bang, bang.

Robert's feet keep hitting the steps as we make our way down, but there's hardly anything we can do about it. We wouldn't be able to lift him higher if we tried, so Stacey and I continue steadily, doing our best to not collapse under his weight. By the time we reach the bottom of the stairs, my neck and shoulders feel stiff, even though we've barely gone down one floor and still have a long way to go before we get to the Plaza.

"Let's just make it out of the building," Stacey pants, nodding at the hallway ahead of us. I'm sure she's thinking the same thing I am—that we can take a small break outside while we call an Uber.

Ninetieth Street is slightly more alive now than it was a half hour ago. The air feels warmer, the sunlight is brighter. A car drives by. A woman pushing a stroller is wandering along the sidewalk without a care in the world, while the sounds of the city buzz somewhere in the distance. Luckily, no one seems to be looking our way, so we lower Robert onto the front steps of my building and lean him back against the metal railing with the hope that it'll look like he's just relaxing.

I look down at my phone. "The Uber is seven minutes away."

"Good." Stacey clutches her chest as she sits down on the steps next to Robert. "That's good—gives us more than enough time to rest."

It feels like we've barely caught our breaths, however, when a gray Toyota pulls over in front of us, and the driver lowers his window.

"David?" he asks.

"Yeah," I reply, jumping to my feet. "That's me."

He watches us intently as we grab hold of Robert's arms again and carry him toward the car.

"What's wrong with him?" he asks as I open the back door.

"Had one too many drinks last night," Stacey answers quickly. Good thing she has acting skills, because my heart is stuck in my throat. "Nothing to worry about, truly."

Even from an angle, I'm able to tell the driver is frowning. "Just make sure he doesn't throw up."

"That won't be a problem. Not a problem at all."

We shove Robert into the car headfirst, and once he's halfway onto the leather seats, we lift his legs and place them safely inside. Stacey slams the door shut, and then she and I run around the car so we can hop in from the other side.

"All righty," she says casually. "Robert, David, are you two okay?"

No answer comes from Robert's end, but I manage to clear my throat and say, "Yeah. I'm okay."

"We're good to go, then!"

The driver pulls away from the curb, and that's when I start to feel like I'm choking. I'm actually not okay—not at all. *None* of this is okay—not the way the driver keeps sneaking glances at us from the rearview mirror, not the nausea that is swirling around inside my stomach, not the fact that I've somehow found myself here, sitting in the back of an Uber on my way to the fucking Plaza, with my literary agent on one side and the dead body of the guy I slept with last night on the other.

CHAPTER SEVEN

Stacey remains nonchalant during the drive, her head bobbing gently with the movements of the car.

"Beautiful day, isn't it?" she says, sneaking a glance out the window as we're speeding down Central Park West. "And a Friday, too."

"Stacey, could you just—"

Take this more seriously? I wish I could say. Before I can get the words out, I catch the Uber driver staring at me again in the rearview mirror.

"Crack open a window?" I finish my sentence in a small voice. "It's a bit stuffy in here."

She clicks the button to lower her window slightly, and a cool breeze starts whipping through my hair. I just want this to be over already. I want to go back home, close all the blinds, scream into a pillow for an hour or two, and try my best to forget that any of this ever happened.

We're approaching the corner of Fifth Avenue and Central Park South, and the Plaza Hotel is becoming visible through the windshield, when a thought comes to mind—one that makes my stomach churn and my hands feel numb.

I don't know his room number.

Fuck. This was such a stupid idea. How are we meant to bring him upstairs when we don't know exactly where we're going? How are we supposed to walk through the crowded lobby, carry him past suspicious doormen and security guards, and drop him off in his room when I can't even remember what floor his suite was on?

"Here we are," the driver announces. "The Plaza Hotel."

I don't think I can do this. I don't think I'll even be able to get out of the car. I should just ask the driver to turn around and bring us back to my apartment, if only I could manage to get the words out.

"Everything okay?" he asks, turning to look at us over his shoulder.

I'm breathing fast all of a sudden. Stacey's window remains cracked open, but now that the car is standing still, there's no breeze coming through it.

I clear my throat. "Yeah. Could you just...could you drop us off over there instead?" I ask, pointing at the little park that's right across the street from the hotel.

Stacey's face crumples into a frown. "Are we sure about that?"

"Trust me."

The driver hits the pedal softly to pull out of his parking spot and takes us a few feet further, stopping on the opposite side of the road.

"Is this all right?"

"Perfect."

I lean over to open the door on Robert's side, but the second I do, his limp body topples over like a rag doll. I manage to grab his arm just in time to stop him from falling out of the car, and then I throw a desperate glance at Stacey, begging her to come help me.

"Oh, dear."

She gets out, runs over to the other side, and a second later she's there, holding Robert up. It takes all of our effort to pull him out, and by the time we've managed to get him into an upright position, I'm almost sure the Uber driver has figured out something's very wrong.

"Don't worry, love," Stacey says loudly to Robert. "We'll get you up to your room in no time."

I can feel the driver's gaze on our backs as we stumble into the park, but he doesn't say anything. As soon as I hear the car driving off into the distance, I let out my breath, telling myself that at least the first part of this nightmare is over.

Pulitzer Plaza is empty save for a couple of tourists walking around, the cars driving down Fifth Avenue, and a bunch of pigeons basking in the morning sun. Stacey and I carry Robert toward the fountain at the center of the square, and we lower him to sit on the ledge.

"Well?" Stacey asks as we take a seat on either side of him. "Are you planning to explain why we're here?"

"I...I don't know the room number."

"What?"

A few pigeons jump up, flying off to a different area of the plaza.

"You couldn't have mentioned that earlier, could you, darling?"

"I didn't think of it!" I screech. "I met him in the lobby last night, so all I did was follow him upstairs."

"We'll have to ask the front desk, then," Stacey says, her tone turning very serious. "They'll be able to tell us where to go."

"I...I'm not sure I like that idea. I don't want us to attract any more attention than we need to."

"Well, what else do you suggest we do?"

I press my face into the palms of my hands, making everything around me disappear—Stacey and Robert, the park, even the sunshine. For a moment, all I can see are stars flashing behind my eyelids...but then another image comes into focus. A hand pressing a button with the number 16. I just have no way of knowing if this memory comes from the hotel or from one of the other elevators Robert and I rode in last night.

"Sixteen," I mumble, opening my eyes.

"Pardon?"

"I think we were on floor sixteen. If I'm right, I should be able to retrace our steps to the correct door once we make it out of the elevator."

Stacey bites her lower lip. "I don't know. Perhaps we should—"

"I'll go up there. I—I'll go into the hotel, make sure I find the right room, and then I'll come back to get you."

She widens her eyes at me. "You're not suggesting I wait out here with him, are you?"

All of a sudden, the thought of Stacey sitting in a public park seems completely absurd. Even now, seeing her in her canary yellow suit and high heels, I can't deny she looks out of place—a fish out of water. Add to that a suited man slumped on the ledge of the fountain beside her, and you may as well have a weird realist painting.

"I'll be quick. It'll only take me a few minutes."

Stacey doesn't seem convinced. She stares at me with a deep frown on her face for what feels like a long time, but in the end, she gives a small nod.

"Very well," she says. "For the love of God, though, don't leave me out here too long."

"I won't. I promise."

I jump off the fountain and start making my way toward the front entrance of the hotel—across the street, up the front steps, and through the doors. It isn't until I'm approaching the grand chandelier that my mind transports me to last night. The anticipation, the awe, the thrill of following Robert down this very same route toward the elevators. How very different it all feels now. How very sad.

Still, I keep moving my feet forward over the carpeted floors, trying my best to channel Robert's confidence, to imitate the way he strolled through the hotel. I can't tell if anyone is staring at me, but there's a near-certainty in the back of my mind that someone must be—that I'm being watched closely, that the employees and other guests know I don't belong here. That somebody is going to tap my shoulder at any moment, ask me to hand over Robert's key card, and order me to leave the premises.

By the time I finally make it into the elevator and hit number 16 on the pad, I feel as though I've run a marathon. At least I've made it. I am here, past the most crowded areas of the hotel, and no one has questioned me. Yet.

When the elevator doors open, I step out warily. It all seems vaguely familiar to me, but I suppose every floor would look the same: stark white walls and ceilings, bright lights hanging overhead, blue carpeting with patterns of gold. I keep my eyes and ears alert as I move down the hallway, ready for a housekeeping employee or cleaning cart to jump out, but my surroundings remain eerily silent.

Finally, I reach what I think is the correct door. With a shaking hand, I pull the key card out of my pocket, tap it against the reader, and hold my breath.

The light turns green.

Oh, thank God. I sneak into the room, close the door, and press my back against it, letting out a long sigh of relief. Since I first realized Robert was dead, I haven't been able to breathe properly. It's as if there's been a weight on my shoulders all morning, but in this moment, I'm able to release some of the tension.

Housekeeping hasn't been in the room, that much is certain. There are still traces of my night with Robert—a champagne cork left on the counter of the bar, squashed pillows on the living room couch, pulled back curtains at the window.

My heart aches more and more the deeper I step into the room, and a sharp pain stabs at my chest when I think of all the things that happened here last night.

The way Robert kissed me by the window while the city sparkled in the distance.

The certainty in his hands, in his mouth, in his every movement as he made me forget where my body ended and his began.

The softness in his voice when he whispered, *You're really something, aren't you?*

The playfulness in his eyes as he covered up the champagne bottle with a towel.

None of it is ever going to happen again. I will never get to find out what he and I could've become.

That's the thought that breaks me. More than the anxiety of bringing him up here, more than the fear of anyone finding out what Stacey and I have done. It's the idea of giving up all the hope and joy I felt last night, because after going on so many dates in the past year, I finally thought I'd met someone I might be able to build something with. It's the fear of going back to my same old life once all this is over—one where I'm all out of love, all out of money, all out of the things Robert would've been able to give me. It's the realization that I found a perfect man and lost him all in the span of twelve hours. That is what makes my entire body go numb, what makes me stop breathing altogether.

I stumble around, making my way toward the bedroom. The bed is unmade, exactly as we left it before heading out last night. If I close my eyes, I can almost picture the dim lights, the smell of his skin, the taste of his lips.

When I open my eyes again, however, everything seems a lot different. I see not memories from last night, but an empty hotel room—and an opportunity for Stacey and me to finish this once and for all.

I need to get out of here. I need to head back to the park as soon as possible, just as I promised I would. I'm walking out of the bedroom, my eyes firmly set on the front door of the suite, when an unexpected sound chimes, making me freeze on the spot.

A soft beep, which tells me someone has scanned a key card on the other side of the door.

"No, no!" I yell. "No housekeeping!"

It's too late. The knob turns, the door swings open, and a tall, handsome man steps into the room.

"Excuse me?" he asks, staring at me with wide eyes and a shocked frown on his face.

My first thought is that he doesn't appear to be a hotel employee. He's sophisticated, able to muster a level of confidence that is all too similar to Robert's. He looks about the same age, too—early to mid-forties, I'd say. He has silver hair that is carefully pushed to the side, intense blue eyes, and he's wearing what you would expect someone to wear on a weekend in the Hamptons: a smart button-down shirt, a sweater tied around his neck, and pink Bermuda shorts.

There's something wrong here. *Very* wrong. The vague possibility that Robert stole this man's hotel key and tricked me into thinking he was staying in this room crosses my mind, until I remember that all the employees seemed to know and respect him. But then, why is this stranger standing in Robert's suite, holding a key card of his own and carrying a duffel bag over his shoulder?

"Well?" he says, raising his eyebrows at me. "Who are you? Why are you in my room?"

"I—I'm with housekeeping."

His gaze travels down to my clothes: a white polo and dark joggers. With any luck, I might just pass for an underdressed employee.

"What was it that you yelled when I walked into the room?"

"Uh...sorry?"

"It sounded like you said, *No housekeeping!*"

"Oh." I can feel myself sweating through my shirt, but I try my best to keep a straight face. "I meant: *No, no! Housekeeping!* I just… didn't want you to walk into a dirty room—not while we're working on it, that is."

"Where's your housekeeping trolley?" he asks, looking at me intently.

"It's just next door. My colleague is finishing up with the suite beside us, so she'll bring it over in a second."

I have no idea where this quick thinking is coming from, or whether it's even working. My hope is that all the media training I've done has paid off—that the skills I learned doing events and interviews for *The Millers* will end up being good for something other than book promo.

"And your name tag?"

"I…believe you've caught me," I say, sneaking a glance down at my chest as if expecting to find a tag there. "Breaking dress code policy, aren't I? I'll need to run down and get my tag right away. I do hope you won't tell my manager about this."

He doesn't seem amused, so I point a finger at the door.

"I can give you some privacy. I'm sorry to have bothered you, Mr.…?"

"Donovan. Corey Donovan," he says curtly.

"Of course. I do apologize, Mr. Donovan. We'll return to make up your room later."

Without waiting for his response, I make a move toward the door. I'm nearly there, so close I can almost touch the knob, when he clears his throat.

"You wouldn't have seen my husband around here by any chance, would you?"

Suddenly, it hits me again—the sharp pain in my chest, except this time, I might actually be bleeding. He has sunk a knife into my heart, making me feel a sting that's unlike anything I've ever felt before.

"Your—your husband?"

"That's right. Dark hair, more likely than not to be wearing a suit? He checked in yesterday, so I'm assuming he slept here last night."

He was married. He was fucking *married*! And now his *husband* is standing here, asking where he is. It takes me a few seconds to comprehend this, to realize that this is actually my life and not the plot of some weird book I dreamed up.

"No," I say. "I haven't seen him." The words slip out of my mouth without me realizing. I'm not sure if they came out in a strong or weak voice, not sure if I managed to be at all convincing. Either way, it doesn't seem to matter. Robert's husband makes a move toward the bedroom, and I take that as my cue to get the hell out of here.

I have no idea which way is left or right, where the hallway starts or ends, or how to find the elevators. Somehow, my legs carry me in the right direction, and all of a sudden I'm surrounded by soft lighting and wood paneling, descending toward the lobby.

I'm so fucking stupid. What kind of person finds themself in this situation? What does it say about me that I started dreaming of a future with a man I'd only known for a few hours—without even knowing his last name, without ever suspecting that he might be lying to me about his age, his relationship status, and probably a million other things? How desperate does anybody need to be to fall for all the bullshit he fed me? How lonely?

The elevator doors open, and I rush through them. It's busier on the main floor now than it was earlier, and this time, I *do* know there are countless gazes following me. A bellman pushing a luggage cart throws a quick glance at me, and I can just tell he knows I'm up to no good. An old lady wearing a pearl necklace narrows her eyes at me in a way that says, *How cold-hearted are you, treating a poor dead man like that?* The lips of a small girl carrying a stuffed animal seem to mouth: *Good job. You've managed to ruin your entire life.*

I shouldn't have followed Stacey's advice. She always knows what to do in the publishing world, always has the right answers, so I suppose it's only natural that I would do as she says, but I shouldn't have listened to her this time. We should've just left Robert on my bed, called 911, and dealt with the fallout. Instead, we now have a dead body sitting in a park, a shit ton of cameras documenting my little trip to Robert's suite, and a resentful husband who has seen my face and won't hesitate to point a finger at me once we're in front of a jury.

In the midst of all the anxiety swelling in my abdomen, I am able to formulate a single clear thought—one that brings me all the comfort, and warmth, and peace I need right at this moment.

Jeremy.

I wish he was here with me. He's the only person who could make all of this go away, who could find a way to make every single one of my problems disappear.

It was ridiculous of me to even compare Robert to him. No one could ever come close to the stability and safety that Jeremy made me feel. So what if Robert was smart, classy, and confident? Jeremy was also all of those things, and so much more. He was a warm hug on a winter night. A shoulder to cry on. The very definition of home. And that's all I'm craving right now—just a little bit of him. Just the sound of his voice, a kiss on the top of my head, and the promise that everything will be okay.

But it's pointless to even hope for any of those things, because he's no longer a part of my world. I mean...I really need to find a way to stop thinking about Jeremy so much. I should stop keeping an open space in my life for him, should stop having him top of mind at all times, because he broke my heart, and he turned his back on me, and—

Holy shit.

He's right here. In the Plaza.

Jeremy is staring at me from across the lobby, and he looks every bit as shaken as I feel.

CHAPTER EIGHT

I used to think love wasn't meant for me. Money? Maybe. Success...
why not? I always had my dad to look up to when it came to those
things—someone who came from Mexico with close to nothing
and worked his ass off until he made it. Someone who defied the
odds and ended up with the beautiful house in the suburbs he was
never meant to have, which was what made me believe I might also
be capable of beating the odds.

When it came to two men in love, well... there were hardly any
examples I could turn to. So I got used to thinking that there were
bigger and better things to go after. I got used to dreaming of a life
where I could make money doing what I loved most—where I could
be on morning shows and bestseller lists, and maybe have a few
casual hookups to make me feel something every once in a while.

I was never looking for Jeremy until I found him. I never imagined how sweet life could be when you have somebody to love and
who loves you back. I never thought I would become the kind of
guy who used the pronoun *we* instead of *I* when making plans, or
the kind whose entire existence could revolve around a man. When
I was with Jeremy, I became all of those things. I learned that buy-
ing movie tickets and making dinner reservations is always better
in pairs, that time has no laws or meaning when you're listening
to a story told by the person you love, and that secrets whispered

beneath the covers after having sex on Sunday mornings are the most intimate a human being can share.

But I also learned just how taunting an empty chair can be when you're having dinner without the man you love, how the seconds and the minutes stop when you're crying naked on the bathroom floor, and how the hardest thing anyone can do is keep secrets, and thoughts, and feelings locked in after you've lost the person you used to share them with.

And here he is. The man who shaped me into who I am now, the one who taught me all those lessons, wearing a navy blue suit that makes his eyes look like an ocean and staring at me as if he'd seen a ghost.

Maybe that's all we are—ghosts of the people we used to be, because that's what he seems to me as well. A ghost with charcoal black hair and a boyish quality to his face that makes him look much younger than thirty-one.

"David?" is the first thing he says. Even now, the sound of my name on his lips makes me shiver.

"Jeremy?"

"What are you doing here?"

"I had a...work meeting," I manage to say. "You?"

"Same, actually," he answers. "I'm about to head in now." He nods vaguely toward the restaurant at the back of the lobby—the Palm Court, I think it's called.

"Are you..." I begin, without even knowing what I'm about to ask. I have too many questions for him—too many things I want to know after nearly a full year of not seeing or talking to him.

Somehow, he catches on to my inability to complete the sentence, and he finishes it for me. "Still at the same job? I am, yeah."

Jeremy's an investment banker. The job itself is way more boring than anyone would suspect, but the money is also better than you'd imagine. We used to split most expenses while we were living together, but it was the extra money Jeremy brought in that allowed us to move into our two-bedroom on the Upper East Side. It was his salary that paid for fancy dinners and summer weekends in the Hamptons, that gave us a life that felt straight out of a movie.

"I got a promotion, though," he adds.

"That's amazing."

"Thanks. And are you..."

"Still writing?" I ask. "Yeah. At least trying to, anyway."

"Good," he says, smiling a little. "I'm excited to add your next book to my shelf."

A wave of warmth rushes through me. Jeremy was always my biggest fan, my most enthusiastic reader—that is, until it became impossible for him to keep encouraging me to pursue a career that was doing me more harm than good.

"How's your mom?"

"She's doing great," he replies. "Trying to keep busy, as always. She decided to rent a house in the Hamptons for the summer."

"Nice. I'm glad to hear."

He lifts an eyebrow. "Your dad and Sheila?"

"Oh, they're as horrible as ever."

That's when it happens. He lets out a laugh, his eyes sparkling in the light of the chandelier, and I'm transported to a different lifetime—one in which it felt as though Jeremy and I were unbreakable, as though nothing and no one could've ever torn us apart.

It's hard now to understand exactly what it was that broke us. It's the question I've asked myself endlessly over the past eleven months—*why?* But I suppose it's not actually as complicated as I've made it out to be.

The truth is, as much as the publication of *The Millers* was a blessing, it was also a curse. In the months after it came out, I started losing myself, little by little. After years of turning writing into my safe place—the only one I could escape to when I was feeling sad, fearful, or upset—I wasn't entirely prepared for what it meant to let other people access that part of me. By the time I began working on my second book, I started feeling as though writing was no longer a refuge to turn to—not when there were editors, reviewers, and readers waiting to see what I came up with next. People with expectations and demands that I suddenly needed to meet.

I became consumed by the pressure. I stopped being able to see the line between David Alvarez (the person) and David Alvarez (the bestselling author). I spent the better part of a year trying to write a new novel that would be a worthy follow-up to my first, and when the dreadful reviews started pouring in for *Walking Home*, I completely lost it.

I started drinking more and sleeping less. I would toss and turn at night, keeping Jeremy awake while unspoken tension lingered in the air around our bed. I was depressed, anxious, and angry. I was watching in real time as the whole world turned its back on me—first my family, then the reviewers who had once praised me, then the readers I'd disappointed, and finally the publishing team that had placed all their faith in me—and I was trying desperately to hold on to them, trying to get people to turn back around, to see me, to not dismiss me so easily.

The worst part was that I no longer had that safe haven to go to, no longer had the ability to reach for the solace I used to find in my own writing. The coping mechanism I'd spent my whole life lovingly crafting for myself had come crumbling down, and then I had nothing and no one left. Not even Jeremy, because all I did in the end was push him away.

Jeremy tried. I wish I could place all the blame on him for leaving me, but God, did he *try*. He listened, provided advice, and dried my tears. He found me a therapist and sat with me in the Uber on the way to and from each appointment, holding my hand as I recounted what had happened during my latest session. He just couldn't find a way to fix me. He couldn't find a way to put the pieces of me back together, and he came to the realization that the only way to save himself from also breaking was to get away—to look for an apartment of his own, move out, and seek some peace.

So, no. I don't blame him. I have wished he had never come into my life, and I've cursed his name a million times, and I've spent all of last year wondering why things had to turn out this way, but I've never truly faulted or hated him. I love him. Always have, always will, even now that we're standing here acting like strangers and not former lovers.

"You look good," I mutter. It's my way of saying that I miss him, that I hope the distance has brought him all the peace he desired, that the last thing I ever wanted was to hurt him.

"Thank you, David," he replies, which feels almost like his way of saying that I *don't* look good—that he can tell I haven't really changed much, that he knows something sketchy is going on right at this moment. Something I haven't told him yet and likely never will.

"Will you . . . be in the city all summer?"

Jeremy nods once. "For the most part, yeah. You?"

"Same." A few terrifying images flood my mind—all related to the possibility that I'll be spending my entire summer at Rikers Island. Explaining to Jeremy through a glass wall how I ended up there. Having phone conversations with Pa and Sheila in which they tell me they won't bail me out and won't help me pay for a lawyer. Sleeping alone in a dark cell, wondering if or when I'll ever get out.

I clear my throat, trying my best to push it all away. "Maybe . . . I don't know. Maybe we could hang out sometime? Catch up?"

"Oh, David," Jeremy sighs, looking down at his feet. "I didn't want to tell you like this. It's just that . . . I'm seeing someone."

"Oh."

"Yeah." He presses his lips together. "It's only been a couple of months…but maybe it wouldn't be wise for you and me to start spending time together again right now."

"Totally." Is it me, or did this place suddenly get really hot? "No, yeah. I get it."

We stand still for a moment, staring into each other's eyes, and I have to fight the urge to hug him, to kiss him, to sink down to my knees and wrap my arms around his legs while saying that allowing him to slip away was the worst mistake I've ever made.

He takes a deep breath, preparing to say something, and I inch closer to him, hoping he's about to tell me that he's changed his mind—that we should drop everything right at this moment and go catch up over coffee. That we owe it to ourselves to try again.

"I'm, uh…running a bit late," he says instead, pointing toward the restaurant.

"Of course. Yeah, I also gotta get going. I should really get back to…" *To the dead body I have waiting outside.*

"Sounds good. Take care, David."

"You, too."

I watch him walk away until he disappears from view. Then, I turn around and make my way toward the front doors of the hotel, somehow putting one foot in front of another even though my legs feel like they're going to collapse under my weight.

When I step back out into the morning sunshine, a part of me is relieved. After the stuffiness of the lobby, the open space and the cool breeze feel almost like a reward.

"There you are," Stacey says the moment she sees me. "Did you find the room?"

I nod once, but I don't reply. I simply stand in front of her and Robert, my arms hanging limply by my sides. It's as if I'd managed to forget just how hungover I am, but now that I'm remembering, it's all coming back with full force: the headache, the dryness in my mouth, the feeling that I might throw up any minute.

"I was starting to worry you'd made a run for it and weren't coming back. What took you so long?"

Still, I am unable to speak. All I can do is take deep breaths, focusing on the idea of *not* throwing up. When I sneak a glance at Robert, however, the acid rushes up my throat and I turn toward the fountain, spewing the contents of my stomach into the murky water.

"He looks terrible," I pant, leaning my hands on my knees and trying hard not to look at him again.

"He's pale, yes," Stacey says. "That's normal, though. Don't be alarmed."

I can't resist. From the corner of my eye, I sneak another glance. "Why did you lay him down like that?"

Robert is lying peacefully on the ledge of the fountain, his hands folded over his stomach. He could be taking a nap, and I'm sure that's what anyone passing by would automatically assume, but to me the sight of him looks so fucked up.

"Rigor mortis, David," Stacey says, as if I should already know what the hell that is. "Lifeless bodies go stiff after a few hours. We have to keep him lying down as much as we can, or else we risk him getting stuck in a position that might suggest foul play."

I should really be asking more questions about those ex-husbands of hers who died mysteriously. It feels important to know, especially now that she and I are technically accomplices in this whole thing, and if we go down, we go down together, but I can't find the strength to question her. Instead, I sit down, extremely conscious of the way my sweaty shirt is sticking to my skin.

"What are you doing?" Stacey asks. "This is not the time for a break, I'm afraid. We need to get him inside. Lead the way, dear!"

"We can't," I mumble.

"What was that?"

"We can't bring him up to the room."

"I thought you found the right one."

"I did. But then his husband walked in."

Stacey shakes her head slightly. "His *husband*?"

I nod, rubbing my eyes with the tips of my fingers.

"You didn't mention he had a husband," she says.

"Neither did he."

"So you didn't know?"

"Of course not! Do you think I would've done everything I did last night if I'd known he was married?"

"Different people draw the line at different places, darling. I'm not here to judge."

"Well, I draw the line at married!"

I clutch my throat, still feeling the burn of the acid. I'm sure I would throw up again if there was anything left in my stomach, but I haven't had anything to eat or drink today. The realization makes me hungry, thirsty, and sickened all at once.

"This is bad, isn't it?" I say. "He saw me! His husband *saw* me, and we're not gonna—"

"Let's not get lost in the negatives, David," Stacey interrupts me. "We just need to come up with an alternative plan."

"There *is* no alternative plan!" I shout. "Even if we bring him back to my apartment now, we won't get away with claiming he passed away in his sleep. People have *seen* us with him. And his husband will come after me. The police will notify him of where Robert's body was found, he'll recognize me the instant he gets to my apartment, and he'll know I was the one who—"

"Okay, so the circumstances have changed slightly. It's just a matter of figuring out a more discreet way to get rid of the body. We'll just have to—"

"*A more discreet way to get rid of the body?*" I interrupt her. "Are you hearing yourself? This isn't how it was supposed to be! We were only meant to get him back to his hotel room, quick and easy. There's no way we're gonna—"

"Hold on for a minute." Stacey turns toward me with a slight frown on her face. "What exactly do we know about this husband of his? Did he seem like a vengeful person?"

"Yes?" I answer. "I mean... I don't know! I barely even talked to him."

"What else do you know?"

"He said his last name was Donovan. Corey Donovan, I think, but he didn't—"

"*Corey Donovan?*" Stacey repeats, and I nod. "What did he look like?"

"He was well dressed. He was wearing a—"

"Physically, David! I meant physically."

"I don't know. I guess... about the same age as Robert. With blue eyes and gray hair."

"Oh, dear. That can't be good."

"What?" I ask, my heart skipping a beat. "What can't be good?"

Stacey purses her lips. "This husband... it couldn't be *the* Corey Donovan, could it?"

"Who the fuck is that?"

"The news anchor!"

"I don't watch the news!"

Stacey fumbles with her phone, types something into the keyboard, and holds the screen up for me to see. "I'm talking about *this* Corey Donovan!"

It's him. Smiling on a red carpet, wearing a three-piece suit. Same silver hair, same penetrating blue stare.

We're absolutely fucked. What's an expression greater than *absolutely fucked*? If it exists, then that's what we are. Why couldn't Robert's husband be another finance guy? Or a flight attendant? Or an accountant? Why does he have to be a damn news anchor on CNN with a primetime show, millions of viewers who probably hang on to his every word, and a platform to expose Stacey and me?

"Regardless of who his husband is," Stacey says after a moment, "I thought you should also know that I went through his pockets while you were inside the hotel and found *this*."

She holds up a small plastic bag filled with white powder.

"*Cocaine?*" I ask.

"I'm not inclined to try it out for confirmation, but yes. That's what I think it is."

I'd say that explains all his trips to the bathroom. It explains why he needed to pee so badly at the end of the night even after all the times he'd already gotten up to "pee" throughout the evening. The motherfucker. He must've been high the whole time, excusing himself to go take another hit when he started sobering up. In the meantime, there I was, eagerly waiting for him to return to our table so he could keep feeding me lies about himself, about the two of us, about how special he thought I was.

I take the bag from Stacey.

"What are you doing?"

"I'm getting rid of it." I open it and dump the contents into the fountain. "The last thing we need is to add a drug possession charge to our crimes."

"Good thinking," she says. "This could've also reacted poorly with the alcohol and the Xanax. Wouldn't want anyone thinking it was you who gave him the cocaine on top of that."

"Oh, fuck. I hadn't even thought of that." I crumple the empty bag and cast it aside.

"Don't worry, love. It'll be all right in the end—I really do believe that."

"Yeah," I reply. "I hope so."

"Now," Stacey says firmly. "It's nearly nine, so I should really get going."

"*What?* Get going to *where?*"

"The office. Where else?" Stacey gets on her feet and swings her bag over her shoulder.

"Don't we have something important to take care of first?" I sneak another glance at Robert, who's still sunbathing on the edge of the fountain.

"I have a meeting to get to. A meeting with Jackie, in fact."

"Jackie?" I jump from my seat, staring into her eyes. "Jackie Morales is coming to your office? *Today?*"

"She is. We have plenty to discuss—your new proposal for book three, among other things."

"Why didn't you tell me this before?"

"I wasn't aware I needed to keep you up to date on the meetings I have in my calendar."

"You do if you're meeting with my editor on the same day we're trying to move a dead body!"

A pair of tourists—European, by the look of them—turn sharply toward us. I smile vaguely at them from across the plaza, trying to seem relaxed so they'll think I'm joking.

I lower my voice. "You can't abandon me. You can't leave me to do this all by—"

"Who said I was leaving you?" Stacey says with a small shake of her head. She holds my gaze, unspoken words hanging from her lips, and then she smiles out of the corner of her mouth.

"You're ... not saying we should *all* go, are you?"

"That's exactly what I'm saying, David."

"We can't do that!"

"Of course we can."

"We *cannot* bring a dead body to your office building."

"Why not? I'll take the meeting with Jackie in the boardroom, and we'll leave him inside my office. It'll be quiet, it'll be private, and it'll be the perfect way to keep him out of the spotlight while we figure out what to do next."

I'm torn. What would be worse? Walking into the crowded lobby of a Midtown office building carrying a corpse? Or keeping Robert out here in the open where anyone can see us?

"Fine," I say under my breath. "Let's do it, then."

And just like that, we're on the move again. Supporting the weight of a dead man on our shoulders. Hailing a cab on Fifth Avenue while hundreds of people walk and drive by, blissfully unaware that they're witnessing a crime. That's something positive to be said about New York, I suppose—as long as you're not a slow walker, no one cares what you do.

Nobody slows down long enough to take a good look at Robert, nobody bothers to question what's wrong with him, even though we're at one of the busiest intersections in Manhattan. Stacey was onto something when she said it'd be easy to convince people that he's drunk, because the mere idea of us actually carrying a corpse down the street would feel a bit too far-fetched to people watching—even to longtime New Yorkers who have seen it all before.

"Watch his head," Stacey says as we slip Robert into the back of a yellow taxi.

"Nah, it's fine." At this point, I wouldn't mind getting him a little banged up. The lying bastard.

Stacey was right about the rigor mortis thing, though, because

Robert's body is a lot less bendy than it was earlier. In the end, our only option to fit all three of us inside the car is for Stacey and I to sit side-by-side and have Robert sprawled on top of our laps.

"Onward!" Stacey shouts once all the car doors are closed. I swear, there's a part of her that appears excited, as if we were riding a roller coaster or going on some sort of twisted adventure.

The driver hits the pedal, and Stacey's words from earlier start spinning around in my head. *It'll be all right in the end—I really do believe that.*

Of all the bad decisions I've made in the past twenty-four hours, I'm still uncertain whether calling her was the worst one. But if one thing is true, it is this: the only way this situation could've been worse is if I'd had to face it alone. Say what I may about the quality of Stacey's advice, she was the only person I was certain would answer the phone in my moment of need—and she did. She showed up at my doorstep, she offered to help, and she is still here, willing to remain by my side despite everything.

So I can't say calling her was a mistake. For now, at least, I allow myself to trust her, to share her optimism—because, as long as Stacey is by my side, there's always the possibility that we'll manage to get away with all this, that we'll find a way out of this mess.

Together.

CHAPTER NINE

A piece of good news: the taxi ride is pretty short, even with morning traffic. The bad news is that once we're about halfway to Stacey's office, Robert's body starts to smell like farts.

"Unfortunate, but also normal," Stacey mumbles into my ear, softly enough that the driver won't hear above the sound of the music. "Dead bodies release gas. We'll power through, darling. Don't you worry."

The rest of the trip to her office works out well enough—until the three of us find ourselves stuck inside the revolving door of the building, our bodies pressed against the glass with absolutely no room to move.

"We should've taken the automatic doors," Stacey groans, squished between Robert and the back of the door.

"Slowly," I say. "Come on."

Taking mini steps, Stacey and I manage to push our way forward until we're released on the other side.

"Elevator. Now," Stacey pants, her eyes firmly set on the back of the lobby. She's getting tired, and I don't blame her. My back and shoulders ache from supporting Robert's weight, and my knees feel like they're about to buckle.

Even though a few necks turn in our direction, no one's gaze lingers for too long. The security guard at the front desk rises from his seat when he sees us approaching, but as soon as he spots Stacey, he flashes a big smile.

"Going all right, ma'am?"

"Ah, it's just going, Larry," she answers casually, her neck bent forward beneath Robert's heavy arm. "At least it's Friday, am I right?"

"Amen to that, ma'am. Do you... need any help there?"

"Not at all, Larry," she replies as we keep moving. "Just bringing an old friend up to the office, but you're kind for asking. Very kind indeed."

Whatever Larry says in response, I don't find out, because a moment later we're sneaking into an elevator. Stacey hits the button for the forty-second floor and the doors begin to slide closed, thankfully blocking us from view, but then—

"Hold the elevator, please!"

Before either of us can reach for the Close button on the panel, an arm sneaks in, blocking the doors and forcing them back open.

"Oh, Stacey! David! What a surprise."

It's Jackie Morales. *The* Jackie Morales. The powerhouse editor, the one who made the publication offer for *The Millers* that changed my life, the one who holds the future of my career in her hands— *that* Jackie Morales is standing in front of us, sharing an elevator with me, Stacey, and a dead man.

"Jackie!" Stacey and I say at the same time, and I immediately worry that our shrill voices and fake smiles will alert her that something is wrong.

The doors slide closed, trapping us inside this tiny metal box, and we start ascending.

"David, it's been a while since we've last spoken," Jackie says. "I didn't realize you were going to be here for the meeting."

"Oh, I won't."

"He won't. He's just—"

"And who is this?"

Her gaze falls on Robert.

Damn it. Here comes the nausea again. "Funny you should ask. He happens to be—"

"A potential client," Stacey blurts out, and Jackie and I both turn toward her. "Yeah, he...he's a debut author I've been thinking of signing. Wrote one hell of a good novel."

Jackie tilts her head slightly. "Oh?"

"We're just coming back from a breakfast meeting. I thought I'd invite David along so he could tell him about his experiences in publishing, but *someone* had one too many mimosas, isn't that right?"

"Ah, yes," I reply quickly. "*So* many mimosas. We should've cut him off sooner, but we were having too much fun, I guess."

An awkward smile. I can tell Jackie is a little uncomfortable, a little uncertain of what to do. She's a full decade older than me, with shiny black hair and big brown eyes. Today, she's wearing bold red lipstick and a flowery summer dress, and she is carrying a tote bag filled with what I can only presume are publishing secrets.

"Why not just put him in a cab home?" she asks in a whisper, sneaking a worried glance at the unmoving body perched on top of our shoulders.

"That is a great question," I reply, looking over at Stacey. "Why *didn't* we do that?"

"Well, we couldn't just leave him to fend for himself. Not in this state. I...I make sure to treat my prospective authors as well as I treat the old clients, of course."

"You know how things are done on your side of the industry better than I do," Jackie says. Even though her lips are pressed into a smile, I can't help but worry that she *knows*. She can tell we're carrying a dead body, and she's just too polite—or too terrified—to point it out.

If I thought my career was over before, I was wrong. *Now* it's over. It won't matter if I come up with a great premise for my third novel, won't matter if I write an amazing proposal. Jackie's never going to offer me another book deal—not after this. I wouldn't be surprised if she tells every single person in the industry how deranged David Alvarez and Stacey Hixon-Jones are, and to never, ever work with either of them again. But I suppose the more pressing matter is whether or not she'll call the police the instant we get off the elevator. It'll be a miracle if she doesn't.

A heavy silence falls while all three of us stare up at the little screen that's flashing with the floor numbers: *31, 32, 33.* We are fast approaching the forty-second floor, and we're so very close to getting there, when a loud farting sound fills the air around us.

"Oh, my!" Jackie gives a small jump.

I cover my nose. "Wow, that is just..."

"The poor man really can't hold his alcohol." Stacey shakes her head. "I don't think I'll be signing him now. Not at all. I'm just sorry you had to be here for this, Jackie, dear."

Jackie makes a motion with her hand that seems to signal it's all good, but she doesn't say anything. She appears to be holding her breath up until the moment we all step out of the elevator.

The glass door of the office swings open just as we're approaching it, and Stacey's assistant, Josh, greets us with a bright smile.

"Good morning, y'all!"

I can't help but wonder if he stands in the reception area every single morning, waiting for Stacey's arrival just so he can get the door for her. He hasn't been with the agency for too long, but I like him. He reminds me of a younger me—a gay guy right out of college, with a deep desire to make a name for himself in publishing and an eagerness to help that at times borders on annoying.

"I've got the boardroom all set up for—"

"We may not use it after all," Stacey says, her voice strained as we carry Robert into the cool, brightly lit room. "Jackie, what do you say we go out for breakfast instead? My treat."

Jackie frowns. "I...thought you just came back from breakfast."

"Well, they do say it's the most important meal of the day. May as well have it twice. Josh, sweetheart—" He takes a few quick steps forward to come stand in front of us. "Please make sure Jackie has something to drink while David and I guide this poor man to my office. We won't be long."

Josh gives a sharp nod, and Stacey and I turn away to walk down a long hallway. As soon as we step into her office and push the door closed behind us, we both let out loud grunts.

"Where should we leave him?" I ask.

"Just on the carpet. The carpet will do."

Somehow, my shoulder and back pain gets worse once we've laid Robert down. We're both breathless, and I know we could use a solid moment of rest and a cold glass of water, but Stacey doesn't slow down. She goes up to the thermostat and presses the arrow pointing down.

"What are you doing?"

"Lowering the temperature," she says. "The cooler we keep the body, the better. It's basic forensics, David."

I don't have the energy to argue. My mind is still spinning with the fears that manifested in the elevator.

"Jackie," I pant. "She—"

"—hasn't got a clue what's going on," Stacey assures me. "She might have, for a moment. But we were saved by the bell—or the flatulence, in this instance."

"What?"

"I don't think anyone expects dead bodies to fart the way Robert did back there," she says. "You know who *does* fart? Drunk men. It all aligns with our story."

"I'm not sure that's—"

"Just relax, darling. I'll go take this meeting, but I'll return as soon as I can."

"Can't you just—"

"You know as well as I do that we need to keep Jackie happy," she interrupts me. "Have a drink. Get some rest. I'll be back."

I don't have the opportunity to say anything else. She turns around and walks out, leaving me all alone with Robert.

The door swings shut slowly while the sound of her high heels echoes against the walls of the hallway. Right before the lock clicks into place, I hear Stacey's voice: "Jackie, love, are you ready to head out?"

I wait a few minutes and then step out of her office myself. I head straight for the bathroom and lean over the sink, splashing my face with cold water. I don't know how long I remain here, dripping all over the floor and watching the tap running. What I do know is that I simply cannot bring myself to look in the mirror.

"David!" Josh says to me when I exit the bathroom. "What can I get you? Something to drink, maybe?"

My first instinct is to turn him down. But then, when I realize just how thirsty I am, I ask for a glass of water and a coffee—a strong one, preferably.

"I'll bring those right over. Why don't you wait in the board-room? You'll find snacks in there, too."

There is a platter with all kinds of fruit and pastries set up on the long table in the boardroom, surely intended for Stacey and Jackie to peck at during their meeting. I reach for a croissant and stuff it into my mouth, chewing as fast as I can.

"Here you go—a coffee and a water," Josh says, appearing suddenly. He sets a mug and a tall glass over the table. "Feel free to make yourself comfortable in here until Stacey returns."

"No, no," I say. "I'd rather wait in her office."

"Are you sure? You can—"

I pick up the coffee mug and empty it in a couple of gulps. The liquid burns on its way down, but I don't care. I wipe my mouth, grab the glass of water, and once that's done, I turn toward Josh.

"I'm sure. Thank you."

Inside Stacey's office, I go straight for the windows and lower all the blinds. I turn off the lights, and then I sit on the carpet in a corner of the room, hugging my legs and staring over at the shape of Robert's body resting beside the desk.

You wouldn't have seen my husband around here by any chance, would you? Corey Donovan's voice rings inside my head. A moment later comes my own voice, repeating the same words again and again: *He was married. Married!*

I reach into the pocket of my pants and pull out my phone. I type Corey's name into Google, and a million search results appear, starting with a preview of his Wikipedia article: Corey Donovan is an American broadcast journalist and political commentator. He is the primary anchor of the CNN show *Tonight with Corey Donovan.*

I click on the Images tab. There are thousands of photos of him—on stage at an awards ceremony, smiling as he opens an envelope. Wearing camouflage and a helmet, on assignment in a war zone. Sitting behind a desk on the set of his show, facing the camera with puckered lips. And then, once I've scrolled down enough to get past the most relevant results, an image of him and Robert pops up. They're standing on a red carpet holding hands. The caption reads: Corey Donovan attends movie premiere in Hollywood with longtime partner. Robert's name is not mentioned. It doesn't even specify that they're married. He must not have enjoyed the attention that came with his husband's profession, must've not liked being in the spotlight.

For the longest time, I stare at the photograph. I just can't understand how any of it happened—how it was that Robert came to the decision of opening a Grindr account, and lying about his age, and fooling guys into thinking he was an eligible bachelor. It could be that, despite the big smiles he and Corey displayed for the camera on the day of that movie premiere, theirs wasn't a happy marriage. Maybe Corey always prioritized his career, always craved the spotlight more than he did Robert's love and affection. Maybe Robert felt neglected. Maybe he was trapped in his relationship and had to form an alternative identity to cope—one where he was single and available. One that would allow him to get the devotion Corey refused him, even if it was from strangers, and even if it was only for one night.

Or they might've had a good marriage. Maybe they were some of the lucky ones—the kind of gay men who find their person early on in life and get to spend decades feeling safe, loved, and wanted—and Robert simply wasn't satisfied. Maybe he wanted more. Maybe his fragile ego needed the attention of other men—younger men—so he could feel worthy, important, and desirable.

Sitting here in the dim office, staring at the silhouette of his body, I can't help but suspect that the second version of the story is more accurate.

Then again, there could be a third option—one in which they had an open relationship. There are plenty of couples who do it. Couples that are used to spending long stretches of time apart and agree to find company on the side whenever they're traveling. Couples that just want to add a bit of excitement to their sex lives.

Couples that love each other deeply, but can't find a way to satisfy each other sexually, so they decide to seek that enjoyment elsewhere. But if that was the case in Robert's marriage, why wouldn't he have said so? It wouldn't have been the first time I've hooked up with a guy who was in an open relationship. So why would he have lied, pretended to like me, and led me to believe we were on the verge of starting something new?

I'll probably never know the right answer. Perhaps, no matter how hard I try to rack my brain, all I'll be left with is this: the humiliation of being lied to, the heartbreak of believing that he was someone he wasn't, the fear that I'll spend the rest of my life regretting last night's encounter, and the certainty that I'm not good enough. Not good enough for a steady, successful career, not good enough for my family, not good enough for an exciting, genuine love story.

If only Jeremy could see me now. If only he could see the state I'm in, the mistakes I've made, the way my life has gone off the rails since he walked out on me. I wonder what he would say—whether he would feel any type of regret for leaving, or whether he would take it as further confirmation that he made the right decision.

It's just that... I'm seeing someone. The memory of his words burns somewhere inside me. Somehow, despite everything that has happened today, and despite the fact that I'm sitting here facing the possibility of going to jail for improper treatment of a dead body—or maybe even manslaughter—this is what hurts the most.

I miss you, I say somewhere deep down. Even though the words don't leave my lips, and even though he's not even here, it feels as though he can hear me. *I'm so lost and I have no idea what to do. I wish you were here.*

The optimism I felt in the cab on the way over all but disappears. Because how are we meant to get rid of Robert's body? How are we meant to get away with this when half of New York has seen us lugging a dead man around? How am I meant to ever recover from any of it?

These are the last thoughts on my mind before my heavy eyelids close, and I fall into an uneasy state somewhere between sleep and wakefulness.

CHAPTER TEN

By the time Stacey returns, I'm awake and fully alert again. Despite my little nap, I haven't moved an inch. I'm still on the carpet, my back against the wall and my arms wrapped around my legs while I stare straight ahead—sometimes at Robert, sometimes at the outline of buildings through the translucent blinds, sometimes at nothing in particular.

"Lord, it is *chilly* in here!" she says the moment she walks in.

"Is it?" I ask, my voice barely there. "I hadn't noticed."

"And why did you close all the blinds?"

I shrug in response.

"Oh, David." She sighs. "David, David…"

She drops her bag onto the desk with a heavy thud and comes to join me on the carpet. For a while, she just sits beside me, matching the rhythm of her breath to mine, but then she clears her throat.

"Aren't you going to ask how the meeting went?"

"It doesn't matter."

"Oh, but it does," she says, leaning closer to me. "Jackie is excited. Very excited, in fact."

"About what?"

"Reading your proposal, of course! I didn't mention any specifics, but I might've really sold her on it. She thinks it'll be the greatest novel that has ever crossed her desk."

"There *is* no proposal."

"*Yet*," Stacey replies. "There will be one soon. Call it my literary instinct—I just have a feeling."

"There'll be no more books," I say dryly. "No more trying to prove myself to anyone. If we manage to stay out of jail, I'll just... disappear. Find a place somewhere in the woods and hope everyone forgets me."

"That's a tad dramatic, dear. Save the emotion for when you're working on your proposal."

"I *don't want* to write it."

"You can't give up now! Not when you've been handed the perfect story to tell."

"Is that what this is, then?" I say with a snort. "Life handing me a story? Cause if that's the case, life must have a sick sense of humor."

"Don't be discouraged. I truly believe things happen for a reason."

"Except that, in this case, *you* were the reason! Stacey, if we'd just left him on my bed, none of this would be happening!"

"But you also wouldn't be dangerously close to something great! Think of all the possible angles for your next book. A guy wakes up in bed next to a dead man and has to figure out what to do with the body—it could be a thriller, it could be a comedy, it could be a cozy mystery. Or even a literary novel about the fragility of life. It simply has too much potential."

"That's why you suggested moving the body, then?" I ask, turning sharply toward her. "To get me *dangerously close* to a story idea?"

Stacey lifts her eyebrows slightly, her lips pressed into a straight line. "Well, I... no, that wasn't it."

"*Stacey!*"

It's hardly a secret that she's been desperate to sell a big book. She hasn't had one of those in a while, and I can't imagine how heartbreaking it's been for her to watch so many of her clients leave her in the last year—clients whose careers she has built from the ground up, and who have heartlessly shoved her aside to sign with younger, savvier agents. I have no idea what it's felt like for her to be shut out by an industry she's helped shape over the span of four decades. What I *do* know, however, is that convincing me to move a dead body for the sake of boosting both of our careers was definitely *not* the right thing to do.

"I stand by what I said back in your apartment! We had to take a chance. Allowing the cops to flood your home would've been like giving up, and you and I may be many things, but we are *not* quitters." She lifts her chin slightly. "And it may also be true that you needed a little push to get out of your comfort zone—to start living a little, so you can come up with a great idea for your next book."

"This is not my idea of *living a little*," I shriek. "Oh my God. I can't believe this." I sink my head into the dim gap between my stomach and legs. "I might spend the rest of my life in prison because you thought I should *get out of my comfort zone*."

"Or…you could get away with it, not go to prison, and write the next great American novel. You could make a new career out of this, David, and at one point you might look back with gratitude for everything that has happened today."

"I can't write a book about this. It's too fucked up."

"I hope you won't allow yourself to be held back by a sense of self-righteousness, dear," Stacey says. "Or worse—by a sense of sympathy toward him." She points vaguely in the direction of Robert's body.

"It just wouldn't feel right—making money off his death."

"He was not a good man. Trust me, David. After five marriages, I can tell the difference between the good ones and the bad ones from smell alone."

I wish I had that instinct. I wish I was able to differentiate between the guys who want to date me and the ones who want to fuck me, lie to me, and ruin my life. It would've saved me from more than one awful situation.

"How is that even possible?" I ask, lifting my head up from my little hideaway. "*Five* marriages?" I don't understand how anyone could find that level of connection with five different people—how it is that Stacey has fallen in love with someone so deeply that she would decide to spend the rest of her life with them five separate times.

"That's a good question, darling," she says, staring ahead at the closed blinds. "I ask it to myself sometimes."

"You're lucky. It's five times more than I'm ever likely to get married."

"Lucky is one way to put it," she replies, still not looking at me. "I've also experienced heartbreak many times. Many more than you."

She can make herself out to be a victim all she wants, but I know the truth: she is more fortunate than most. Isn't it a privilege, really? To want and be wanted back? To have loved and lost—not once, not twice, but *five* times?

"You'd think that the end of a marriage wouldn't hurt, after all the times I've been through it, but it does." She shakes her head. "Every single time, it breaks me. The last one, especially."

"Why the last one?"

"I loved him. He was a silly old goat. He fell asleep halfway through every single movie and television show we ever watched together, he couldn't work a smartphone to save his life, and he snored like a whale. But I really did love him."

"Why did it end, then?" I've never known much about Stacey's life outside the book world. Other than semi-frequent mentions of lawyers, and court dates, and divorce settlements, she's never opened up to me like this, never shared any details about her last ex-husband, even though I'm pretty sure the marriage ended barely a few months ago.

"Same reason as every other one," she answers. "Pride. Heedlessness. Disdain. There's just something particularly hard about a marriage ending when you're so far down in life. I'm not twenty-eight anymore, dear. This time, it felt like my last chance, my last hope for one more love. Now there's only the prospect of a long, lonely life ahead."

There's something about what she's saying that brings pain to my heart. Perhaps it's true that I'd rather be in my position than hers, because at least I have hope to hold on to. There's always the possibility that I'll sit next to a handsome stranger on the subway and start a conversation. Or bump shoulders with someone at a bar. Or swipe right on an app. And it might just be the hope that drives me—far more than the thought of getting back together with Jeremy, far more than the actual idea of a relationship or marriage. If you took that hope away from me, I don't know what I would do with myself. I'd have nothing.

I wish I could share some words of wisdom. I wish I could figure out a way to comfort Stacey, to convince her that if she's done it five times before, she can do it again. Instead, I blurt out the one thing I should definitely not say.

"Is it true? The rumor that you killed some of your ex-husbands?"

Slowly, she turns to face me.

"David," she says pointedly, "there are only two things you should never ask a woman: how many fake designer pieces she owns, and whether she's killed any of her husbands."

"So it *is* true?"

"What do *you* think?"

There's something in her face that makes me suspect it's all a big joke to her—that she may have even started the rumors herself as a way to scare away mediocre men. Then again, there's something about her tone that makes her question feel like a dare—to press further and find out for myself if she's capable of murder.

"That…the rumors are ridiculous?"

"Right answer." I could be wrong, but I'm pretty sure she's smiling to herself.

"Besides," I add, "you're hot as hell. Anyone would be lucky to have you."

She laughs. "Darling, there's no need to lie."

"I'm not lying. You're gorgeous, and fucking smart, and you always have the answer to everything. I couldn't ask for a better agent."

"David, you mustn't—"

"It's true. I think…" I swallow hard. "I think you're my best friend. The only one I have, at least."

Stacey nods slowly. "This may surprise you," she says, "but friendship can have a way of evading women in their sixties. I'm also lucky to have you, dear. I always look forward to our meetings—more than with most of my other clients." She coughs once, as if there was suddenly something stuck in her throat. "I might even go so far as to say…you're one of the few people I'd consider myself to be on friendly terms with. My *best friend*, if you will."

Warmth. Spreading in my chest, in my stomach, reaching every corner of my body. If only Stacey and I could stay here and never have to leave. We'd have everything we need—good company, alcohol, and an all-too-eager Josh waiting right outside, ready to bring us snacks, and water, and whatever else we may desire. We could shut everything and everyone out—all the failed romances, all the fear of loneliness, all the men who don't deserve us—and just exist in this little corner of her office forever.

But there's a dead man right in front of us. And we need to figure out what to do about him. Soon.

Stacey may as well have read my mind, because she clears her throat. "We've found ourselves in an interesting dilemma," she says. "What are two unlikely best friends to do with a dead body?"

The question seems to linger in the air around us, echoing against the walls of Stacey's office.

"We could…" I don't want to say it out loud. I don't even want to imagine it, but what if we're left with no other choice? We have to consider every option. "Tie big rocks to him and throw him in the Hudson?"

I cover my mouth with a hand, unable to fight the feeling that I've cursed—that I've spoken the unthinkable.

Stacey, however, doesn't seem to be the least bit fazed. "We certainly could," she says, nodding. "But it would leave too many loose ends. This could easily turn into a missing person investigation, and you can bet the police will trace his disappearance back to us."

"We're fucked, then."

"Not quite. This just means our options have become narrower: We can't throw him in the Hudson, can't feed him to a tiger, can't drive him out to Long Island and bury him on the side of the road. We could, however, find another resting place for him. Leave him in a public spot—a park in the city, perhaps. He could've been walking back to his hotel from the bars last night and collapsed on a park bench."

"Doesn't that also leave loose ends?" I ask. "People may ask exactly how and why he ended up there. And if the police check CCTV footage around the city to explain it, well…"

"Excellent point."

"So? Are we ready now to admit that we're fucked?"

"Not yet. If there's anything I've learned after four decades of editing manuscripts, it's that every plot hole has a solution. We just haven't figured it out yet."

I set both my hands over the carpet and prop myself up, every single one of my muscles protesting in pain. Taking slow steps forward, I approach Robert's body and lean down over him.

"What are you doing?" Stacey asks from behind me.

"Looking for his phone."

I can't believe we didn't think of this earlier. That cell phone could hold all the answers we're looking for. It could reveal to us the details of Robert's trip to New York—the people he was going to see, the things he was going to do, the places he was going to be. It could help us come up with a new plan for where to leave him—if only I could find it.

My heart beats fast as I sneak my hands into the inside of his jacket and touch the pockets of his pants, but there's nothing. Not even his wallet.

"It's not here," I say, panic rising in my chest. Could we have forgotten his phone back at my apartment? Or did we drop it somewhere along the way—maybe in one of the taxis? My mind is racing with the possibility that this is how we'll be found out: by a good Samaritan simply trying to return a lost cell phone, when I catch a glimpse of Stacey out of the corner of my eye. She's holding up Robert's phone with a smirk on her face.

"*What?* Why do *you* have it?"

"I figured I'd take it with me for safekeeping, along with his wallet. I found the phone in his pocket while you were inside the hotel earlier." She frowns a little. "That was also when I found the cocaine, oddly enough."

I move toward her quickly. "Well?" I ask. "Have you gone through it?"

"I have not."

"Let's do it, then."

I reach for the phone, but Stacey moves her hand away to stop me from taking it.

"I've turned it off. And I don't think it's a good idea to turn it back on."

"What are you talking about? We gotta check if there's any—"

"Location tracking, darling. We can't forget about that. I turned it off immediately after I found it, so as it stands now, the last known whereabouts of his cell phone are right outside the Plaza—a perfectly reasonable place for Robert to have last been seen. If we turn it back on now, then—"

"People could know he was in this building."

"Exactly."

Fuck. Why can't any of this be easy? I start pacing around the office, my hands on my waist and my brain working in overdrive, but no answers come to me, and even Stacey seems to have no clue what to do next. I feel her eyes following me as I move back and forth, back and forth, until I stop suddenly and turn to face her.

We both say it at the exact same time: "What if…"

Stacey's eyebrows shoot up. "Are you thinking what I'm thinking?"

"Maybe. What are you thinking?"

"I know a guy who may know a guy," she says. "A hacker. There might be a way for us to access the contents of his phone without activating the location services."

"Oh."

"Why? What were you thinking?"

"Just that we should go back to the Plaza and turn on his phone there."

"Yes," Stacey says, getting up from the carpet. "I like your idea better."

We stand motionless for a moment, staring down at Robert.

"Do we…"

"Leave him here?" she says. "Yes, I'd say so. I'll lock my office on our way out."

I make a move toward the door. My hand is on the handle, and I'm about to pull it open, when another thought comes to me.

"Maybe we don't have to go all the way to the Plaza," I say, turning around to face Stacey. "All we need is a public place—somewhere that isn't traceable back to us."

Stacey shrugs. "Times Square is right down the block."

"That could work. Even if anyone reviewed the cameras, it would be impossible to tell which person in the crowd had Robert's phone—or whether he was there himself."

"That's just what we need."

We step out of the office and start making our way down the long corridor. We're halfway to reception when Josh's head pops out of a door, making us both jump.

"Need anything?" he asks.

"Not at all," Stacey says, swinging her bag over her shoulder. "We're stepping out for a few minutes. Please make sure no one goes into my office."

Josh nods once. "No problem."

"Are you sure we can trust Josh to stay out of your office?" I ask once we're waiting for the elevator.

"Oh, I'm sure," Stacey replies. "That boy wouldn't dare challenge a request from me. Not even if his life was on the line."

135

CHAPTER ELEVEN

Times Square is as busy as ever. There are tourists, and a naked cowboy strumming his guitar, and costumed characters looking for unsuspecting victims to snap a photo with.

And then there's me and Stacey, standing in the middle of it all, staring down at the phone I'm holding in my shaking hands, which I can't help but feel is a bomb that might go off any second.

"Are we ready?" I ask, sneaking a glance up at Stacey's face.

"Just do it."

I hit the side button, and a logo pops up against the dark background. A few excruciating seconds later, the home screen appears—an image of the ocean I have no doubt was taken in Malibu—along with the time, date, and a prompt saying: Swipe up to unlock.

"Damn," I say, staring down at the keyboard where we're meant to enter the passcode. "I have no idea what it could be."

"Give it a second," Stacey says. Her gaze is still fixed on the phone, as if she knows something I don't.

Sure enough, when the phone connects to the network, notifications start popping up on the screen.

My stomach lurches when I see Corey's name: Hey. Just made it to the hotel, he texted Robert at 8:42 a.m. Where are you?

I'm heading out soon. Meeting Anderson and Andy for brunch

in Tribeca, he sent barely twenty minutes ago. You can join us if you're free later.

I let all my breath out through my mouth. At least they're casual messages and not desperate *Where are you?!* texts. This should buy us some time.

I scroll down, reading through the other notifications that have appeared—mostly work-related stuff, by the look of it. Rob, I just sent you the reports you needed for the Henderson account, a text reads. Let me know if you want to discuss. Right below it is an email notification, which seems to contain the reports in question.

And then there's a series of WhatsApp messages that make my body temperature rise, my hands start to sweat. Hey, handsome, someone named Ryan said. Yesterday was fun. Would love to stop by your hotel again at lunchtime if you're . . .

"Son of a bitch!" I yell. If we were anywhere else, I'm certain people would have turned to look at me, but in the madness of Times Square, my voice gets lost in the crowd. "How many guys did he fuck yesterday?"

"He was keeping busy, that's for sure," Stacey says, looking at the screen from over my shoulder.

I want to know more about this Ryan guy. I want to unlock this freaking cell phone so I can figure out who he is, what he looks like. I want to understand if he was just another Grindr fling or someone Robert met up with regularly. I want to find out if he was fed the same lies I was.

Before I can begin to guess potential passcodes, though, I get to the final notification at the bottom of the home screen—an email from Hilton Hotels. We Hope You're Enjoying Your Stay at the New York Hilton Midtown, the subject line reads. Below it, in smaller letters, the email preview says: Let us know if there is anything we can do to make your visit more enjoyable.

"That's odd," Stacey says behind me. "Why would he be getting this email? He's not staying at the Hilton."

I turn toward her. My mind has already arrived at a conclusion, but I can't bring myself to speak it out loud, so I'm left with no option but to watch as Stacey connects the dots herself.

"Then again," she adds, "he did have a key card for the Hilton in his wallet." She gasps. "You don't think he—"

"Had two hotel rooms in the city?" I complete her sentence. "Yeah, I do!"

"Why would anyone do that?"

"Why did Robert do any of the things he did? To stick his dick inside other guys!"

"Now, don't be crass, darling. I'm—"

"The Plaza was probably meant for him and Corey only," I say. "So he must've gotten a second, cheaper hotel room nearby so he could get some action on the side."

"If that's the case, why wouldn't he have invited you to the Hilton? Why bring you to the Plaza?"

A few cars honk behind us on Seventh Avenue. I search my surroundings, almost hoping to find the answer written on one of the flashing billboards, but they aren't there. There's only noise, and people scurrying like ants all around us, and a feeling of uneasiness in the pit of my stomach.

"I have no idea," I admit finally. "But we need to look into it. If this is true—if there's another hotel room we can leave him in, away from Corey's prying gaze, then—"

"It'll all be over."

"Exactly."

She pushes her glasses up her nose. "Onward to the Hilton?"

"Let's go."

I hit the side button to turn off Robert's phone, and we turn around urgently, trying to make our way through the crowd. I swear, Times Square has gotten twice as busy in the ten minutes since we arrived, because now there's hardly any room to move. We settle into the slow pace of the masses, taking small steps forward, while the image of Robert's dead body lying in Stacey's office spins around my head, reminding me that we have absolutely no time to waste.

We're reaching the end of the funnel, finally about to break free from the crowd, when two women wearing identical Minnie Mouse costumes appear in front of us, blocking our way.

"How about a photo with the Minnies, huh?"

Sixth Avenue has never seemed more overcrowded than it does now. It's not even eleven yet, but everyone seems to be out and about—office workers inexplicably walking around despite the fact that lunch hour is still a while away; cars driving up the avenue in droves, as if there were an unmissable event they were all trying to get to; tourists who seem to have randomly decided this is the new hot place to be in the city.

Stacey and I rush through it all, jaywalking at red lights and apologizing every time we accidentally hit someone's shoulder, and we don't slow down until we've walked through the revolving doors of the Hilton hotel.

The lobby is wide and open, with shiny white floors and big columns here and there breaking up the space. The wood-paneled reception desk is on the far left, and several employees are busy behind it, talking to guests, answering phones, typing into computers.

"How do we do this?" Stacey asks. She's holding up the Hilton key card we found in Robert's wallet, and she's breathing heavily from our run.

"We need his room number," I say, panting as well.

"Well, how do we get that?"

There are no memories to reach toward this time, no images of Robert pressing a button inside an elevator that I can summon. There's only this card and the hope that our suspicion of him having a second hotel room in the city isn't entirely, ridiculously wrong.

Suddenly, a phone rings somewhere in the background, and my eyes fall on an employee as she lifts the receiver up to her ear.

"We should call them," I say.

"What?"

"We'll call the front desk and ask for Robert. We—we can just pretend that we need to talk to him. Maybe they'll be willing to tell us the room number and connect us to it—and then we'll know where to go."

"Brilliant," Stacey says, reaching into her purse for her cell phone. "Absolutely brilliant."

I look up the number for the hotel and read it out loud for Stacey to type into her keypad. She then hits the Call button and presses the phone against the side of her head.

"Hi, there," she says a second later. Looking over her shoulder, I spot a dark-haired employee standing behind the desk, who I'm pretty sure is the person who answered her call. "I'm looking for Robert Wallace. Would you be a sweetheart and connect me to his room?"

The employee types something into a computer. Even though I'm too far away to hear him, I'm able to make out the vague sound of his voice coming through Stacey's phone and read his lips as he says, "Certainly. Just a second, ma'am."

"Oh, by the way," Stacey adds quickly, "what *is* his room number?"

"I'm unable to divulge that information, unfortunately," he says. "But I can direct your call up to Mr. Wallace. Please hold."

Stacey remains on the line for a few seconds. Once it becomes clear that Robert's room is indeed empty and no one is picking up, she lowers the phone.

"Well, that's that," she says, hitting the End Call button more forcefully than she needed to.

"What do we do now?"

She turns slowly on the spot, looking around. Her eyes scan the lobby, and I can just tell her mind is hard at work. "We could always go floor by floor, trying different rooms until we find the right one," she says finally.

"That'll take forever. And someone will figure out what we're doing and report us to security sooner rather than later."

"Fair enough."

"I guess we could try to pull an Anna Delvey—slap a hundred-dollar bill on the front desk and demand to be told Robert's room number."

"I have no idea who you're talking about," Stacey says. "But it wouldn't be wise to call attention to ourselves like that. Last thing we'd want is for hotel staff to tell the police two perps were trying to get up to Robert's room shortly before his body was found."

"We're screwed, then." So close, yet so far... and so absolutely, undeniably screwed. I can't believe we're here, holding a hotel room key and an answer to how to get rid of the body, and a stupid technicality is what's stopping us from finishing this once and for all.

"A delivery, maybe," Stacey says suddenly. "We could pretend to have a package for Robert and see if they'll let us bring it up to his room."

I nod quickly. I like this idea. I'm almost certain that we could make it work, except...

141

"We don't have a package."

"That can be easily solved, dear."

"Do we ask Josh to bring over a box of books?" Stacey's office building is only a couple of blocks away. I'm sure he could make it over in a matter of minutes.

Stacey presses her lips into a smile. "I can think of a better way to do it."

Without telling me what she's planning or who she's calling, she brings her phone up to her ear again and frowns slightly while it rings.

"Hello," she says a moment later. "I'd like to order a large pizza. No, just cheese is fine."

I have to resist the urge to hug her, forcing myself to keep my arms firmly by my sides while she listens to the person talking back on the phone.

"The Hilton hotel in Midtown," she says. "Now, please listen very carefully: I'd like the pizza delivered directly to the room. When the delivery person arrives, they should go straight to the front desk and ask to be let up to Robert Wallace's room. Yes, Robert Wallace. As soon as possible would be great. Thank you very much."

When she hangs up, I'm unable to hold myself back any longer— I close the distance between us, wrap my arms tight around her, and whisper, "You're a genius."

"First we have to make sure this works," she replies, trying to wiggle herself out of my grasp. "*Then* you can call me a genius."

We wait near the front desk, perfectly within earshot of what the guests and employees are saying, keeping an eye out for any pizza delivery guys.

Every once in a while, Stacey will sigh loudly and say things like, "Where *is* your father? He said he'd be here ten minutes

I MIGHT BE IN TROUBLE

ago!" I don't think anyone is giving much thought to our presence, but I suppose it's still good to shout out an explanation as to why we're lingering here, in case any suspicious employees are wondering. Besides, the thought of Stacey being my pretend mother—or stepmother—is oddly comforting. That is, until I start thinking of Sheila, and the comfort is replaced by a subtle headache.

I don't think we've been waiting for too long—fifteen, twenty minutes, maybe—by the time a freckly kid comes in through the revolving doors, balancing a pizza box in his hands.

For a second, he seems confused. He looks around the lobby, uncertain where to go, but when he spots the reception desk, he walks confidently toward it and casually passes by the spot where Stacey and I are standing, clueless to the fact that we're watching his every move.

"Pizza delivery for Robert Wallace," he says to one of the men working behind the desk—the same one who answered Stacey's phone call earlier.

The hotel employee—Kirk, according to the name tag on his chest—nods once and reaches for the phone. He pouts his lips while he waits for an answer that will never come.

"Sorry," he says to the delivery guy. "No answer."

"Try again, maybe?" the kid replies, and so Kirk tries again a second time, and even a third, before hanging up the phone assertively.

"Are you sure you have the correct name?" he asks.

"I'm sure, yeah. I...I was actually asked to deliver the pizza straight to the room. Could I go up there, try knocking on this guy's door?"

Stacey and I hold our breaths, listening intently. This is it—this is where Kirk nods, speaks the room number out loud, and grants the poor kid access upstairs.

But that is not what happens. With the same unwavering, almost mean tone he used when talking to Stacey on the phone, Kirk says, "I'm not allowed to do that. Unless Mr. Wallace answers the phone, I can't just let you go up there."

"What am I supposed to do with this pizza, then?"

"You can leave it here, if you want. Once Mr. Wallace is ready, he can come down to collect it himself."

"I can't just leave it. It's not paid yet."

A pang of guilt hits me. I don't want this kid to get in trouble. I wish I could pull out a twenty from my pocket and hand it to him, just so he has something to bring back to his manager at the pizza joint, but I remain still.

"Don't give up, now," Stacey says under her breath, her eyes firmly set on the two guys. "Come on. Try harder."

But the pizza delivery kid doesn't. Looking dejected, he turns around and carries the pizza across the lobby, back in the direction of the revolving doors.

Meanwhile, Stacey and I remain frozen, likely looking just as dejected. This feels like the end—the end of our attempts to get rid of Robert's body, the end of the possibility that we might get away with this. The end of everything.

There must be other ways to get Robert's room number that we just haven't thought of yet—maybe even ways to break into his phone and seek more answers there—but I'm not sure any of them will work. I'm not sure either of us has the energy to go on much longer.

"Where do we go next?" I ask.

Stacey's lips tremble. She must be as afraid of speaking the answer out loud as I am of hearing it—back to the office, back to the dead body, back to square one.

Before she can get the words out, however, a man wearing a brown UPS uniform rushes past us, goes up to the front desk, and slaps a small box right in front of Kirk.

"Package for room fourteen-oh-one," he says. "A Mr. Robert Wallace?"

Everything in the lobby seems to freeze in that moment. I'm almost certain that I misheard, that the UPS guy spoke someone else's name—but when I sneak a glance at Stacey, her mouth is twisted into a smile.

Trying to stop myself from pulling her in for a celebratory hug, I smile back.

CHAPTER TWELVE

When I was little, I used to like playing with dolls.

My father never said anything about it, never explicitly told me not to. When I look back on it, though, it isn't hard to see how much it must've irked him. Every birthday, every Christmas, he'd buy me brand-new cars, planes, and trains, which I'd play with for a day or two only to return to my dolls, figurines, and stuffed animals. I spent my childhood thinking Pa was simply bad at choosing presents, but a few years ago, the truth finally clicked: those gifts were no accident. They were his attempts to get me to start playing with toys he deemed appropriate for a boy.

My mother, on the other hand, never seemed to mind which toys I did or didn't enjoy playing with. She'd sometimes sit down with me when I was playing teatime, drinking air from plastic cups and making polite conversation with our fellow guests, none of whom talked back. Ma caught on to my interest in dolls pretty early on and made sure I had enough of them to play with—but my favorite by far were a pair of Mexican dolls that she kept tucked away in her closet, which she'd gotten from her grandmother as a child and had probably been saving for the daughter she'd once dreamed of having. We never got the opportunity to talk about it, but she must've known how much I loved them. She must've noticed how I would sneak into her closet, bring them out for an hour or two, and then put them back exactly as I'd found them.

The dolls had big eyes, braided hair, and wore beautiful hand-stitched dresses. Mara and Mora, I called them, uncertain whether my mother had given them different names when she was a little girl.

I have no idea where they ended up. I don't know if Pa and Sheila got rid of them, or if they're still hidden away somewhere in the house. But now, staring down at Robert's body, I'm reminded of those old dolls—still, lifeless, with the trace of a smile permanently etched upon their faces.

That's all he is, I tell myself as Stacey and I stand over him. *A doll. A big, realistic, wax-skinned doll.*

I don't manage to convince myself of it, of course, but at least the thought stops me from vomiting up the coffee and croissant I had a while ago.

"We need to change his clothes," Stacey says suddenly, as if supporting my delusion of seeing Robert as a toy.

"Why?"

"Security cameras, dear," she says. "The more we can disguise his identity as we move through the hotel, the better."

"Yeah," I say. "That's a good idea."

Instinctively, I look down at my own clothes. I suppose we could try fitting them on Robert, but I have no idea what I would wear then. It's not like I have anything to change into, and putting on a dead man's suit would be out of the question.

Before I can point any of this out, Stacey walks toward the door of her office, opens it a small crack, and pokes her head out.

"Josh, sweetheart?" she says.

Josh's voice answers immediately. "Yes, Stacey?"

"You wouldn't be planning on going to the gym after work by any chance, would you?"

"I...am, yeah."

"Fabulous! Does that mean you've brought along your gym bag?"

Even though I don't have a direct view of him, I can just imagine the confused look on Josh's face.

"Yeah," he replies. "Yeah, I brought it."

"I will need to borrow it."

"Okay," he says. There's no hesitation in his voice, no sign of alarm. "I'll just take out my things and bring it right over. It'll take me one—"

"No, no," Stacey says. "You can leave your clothes inside. In fact, we're gonna need them, but you'll get everything back, dear, I promise."

If Josh is in any way suspicious about this request, we don't find out. After a few seconds of waiting, Stacey withdraws back into the office, holding a gym bag and smiling to herself.

"I'll need your help," she says, taking out a pair of Nike sweatpants from the bag. "Come on, we must hurry."

The sweats are stretchy enough that we're able to fit them over Robert's suit pants, one heavy leg at a time. *Just a doll, just a doll*, I keep repeating to myself, but staring at him from up close, Robert looks more dead than ever.

"This is fucked up," I mumble as we fix the elastic band of the sweatpants around his waist.

"It'll all be over soon, David," Stacey says, her voice coming out a bit muffled, which tells me she's holding her breath. She's better than me at disguising it, but she must also be having a hard time with this.

At least she's right—soon, this will all be behind us. We stuck around the Hilton lobby just long enough to watch Kirk sign for the

UPS package, and then we headed straight for the elevators and up to the fourteenth floor. Almost miraculously, the key card worked on room 1401. Once we'd made sure that housekeeping still hadn't come by to clean the room, and that the DO NOT DISTURB sign was securely attached to the front of the door, we ran out and rushed back to the office with our minds set on one thing only: getting here as fast as possible so we could return to the Hilton with Robert's body.

With a bit of difficulty, Stacey and I remove his suit jacket. She steps away while I start unbuttoning his shirt, and an instant later, she lets out a grunt.

"Well, this simply won't do."

I turn to look at her over my shoulder. She's holding up a stringy tank top, which looks exactly like the type of thing Josh would wear to the gym.

I suppress a smile. "Isn't there anything else in there?"

"A Red Sox baseball hat," she answers. "Oh, I'll need to have a chat with Josh about that."

"We can use it," I say. "It'll hide his face."

"I know, David, but what about the shirt?"

I guess I could put on the tiny tank top and give Robert the shirt I'm wearing. I'm about to suggest it when Stacey rushes toward the office door.

"Josh, love?" she shouts out.

"How can I help?"

"Could you look inside the closet for my raincoat, please? The long beige one?"

By the time we're done dressing Robert, he looks absolutely idiotic—sweatpants, sunglasses, a baseball cap, and a women's trench coat—but at least he doesn't look much like himself.

"Perfect," Stacey says with a nod of approval. "Are we ready for this?"

The truth is I'm not at all ready, but I lean down to pick up Robert anyway.

"Did he get heavier?" I ask as I swing his arm over my shoulders.

"Not heavier," Stacey replies, doing the same with his other arm. "But definitely stiffer."

The office feels busier than earlier, though it's definitely emptier than usual. Most of the other agents and assistants are probably working from home today, but we can still hear voices and phones ringing as we make our way down the hallway toward the main entrance.

"Heading out again?" Josh asks, appearing unexpectedly.

"We are," Stacey replies, throwing him a quick glance. "Just taking our friend home, but we'll be back soon."

"Do you…need help?"

"Maybe just with the door. Thank you. Thanks very much indeed."

As we sneak into an elevator, I can't help but wonder what's going through Josh's mind. I wonder whether he realizes we've put his gym clothes on a dead man, and whether his loyalty to Stacey has any limits. How ironic would it be if Josh was the one who ended up turning us in to the police?

For now, at least, I try my best to push that thought aside. We have much more pressing matters to take care of.

We hail a cab on Sixth Avenue to take us to the Hilton. It's literally two blocks away, but by now we're too exhausted to carry Robert even short distances.

"It'll be a quick trip, I'm afraid," Stacey says to the driver after telling him where we're going. "Our friend here is simply too tired to walk."

"Not a problem, ma'am," he replies. "It's all good."

I should *hope* it wouldn't be a problem for him—we'll probably end up paying him fifteen dollars just to take us down the avenue.

If there's one positive thing to be said about everything that has happened today, it's that Stacey and I have gotten shockingly good at maneuvering the process of getting dead bodies into and out of cars. When the taxi comes to a stop in front of the Hilton, we manage to pull Robert out seamlessly, despite the fact that his limbs barely bend at this point.

We enter the hotel through the automatic doors and find ourselves face-to-face with a bunch of frat bros who are on their way out.

"Yo, that guy is *wasted*," one of them says to the rest of the group. I'm not sure if he intended for us to hear or not, but Stacey and I keep going as if we hadn't.

Another guy hits the first one with an elbow. "If we don't end up like that tonight, I'll be wanting a full refund for this trip."

Trying our hardest not to make eye contact with anyone else, Stacey and I move quickly in the direction of the elevators.

"Almost there," Stacey whispers to me once we're on our way up to the fourteenth floor. "Remember, dear: in and out."

"Trust me, I know."

I can't wait for us to be riding the elevator on our way down. I wonder what we will do after Robert's body is out of our hands. Am I meant to just go back home while Stacey returns to the office? Will she suggest staking out the front of the hotel, keeping an eye out for police? Or will she want to go to a bar and drown our sorrows in alcohol?

Somehow, I know it'll be the third option. And I'm desperately looking forward to it. I am more than ready to down one whiskey shot after another, until the memory of this whole day starts to fade into a dark corner of my consciousness.

My entire body seems to be screaming in exhaustion as we carry

Robert out of the elevator and down the hallway. The scream nearly reaches my throat, but I manage to stop it when I think of the people behind these doors. Any of them could be about to step out of their room. Any of them could hear suspicious sounds and decide to come out to check what's happening. Any of them could completely ruin our plan of sneaking into and out of Robert's room without being seen.

"The key card," I pant, staring hungrily at the door of room 1401.

Stacey fumbles with her purse. She pulls out the card, scans it, and pushes the door open with a foot. Like light at the end of a tunnel, the sunshine coming through the windows blinds us, but we don't slow down—not to bask in this feeling of triumph and hope, not to catch our breaths, not to think about the fact that we've finally made it. We go straight for the bed and lay Robert down gently.

"Careful, darling," Stacey says to me. "Don't touch any surfaces— no fingerprints, remember?"

We wiped his phone and wallet while we were in the taxi, which I hope was enough to remove any traces of us. With a gloved hand, Stacey sets them both down on the bedside table, and then she turns toward the body.

"Quick," she says. "Let's take all this stuff off him."

I remove the hat from his head, the sunglasses from his eyes. Stacey undoes the waist belt of the trench coat, and together we slip it off his shoulders, replacing it with his suit jacket. Once the sweatpants are off, we tuck his shirt into his pants, fix all his buttons, and then, finally, we take a step back to look at him.

He's lying there peacefully, looking at ease. He could be sleeping, just enjoying a little nap, or even resting his eyes. At least that's what I tell myself, trying hard not to think about his pale, waxy skin, the odd position of his arms, or the way his mouth has fallen slightly open.

"It's over," I whisper, breathing heavily. I'm not sure why, but I feel the need to cry all of a sudden. "It's really over."

"It is," Stacey says, sounding just as relieved. "Now, how about we go grab a few drinks to take the edge off?"

I knew it. I am so ready for us to get to the bar. I've never needed a drink so badly in my life.

We start moving toward the door, our eyes searching the room carefully to make sure we haven't forgotten anything. But then, at the exact same moment Stacey's hand wraps around the doorknob, a knock comes from the other side.

"Mr. Wallace?" a woman's voice shouts. "Mr. Wallace, just a gentle reminder that checkout was at twelve o'clock."

I have stopped breathing. I have stopped moving. I'm not even sure my heart is beating. The only part of my body I still have control over are my eyes, which meet Stacey's, desperately searching for answers.

Another loud knock. "Mr. Wallace, are you in there?"

Why didn't we think of this before? I guess we'd assumed he had this hotel room for the whole weekend—that he'd want to keep his side playground during his entire visit to New York. The lying fuck must've only had it for one night. He must've just been trying to avoid bringing guys to his empty suite at the Plaza, out of fear that any of the employees would expose him once his husband arrived.

Nice to see you, he said when we first met. So cunning. So discreet. Always walking a few steps ahead of me, always putting on a performance—not only for me, but for anyone who might've been watching.

Then again, there's the question Stacey asked earlier. If he had a second hotel room, why did he invite me to the Plaza? Why didn't he ask me to meet him at the Hilton instead? Why would he have risked being seen with me?

"What do we do?" I ask Stacey in a whisper, but she doesn't have an answer.

A final knock comes—a softer, lazier one. It's a knock that suggests the woman on the other side of the door is giving up, and she'll either leave or enter the room using her own key.

She chooses the latter.

I'm not sure exactly how it happens. One second we're there, listening to the door beeping, about to be discovered, and the next, Stacey is pulling hard on my arm, and we're stumbling into the bathroom.

It's over, I tell myself as we sneak into our hiding place behind the bathroom door, except this time, no relief comes with those words. There is only a razor-sharp, paralyzing fear. *It's really over.*

We've been too stupid, too careless. I guess we had it coming. I don't know how either of us ever managed to convince ourselves that we were going to get away with this, because the truth has never been clearer: We should've never started any of it in the first place. We should've left the body on my bed. I never should've listened to Stacey.

It all happens in slow motion—or at least that's how it feels. We hear the front door of the room opening, the woman's shoes stepping softly over the carpet, and then her voice.

"Mr. Wallace, I apologize! I didn't realize you were in here."

A long pause, during which Robert's response doesn't come. The woman—a housekeeper, I'm ready to bet—is probably debating her next move. I can almost feel her indecision floating in the air—the choice between running out of the room and giving a sleeping guest the privacy he deserves, or approaching him to make sure he is indeed sleeping, because he looks just a little off, even from a distance.

"Mr. Wallace?"

More cautious steps moving forward on the carpet. From the

slim gap between the bathroom door and the wall, I see her shadow falling across the bed. And then, a scream.

"*Oh, Mr. Wallace!*" she yells. "*Help! We—we need help!*"

This is the last thing we need—someone yelling desperately for help, more people coming in to see what has happened. The housekeeper's shadow retreats as she turns around to run out of the room—but all of a sudden, a loud bang comes, almost as if she'd tripped and fallen.

Stacey holds my gaze as we wait motionless. I don't think I've ever seen this type of terror in her eyes. She looks absolutely, irrevocably defeated. Even she knows that we have lost, and that it's only a matter of time before we're taken out of here in handcuffs.

The silence stretches on, and still, we wait. The housekeeper is no longer yelling for help. It didn't sound like she went very far, but she also doesn't seem to be getting up.

"Do we go check what's happened?" I ask Stacey in the faintest of murmurs.

She doesn't react—I don't think she even heard me. Her eyes remain as horrified and unblinking as they were a moment ago, but then she gives a small nod.

"We have hardly anything left to lose," she says, her voice just as weak as mine.

We move silently, stepping out of our hiding place to find the housekeeper's body splayed on the carpet by the entrance, looking just as lifeless as Robert's.

"Is she...?"

"No," Stacey whispers. "I think she just passed out from the shock."

"What do we do?" I ask.

Stacey presses her lips together while she stares down at the housekeeper. A moment later, she starts moving over the carpet carefully, so as not to step on the woman. Once she reaches the other side, she stops at the doorway, turns around, and lifts her eyebrows at me.

"Well?" she asks. "Are you coming?"

Following the same step pattern, I walk around the housekeeper and join Stacey at the door. We take one last look at the hotel room—the sunlight filtering through the windows, the half-open bathroom door, the two bodies lying there.

And then we nod at each other, turn toward the hallway, and break into a run.

We don't take the elevator. Instead, we head for the emergency exit at the end of the hallway and rush down as fast as we can, twisting and turning in the stairwell.

When we reach the ground floor, Stacey and I push the door marked EXIT TO STREET LEVEL, not even stopping to think about the possibility that it might set off an alarm. It only crosses my mind an instant later, once we've stumbled out, and I come to the realization that no alarms are ringing. All we can hear are cars beeping, the huff and puff of our own heavy breathing, and the constant murmur of the city all around us.

"She saw us," I pant, leaning against the wall of the building and clutching my chest. We've come out of the hotel from the side— onto 54th, I'm pretty sure, because the Ziegfeld Ballroom is right across the street. "She definitely saw us."

"No one saw, darling," Stacey responds, also clutching her chest. "We're in the clear."

I feel sick. I want to disappear. I want to collapse right here on the side of the road and never wake up, but I manage to remain upright.

The seconds stretch into minutes, and still we wait. People and cars move down the street. Sirens wail every now and then, bringing horrible images to mind—police cars coming to a screeching stop right in front of us, red and blue lights reflecting off Stacey's terrified eyes, crowds gathering to watch as we're put under arrest.

Time after time, my fears are proven wrong when the sound of sirens fades into the distance. But then, what starts as a faint wailing becomes stronger and stronger, ultimately coming to a stop somewhere nearby, and I'm almost sure that if we walked around the corner onto Sixth Avenue, we'd find an ambulance and police cars parked right in front of the hotel.

"This is meant to happen, darling," Stacey says, making me think of paramedics and cops walking quickly across the lobby, on their way to the fourteenth floor. "Someone must've called 911 by now. Do not worry, though. Nobody saw us inside his room."

"Yeah," I say. My lungs ache with every inhale and exhale. "I hope you're right."

I'm not sure what we're waiting for, because there's truly nothing for us to do anymore. Nothing except get far away from here and hope no one will come after us. At some point, Stacey seems to realize this, too, because she steps away from the wall we've been leaning against and turns toward me.

"We may as well get going, dear," she says, rearranging her bag over her shoulder. "Unless…you want to go around and see what's happening at the front of the hotel?"

"No," I say firmly. The last thing I want is to watch the paramedics wheel away a body bag. "We should go."

We start walking down the street toward Seventh Avenue, in the opposite direction of the main entrance to the hotel.

"At least that's over," Stacey says suddenly. "I'll be glad to put all this behind us. Very glad, indeed."

I don't respond. It's not that I don't want to put all this behind me—it's just that I don't know how I'll ever be able to do it.

"Now all there's left to do is write the book, darling." Stacey lets out a chuckle, but I don't laugh in return. Instead, I stop in my tracks, my face feeling very hot.

It's not too late to stop myself. The last thing I should be doing is allowing the fury that's bubbling in my chest to get the best of me, but I just can't keep the words from flying out of my mouth. "What the hell, Stacey?"

She turns to face me, frowning slightly.

"David, what's the matter?"

"All there's left to do is *write the book*?" I repeat. "Could you not make this out to be a big joke for *once*?"

"I'm dead serious," she replies. Even though I'm shouting, she manages to remain composed, and it's driving me crazy. I'd far prefer it if she were yelling, or crying, or showing whatever type of emotion—anything to validate all the guilt, terror, and despair that are eating me up inside. Anything to reassure me that I'm not alone in feeling that we've done something horrible, and that we'll be haunted by it for the rest of our lives.

"How am I meant to write about this, Stacey?" I yell, throwing my hands up. "This wasn't a fun little adventure I can spin into a story. We got rid of a *dead body*, for crying out loud!"

I don't care who's around. I don't care who might be listening. I don't even care that we're merely half a block away from the hotel. Nothing matters anymore.

"Not all of us have prior experience with this kind of thing," I continue, my face feeling hotter and hotter every second. "You may go to sleep tonight feeling perfectly at ease knowing you've killed two of your husbands and treated a dead man as if he were a mannequin, but I can't just brush this whole thing off. I can't pretend it's okay. *None* of what happened today is okay!"

Stacey's expression shifts at the mention of her dead husbands. For a moment, I worry I've gone too far. I worry that she's gonna start yelling back, that she's gonna go off on me for accusing her of killing them.

Taking one step closer to me, she clears her throat. "Yes, this was a god-awful day," she says calmly. "And yes, we were forced to do god-awful things. But it is *done*, darling, and we might as well make the most of it, instead of letting it ruin us forever. You don't have to start writing tomorrow, or next week. But if you don't find a way to channel all this anguish into your next book, then it will all have been for nothing."

"Maybe it *was* for nothing!" I yell. I am tainted, broken, ruined, and it's all Stacey's fault. To think that I might want to write about this is fucking ridiculous. I'm done with this industry, done with those stupid dreams I used to have, done with everyone and everything that's ever made me feel like a failure.

Stacey raises her eyebrows gently at me, as if asking for leniency. "I suppose you don't want to join me for drinks after all."

"No, Stacey!" I say, my voice coming our harsher than I intended it to. "No, I don't."

She nods, pressing her lips together. Her lipstick looks smudged. Her bright yellow pantsuit, which was freshly ironed this morning, is crinkled, and her hair is all over the place. I know none of this has been easy for her, either, but I cannot find it in me to feel compassion for her right now. I can't feel sorry for either of us—not after everything we've done.

"Darling, I—" she begins, but her words get caught in her throat. She swallows hard and tries again. "I was only trying to help."

I know, I wish I could say. *I'm so grateful you were there. I have no idea what I would've done if I'd been left to face all of this alone.* But I can't bring myself to say any of it. All I can do is stand here in front of her, wishing that she would stop looking at me this way—as if she were begging something from me, and I was refusing it.

159

"Either way," she says, turning away from me. "I'll be expecting your pages soon—whatever it is you choose to write."

With that, she starts walking down the street, her high heels banging against the sidewalk with every step she takes.

I remain frozen on the spot, my eyes fixed on Stacey's back until she reaches the end of the street, turns a corner, and disappears from view.

PART II

CHAPTER THIRTEEN

How many words does the average person speak in a day? One thousand? Ten thousand? A million?

In the weeks after Jeremy and I broke up, I had the strangest realization: my daily word count had gone way down. When he moved out of our apartment, I was left with nobody to talk to—no one to share long conversations or random musings with, no one to turn to and say, "I love this song," or "I put too much sugar in my coffee," or "I might go to bed early tonight."

My throat became dry from lack of use, my chest heavy with unspoken sentences, and I became deeply aware of the number of words that came out of my mouth every day. Saying "Thanks" to a neighbor holding the door for me on my way out of the building— that was one. Mumbling "Excuse me" to a stranger as I stepped into the deli by my apartment—another two. Ordering my morning coffee—a dozen, at least.

I never made it above one hundred words. Sometimes, I would sit around the apartment and just talk to myself, out of a sheer necessity to use my voice. "I should hop in the shower," I'd say. Or "I gotta pay off my credit card bill." Or "I haven't seen it rain like this in a long time." Of course, I wouldn't add those sentences to my daily totals. Words hardly matter unless there's someone there to listen to them.

For the past few days, my word count has been zero. There have been no trips to the deli, no morning coffee runs, no evening walks through Central Park. Not even sentences spoken out loud for my own benefit. There's been nothing, really, except for the four walls of my apartment.

I'm used to feeling a bit claustrophobic in here. I've always wished this place was bigger, that the kitchen wasn't visible from my bed, that the couch was in its own separate room and not floating in the middle of the apartment. Lately, though, I've found myself wondering why there's so much space, so much emptiness. I've been feeling naked, exposed, wishing I could bring the walls closer together to make the place feel a little safer.

A few people have called, and texted, and emailed. Stacey, trying to make sure I'm okay. My dad, confirming I'm still planning to come to Jersey for Father's Day. My publicist, asking if I'm willing to endorse a book by a debut author. I haven't replied to any of them, but I've made sure that my read receipts and out-of-office emails are on, just so people will know I'm not dead.

In my darkest moments, I wish I *were* dead. This is no way to live—sitting around in the same pair of dirty sweatpants, ordering barely enough food online to keep me going, scrolling desperately through my phone for updates and flinching every time a new article containing Corey Donovan's name pops up. On the *New York Post*, which broke the news that his husband had been found dead in a hotel room. On TMZ, which revealed that the police were not treating it as a suspicious death but were in the process of carrying out an autopsy. On social media, where Corey was trending for the entire weekend.

Robert's name has hardly been mentioned. An entire man, erased. His life and death are only talked about through the lens of Corey. Sending my deepest condolences to Corey Donovan, a handful of celebrities have written in their Instagram stories. Corey Donovan is taking a leave of absence from his primetime show, and it is unclear when he will return, the *New York Times* said. A few twinks have been joking around on TikTok, offering themselves up to Corey for whenever he's ready to jump back into the dating scene.

It is late on Tuesday night when I'm lying on the couch in the dark, scraping a spoon against the sides of an empty ice cream bowl, and my phone pings with a familiar sound—the email alert I've set up for articles about Corey.

Autopsy Report Released in Case of Corey Donovan's Husband's Death, the headline reads. I prop myself up to a sitting position, sending the spoon flying out of my hand. It lands with a loud clatter on the floor, but I don't make a move to pick it up. Instead, I click on the article and hold my breath as I skim the text.

... was revealed to have had high alcohol levels in his blood, as well as other drugs, including cocaine and Xanax... cause of death was a cocaine-induced stroke... consistent with initial reports, which said no foul play was suspected... concluded Wallace's death was accidental... findings will be discussed further at a press conference on Wednesday.

I hold the phone in front of my eyes for the longest time, the bluish light blinding me. *Stroke. No foul play. Accidental.* Those words flash before me, but they don't seem real. It feels as if someone has put them there as a sick joke, trying to trick me into a false sense of security.

Even long after I have lowered my phone and gone back to the freezer to get a second bowl of ice cream, I keep waiting for a knock at the door, or the sound of sirens on 90th Street, or the glow of blue and red lights flashing through the windows. None of it comes, but still I wait, confident that Stacey and I won't be able to get away with this. Confident that someone will speak up saying they saw something suspicious, that the coroner will find a strand of hair or a trace of DNA on his body and link it to us, or that the police will start piecing certain inconsistencies together—like the pizza that was ordered to Robert's room shortly before he was found dead, or the footage from the hotel security cameras showing a peculiarly dressed man being carried across the lobby.

We might just be in the clear, darling, Stacey texts me after the press conference ends on Wednesday. As long as the police declare his death non-suspicious, there's no reason anyone should look further into it.

I don't respond. The days keep passing, and I simply carry on with my routine. Wake up, check phone. Sit on couch, check phone. Order food, check phone. Look out the window, check phone.

At night, I have trouble sleeping. I wake up every few hours feeling like I'm drowning and gasping for air, reaching for the emptiness around me as if hoping to find a hand to pull me back to the surface. Night after night, there's nothing. Sometimes, I'm able to lull myself back to sleep. Others, I move to the couch, regardless of the hour, and scroll through my phone until the sky outside the windows starts to turn lighter.

Soon enough, I lose track of the date and the hours and the minutes. It's getting comfortable, truly—ignoring reality. Ignoring the fact that I don't have any money to pay next month's rent and will likely end up getting evicted. Ignoring the fact that someone could come knocking on my door at any moment and take me away. Ignoring the fact that I've become a shadow of the person I used to be, and that this is the last thing I ever imagined for myself. But then, without warning, something happens.

I start to write.

In the morning, in the darkness of the night. By the window while soft summer winds rattle the leaves of the trees along the street, and in bed on days when I'm feeling so weak that words become my only form of sustenance.

I write about a guy, twenty-eight years old and with everything going for him, whose biggest enemy is his lack of self-confidence. A guy who grew up with a fractured sense of belonging and identity, and who now feels forgotten, left behind, cast aside—by his family, his former friends, and his ex-boyfriend. A guy whose entire life has become a mess without him even realizing it, and whose most desperate wish is simply to be seen, to be wanted, to be loved. I write about nights of loneliness, nights of casual sex, and nights of self-destructiveness—and then, about a morning on which the main character wakes up to find the dead body of a man he doesn't recognize in his bed.

And it is my favorite thing I've ever written.

The words flow out of me in a way that they never have before—not even when I was writing *The Millers*. My waking hours are consumed with the thought of this character—so much that I start checking my phone only once every several hours, and then not at all. Come midnight, I fall asleep easily, exhausted after a long day of work, and dream of new directions to take the story in. Other images sneak into my dreams, of course—champagne glasses clinking against each other. Shoes stepping lightly over carpeted floors. Bodies sweating on the dance floor.

At first, the images feel like nightmares—they force me awake, leaving me feeling cold and desolate. But then, when I start incorporating them into my writing, reliving them becomes almost cathartic.

It's nearly effortless, the way I start to remember what it used to feel like to write before I became published, before *Walking Home* failed, and before I started prioritizing people's opinions over my own passion. I begin to feel inklings of the hope, the joy, and the

167

comfort that pen and paper used to bring me when I was younger, and a part of me that I thought had died long ago slowly comes back to life.

I'm not really sure what the point of this book is. I don't even know what's going to happen in the end, but I decide one thing pretty early on: this is a thriller. And as I write about a character whose entire world has been turned upside down—someone desperately seeking answers about the identity of the dead man in his bed and about what happened the previous night—I feel strangely safe. Because this time around, I'm in control. I get to call the shots and take these fictional characters in whatever direction I want them to go. More importantly, I'm not at risk of being betrayed by a dishonest man, or by my own clouded mind after drinking too much, or by the surprises that waking up after a wild night can bring. I am just wrapped in a blanket inside my apartment with a pen in my hand and a notebook on my lap, and as long as I'm here, no one can hurt me.

I don't even know how long it takes me to write three full chapters. Time has little meaning to me anymore, so it may very well have been two weeks, or two months, or two years. As I type *Chapter Four* into my laptop on a cloudy day in mid-June, however, I realize something: I have a full proposal in my hands, even though I wasn't trying to write one.

I spend the rest of the day pacing around my apartment, thinking, thinking, thinking. I can't send this to Stacey, can I? I can't pitch this story to Jackie—not after she saw us with Robert in the elevator. I shouldn't try to make money off of what happened that day. But then, in a moment of weakness—a moment of desperation, as I think about the fact that the month is halfway done and I have no cash to pay July's rent with—I sit at my desk and type out an email.

Here's what I've been working on, I say to Stacey. Maybe you were right—maybe I needed to write about all this.

The next morning, I wake up to an email from her.

I just finished reading, she replies without any of her usual enthusiasm. I'll share with Jackie and the team at Wagner. More soon.

There's something about the thought of other people reading my words that terrifies me. It almost breaks through the safety I've started to feel lately. They may as well be in the room with me, looking over my shoulder while I work on the next few chapters.

Despite that, the urge to tell the story is just too strong. My desk keeps pulling me toward it, my pen keeps begging to be picked up, the blank pages keep asking to be filled.

And so I write.

When I wake up on the third Sunday in June, there are no dead men lying beside me, of course, but there *is* a text from my dad that shocks me nearly as much.

What time are you planning to be here?

Fuck. Going to New Jersey for Father's Day is the last thing I want to do. If you gave me a choice right now between facing my father, Sheila, and Billy, or getting rid of another corpse, I'd probably choose the corpse.

Still, I lift my head up, sit back against the bed frame, and type out a half-hearted response.

Not sure yet. Gotta look at the train schedules.

My dad answers almost immediately. The earlier, the better. Sheila is making Mexican food.

Ugh. My will to get myself to Penn Station has just gone down by half. I'll never understand why Sheila insists on cooking Mexican

169

food. She knows Pa and I both love authentic Mexican dishes. She also knows her version of them is the furthest thing from authentic. Does she not know we slurp her food down just to limit the amount of time it spends in our mouths? Or has she fooled herself into thinking that we love it, and that we're somehow grateful to her for "honoring" our culture?

I'll let you know when I'm on my way.

Great, he replies. Would you mind bringing dessert?

I don't write back. God knows I don't have the time or the money to stop and pick up dessert for four people. Hopefully the fact that I didn't cancel at the last minute will be enough to keep my dad satisfied today.

Putting on jeans is the strangest feeling after all these days in sweats. They cling to my skin, bending uncomfortably with every move I make. After weeks of not brushing or styling it, my hair is untamable. I'm long overdue for a haircut, but my checking account is officially empty, and my credit card debt has skyrocketed over the past few weeks, so any expenses unrelated to food and rent will have to wait until…well, I don't know until when, exactly. I settle for pushing my hair back, grab my keys and wallet, and turn toward the door.

I'm not even halfway there when my legs freeze, preventing me from moving any closer. It feels wrong to leave, wrong to step outside the safety of these four walls, wrong to expose myself to the dangers of the world that lies beyond my windows. Sneaking a glance over at my desk, I can't help wishing I could just sit down and work on my new book all day. It feels almost like a betrayal to choose New Jersey over my manuscript. I'm getting awfully close to a good scene—one in which the main character realizes the dead guy's phone is ringing. I'm not sure yet who will be on the other side of the call when he picks up, but I'm eager to figure it out.

But my dad is waiting. And so are Sheila and Billy. Taking a deep breath and holding the air in my lungs for as long as possible, I go up to the door and sneak into the hallway.

The sunlight blinds me when I step out of my building. The air is warm, and the Upper West Side is humming gently with the serenity of a Sunday morning. It's a lot less scary than I'd made it out to be, honestly—rejoining society, walking down the street, taking the subway. I make it to Penn with several minutes to spare before my train, so I stop by the Krispy Kreme inside the station and fish a few leftover quarters and dollar bills out of my wallet to pay for a dozen donuts, which at least Billy will love.

The instant Sheila opens the door, however, she pouts. "Oh, David, donuts?" she says to me. "You know we've been trying to lower our sugar intake!"

"I . . . didn't know, actually."

"Never mind, then," she says. "I'll throw these out before your dad and Billy see them."

She takes the box from me and rushes off to the kitchen before I can say anything—before I can ask her to keep the donuts in a safe place for me until I leave, instead of shoving them in the trash.

"David!" my dad's voice comes suddenly. "You made it!"

I turn toward the staircase. He's coming down slowly, holding on tight to the handrail.

"I did, yeah."

"A lot later than we'd hoped, but at least you're here."

I swear, I cannot spend longer than a minute inside this house without being made to feel inadequate. *Deep breaths*, I tell myself. *Deep breaths, and you'll be back in your apartment before you know it, working on the new book.*

"The food is ready," Pa says once he reaches the bottom of the stairs. "It's been ready for a while, but why don't we step into the living room first and have a drink?"

"Yes!" I say a little too eagerly. "A drink sounds great."

Pa pours me a mezcal without asking what I want, and we sit side by side on the couch, staring at each other awkwardly.

"Happy, uh...happy Father's Day," I say, making a slight motion with my glass.

"Thank you," he says, lifting his own glass as if making a toast. "Thank you very much, mijo."

We each take a sip. After not drinking for the past few weeks, the mezcal may as well be jet fuel, but once I adjust to the taste, I go for a longer sip.

"How's..."

"Life? It's great," I lie easily.

"And New York?"

"Better than ever."

"Jeremy?"

The mention of his name burns more than the mezcal. I haven't been thinking about him lately. I've been *forcing* myself not to think about him. Or his fancy promotion. Or his new boyfriend.

I take another gulp. "Still taking time apart."

"That's a shame," Pa says, staring down at his glass. "A real shame."

In the back of my mind, I'm reminded of the last time I was here. It all feels a little too fresh—the harshness in my dad's voice when he told me he couldn't lend me any money, the disappointed look in his eyes. I'm not sure if he's aware that my economic situation has only gotten a million times worse in the past month, or whether he's even planning to ask. All I know is that this would be the perfect opportunity to beg for his help again, because I have no idea what I'm going to do if I can't come up with some cash soon.

Staring at him out of the corner of my eye, I can't help but wonder what he would say if I dared to speak up. Would he find it in himself to feel any compassion for me this time around? To resist his instinct to reprimand, and just transfer me some money?

Perhaps the old him would have. The person my dad used to be when I was little might have found it easier to lend a helping hand—or at least I'd like to *think* that. He was never around much back then, so when I look back on my childhood, most of what comes to mind are images of my mom. As for my dad, well... he only drifts into my memory around the time he started dating Sheila, and by then, he was already a changed man—already the person who was all too focused on building his own life back up after his wife's death rather than meeting the needs of his teenage son.

Still, there's hardly anything to lose by asking for help again— even if he turns me down. I'm trying to find the right words to say, trying my best to gather the energy to start this conversation, when Sheila reappears suddenly, stopping at the entrance of the living room.

"Are we ready for tacos?" she asks.

"I believe so," Pa says, his face lighting up as he looks at her. "David, are you ready?"

I down the rest of my drink and try not to grimace as the mezcal makes its way down my throat. "I am now."

Billy is already waiting at the table when we step into the dining room, wearing his Sunday best—a button-down shirt and a blazer that makes him look more like a middle-aged car salesman than a ten-year-old kid.

"Hey, Billy," I say, throwing a nod in his direction.

"Hey."

I take the seat across from him, while Pa and Sheila sit at the ends of the table.

"What a feast!" Pa says, holding the palms of his hands open as he stares down at the food.

"Oh, it's nothing, it's nothing," Sheila answers, smiling proudly to herself.

Pa can fake it all he wants, but I can see the apprehension in his eyes as he fills his hard-shell taco with toppings—ground beef, lettuce, cheddar cheese, and sour cream. A middle finger to what tacos should be, but he wouldn't dare point that out to Sheila. Happy wife, happy life, they say—and my father has always taken that very seriously.

"Lovely," he says after taking the first bite. "Just perfect."

"So..." I say. "How's everything, Billy?"

"Oh, he's been doing great," Sheila answers for him.

"Any fun plans for the summer?"

"The three of us are going to Puerto Vallarta in August," Sheila says. "Before school starts up again, of course."

"Nice. Any other fun stuff going on?"

"He's been spending a lot of time with friends, isn't that right, Billy?" she replies. "He's got a good group of them in the neighborhood."

Can you let the kid answer a single fucking question for himself? I nearly ask. "Amazing," I say instead, going for a bite of my taco.

Billy stares at me warily while I chew. I wonder if there's something else to this whole thing—if he's been told not to address me directly. It would be absolutely insane, but I can't say I'd be surprised. I can just imagine Sheila feeding him poison about me—telling Billy not to trust me, not to follow in my footsteps, not to grow up to be like me.

"How have you been, David?" she asks, turning toward me suddenly.

I swallow hard. How *have* I been? I don't even know. Barely surviving, I'd say. Still breathing, but sometimes wishing I wasn't. Relying on ink, and paper, and words to keep me living.

This is not how I wanted my return to Morristown to be. I was meant to come back victorious. I was meant to come back as a new person. I wanted to sit here and tell them that my publisher was giving me another chance, that I'd sold my next book for a decent amount of money, that I was on my way back to capturing the success that slipped through my fingers after *Walking Home* was published.

Instead, I'm sitting here feeling even more broken than last time.

"I've been doing well," I say, smiling with my lips pressed together.

Sheila's eyebrows shoot up. "Is that right?" she asks. "Because you look absolutely *ghastly*. I mean, I didn't want to point it out, but..."

"Oh. Um...thanks, I guess?"

"It wasn't intended as a compliment, David," she continues. "We worry about you, you know?"

"You do? That's nice."

"Of course! Alberto, tell him."

My dad looks up from his plate. He doesn't seem the least bit grateful to be dragged into this conversation—taking my side against Sheila has rarely led to anything good for him.

He clears his throat begrudgingly. "We do worry about you, David."

"You don't have to," I tell him. "I...I'm actually doing great."

My dad frowns. Lowering his voice, as if hoping it will reach my ears only, he asks, "You...are?"

"Mm-hmm. Better than great. I've completed a proposal for my next book and sent it to my agent."

"You...have?"

I nod confidently. "She loved it. She won't stop talking about how it's my best work ever, and how it's gonna launch my career in a new, exciting direction."

Sheila leans forward in her chair. "What's it about? Not about us, hopefully—not again." She lets out an airy laugh.

"No, Sheila," I reply. "It's not about you."

"Wait a second," Pa says, staring at me just as warily as Billy has been all through this meal. "Has your editor agreed to publish the new book?"

"Not yet. But she will—it's only a matter of time, really."

We fall silent, my words echoing against the dining room walls. Why the fuck did I have to say all that? I shouldn't have taken it that far. It's only going to make it so much worse when I come crawling back in a few weeks with the news that my publisher has rejected it. *You told us you were turning your life around, David! We can't trust a thing that comes out of your mouth, can we?* my dad will say. He will feel no sympathy once I tell him an eviction notice has finally come in the mail. He won't offer any help, won't give me any money, won't move a single finger to prevent me from falling into ruin.

"I, for one, am thrilled to hear all this," Sheila says, reaching for another taco shell.

I narrow my eyes. "Are you?"

"Absolutely," she replies, sounding offended that I'm doubting her. "I can't tell you how glad I am to hear you're doing better. I took no joy at all from seeing you a few weeks ago, looking so... *defeated*, and *wretched*, and *lonely*."

I bite into my taco, chewing aggressively.

"Really, David, it was an awful thing to witness. I could hardly bear the thought of you giving up on yourself like that—just moping and going around asking for pity. It was pathetic, truly. *So* very sad."

I close my grip around the taco so tightly that the shell crumbles in my fist. Before Sheila can say anything else, Pa coughs loudly.

"Did, uh..." His eyes move fast as he tries to think of a change of topic. "Did you have a chance to pick up dessert, David?"

"Actually, I—"

"He must've forgotten," Sheila interrupts. "Could happen to anyone, I suppose. Especially to David. He can be so aloof at times, can't he?"

The heat is rising up my neck. I can feel my face turning red. I open my mouth, ready to say something I'm sure I'll have to pay for later, but then—

My phone rings. They all scramble in their seats—Pa, Sheila, and even Billy, touching their pockets to check their own phones—but I know it's not them. There's a vibration against my thigh.

I pull my cell phone out and look down at the screen. It's Stacey. Calling on a Sunday. Reaching out after weeks of near silence.

A hundred different scenarios flash through my mind. I haven't been checking the news as closely lately, so I have no idea what the latest developments might be, but something must've happened. Someone must've spoken out about what they saw. The police must've discovered something incriminating.

"David, we're eating," Pa says. "Can't you—"

"I have to take this."

I don't give any more explanation than that. I push my chair back and walk out of the dining room, across the foyer, and out of the house.

Standing on the front steps, I hit the Answer button and press the phone against my ear.

"Stacey?"

"You did it, David."

"What do you mean?" My hand instinctively travels to the left side of my chest. My heart seems to have stopped beating. "What did I do this time?"

"You *did* it," Stacey repeats. She pauses dramatically, as if expecting me to guess what's going on, but I still have no idea. "Jackie loves the proposal!"

No words come to me. No reaction. Just a cold, sobering feeling of disbelief, because this doesn't make any sense.

"But…" I mumble once I find my voice. "But I only sent the pages earlier this week."

"I know that."

"And…today is Sunday."

"I'm well aware, darling. Jackie ripped through the proposal yesterday and couldn't wait a minute longer to tell me how excited she is about it."

"You—you've spoken to Jackie, then?"

"Sure have. I dialed your number as soon as I got off the phone with her."

I let my breath out slowly. "What else did she say?"

"That I was right—I promised her something new, raw, and provocative, and you delivered. She's sharing with the rest of the team tomorrow, and if all goes well, we should have an offer by the end of the week."

An offer. To publish a third book. To tell another story. To prove to readers, reviewers, and to the rest of the world that I am more than my first two novels. A chance to continue doing what I love most, keep paying the bills, and fix all the things that have broken in the past year.

"Are you there, dear?"

"I'm here." I'm not sure if I'm holding back tears or laughter, but there's something in my throat that won't let me speak normally. "I don't know what to say."

"Say that you'll have a celebratory drink tonight. And that you'll work hard to do this story justice."

A small laugh comes out of my mouth. "Okay," I reply. "I can do those things."

"I'm proud of you, David," she says, her tone softening. "Now, go write. I'll talk to you soon."

I clutch the phone tight against my chest after we hang up, fresh tears pouring from my eyes. I blink fast, trying to make out the world around me. Everything looks brighter all of a sudden—the blue sky, the white houses along the street, the green grass on the front lawn. It's all a little more charming than it was before.

I need to fix myself up, go back inside, and finish eating, but the tears won't stop, so I allow myself a couple more minutes before drying my eyes on the sleeves of my shirt and turning toward the front door. As I walk back to the dining room, listening to the sound of my family's voices, all the joy, and the triumph, and the relief start to fade away. With each step I take, I become a little more anxious, a little more flustered.

That's when I realize—I want to go back to my apartment and keep writing. I want to get lost in the pages and not think about anyone or anything until I'm finished. And, more than anything, I do not want to be here, do not want to eat shitty tacos, do not want to put up with passive-aggressive jabs when there are bigger and better things for me to be doing with my time.

They all look up at me when I return to the dining room. Pa is wiping his hands on a napkin, Sheila is mid-bite, and Billy looks like he's going to puke. I think someone says something—my dad, maybe, asking if everything is all right, but I don't care enough to answer.

I clutch the back of my chair. I watch their faces turn from indifferent to concerned to disappointed all in the span of one second, as they realize what I'm about to say before the words leave my mouth.

"I have to go."

CHAPTER FOURTEEN

I was so young when I got the offer for *The Millers*. Too young, perhaps. "Only twenty-four and already signing a major book deal," some people said. "One can only imagine what you'll be accomplishing by the age of thirty!"

I used to take so much pride in that, all too aware that I was being given the opportunity to experience an author's wildest dreams before my frontal lobe was even fully developed. Looking back, though, I can't help but wonder what things would've been like if I'd been a bit older at the time of signing my first deal. I wonder whether I would've found myself in the same position—crumbling under the pressure, failing to produce a worthy follow-up, allowing my success or lack thereof to alter every single aspect of my life.

It all happened so quickly back then. Being on submission, as industry people like to call the process of sending a manuscript to publishers for consideration, usually takes a long time. Editors have to sift through hundreds of manuscripts, find the ones they're passionate about, and make a case to the acquisitions board at their imprint that the book they've fallen in love with is worth publishing. It can be months before you hear any news, but when Stacey sent out *The Millers*, barely twenty-four hours passed before the first editor replied, saying she had read the entire manuscript and was planning to make an offer the following week.

Other editors followed soon after. I had one call after another, during which I was told how excited everyone on the team was about my book, how strong my voice was, how thousands of readers were bound to become obsessed with my work. I was over the moon, of course. I vividly remember the giddiness, the astonishment, and the pure, unfiltered joy I felt as I realized my biggest dreams were coming true.

It's all a lot different now, as I prepare to chat with Jackie on the phone, but I can still feel some traces of hope and anticipation. Things that remind me my dreams are not dead yet, that amazing things could still happen to me, that my life and my career are not yet over.

Just as the time on my cell phone changes from 1:59 to 2:00, a knot appears in my throat, which makes me worry I won't be able to speak at all. When the phone rings a few seconds later, though, I answer it easily.

"Hello?"

"David! It's me, Jackie."

"Jackie," I reply in a whisper. "Thank you so much for calling. I'm so—"

"Trust me, the pleasure is all mine," she says. "I know Stacey must've already told you, but your proposal just blew me away."

"Stacey did mention it. I just can't believe it yet."

"Well, start believing it. This new book is exactly what I've been hoping to find in my inbox. Everyone is going crazy over thrillers right now, and you've nailed it—the voice, the tension, the reveals. I mean…I almost fell out of my chair when the main character found the dead body in his bed."

"Well, I'm so—"

"I'd love to hear about the inspiration behind this book. How did you come up with it?"

"It's, uh..."

Does she suspect something? Or is this a valid question to ask on a pre-offer call? I don't remember if any editors asked me the same thing when I spoke to them about *The Millers*, but they must have. Okay, yes, they definitely did. It's not at all unusual for Jackie to be curious about this.

"I just...woke up one morning and thought of it." At least this part is somewhat true. "It's a question so many of us ask ourselves at one point or another, isn't it? Would we be capable of killing someone? What circumstances would it take for anyone to do something as horrible as that?"

My stomach clenches at the thought of being responsible for Robert's death, but I try to suppress it. *It was the cocaine that caused the stroke*, a voice tries to remind me somewhere in the back of my mind. *There's no way you could've prevented that!*

I press my nails into the palms of my hands, forcing myself to remain in the present moment. "But also..." I continue, my voice coming out a bit muffled, "what if there was a possibility that you'd killed someone, and you just weren't sure whether you did or not? Would you even want to know? And...where do you draw the line between guilt and innocence? Between being complicit...or being a victim yourself?"

"Incredible. Just fantastic," Jackie says. The enthusiasm in her voice reminds me that we're talking about fiction and not my own fucked-up life. "It sounds like you're thinking through the themes very carefully."

"I'm...trying to, at least."

"Do you have an outline I could look at? Or a synopsis? It would be great to get a sense of where the story is going before you complete the manuscript."

"I don't, actually." This is highly unusual for me—I'm an obsessive plotter, and Jackie knows it. My outlines tend to be so detailed that they could be full-length novels in and of themselves. "I'm figuring this one out as I go—trying something new. But if you need me to, I can try to pull something together."

"That might come in handy, if you can send it over. But don't worry about it too much—crafting the story as you go might help you heighten the element of surprise. Just make sure to keep readers on the edge of their seats."

"I will. Hopefully even falling out of their chairs."

Jackie laughs—a hearty, genuine laugh. "I'm so happy to get to work with you again, David. Very happy, indeed."

"Me too, Jackie. *So* happy."

"The wheels are turning over here. Everyone else has read the proposal."

"Are you about to tell me they all hate it?"

Another laugh. "No, no," she says. "We're all on the same page. They'd have to face my wrath if they weren't, because I really, really want this book."

The thought of Jackie fighting for me in-house brings a warm glow to my heart. It makes me feel so grateful to have her on my side. It also makes me wonder—how much heat did she face after my second novel underperformed? How many times did Jackie have to hear that she shouldn't have bet on me, that she should've asked me to do at least one more round of edits? How long did it take her to recover from that whole situation?

Maybe I got it all wrong after Stacey told me Wagner had rejected the option for my third book. I'd pictured Jackie turning away from my work, too afraid to put her name on the line for me again. But what if that wasn't the case? What if she read the previous proposal and loved it? What if she fought for me, and tried to get everyone to agree to publish it, and she just couldn't change people's minds? What if she was heartbroken about letting that project go, wishing desperately for another proposal from me to cross her desk—one she could champion?

It can't be easy for her, as the only Latina editor at her imprint. I know how hard she's worked to make it to where she is today. Just how lucky I am to have the opportunity to work with her—with someone who gets me, and my stories, and what I'm trying to say— I'm only just realizing it now.

"I'll be in touch with Stacey between today and tomorrow."

Thank you, I would say, if the words weren't caught in my throat. *Thank you for giving me another chance, for believing in me, for fighting for me and my stories.*

"Sounds good, Jackie," I reply instead. "Chat soon."

Stacey's office is as pristine as ever when I step in on Thursday morning—the white carpet, the smell of perfume, the vases filled with blooming peonies. It doesn't seem at all like the kind of place that would've sheltered a dead body for several hours. Even the thought of it is absurd.

"You're early, dear," Stacey says to me. She's sitting at her desk, glasses on, hair freshly blow-dried, hands neatly folded over the table.

"Yeah."

"I wish you'd given me a heads-up that you were planning to be early."

"I didn't plan it. I just—"

"I wanted to have champagne waiting for you. Josh is getting it ready just now. It was meant to be a surprise."

She smiles, and the energy around us changes. From one instant to the next, it all feels lighter, easier, familiar—like two best friends reuniting after a long time apart.

"You have the offer, then?" I ask as I sit at the desk in front of her, my legs shaking uncontrollably.

"I do."

"And?" I stare at her uncertainly, wondering if I'm the only one who has felt the shift in the air around us—if she's ready to move past everything, forgive the way I pushed her away after we got rid of Robert's body, and forget the fact that I blamed her for everything.

Her smile widens. "It's a good one."

I lean forward in my seat. "How much?"

"A hundred thousand for world English rights. It's lower than what we got for your first two books, but don't be too disappointed. They were bound to be less aggressive after what happened with *Walking Home*."

I don't have anything to say to that. I stopped listening after I heard "hundred thousand." Holy fuck. *One hundred grand for my next book.*

"But..." Stacey adds, and my stomach gives a painful lurch.

"There's a *but*?"

"There is."

"Maybe I don't wanna hear it. You can tell me some other day. For now, let's just leave it at a hundred grand for world English rights." I throw a glance at the door. "Where's the champagne?"

"Trust me, David, you'll want to hear this *but*," Stacey continues confidently. "I managed to bring them up to a hundred and thirty."

"A hundred and thirty *thousand*?"

She raises her eyebrows, and just like that, fireworks explode inside me. It's over. It's really, truly over—all the anxiety, all the insecurity, all the sleepless nights I spent wondering if I was ever gonna get to publish another book. No more feeling like a one-hit wonder, no more fearing I would spend the rest of my life chasing

185

after the high I experienced when *The Millers* came out. This new book is going to change everything. It's going to give me my life back.

"Jackie wants to make it their lead title for next summer. That is, if you're willing to work on a tight editorial schedule."

"Yes," I say quickly. "I am."

"And this time around, we'll need to be more careful about not forgoing quality for the sake of pumping the book out faster."

"Agreed. I won't let that happen."

"Very well," Stacey says, putting her hands together. "In that case…we'll ask the folks at Wagner to start working on the contract."

"When do you think we'll get it?"

"A few weeks, perhaps. The terms should be just about the same as before, which will make the process a lot smoother. And I already talked to Jackie about keeping a three-payment structure, so we'll get the first third as soon as the contract is signed."

"Okay," I say, looking out the window. "Okay, I'm glad to hear that."

"I know how badly you need the money, dear. I'll get it done as quickly as possible."

"Yeah, it's…it's all good."

It's not good—not really. Rent is due in a few days, and my bank account is empty. Now that I know the first third of the advance is coming soon, at least there'll be some hope to hold on to, but I'll still have to find a way to cover the bills until the money arrives.

"Chin up, darling," Stacey says. "This is the opportunity we've been waiting for."

It might be unnoticeable to someone who doesn't know her well, but today she seems much more like the person she used to be when she first signed me. There's a gleam in her eyes, a certain pep to her mannerisms that's been absent for a while. And in this moment, more than being happy for myself, I feel happy for Stacey. It's no secret what this will mean for her—being able to prove to everyone who doubted her that she's still got it, that she's still as capable of closing big book deals as she was a decade or two ago, that she's still among the best in the industry.

The office door swings open suddenly, and Josh appears, carrying a bottle of champagne and three glasses.

"Am I interrupting?" he asks, stopping at the doorway.

"No, no, sweetheart. Your timing is absolutely perfect."

He smiles as he comes up to the desk. The bottle pops with a loud bang, and he pours a glass for each of us.

"Cheers," Stacey says. "To all the great things this new book will bring."

Josh looks over at me. "Congratulations, David."

I meet his eyes and Stacey's briefly as we clink our glasses together, and then I go for a big swig.

The taste of champagne brings all sorts of conflicting emotions to my stomach. A rush of victory, because barely a month ago I was sitting here thinking my career was over, but also a sinking feeling, because the last time I drank champagne, I was with Robert. Deep optimism after having felt nothing but despair over the past few weeks, but also paralyzing fear, as I look ahead at what's coming.

While Stacey and Josh sip from their own glasses, smiling and talking about what a huge success this book is bound to be, I realize something: I may have made a huge mistake. Maybe I should've written this manuscript only for myself, and then shoved it into a drawer. Maybe those chapters were never meant to be read by anyone. Maybe I never should've sent Stacey the proposal or allowed her to share it with Jackie and the team at Wagner.

It seems a bit extreme now, doesn't it? The thought of writing a whole book inspired by what happened with Robert. I mean... it wouldn't be the first time I've made a bigger deal out of a situationship than I should have, but this may be taking things a bit too far. Because, if I choose to publish a novel based on him, I may just be condemning myself to relive that awful day for the rest of my life—not only through the next several months, as I work on multiple rounds of edits, but also over the years and decades, as people ask me questions about the inspiration behind the story. I may be choosing to etch the memory of this man in ink and paper, to preserve the worst day of my life in a book that will live on long after I'm gone. I may be turning Robert into a permanent part of my own story.

"I'll leave you two with the rest of the champagne," Josh says, pointing at his near-empty glass. "Let me know if you need anything."

"Thank you, love."

He steps out of the office, leaving behind a resounding silence. Stacey and I remain standing, drinking and occasionally meeting each other's eyes, but neither of us says anything.

After a while, I go back to my seat. Stacey sits in front of me and pours us fresh glasses of champagne.

"Allow yourself to enjoy this moment, darling," she says. "You can worry about everything else tomorrow."

I accept my topped-up glass from her and drink up. I know she's right. With everything that has happened in the past year, I owe it to myself to celebrate—to pat myself on the back and make the most of today—if only I could get rid of these dark thoughts.

The champagne flute feels fragile in my hand suddenly, and I become all too aware that if I gripped it just a little tighter, it would shatter between my fingers. Setting it down over the desk, I push my chair back and move toward the window.

The city outside is exactly as it should be. Cars beeping on the street below, tiny figures moving up and down the sidewalk, the windows of buildings concealing the lives of thousands of people. It really is just another day in Manhattan, except it all feels different somehow. I find no comfort in the thought of the people hiding behind all the glass and steel. No matter what any of them may be going through—no matter how miserable any of them may be right now—no one is going through the same things I am. Not even close. And nothing could shield me from the loneliness this realization brings.

"Is it a mistake?" I ask, my back still turned toward the office. "Writing about this? About him?"

I'm hoping Stacey will give me a definitive answer, one way or the other, because that is what she does best. But then she clears her throat and says, "I don't know," and the uncertainty in her voice hits me like a kick to the stomach.

"What I do know," she says after a moment, "is that this proposal is your best work in years."

"But what about everything else? Jackie, and Corey, and the police? Putting this story out there...won't someone make the connection eventually? Are we setting ourselves up?"

"We have been lucky, darling," Stacey says. "I don't fully understand how and probably never will, but we can't deny that it has all turned out better than either of us could have ever hoped. Maybe we should be thankful for that instead of doubtful."

"What if Jackie becomes suspicious, though? What if the story reminds her of that weird encounter we had in the elevator, and she catches on to the fact that the dead man I'm writing about is the same one she saw us with?" I ask. "Or Corey—he could stumble upon the book and remember seeing me inside his hotel suite. He'll connect the dots in no time! And—and what about the police? I mean, what if their investigation isn't over yet? It's only been a few weeks—they could still get their hands on more evidence and track us down. What if they uncover things about what happened that day, and then they take this book as a written confession?"

"Don't think I haven't asked myself all these questions, David," Stacey says, peering at me over her glasses. "When it comes to Jackie...if she were at all suspicious, she wouldn't be offering you a book deal, would she? Corey is hardly a risk. I doubt he'll even remember meeting you by the time this book is on shelves. As for the police, well...that's what I've been doubting the most. Did they simply miss crucial details about what happened to Robert? Perhaps. Is their investigation not finalized yet? Certainly possible, though it would raise the question of why it's taking them so long to point their fingers at us. What I'd say is more likely is that they didn't bother to look—the man fell asleep in his hotel, and he just never woke up. That may very well have been the start and the end of it for them...and I think we'd be better off accepting it as the end for us, as well."

"What do you mean?"

"There's no use in wasting our lives being tormented by the vague possibility that someone might connect Robert's death to us. The best thing for you and me to do at this point is carry on," Stacey says. "If, for you, that means publishing a book about it...I don't see why you shouldn't."

"It just feels wrong," I reply, turning to look at her. "I mean... *is* it wrong?"

"There's something in those pages, David. I saw a trace of it when I first read *The Millers* years ago, but you've managed to bring it to the forefront in this new story. Something raw, and earnest, and human. If this book allows you to be vulnerable and grow as a writer, then...how could it be wrong?"

I turn toward the window again, crossing my arms.

"We could still turn down the offer," Stacey adds slowly. "We could come up with a reason why you've decided not to pursue this manuscript. But then..."

"We'd be back where we started."

"Exactly."

It's that thought that scares me most of all—going back to the beginning. To a situation where I had no money, no good ideas, and no hope for a future in publishing. Turning down the offer would make it all meaningless, wouldn't it? Every single decision Stacey and I made to save my career, to protect my reputation, to move Robert's body out of my apartment—it would all have been for nothing.

"Well?" Stacey asks me after I've been silent for too long. "What will I tell Jackie?"

I swallow hard. "To send the contract. The sooner, the better."

"Excellent. I will most certainly do that."

"I just have one last question."

"Ask away."

"It's...about us. You and me."

"Oh?"

"Are we...okay?"

"We're about to get a big check for your next book, darling. I daresay we're more than okay."

"You know what I mean."

Stacey removes her glasses and sets them carefully on top of the desk. "Yes, David. We're okay."

"I am sorry, you know?" Every single one of my instincts is telling me to look down at the floor, but I force myself to keep looking straight into her eyes. "For yelling at you, and...for the things I said."

"I know. It's water under the bridge now."

I nod. Letting out a deep breath through my mouth, I step away from the window.

"I guess I should go. Thanks for the champagne, and everything."

"Of course. I'm glad you enjoyed it."

I smile at her. She smiles back, and I take that as my cue to leave. Just as I'm approaching the door, however, Stacey clears her throat loudly.

"David?" she says. I turn around to find that her lips are pressed into a gentle smile. "If you'll remember, it's been established that you are my best friend and I am yours. And if there's one thing I've learned after decades of reading books, it's that best friends can make it through anything, dear."

I laugh a little. "Right. Yeah, I suppose that's true."

"Now, go write the next great American novel!"

CHAPTER FIFTEEN

There's never really a good moment to reach out to your ex—not to say, "I miss you," not to say, "Can we talk?" Even a casual, "Hey! I thought of you the other day and figured I'd see how you're doing!" can be a terrible idea.

But texting to say, "I'm completely broke and need to borrow five thousand dollars" has got to be the absolute *worst* way to reach out to an ex. Or... is it?

I sort of like the honesty of it. There's something to be said about the directness—no bullshit, no mixed signals. Would Jeremy appreciate it, though? Would he understand that I'm just asking for help and trying to interfere in his life as little as possible, or would he think I'm attempting to use him as my personal ATM?

This is what I've been thinking about for the last hour. I've been sitting on the couch, watching as the early morning light shifts outside the windows and turning my phone over in my hands again and again, searching for the will to type out a message.

Monday is the first of the month, and the three thousand five hundred and seventy-eight dollars I used to have in my bank account is all gone, not to mention that I'm a mere twenty-eight bucks away from reaching the spending limit on my credit card. I could always tell my landlord that I have money coming—that it's only a matter of time before my next book deal is signed and a third of the advance is in my hands—but I doubt it'll matter much unless the ink is dry. Turning to my dad and Sheila is out of the question, obviously. I've played around with the idea of going on Grindr and looking for a generous daddy to pay my bills for the month…but I'd rather not, if I can avoid it. That leaves me with one option—my last resort, which I hadn't even wanted to consider until now. Jeremy.

Hey, I type. I'm completely broke and need to borrow five thousand dollars.

Okay, maybe that's not it. I hit the Delete button and start again: Hey. I'm sorry to reach out so randomly, but I really need some help. Can we talk?

That's better, I think. Direct, no bullshit, no mixed signals. Holding my breath, I press Send and put the phone face down on the couch, telling myself I need to find a distraction. The last thing I want is to spend all day glued to the screen, waiting for his answer.

I should hop in the shower, get some coffee in me, and start writing, but before I can get up to do any of those things, my phone pings.

Of course, he says. I'll be done work around seven. We could meet somewhere around my office.

That works. Just let me know where.

I spend the entire day in a state of agitation. I go for a shower, but the water's too cold, so I hop out almost immediately. I pour myself a cup of coffee, but the liquid's too hot, and I burn my tongue. I sit at my desk and try my best to write, to keep my promise to Stacey that I'll do this story justice, but I just can't find a way to focus. Not today.

By the time six p.m. rolls around, I feel as though it's been days and not hours since I texted Jeremy. I get dressed, making my best attempt at looking composed, and head out of the apartment.

He never wrote back specifying where to meet him, which isn't all that unexpected. Some days, work is so insane for him that he barely has time to eat, let alone answer texts on his personal phone, so I just show up in front of his office right before seven.

Over the past year, I've rarely had a reason to come to this part of the city. Beyond Fifth Avenue, Midtown East is just a collection of skyscrapers and people in suits. There's none of the charm of Midtown West—none of the Broadway theaters, none of the piano bars tucked along the West Forties, none of the cute restaurants in Hell's Kitchen.

As I approach the main entrance of Jeremy's office building, memories come rushing back—memories of hot summer days when I'd walk here from our apartment just so we could have a quick lunch together, and of crisp autumn evenings when I would meet him outside work so we could head to dinner.

Looking into the lobby through the glass walls, I remember the rush I used to feel every time he appeared. I remember the way his face would light up when he saw me waiting, and how the muscles in his back seemed to loosen when we hugged, as he let go of all the tension and stress from his day.

This time around, there isn't any of that. There's only a strange wariness to our interaction—from the moment we meet each other's gaze through the glass as he walks across the lobby, to the moment he comes to stand in front of me and both our bodies twitch, neither of us certain whether we should go in for a hug or not.

"Hey," he says.

"Hi," I reply. "Thank you for making time for me. I'm—"

"You don't have to thank me, David. Is everything okay?"

"Yeah, it's, um…" I nod vaguely, looking over his shoulder at other people stepping out of the building, and he seems to get the message—that I'd rather not talk about what's going on out here on the sidewalk.

He reaches for his tie, loosening it a little. "Come on," he says. "Let's go find somewhere we can chat."

We settle for a Starbucks right across the street. He orders a cappuccino for himself—decaf, of course, otherwise he'll have trouble sleeping—but I get a regular latte. Once we're sitting in a corner by the window, he looks up at me with his calm blue eyes.

"So . . ." he says.

"So," I say.

"You need help." It isn't a question. It's a simple fact—the reason we're here. I didn't intend for it to be this way, didn't want for it to feel purely transactional, but I guess that's how it's going to be. I need something, and he's sitting right across from me, ready to hand it over.

"I do." I bring my cup of coffee up to my lips but set it back down as soon as I feel the heat radiating from it. My tongue is still burned from this morning. "I'm sorry, Jeremy. I—I don't want you to feel like I'm using you. I wouldn't have reached out unless it was really—"

"David," he says, "don't you remember what I said? I made a promise to you, and I fully intend to keep it."

I've been trying not to remember. It hurts too much to remember— to think of his arms around me, my tears falling on his chest, his lips on the top of my head, and the whisper of his voice: *Even if we're no longer together, I'm still here. You will always have me, David. If you need me, I will always be there for you.*

We were sitting on the couch. Or standing by the doorway. Or on the street outside our apartment building, hugging beneath a cloudy sky. I'm not certain which one it was. There were so many conversations, so many attempts he made to explain why he had to leave, and so many attempts I made to get him to stay, that they've all blended together in my memory. What I do recall is that, when

I MIGHT BE IN TROUBLE

he said those things to me, I didn't believe him. I knew how it was gonna go—he was going to try to keep his promise for five or six months, until other things got in the way. Work, or new relationships, or the distance itself. He was going to build a new life, I was gonna put the pieces of my old one back together, and the promises we'd once made—to spend the rest of our lives together, to never stop loving each other, to always be there for the other no matter what—would be forgotten in time.

"Well?" he asks. "Do you?"

"Do I what?"

"Remember."

"Yes."

He stares at me for a long moment, as if he knew just how hard I've been trying to forget. To surrender the idea of us, let go of any hope, and erase the memory of all those promises.

"What is it you need?"

I reach for my cup of coffee and drink from it, not stopping to think about the heat this time. "It's, uh...money."

"How much?"

"Just enough to get me through the next several weeks. I'm—"

"How much, David?"

"Five thousand dollars."

There's no widening of his eyes, no twitch of his eyebrow, nothing to suggest a negative reaction to what I'm asking for. Nodding once, Jeremy says, "I'll transfer you tonight."

"I'll pay you back," I say. "I promise. I only need to get—"

"David," he says firmly, and I fall silent immediately. "Allow me to help you. I want to do this for you."

I feel so small in my chair all of a sudden, like a child speaking to a wiser and more experienced adult. Money has never been an issue for Jeremy, I know that much. He grew up on the Upper East

Side, went to all the best private schools in Manhattan, breezed his way into Yale. And when his dad passed away a few years ago, he left a big inheritance, which Jeremy had to split with his mom and brothers but still left each of them with a more-than-comfortable amount.

There's also his latest promotion. I have no idea how much money he's making now, but I can only assume it's considerably more than he used to when we were together. Five thousand dollars is not a big deal for him. Still, I need him to know that this is a loan, that I don't want to be a charity case, that I'm not doing as badly as he thinks.

"I got another book deal."

His eyes sparkle. "You did?"

I nod. "It's not official yet. We haven't signed the contract, but I got an offer."

Jeremy leans forward to grab my hand. He squeezes, and I squeeze back, and through his touch he communicates all the things he's not saying out loud—how happy he is to hear this, how proud of me he feels, how he wants nothing but the best for me.

But then, as the seconds keep passing and he keeps squeezing, I realize this might just mean something different: That holding my hand is a compromise he's making. That he is settling for this but is in fact wishing we could do more—that he wants to hug, and jump, and spin around with me. He wants us to put on fancy clothes and go out to celebrate, but for tonight, this squeeze will have to be enough.

"It's, um…it's a good offer," I say, letting go of his hand gently.

"Same editor?"

"Yeah. Same editor, same publisher, same everything."

"And that's a good thing, I'm guessing?"

"Yes," I reply, smiling a little. "It's a very good thing."

"Amazing."

"The money shouldn't take too long. I just need something to tide me over until the first payment comes, but I'm—"

"If you're struggling with money, you can always come to me."

"I know. But I don't want it to be that way. I promise I'll repay you. It's just a matter of—"

"David," he says again, this time a little more forcefully. "We can talk about that a different time."

"Okay," I say, staring down at my hands. "What do you wanna talk about, then?"

"You," he answers. "I'm so proud of you."

I feel my face turning red. He doesn't know what I've gone through to get the book deal, has no idea where the inspiration for this next novel came from. I doubt he'd be very proud of me if he did. If the truth ever came out, would Jeremy be willing to hear me out, to wrap his head around my explanation as to why I made the terrible choices I did? Would his offer to be there for me no matter what still stand? Or would he swear me off forever, convinced I'm no longer the person he once fell in love with?

"I want to hear about you instead," I say, eager to change the topic. "How's life?"

"Good. There isn't much going on. Nothing I didn't mention last time I saw you, at least."

The thought of running into him at the Plaza still stings. I hate the fact that our first encounter in almost a year was so rushed and uncomfortable. Why couldn't we have caught up on a night like this instead, over coffee, at a cozy table by a window, underneath warm lights?

"So, the promotion..."

"Has been a lot of work, but a good change overall."

"And your mom..."

"In the Hamptons for the summer."

"And that guy you were seeing..."

"He's...doing well."

"Who is he?" A part of me doesn't want to hear the answer. I'd rather he be anonymous—the outline of a shadow in my mind and nothing more. But I also want to know who has taken my place in Jeremy's life—who has been waiting for him outside the office to go get lunch, and sitting next to him in dimly lit bars in the East Village, and waking up next to him on Sunday mornings.

"His name is Julián."

"Julián? Wow. You really are into Latinos, aren't you?"

He laughs, the corners of his eyes crinkling. "And writers, too, apparently."

"Oh." *Please don't let it be someone I know, please don't let it be someone I know.* "He's a writer?"

"A journalist. But yes, he writes for a newspaper."

Thank God. I don't think I could've dealt with the idea of Jeremy sleeping with another novelist.

"We've been taking things slow," he says. "But...we connected."

Connected in the same way you and I did? I wish I could ask. I wonder if their first date went on way longer than it should have because they couldn't stop talking. I wonder if they've started to feel as though every second not spent together is a moment wasted, or if the words "I've fallen in love with you" are bubbling inside their chests after barely a few months of dating, begging to be confessed out loud.

"How about you?" Jeremy asks. "Are you seeing anyone?"

I think of Robert. I think of Shane, and all the other men that came before him, none of whom have meant much more than a night of sex and a distraction from missing Jeremy.

"Not really. I mean, I've been going on dates, but..."

He nods, signaling that he doesn't need any more explanation than that.

"I just wish…" I start, without even knowing where I'm going with this sentence. What *do* I wish? That things had been different between us? That I had also found someone else by now? That his new boyfriend wasn't a 2.0 version of me?

"I know," Jeremy says, even though he can't possibly know what he's agreeing with. "Me too."

As I stare into his ocean blue eyes, I finally realize what I wanted to say: *I wish we could try again.* There's just no way I can speak those words out loud. Not after all this time, not now that he's moved on.

While we sit here, finishing our cups of coffee and making small talk, my mind keeps spinning with other things I would say, if only I was a little braver. *It's not the same as it used to be. I'm much better now. This new book will change everything for me.* I want to make him see that I'm a new person, that I won't let the pressure of publishing consume me this time around, that if we were to get back together, I wouldn't let anything get in the way of us—not again.

But I keep swallowing back the sentences, keep pressing my lips together to stop myself from saying anything I shouldn't. More than once, I remind myself that remaining silent is for the best, because things are finally over between us. The simple fact that we're here tonight is proof of it—proof that we're able to spend time with each other as something other than lovers, proof that there's no more resentment or unresolved business here. No more hope, either, because any remaining longing I may have had for the idea of us is slowly slipping through my fingers.

At least I have my writing. I have the renewed passion my next novel has brought into my life, and isn't that better, somehow? Doesn't that mean I have the power to find all the love and comfort

I desire within myself? Doesn't this give me the freedom to redis-cover my relationship with my craft without any distractions, without any reservations, and without any fear of disappointing anyone?

It *is* much better this way, I tell myself as I start to tune out Jer-emy's steady voice. Because writing is the only constant I've ever had, the one true love of my life. After my mom died, my stories were there to comfort me, to allow me an escape from reality. During my high school years, when I hadn't yet come out and the girls wouldn't hang out with me because I was too boyish, and the boys wouldn't hang out with me because I was too girly, I would spend my evenings creating worlds where I could exist as someone else, someone different. On lonely weekends at the start of college, while everyone else was out par-tying or hanging out with their friends, I would shut my door and get lost in the pages of my notebook, dreaming of a life where I'd be able to share my stories with other people. And now, my writing is still here to give me a reason to exist, to inspire me to keep going, to give me hope and help me understand why certain things happen the way they do.

My family may resent me. Publishing may turn its back on me. Jeremy may carry on without me, but words will always be there, patiently waiting to be laid down on the page. So, no. There would be no point in saying any of the things I want to say, or in trying to get back together with Jeremy. Because he's proven that he's capable of leaving me, but my stories will always stay.

By the time we finish drinking our cups of coffee, I feel exhausted. Caffeine does that to me sometimes—it soothes me, puts me to sleep instead of revving me up.

The night air is warm when we step out of Starbucks. There's an odd sense of anticipation all around us—like there's a massive party happening elsewhere in the city, and everyone is expecting us to join them. But we both know the evening is over. We're going home, and there's nothing left for us to do here.

Jeremy turns toward me and stares into my eyes with a somewhat pained expression on his face.

"It's good seeing you, David," he says.

"You too, Jeremy. Thank you for—"

"I'm happy to help. The money should be in your account by tomorrow."

I have nothing to say—no more ways to thank him, no more promises to make about paying him back—so I just stand here in front of him, waiting for him to make a move.

Jeremy opens his arms slowly, as if to give me a heads-up that he's going in for a hug. I take him in my own arms and breathe in his scent, touch the muscles on his back with the palms of my hands, feel the scruff of his beard against the side of my face.

Just like that, all my resolve crumbles. Despite everything that was going through my mind earlier, the truth is that I never want to let go. A part of me wishes I didn't have to, but I don't really have a choice. We step away from each other and, with one last gentle smile, we start walking in separate directions.

Instead of heading for the nearest subway station, I decide to walk to Sixth Avenue so I can hop straight on the B train and avoid having to transfer. I'm about halfway there, crossing Madison Avenue with a cool shower and warm bed on my mind, when I come to a sudden realization: I don't want to go home.

I don't want to step into a dark, empty apartment, don't want to spend the night alone. It's at moments like these that I wish I had a friend in the city—someone I could call and ask if they're free for a drink. Perhaps I could do it by myself—go to a bar and drink until I stop caring about the idea of returning to my shitty studio apartment on my own. Or maybe...

I pull my phone out of my pocket and swipe sideways on the screen until I find the Grindr logo. I haven't used it since the night I met Robert. I've been trying my hardest to avoid it, but tonight it feels like a saving grace.

Hey, I say to one of the first guys that pops up. Would be fun to meet up for a drink. He's thirty-two, with a big smile and a caption that says: Drinks?

Another guy that catches my attention is one with a shirtless pic. He's wearing gym shorts, and I can tell he's packing underneath. Hi, I write. What are you looking for?

I also message a third—a handsome man with long brown hair and a caption that says: Up for anything.

I stop at a red light and lower my phone, thinking I'll give them all a minute to reply. At least one of the three should work out.

The light turns green. I'm about to move my legs forward when my phone vibrates in my hand, and I look down to find two new Grindr notifications and a text message from a familiar name: Shane. The same Shane who made me pay the entire bill on our first date, the one who was so fucking loud during sex, the one who gave me that gonorrhea scare.

How's it going, handsome? he said. Up to much tonight?

This feels almost like fate. I haven't heard from him in weeks, and he's suddenly here, readily available at a moment when I'm desperate for company. Maybe he saw me on Grindr and decided to text instead of messaging me on the app. Or maybe the stars aligned, and he thought of me at precisely the right time.

I should check Grindr to see what the other guys replied...but, if I'm being honest, I'd rather save myself the awkwardness of a first encounter. At least I've met Shane before, so there should be some level of comfort there that won't exist with either of the other options.

Funny you should ask, I reply to him. I was literally just trying to come up with a plan.

I have beer at my place, he says. Wanna come over?

I should drop this. Nothing good has ever come from going on Grindr when I'm feeling sad, vulnerable, or alone. The best thing would be to turn my phone off and head straight home, but then I think of Jeremy. I think of his liquid blue eyes, and the way I convinced myself not to say any of the things I wanted to say, and the fact that there's someone new in his life—someone he *connected* with, whatever the fuck that means.

I don't know anything about his new boyfriend, other than his name and what he does for a living, but as I approach Fifth Avenue, a face appears in my mind—one that looks an awful lot like my own. Julián—or this imaginary version of him, anyway—is holding on to Jeremy's hand possessively, and he's sneering at me as he occupies the place beside him that used to be mine.

I stop in my tracks. I lift my phone up, click into the text conversation with Shane, and start typing.

What's your address?

CHAPTER SIXTEEN

Life has been good this past month. I mean that. The rent is paid, there's food in the fridge, I've been getting dick on the regular (granted, it's not a very big dick, and it comes with the unfortunate condition of being attached to Shane, but it's regular dick nonetheless), and so far, the police haven't come knocking on my door asking about Robert.

Most importantly, though, I've been writing. It's all I ever feel like doing, honestly. While I'm on the subway, making my way down to Shane's apartment, I daydream about the book, plotting out the next few scenes I'm meant to draft. On nights when Shane and I are sitting beside each other at a bar, trying to get through the small talk as quickly as possible so we can go have sex, I'll stop responding suddenly and pull out my phone to type an idea into my notes app. Even when I'm on all fours on his bed and he's railing me from behind, I picture myself getting back home and working on my novel.

"Good luck with your writing, handsome," Shane usually tells me after we've finished and we're moving toward the door of his apartment. "Hope you'll get published soon."

I don't think it's clicked with him that I'm already published, or that I have an offer for a third book, even though I've explained it to him multiple times. He keeps making references to "hustling toward the dream" and "making things happen with my little stories," so I've learned to just nod along and thank him. It's not like I'm hanging out with him for his intelligence or active listening skills, after all.

The contract is slightly delayed but should be coming very soon, according to Stacey's latest update, and I've agreed to have a first draft over to Jackie by mid-August. I would be worried about meeting such a tight deadline, if it weren't for all the long writing sessions I've been doing lately, which have already gotten me near the seventy-five percent mark of the book.

I write in the morning while the soft sunshine draws patterns around my apartment, sitting in the middle of Central Park on warm evenings, and surrounded by dim light late at night, filling pages faster than I ever could've anticipated. It's been refreshing, allowing myself to be consumed by this story. It's what has helped me take my mind off the investigation into Robert's death—for the most part, that is.

At times, when my thoughts start going dark places, I can't help but worry that we left too many loose ends, that it's only a matter of time before our carelessness comes back to bite us in the ass. It's at moments like these that I pack up a pen and notebook and go for long walks around the city, and that's how I'm able to push the anxiety away. No matter how real or present the danger may feel, getting lost in the world of my novel always has a way of making me feel safer. It's during these walks that I've been coming up with new ideas, piecing together the rest of the plot, and figuring out a satisfactory conclusion. Part of this has involved going back to revise the first few chapters to turn the main character into a writer—one who is using his research skills to find out the identity of the dead man in his bed, who manages to craft a convincing story to tell the police when they come asking questions, and who is attempting to understand the things that have happened to him through his art.

And these changes have made all the difference in the world—not just to the book, which has grown so much more complex than it used to be, but also to me. There's something about writing a character who's a mirror image of me—and a story that's a loose reflection of a traumatic experience I had—that feels cathartic, that has brought meaning to the most senseless part of my life.

I'm working at home on a Wednesday evening in August, feeling the pressure now that I have a little over a week to write the final twenty-five percent of the novel, when my phone pings with a text from Shane.

Hey. Wanna come over?

My first instinct is to say yes. I'm not one to turn down a dick appointment. It's the way things have been working lately—Shane texts when he's horny, and I appear at his doorstep thirty minutes later, no questions asked. But I haven't met my word count goal for the day yet, and if I go to Shane's, I'm unlikely to be very productive afterward.

Hey, I reply. Maybe later in the week?

Sounds good, handsome.

It's Saturday by the time he texts again. I'm sitting near Belvedere Castle in Central Park around sunset, balancing my laptop over my legs, when my phone dings.

What's up tonight?

I roll my eyes. I've been working on the final chapters, nearing a final reveal where the main character realizes the dead man in his bed was actually murdered, and he's been set up by a dangerous killer who's been lurking in the shadows the whole time. I'm hoping to make these scenes feel absolutely heart-stopping, so this distraction couldn't have possibly come at a worse time.

I'm writing, I reply. I set my phone on silent and shove it inside my tote bag, promising myself not to check it again until I've left the park. Now that I've been interrupted, though, I can't get back into a rhythm. Barely a couple of minutes later, I reach for my phone again.

But it's Saturday, Shane replied. You should take a break. I can buy us a drink somewhere.

He doesn't usually offer to buy drinks, so he must be really eager to get laid.

Sorry, I write back. Tonight doesn't work.

I pack up my things and head home, thinking I'll have a quick dinner and a shower, and then write into the night.

The following week, on Tuesday, I'm sitting at my desk, typing furiously into my laptop. It's almost nine p.m., but I haven't showered, haven't left the apartment, have barely eaten today. My deadline is only two days away, but no matter how many times I've rewritten the second-to-last chapter, it doesn't feel good enough.

Tonight, however, the words are finally flowing, and I'm almost certain I'll be able to finish this goddamned chapter. If I tried hard enough, I might even manage to get all the way to the end of the book before going to bed.

That's what I focus on as I type—what it'll feel like to complete the manuscript two full days before my deadline. I'm in the zone, experiencing all the tension and emotions that the main character is describing, when I hear a knock on the door.

My heart stops. My hands drop away from the keyboard. No one ever comes knocking—no one except for delivery drivers, and I haven't ordered anything. I have no idea who could possibly be looking for me at this hour on a Tuesday.

That's when I realize—it's happening. It feels so obvious now, the fact that this was going to arrive eventually. Stacey and I have been so naïve, assuming no one would ever come after us. I'm ready to bet that the police are standing on the other side of the door.

A second knock comes, louder than the first, but I'm still incapable of moving. They may just have to tear the door down, because I don't think I'll be able to willingly get up to meet my fate. I won't be able to separate myself from my desk, from my laptop, or from my manuscript and accept that I'll be spending the rest of the night in jail.

As the silence stretches on, I start to consider that whoever is out there may not have realized I'm home. I wasn't being loud, so maybe I could wait it out. Perhaps they'll just leave.

But then, when yet another knock comes, I jump out of my chair. I suppose it would be wise to at least take a look at whoever's come looking for me. I need to see what I'm up against.

I step lightly over the wooden floors, getting closer to the door. Slowly, I lean in to look through the peephole and...motherfucker. What the hell is *he* doing here?

"Shane?" I say as I open the door, my voice coming out unkinder than I meant it to.

"Hey, handsome," he says. He looks as perfect as ever—light brown eyes, pushed back hair, smooth chest peeking from above the V line of his shirt. "I texted about a million times, but you didn't reply."

"I haven't been checking my phone," I say, letting all the anxiety out through my breath. "I've been busy."

"Yeah, I know how hard you've been working. That's why I decided to come to you—to help you relax for a while."

I glare at him. I don't know if he's been drinking or not, but I can't believe he would just show up out of the blue. "How did you even get into the building?"

"I waited outside until someone let me in," he replies casually. "So...can I come in?"

The old me would've said yes. Barely a few months ago, I wouldn't have been able to resist a good-looking guy standing at my doorstep. I would've pushed everything aside to accommodate him, regardless of the hour, any deadlines, or how much work I had to do. But I feel like a different person now. I owe it to myself to say no, to close the door and go back to my writing.

"I..."

He gives me a sultry smile. "It'll be fun."

"No!" I yell. The temptation is just too strong. I make a move to shut the door, but he stops it with his foot.

"What's wrong?" he asks. "I thought you wanted to meet up."

"I can't do it, Shane," I answer, sounding a little desperate. "I'm sorry. I have to get back to work."

I push the door closed and lean back against it, holding my chest.

"David!" Shane says from the other side. "Come on! Are you seriously gonna leave me out here?"

I don't reply. I force myself to move away from the door, afraid that if I don't, I'll just open it again and let Shane inside.

"I promise I'll make it worth your time!"

I take my seat at the desk. I shove my earbuds into my ears and start playing music, trying to ignore Shane's begging, telling myself this is the right decision. I may not have a man to keep me company, but I do have words to write and a story to finish.

And those things count a hundred times as much.

I wake up the following morning feeling disoriented. I can't remember what time I went to bed, but I do know I didn't write as much as I wanted to. I managed to finish the second-to-last chapter, but I didn't finish the manuscript.

For a while, I just stare at the ceiling, vaguely aware of a headache coming on. My mouth feels dry and my stomach slightly upset, almost as if I'd been drinking. When I remember that I didn't have a single drop of alcohol last night, relief sweeps through me. Perhaps I'm just dehydrated.

I roll over, sit up on the bed, and reach for my phone. My mind is slow to register everything that's on the screen—the time, which tells me I overslept; the date, which is one day before my deadline; about a dozen texts from Shane, in which he said he could return to my apartment in case I'd changed my mind; and three missed calls from Stacey.

It's the last notification that forces me awake and makes any trace of a headache immediately disappear. Getting up from bed, I hit Redial.

"David," she says when she picks up. "David, we need to talk."

"What happened?"

"It's . . . it's nothing to be worried about, dear," she replies, even though her voice suggests that there is, in fact, *a lot* to be worried about.

"Just tell me," I say. "Did Wagner take back the offer?"

"That's not—"

"Is Jackie leaving the company?"

"No, she's—"

"Are *you*?"

"No! I'm simply—"

"What is it, then?"

Stacey sighs into the phone. She seems to be having a battle with herself, debating whether to deliver the bad news or not. But then she says, "Come to the office and I'll explain."

"Now?"

"Yes, now. It would be best to talk about it in person."

Oh God. This will never end, will it? I'll have to live the rest of my life on the edge of my seat, knowing that everything could go to shit at any moment.

"I'll be there as soon as I can."

I rush to the kitchen, chug a big glass of water, and then I head into the bathroom to make myself look presentable. Five minutes later, I'm running out the door.

The summer heat is stronger than ever today. Even in an air-conditioned subway car, everything around me feels muggy and sticky, which makes me afraid that Stacey will comment on my sweatiness as soon as I step into her office, but she doesn't. I find her standing by the window, with her back toward me as she stares out at dark clouds closing in over Central Park.

"Stacey?" I ask softly.

She turns around and widens her eyes at me, as if taken by surprise.

"There you are!" she says. "Right on time."

I can't be on time if we hadn't agreed on when we would meet, but I don't point that out. Stacey steps away from the window to take her seat behind the desk, and I sit in front of her.

"Well?" I ask. "What's happening?"

Stacey pushes her glasses up her nose. "I received a call early this morning from Jonathan Wells at Wells and Welsh."

"Okay…" I recognize the name. Wells and Welsh is one of the literary agencies I queried back when I was looking for representation.

"He had a business proposition for us—well, for you, really."

"Oh?" This is not at all the direction I thought this conversation would take. I have no idea why Stacey made it sound like she had bad news on the phone, because this is starting to sound like a *very* good thing.

"Jonathan signed a new client recently. They'll be working together on a memoir, and they're looking for a ghostwriter."

It takes me a second to understand where this is going. "They want it to be me?"

"Yes," Stacey says. "He said they'd love for you to write a proposal. It's a celebrity memoir, too, which would mean good money for you. And Jonathan told me his client is a big fan of your work, so they're very hopeful that you'll agree to it."

"Wow. That's amazing," I say. "Who is it? The celebrity?"

Stacey sighs loudly. "It's Corey Donovan."

I'm falling. Falling, falling, falling, and there's no one to catch me at the bottom. It's only once I've hit the ground that I realize this sensation wasn't only in my mind. I actually did topple over in my chair and fall off it.

"Oh, dear!" Stacey says, jumping out of her own seat to come to my rescue. She offers a hand, pulls me up, and helps me set my chair back into an upright position.

I'm speechless. Even after I've sat back down, I can't seem to escape the feeling that I'm falling.

"Why?" I manage to say after what feels like a long time, even though what I actually wanted to ask was: *Why me?*

"I don't know, darling. All Jonathan told me was that Corey wanted—"

"He remembers." In my mind, I picture Robert's suite at the Plaza. As if I were a spectator standing in the corner, I see myself there, approaching the door, freezing at the sound of a key card making contact with the door outside.

Well? Who are you? Why are you in my room?

I—I'm with housekeeping.

He must've seen right through my lie. *Of course* he knew I wasn't a hotel employee. But why is he doing this now? Why is he asking me to write a book about his life, instead of turning me over to the police?

Stacey shrugs. "It could all be a coincidence, dear."

"A *coincidence*?" I ask, terror rising within me. "Corey randomly decided to write a book and reach out to us less than two months after we got rid of his husband's dead body?"

"We didn't *get rid* of his body. He had a stroke. All we did was move him out of your apartment. That's very differ—"

"*I know that!*" I get on my feet and start pacing frantically. "Corey's trying to intimidate us, isn't he? He's sending a message—he knows what we've done, and he's coming after us."

"That's certainly a possibility, yes."

"What do we do, then?" I ask, my lungs feeling heavy from lack of oxygen. "We have to say no. There's *no way* I'm gonna agree to this."

"I figured you would say that," Stacey says calmly. "But I think we should do the exact opposite. We need to say yes."

"*What?* That would be absolutely insane. We can't—"

"Think about it, David," she adds, and the firmness in her voice forces me to slow down, to stop moving around the office and just listen. "This memoir will get written, whether we want it to or not. Corey could either hire another author—maybe even an investigative journalist—to write it, or ... he could hire you."

"What's your point?"

"If you're the one writing the book, you get to control the narrative. Any other writer may get too close to the truth—and I don't think either of us wants that, do we?" Stacey says. "Corey may be trying to intimidate us, dear, but we won't fall into his trap."

"Wouldn't we be falling into it by saying yes?"

"No, darling. Even if he suspected we had something to do with Robert's death, he can't possibly be certain. From what I gather, the police concluded he passed away in his hotel room and closed the investigation." Stacey narrows her eyes slightly. "I think Corey knows there's more to it, and he may be fishing for answers, but we are not going to give him any. We will do the exact opposite—feed him kindness and pleasantries, until he's convinced you had nothing to do with his husband's death. And, in the meantime, you will write an amazing book that will boost both his career and yours."

"I can't. Stacey, please don't—"

"You know I'd never make you do anything you don't want to," she says. "But I suppose it's true what they say—keep your friends close and your enemies closer."

Is that what it has come to? Is Corey Donovan our *enemy*? Is he also thinking about us using the same logic, trying to get closer to us so he can stab us in the back at precisely the right moment?

"What about my third book with Wagner?"

"You can work on both at the same time, of course."

"That's not what I mean, Stacey. I'm about to publish a novel where the main character finds a dead man in his bed! It's practically a confession—or at least Corey will take it that way once he gets his hands on a copy!"

"Fiction is fiction, David," Stacey replies confidently.

"Except that it *isn't*. Fiction contains truth, and everybody knows that."

"Still, that is your best and only defense—you will say your novel is something you dreamed up. No one will be able to argue against that."

My chest is starting to hurt. I'm breathing fast, and everything around me is becoming bright, even though the clouds outside the window are still blocking the sunlight.

Breathe, David, I can almost hear Jeremy's voice saying. *Yes, just like that. Inhale…exhale.*

I used to get panic attacks all the time—mostly toward the end of our relationship, and mostly publishing related—but I haven't had one in a while. By the time the office comes back into focus and my breathing steadies, I feel strangely weak. Stacey, however, doesn't seem to have noticed anything. She's still sitting in front of me, hands resting over the desk, staring at me calmly through her cat-eye glasses.

"I don't know how I'm gonna do this," I say, breaking the silence.

"One day at a time, darling. Before you know it, you'll have published two more books, and your career will be back on track."

"Not if Corey gets his way. If what you said is true—if this is his way of fishing for answers—then he's going to find them. And then...who knows what he'll do with that information?" My entire body trembles as I consider the possibilities. Will he expose us on his TV show? Turn us over to the police, to be investigated for moving Robert's body? Would he try to turn public perception against us—even try to blame us for killing him?

Stacey has no response. For a moment, I suspect she's envisioning the same things I am: Getting arrested. Being the talk of the industry for months on end, as our very public trials and convictions play out. Going to prison for what we've done.

I'm no lawyer, but a few Google searches I did in the weeks after Robert's death told me everything I need to know about possible jail time. Concealing a dead body carries a sentence of four years in prison. If the district attorney decides we desecrated Robert's corpse in the process, well...that would mean extra time. And if Corey goes so far as to try to prove we actually had a hand in Robert's death and tried to cover it up, we're looking at something far, far worse.

We may be able to strike a plea deal, I suppose—but even if our sentences turn out not to be too lengthy, by the time we get out, there'll be nothing for us to come back to. Our lives and careers will be ruined, and neither of us will get to associate our names with another book ever again.

Thunder rumbles in the distance suddenly, and thick drops of rain start splashing against the windows.

"Did Jonathan Wells say anything else?" I ask in a small voice.

"He asked for a meeting—between you and Corey, so you can chat about the creative direction of the book."

"A *meeting* with Corey? Like...face-to-face?"

Stacey nods. "He's flying into New York next week. I promised I'd sort out scheduling with you and get back to them with a time and day."

"No."

"But—"

"I can't do it. I won't do it, Stacey. It's too—"

"All you have to do is hear him out. Get a sense of what he's after. You don't need to agree to write his book—not yet, anyway. But the more we know about what he's trying to do, the better."

I bite my lip. I can't argue with that. Staring out at the rain falling over the city, I tell myself that I can do this. I can meet Corey for lunch or coffee, pry some information out of him, and not say anything that'll incriminate me or Stacey—or, at the very least, I can *try* to do all of those things.

"I'll need to finish the manuscript I'm working on first."

"Of course. Corey won't be in the city until next week, anyway."

"And I might need an extension. I still have one chapter left to write, and I don't think I'll be able to get it done by tomorrow—not with all this on my mind."

"I'll call Jackie and let her know. I'm sure she won't mind receiving it a few days later than planned."

I look down at my feet. "It's funny. A small part of me had started to think everything was truly behind us—that things were really, truly about to get better."

"It isn't over until it's over, darling. Life gets tough sometimes. Like I've always said, you're tough, too. Don't forget that."

I nod slowly. I don't feel tough at all. I feel weak, tired, ready to give up.

Thunder rumbles again, and this time, a streak of lightning flashes across the sky.

"Can I stay here until the rain stops?" I ask Stacey. "I didn't bring an umbrella."

"Of course, darling. You can stay as long as you want." She throws a glance in the direction of her personal bar cart, which is in a corner of the office. Raising an eyebrow, she says, "Shall I pour us a drink?"

CHAPTER SEVENTEEN

I thought I would feel victorious once I finished writing my manuscript. I thought I'd be happy, excited, proud of myself, just as I was when I completed the first drafts of *The Millers* and *Walking Home*, but there's none of that this time around.

I don't even have a title thought out, so I spend the longest time staring at the blank first page, trying to come up with something. In the end, despite having brainstormed different options for at least a couple of hours, I type out one of the very first ideas I had—*I'm in Deep Trouble* by David Alvarez—and attach the file in an email to Jackie, hoping desperately that she'll like it.

As my meeting with Corey approaches, the days start to go by quickly, but the nights seem painfully slow. I barely get any sleep, so I pass the hours lying in bed, staring at the ceiling and reliving my first encounter with him again and again.

I cringe every time I think of my awkward behavior, my stupid responses. And when I recall the moment I realized Robert was married, the rage I felt on that day returns to my chest, so livid I may as well be bleeding onto my bed.

You wouldn't have seen my husband around here by any chance, would you? Dark hair, more likely than not to be wearing a suit?

Night after night, Corey haunts me. His face and voice become fixtures in my mind, so that by the time our meeting comes around, I've started to think of him almost as an old acquaintance.

Stacey and Corey's agent arranged for us to meet at a French bistro on Christopher Street. It's gorgeous on the outside, with flowers and vines framing the front entrance, and rustic chic on the inside, with wood paneling and mirrors covering the walls.

The hostess leads me to a table near the back, where Corey is already sitting with his back straight and his legs crossed. He looks regal, somehow, in a velvety red blazer and Gucci loafers—all very different from the suit and tie he usually wears on television.

"David?" he says when he sees me, only it sounds less like a question and more like a statement. *David.*

"Yes. Corey?"

He nods once, reaching for a handshake. His grip is so strong that I can't help but feel as though he's trying to inflict pain—which, on second thought, he probably is.

"Please," he says. "Take a seat." There is no *nice to meet you*, no *nice to put a face to the name.* He's not here to waste his time with such pleasantries—not when we both know we've already met once before.

"Thank you for agreeing to lunch," he says as I lower myself into a chair.

"Oh, thank you for…asking if I wanted to grab lunch." Fuck. This whole thing is gonna go terribly, isn't it?

My hands are already sweating, and we haven't even placed our drink orders yet. I don't know how I'm supposed to get through an entire meal. Corey seems to be aware of my nervousness, too, because he stares at me unblinkingly while I dry my palms on the sides of my pants.

His eyes are icy blue, I realize when I meet his gaze. They reveal absolutely nothing about him—not what he's thinking, not what he's feeling, and certainly not what he's hoping to get out of this meeting. In the past two months, I've spent a lot of time thinking about him. I have wondered how he's doing, whether the grief of losing Robert has been too much to handle, even whether he's been busy plotting revenge. But as he looks back at me, he doesn't seem sad or resentful. He is perfectly collected, just as you would expect anyone to be at a business lunch.

"It feels as though we've met before," he says after a brief silence. "Doesn't it?"

My first instinct is to say no. *What are you talking about? We can't possibly have met before!* Instead, I say, "Yeah. I sort of feel the same way, now that you mention it. But you must get that all the time—I mean, your face is all over television."

The corner of his mouth twists upward slightly. "I do hear that often, yes."

"You see, I don't usually have that problem. People may recognize the front covers of my books, but no one knows my face."

"*I* know your face," Corey says, and everything around us goes quiet—the chatter of people sitting nearby, the clanking of forks against plates, the noise of the street outside. It all freezes, leaving behind nothing but a chilly breeze that seems to swoop past our table.

This is it. He's about to confront me. He's going to say he remembers exactly where and how he met me, and he's going to grill me until I reveal the truth about what happened the day Robert died.

But then, Corey says, "I've read your books. The author photo on the back flap is pretty hard to miss, isn't it?"

"You've…read my *books*? Plural?" I ask. Meanwhile, an alarm keeps ringing inside my head as I process all the things he's said and the ones he's not saying—that I'm not a stranger to him at all. That he would recognize my face anywhere. That he's not at all confused about where or when he's seen me before.

"Well, I read *The Millers* a couple of years ago, of course. I only read *Walking Home* recently, and I really enjoyed it."

"You—you did?"

"Mm-hmm. I found your exploration of loneliness very relatable. Millions of gay men go through similar experiences—even if we don't always talk about it. No matter how old I get, I still feel isolated from the world at times. I've never truly understood why that is, but your book is as close as I've ever gotten to an explanation—maybe it's true that growing up in a world bent on making queer people feel worthless has messed us up for good."

"How are we doing over here? Are we ready for drinks?"

Corey and I look up at our server—a middle-aged woman who makes me think of Stacey. I wish so badly she were here, that she would help me field Corey's questions, that she could protect me from whatever's coming next.

"I'll have a Negroni—extra bitter," Corey says.

"I . . . I'll just stick to water."

"Are you sure?" he asks. "Lunch is on me."

"Oh, yes. I'm sure." Nothing sounds better than a drink right now, but I need to stay clear-headed. Getting through this sober will be hard enough as it is—if I bring alcohol into the mix, I have no idea what I might be inclined to say or do.

"Wonderful," the server says. "I'll be back shortly to take your food orders."

She walks away, but Corey doesn't reach for his menu, and neither do I.

"Anyway. Where were we?" he asks, leaning forward to set his elbows on the table. "Oh, right—I was telling you how much I love your work. Funny enough, it was my husband who convinced me to read *The Millers* in the first place."

"Really?" I ask, my stomach turning.

"He wouldn't shut up about it until I finally read it myself. You could say he was a big fan of yours."

An image takes over my mind—of me and Robert lying in bed after sex, breathing heavily.

You look like a . . . like a Daniel, perhaps.

Wow. Close. David, actually.

It all fades away, replaced by another image: we're sitting in a booth, surrounded by red light and crystal chandeliers, and he's whispering that he has a confession to make.

You seemed familiar in your photos. And . . . I realized a while ago why that was.

He was such a fucking liar. He must've known exactly who I was all along. That had to be the reason why he invited me to the Plaza and not the Hilton—he wanted to impress me, to give me a good reason to come over. He must have been set on having his way with me from the moment he saw my photo on Grindr.

"I'm . . . speechless, really," I say, forcing myself out of my imagination and back to the restaurant. "Thank you. That's so—"

"It's not me you should thank. You'd have to thank my husband, except . . . he passed away a couple of months ago."

I hold my breath. "I'm sorry to hear that."

Corey shows no sign of having heard me, makes no attempt to accept my condolences. "It was his death that inspired me to write a memoir, actually. It got me thinking about how short life is, and how many things I want to say before my own time comes. Also . . . after Robert died, I learned things about him that changed everything for me. There's a lot I need to process, and I can't think of a better way to do it than by writing a book."

"Oh?"

"Wouldn't you agree?"

He knows. I'm not sure how, but he must know about the novel I've been working on—the one I turned in to Jackie barely a few days ago. It hasn't been announced yet, and no one outside of Stacey and the team at Wagner knows about its existence, but Corey must've found out about it, and he must be aware that I've written a story inspired by what happened between me and Robert.

"I...I do. Writing can be so therapeutic."

"Absolutely. I'm not an experienced writer, certainly, but that is where you'll come in. I think your voice is exactly what the book needs."

It's funny, somehow—thinking about writing on behalf of Corey. The idea that he and I might be similar enough that he could pass off my voice as his own. Just as Robert was an older, more experienced version of Jeremy, I can't help but feel as though Corey is a mirror of who I'd like to become. I'd love to be as poised as he is, as confident in my own skin. I'd like to be successful, stable, sensible—the exact opposite of who I am now, basically.

Despite that, I find it altogether impossible to sit here and pretend that I'm actually going to sign up for this. This is my opportunity to turn him down gently—to appease him and hopefully walk out of here unscathed.

"I...I have to be honest, Corey," I say. Above his shoulder, I see our server coming back with the drinks. "I don't think I'm the right person for this project."

Stacey will kill me for doing this. I can already imagine the lecture she'll give me about this being the wrong choice—how the last thing we want is for Corey to hire another writer and expose us for what we've done—but I can't bring myself to tell more lies than I already have to.

"Nonsense," he replies. "Your writing speaks to me in a way that no one else's does. That is why, the instant I signed with Jonathan, I told him we needed to reach out to your agent and get you to do it."

"I appreciate that. But...I'm not sure I can."

The server must be able to sense the tension between us, because she doesn't speak a word as she lays down the glasses on the table— water for me, a dark red beverage for him—before sneaking away as quietly as a shadow.

"David," Corey says, leaning closer to me, "it *has* to be you."

"There are much better writers out there—people who actually have experience with memoirs."

"And I don't want any of them."

"Corey, I..."

"We'll let Jonathan and Stacey do the business talk," he interrupts me. "For now, let's enjoy lunch."

We nod gently at each other, and the waitress takes this as her chance to return to our table. When she asks if we're ready for food, Corey and I both get the mushroom ravioli without knowing what the other was about to order.

"Coming right up!" the server says before turning around and leaving us alone once again.

For a while, Corey and I don't say anything. We keep meeting each other's eyes, as if waiting for the other to draw a weapon, but even as the seconds pass, we remain still. That is, until I look down and notice something glinting on his left wrist—a golden bracelet that seems all too familiar.

"You like it?" Corey asks, lifting an eyebrow slightly.

"It's nice, yeah." How funny—I have a bracelet just like it. Jeremy gave it to me on our first anniversary. *From J, with love*, the engraving on the inside says. I used to wear it all the time, but ever since we broke up, I've only worn it on a few occasions, whenever

I've wanted to look classy. Bookish events, or important meetings, or when I've gone to fancy places, like...well, like the Plaza.

"It reminds me of my late husband," Corey says. "I found it on the day he died. Interestingly enough, I'd never seen him wear it, so he must've bought it shortly before his passing. One of his very last purchases, probably."

"Oh?" I reach for my glass of water. No matter how many gulps I take, I can't get rid of the heat that has risen to my face, can't manage to stop my heart from racing. I haven't seen my bracelet in a while, now that I think of it. Not since the start of summer, but there's no way I wore it on the night I met Robert and left it in his hotel room...right?

No, of course not. I would've realized it before—although, to be fair, I *did* have a dead body to deal with the next morning, so I probably didn't have much time to think about lost jewelry. Still, it would be absolutely insane for Corey to be wearing my bracelet. It would mean he knows much more than he's letting on, that he's showing it off to fuck with my head, and well...Corey can't be that much of a psycho. Or at least I hope he isn't, for my own sake and Stacey's.

I clear my throat. "Can I ask you something?"

"Anything."

"You said you found out things after your husband's death that changed everything," I say cautiously. "What were they?"

"If I tell you, will you agree to write my memoir?"

"I can't promise that. But I just...need to know." I look down at the white cloth covering the table. It takes me half a second to realize just how odd my question must have come across, how personal. "I—I mean, it's important for me to get a sense of what you want to write about. That's why we're here, right?"

"Of course," he replies. "Why else?"

So you could intimidate me. So you could trick me into revealing what happened on the day Robert died. So you could gather enough evidence to build a case against me, turn me over to the police, and expose my actions to the world.

He sighs loudly. "He was a liar. And a cheater."

Somewhere deep down, I feel the need to let out a sigh of my own, but I resist it. There's something about hearing those words coming out of Corey's mouth that makes me feel validated. It confirms what I thought I already knew but couldn't be entirely certain of: that Robert was not a good person, that I was right to resent him.

"I don't know where to even begin with all the lies he told," Corey adds, reaching for his own drink. He takes a sip, smacks his lips, and sets the glass back down with a loud thud. "He was found in a random hotel room in the city. The manager wasn't surprised at all—he said people die in hotel rooms more often than you'd think. The police weren't surprised, either. According to them, it all checked out—Robert fell asleep and never woke up. A stroke, according to the autopsy, but I knew from the start that something wasn't right. We had arranged to stay at the Plaza—it turns out Robert had booked that second hotel room so he could sleep with other men on the side."

I try my best to widen my eyes in surprise and imitate the reaction any normal person would have after hearing this. Worried that my face may somehow betray me, I lift my water glass again and use it as an excuse to cover my mouth, at least for a few seconds.

"When I went through his phone, well…there were dozens of messages from different guys. He also had a Grindr account—password protected, so I couldn't get in—but I can only imagine what I'd find if I could access it."

You'd find that Robert's last ever conversation on Grindr was with

228

me. The words hang from my lips, guided by an instinct to get this over with—to just tell the truth—but I manage to keep my mouth shut. I'm suddenly so glad I chose not to order a drink.

"We were open for a while, funny enough," Corey continues. "I was spending a lot of time in L.A. He was spending a lot of time in New York. It felt almost natural for us to seek company elsewhere, but we said we'd stop a few years ago. We agreed to only be intimate with each other, but...I suppose Robert couldn't help himself."

He lets out a small laugh—more a resentful snicker than a chuckle—and I feel the need to match it with a snicker of my own.

"It's a messed-up thing—piecing together the life of someone you thought you knew better than anyone. I'm a journalist—seeking out information is what drives me. I'm sure there's still plenty out there that I just haven't found yet, and...that's another reason I want to write this memoir. I need to understand."

"Yeah," I say, my face feeling very hot again, because I *don't want* him to understand everything about Robert—at least not anything that has to do with me. "Totally."

"The memoir won't be all about Robert, though," Corey says. "I want it to cover everything—my childhood, my journey as a journalist, even my sexuality. I grew up in Missouri, you know? Being a gay teen in that time and place was not an easy thing to do, but I got through it. I escaped my hometown as soon as I could, came to New York, and made a name for myself."

"That's amazing."

"I'll be turning fifty next year. Trust me, I have plenty of material for the book. But perhaps Robert's death could be what ties everything together—the lens through which we look at certain things. Overcoming homophobia and discrimination in the world of media, only to be betrayed by the one person I was meant to trust. Finding love as a gay man, and then losing it in the most sudden and unexpected of ways. Looking back and looking ahead as I'm forced to rebuild my life from scratch at forty-nine years old."

I'm not gonna lie—this book sounds fucking great. If it wasn't for the apprehension I feel toward Corey, I'd be honored to be here, discussing the possibility of working with him. He's someone I would have so much respect and admiration for... if, you know, he wasn't trying to lure me into some kind of trap.

"Well?" he asks. "Does this sound like a story you'd like to tell?"

I am fucked either way—fucked if I say no, fucked if I say yes. But maybe Stacey was onto something. Maybe it's best to have a hand in what Corey says in his book and how he says it. Maybe the only thing worse than collaborating closely with him over the next several months would be to cut him loose, leaving him to find more insidious ways to come after me and Stacey.

"It does," I answer. "It sounds fascinating."

The food comes. While we cut into our ravioli, I sneak glances at him. He looks as regal as ever—not just because of the blazer, but because of the way he's holding his fork, the way he eats his food. I can't help but think of him as a king on a chess board, staying a cautious distance away before he gets ready to strike.

I am terrified of what will happen when he does.

CHAPTER EIGHTEEN

I don't head straight home after lunch with Corey.

We say goodbye outside the restaurant, where a black car is ready and waiting for him. He gets into the back seat, and I start walking down the sidewalk, wandering with nowhere to go.

It isn't until I see a shabby-looking bar on the opposite side of the street that I realize what my subconscious was hoping to find. Looking both ways before crossing, I rush toward the entrance and disappear into a cool, dark interior.

"Vodka soda with a slice of orange," I say to the bartender. This drink always makes me think of Jeremy. It used to be his go-to, the one he bought round after round of during our first date—back when life felt full of possibilities, back when it felt as though we were at the start of something.

Now, I'm at the end.

Corey has a plan—of that I'm completely certain. He never intended to confront me today, never expected to get answers from me easily. He's in it for the long run, and he's not likely to stop until he has taken me down. And then everything I've been working for—the new book, the contract with Wagner, the idea of redeeming myself and saving my writing career—will be rendered useless.

There's something symbolic about it—about the fact that the

same events that gave me a story to tell and a third book deal will be what lead to my downfall. After several vodka sodas, though, I stop caring much. Corey, Robert, Wagner, the book—it all seems smaller than I'd made it out to be, and I like it better like this.

At some point, a man walks through the door and takes a seat on the opposite side of the bar. It's effortless, the way he draws my attention—button-down shirt, salt-and-pepper hair, no ring on his finger, and an air of confidence that I simply cannot resist.

He's in his late thirties, I'd say, with a well-groomed beard. He's not particularly fit, but I don't mind a dad bod—don't mind it at all, actually. In fact, I could use someone like him—someone less vain. Someone without Robert's ego, or Jeremy's stubbornness, or Shane's immaturity. Someone who knows what he wants—and, judging by the way he keeps staring at me from across the bar—he already seems to know *exactly* what he wants.

I'd make a move, if only I weren't so drunk. Or anxious. Or emotional. While I keep exchanging glances with him, sipping on cocktail after cocktail, I make up scenarios in my mind—scenarios where this handsome stranger and I meet under regular circumstances, rather than right after one of the most awful lunch meetings I've ever had. Scenarios where I have a normal life, in which I get to fall in love again and have the things that have evaded me so far.

While I try to get the bartender's attention, wanting to pay the check before I start making some terrible decisions, I realize this handsome stranger and I were probably not meant to have more than these fleeting moments of staring at each other from afar. That normal life, that swoony love story…those things aren't meant for me. They might've been, if I hadn't made so many mistakes over the past few months, but now it's too late.

I cemented my destiny the minute I decided to leave my apartment to go meet Robert, and now, all there's left to do is wait for the other shoe to drop.

———————

Over the next few days, I drink a lot more than I should. I've never much enjoyed drinking alone, but it stops being a choice as much as a necessity. I spend more hours of the day drunk than I do sober, and even though I feel like shit every morning, I can't manage to stop.

Four or five days into my new way of living, I receive a call from Stacey.

"I have news, darling," she says. "The contract is finalized. Jackie sent it through this morning."

"Oh."

"It's in your email. All you have to do is fill out the e-signature, and they'll release the first payment."

"That's great," I say with as much enthusiasm as I can muster. I'm only two drinks in, but I'm feeling woozy already.

"This is a big moment, David. You should enjoy it."

"What about Corey?"

"I haven't heard from him or his agent yet, so you can relax—it may take them a while to put an offer together. Right now, you're better off putting it out of your mind."

"I just...can't."

A long silence comes from the other end of the line, and I can tell Stacey is thinking carefully about her next question.

"David, are...are you drinking?"

I press my lips together. "Maybe."

"It's eleven a.m.!"

"So what?"

"So...the least you could do is ask me to join!" Stacey says. "God knows I could use a few drinks after the week I've had."

"Why?" I ask, shifting positions on the couch. "What's happened?"

"Just drama with some of my other clients. Nothing to concern you with, dear. But really, you shouldn't drink alone in the middle of the day. If we do it together, it's a work event. If you do it on your own...it's just concerning, honestly."

"What else am I supposed to do? Everything's so—"

"Start dreaming up your next book. Spend this time reading, catching up on what's out there in the market. Take up a hobby. There are plenty of ways to keep busy, darling, if only one is inquisitive enough. Besides, editorial notes from Jackie will be here before you know it."

"Yeah," I say. "You're right."

I go to my laptop right after we hang up and open my email. A burst of fireworks goes off inside me when I hit the Confirm Signature button on the contract, but it all vanishes an instant later, leaving behind a muted ringing in my ears and a slight headache. A lot could happen between now and next summer. It's entirely possible that I'll be locked up by the time this book comes out, or that, as soon as Corey exposes me, Wagner will cancel publication.

I spend the rest of the week in a comfortable daze. The alcohol helps, of course, so I keep a bottle on hand at all times. It isn't until the following Friday, when the payment from Wagner arrives, that I manage to come back to life. Thirty-six thousand, eight hundred and thirty-three dollars. This is a lot more money than I've gotten to see in a while—and I couldn't be more grateful for it.

There'll be taxes to pay, and a good amount of cash will have to go toward my credit card bill, but for now, there's something important I need to do. I reach for my phone and call Jeremy.

"Hello?" he answers. There's no hint of familiarity in his voice, no sign that he knows who's calling. I imagine him sitting behind his desk at work, typing hurriedly into his computer, so focused that he didn't even stop to check the name on the screen before picking up.

"Hi," I answer. "It's me."

He's silent for a moment. So silent, in fact, that a part of me wonders if the call has disconnected, until a small sigh comes from the other side of the phone.

"Hi," he says, and all of a sudden, there's something altogether different in his voice—lightness, warmth, comfort. All of the things I had hoped to hear, even though I wasn't at all sure I would.

"Are you at work?" I ask.

"Yeah. Busy day, but I—"

"I can call later, if that's better."

"No, no," he says quickly. "Let's talk now."

"I, uh...I got the first payment for my new book."

"That's fantastic. Congratulations."

"Thanks. I just...wanted to let you know the money is coming your way."

"You don't—"

"I'll transfer it today."

"Please," he says. "David, there's no need to repay me. That money was a gift."

"That's not what we agreed."

"It's what I always intended it to be."

There's a war inside me—between accepting Jeremy's help, and holding on to my pride. Between taking him up on his promise to always be there for me, and not wanting to seem like a charity case.

"I need to pay you back."

"Why?"

"Because if I don't, I'll never be able to ask for your help again. This would become a single grand gesture—a one-time thing."

"That would never happen, David. You can always come to me for help, no matter what."

I swallow hard. "I'm okay for money now. It's really not a big deal."

"And it's not a big deal for me, either. We can argue all day, but it would be a lot easier for us both if you just accepted it as a gift."

"Where does that leave us, though?" I can't help but feel uneasy at the idea of not transferring him the money. It would be like leaving a wineglass half full, a chapter unwritten at the end of a novel, a door open when it should be closed. It would mean leaving unfinished business between us, and I'm not sure I could deal with that—not when I've spent the last year aching for closure.

"I guess…it leaves us as friends," he says. "Friends who rely on each other when life gets tough."

My heart starts pounding, bringing a rush to my chest that has started to become unfamiliar. I've wasted so much time thinking Jeremy hated me—that he resented me for what I put him through, for my inability to prioritize our relationship over my own anxiety, for the way I allowed so many things to come between us. To hear him say that he wants to be my friend—that he'd rather be something than nothing at all—feels a little unreal.

Before I can find a way to respond, Jeremy clears his throat. "I'm sorry," he says. "I just looked at the time, and—"

"You have to get back to work."

"I do. I don't mean to cut this short, but I'm running late for—"

"It's okay."

"I'm happy to hear about the new book, David."

"Thank you," I say. "Now, go!"

He lets out a chuckle, and I do as well. We hang up, but I'm unable to let go of the sound of his laugh, unable to forget the words he said: *It leaves us as friends.*

After a while of sitting here clutching my phone, I realize I can just transfer him the five thousand dollars and be done with it. It's not like I was asking for his permission—it was more of an FYI, after all.

The second I hit Confirm on the transfer, I let out a deep breath. This is exactly what I needed. Closure. But I've barely gotten up from the couch when my phone pings, and I lift it to find an unwelcome notification on the screen: Jeremy Parks III has sent you $5,000.

He can be so *stubborn*. The thing is, so can I. Shaking my head slightly, I transfer the five grand back to Jeremy and set the phone down a little forcefully, hoping he'll accept the money, and that he won't dare return it a second time.

While I head for the closet to get dressed, I find it impossible not to admit that there's a small part of me wishing for the exact opposite—that Jeremy will send the money back to me again, just so we can continue playing this little game.

I waste no time before following Stacey's advice. *Start dreaming up your next book*, she said, so that's exactly what I try to do.

I pack a bag with a notebook and plenty of pens and head out of my apartment, thinking I'll treat myself to a nice lunch. I can do that now, thanks to my own hard work. Thanks to Stacey's grit, Jackie's belief in me, and Wagner's willingness to bet on me again. With the comfort of knowing the first part of the money is in my bank account, I can go back to living my life, away from all the stress that has haunted me for the past year and a half—and maybe even away from the fear and anxiety of what Corey might do.

I head down to the West Village, find a nice patio to sit at, and order myself a full meal—with appetizers and all. I'll have to go back to being responsible with money tomorrow, but for now, I allow myself to relax while I eat and scribble ideas in my notebook, one or two of which may have some potential.

It isn't until I'm nearly done eating that I close my notebook and look up to see where the waiter has gone. I don't find him, but instead, my eyes fall on a man standing on the sidewalk right across the street from the restaurant.

My heart leaps. It's the man who was sitting at the bar the other day, right after my meeting with Corey. He looks just as he did then: handsome, confident, well dressed.

He doesn't seem to notice me, even as I watch him intently. He's typing quickly into his phone, but a part of me is hoping he'll look up and meet my eyes from across the street. An instant later, though, a white car pulls up in front of him—an Uber, most likely—and he hops into the back seat.

For the rest of the afternoon, I can't stop thinking about him. About how crazy it is that we'd coincide twice in a matter of days. Before I know it, a new story idea has taken over my mind—and my notebook. It's a romance, which is so different from anything I've ever written, but feels so *right*. After lunch, I head to a coffee shop just down the street from the restaurant and sit in a corner for a couple hours, drinking overpriced lattes and brainstorming characters and plot points, all but convinced this could become my next novel.

By the time I head back home, all I can think about is putting on sweats and taking the rest of the day off. I shove the key into the lock, turn it, and push the door open, but the instant I step into the apartment, I freeze instinctively.

I know it in my bones, in my scalp, in the back of my neck: someone has been in here.

I can tell from the smell that's drifting in the air—a strong, musky scent that is entirely unfamiliar to me—and the fact that my laptop is not on my desk, where I last left it, but lying on top of my bed. There's a dent in the covers right beside it, as if someone had been sitting there just moments ago.

The door swings shut slowly behind me, and still, I'm unable to move. I should probably be running out of here. I should be rushing down the stairs and out the front door of the building, and then calling the police. Or Stacey. Or anyone. But something is telling me that whoever was here is long gone. There are no dangers lurking under the bed, or inside the bathroom, or behind the curtains. It's just me in here now—me and the lingering presence of the intruder.

Taking a step farther into the apartment, I think of Corey. I think of his prying eyes looking through my laptop, his long fingers searching my things. Could he have been in here? He must've been. No one else would have anything to gain from breaking in. My place would hardly be the most attractive target for a thief operating on the Upper West Side.

Suddenly, my legs carry me forward, and I start opening drawers, doors, cabinets. I search every corner of the apartment for anything else that might be out of place, anything that may have been stolen. But no matter where I look, everything seems to be in order. If it weren't for the smell and the laptop, I might be able to fool myself into believing that no one was here, that I'm only imagining things.

When I open the bottom drawer of my nightstand, however, I hear a small clatter. Shoving aside some papers, I reach into its depths and wrap my fingers around the smooth, golden surface of a bracelet.

I lift it up to take a closer look, and I let out a long breath when I realize it's the one I feared I'd lost. The one Jeremy gave me. With shaking hands, I flip it over to make sure the engraving is exactly as

I remember, *From J, with love*, and then I go sit on the bed, relieved. Of course, I didn't leave it at the Plaza. Of course, it was a coincidence that Corey happened to be wearing a bracelet that was similar to this one. Of course, I've been overreacting.

But then I think of a different possibility—one where Corey broke in and left the bracelet inside that drawer for me to find. Wouldn't that be exactly the kind of thing he might do if he was trying to mess with my mind? Wouldn't that be a great way to gaslight and bully me, and drive me just a little closer to the edge?

Yes is the answer to both of those questions, but it's all a little far-fetched. I refuse to believe Corey Donovan is *that* unhinged.

Maybe no one was in the apartment after all. Maybe the musky smell filtered in through the open crack at the window, and I didn't leave my laptop on the desk as I'd thought. Maybe this is just my anxiety playing tricks on me.

Soon enough, I start thinking about other what-ifs. What if I'm no longer safe—not even in my own home? What if someone really did find a way to get in here, and what if they come back while I'm in the apartment? What would they do to me then?

Sneaking a sideways glance at the door, a part of me expects banging to come from the other side, or for someone to start fiddling with the lock. No matter how long I wait, nothing comes. There's only silence and a lingering question on my mind: *What is Corey capable of?*

A chill runs down my back. But then, shaking my head, I try my best to push it all away. I try to convince myself he wouldn't harm me, can't harm me, even if I don't fully believe it.

In fact, I don't believe it one bit, but repeating this to myself might just be what allows me to sleep tonight—if I'm able to get any sleep at all.

CHAPTER NINETEEN

With the arrival of September comes a change in the air that is near impossible to perceive and even harder to describe. It still feels like summer through and through, but the slightest hints of autumn are starting to appear: crisp mornings, bluer skies. Shorts and T-shirt weather even at night, but with cooler breezes that were nonexistent during the hot, muggy days of August.

Another thing brought by September: the editorial notes from Jackie, which are a lot less daunting than I thought they would be. *Hone in on the antagonist's motivations, so the reader is glued to the page at all times*, she said, along with other comments on character development and reworking the big twist at the end so it feels more earned. Despite her ten pages of notes, there is no mention anywhere of scrapping the entire thing and starting again, which I consider a win.

I'm meant to return the manuscript to Jackie a month from now, so I get to work right away. I spend my days walking around the city, finding places where I can sit down and edit—outdoors, preferably, since I'm very aware that summer will be over all too soon—and my nights at my desk, reading and typing until my vision is blurry.

As the weather changes, so do my feelings about Corey. Sometimes, I tell myself that maybe he'll never reach out again—that all he wanted was the opportunity to speak with me face-to-face, hoping he would intimidate me enough to reveal the details of my involvement with Robert then and there. More hopefully still, I tell myself that he has given up on the idea of writing a memoir, and I'll never have to face him again.

There are other times when the fear and anxiety get to be too much. I keep thinking about the possibility that Corey did break into my apartment last month, that he's only biding his time, waiting for the right moment to ruin my life. I think about all the evidence that he or the police could come across, and I feel sick every time I remember just how careless Stacey and I were on the day we moved Robert's body.

"Still no word from Corey's agent, darling," she says to me during a standard check-in in mid-September. "I could reach out and ask if there are any updates, if—"

"No! Don't ask," I reply urgently. "I'd rather not poke the bear."

"Very well. We'll just assume no news is good news, then."

Somehow, no news feels like *bad* news. I can't help but wonder if this is Corey's way of continuing to play mind games, of lulling us into a false sense of security. So I focus on my revisions, trying my best to seek refuge in the pages of my manuscript.

It isn't long before I come across an additional distraction that helps me keep my thoughts in check: I seem to be running into the same good-looking man everywhere I go—the one from the bar, the one who was standing outside that restaurant in the West Village a few weeks ago. I don't understand how it's possible that we should keep bumping into each other, but it feels almost like the universe's way of telling me that catastrophizing is pointless, and that good things really *can* happen, even in your darkest moments.

I'm at a coffee shop on Columbus, sitting in a corner with my laptop, notebook, and a cup of coffee strategically arranged in front of me like pieces of a puzzle, when he walks in and heads straight for the counter.

"I'll get a regular coffee, please. Black," he says to the cashier in a deep, steady voice. He then goes to sit at the opposite corner of the café and sips his drink slowly.

For the better part of an hour, we play the same game we did the first time we saw each other: throwing stares from across the room, sharing flirty smiles, raising eyebrows. In the end, neither of us is brave enough to make a move, but it doesn't really matter, because we keep having chance encounter after chance encounter. I run into him at a bodega in the East Village, see him jogging while I'm sitting on a bench in Central Park on a Sunday morning, spot him speaking hurriedly into his phone right as I'm about to cross 42nd Street.

Granted, he's a little rough around the edges. I hear him burp loudly one night while I'm sitting at a restaurant in Hell's Kitchen, and I've caught him picking his nose once or twice, but I'm sure we could iron out these small issues when the time comes. I just need to figure out a way to start a conversation—to find the confidence to walk up to him one of these days and say, "It's so funny how I keep seeing you everywhere!"

One such opportunity comes in the last week of September, while I'm at that same coffee shop on Columbus. I'm working through a tricky scene in the third act of the book and starting to dream of next week, when I'll have turned in the revision to Jackie and finally be off deadline. My headphones are on, my fingers are moving fast over the keyboard, and my legs are slightly jittery from all the coffee I've had, when I see someone approaching me from the corner of my eye.

I look up to find him there, smiling gently and pointing at the empty table beside me.

"Is anyone sitting here?" he asks in that deep, sexy voice of his.

My answer nearly gets caught in my throat. "N-no."

He presses his lips into a half smile, and my heart skips a beat. This is it—after all the random encounters and missed opportunities, we're finally here, experiencing our very own meet-cute.

"It's so funny," I begin, "how I keep seeing you everywhere."

He frowns as he takes a seat beside me. "Well," he replies. "I don't know about *everywhere*."

I let out a small laugh, uncertain whether he's joking or not. I mean...he must also have me on his radar, right? It would be pretty impossible for him not to.

"At least that's how it feels to me," I say. "I'm David, by the way."

"Hello, David," he says matter-of-factly.

"Can I ask what yours is?"

"Mine?"

"Your name."

"Oh! My name," he says, turning a little red. He seems quite nervous all of a sudden, which I take as a compliment. In all honesty, I'm a little nervous, too. "I...I'm Jack."

"Hello, Jack," I reply, just as matter-of-factly as he said it.

There's a brief silence, during which I wonder if I've misread this whole situation. Maybe he's just going along with the small talk to be polite—maybe he's not even attracted to men. But then, instead of shifting his attention to his coffee or his phone, he turns to me and asks, "Do you, uh...come to this coffee shop a lot?"

"Not a lot. I mean...I live right around the corner, but I don't typically come here. I prefer exploring new spots around the city," I reply. "How about you? Do *you* come here a lot?"

"Not really, no," he says, his gaze traveling down to look at my laptop. "What are you working on? Every single time I've run into you, you've seemed so busy, typing or scribbling things down."

So he *has* been paying attention to me. "I'm editing a manuscript I wrote," I say, smiling a little. "Like, a novel."

He raises his eyebrows. "What's it about?"

"I'm technically not supposed to talk about it yet," I say, "but it's a thriller."

"A thriller?"

"Mm-hmm."

"Well, color me intrigued. Is there murder in it?"

There's some sort of charm about him that I can't explain. It makes me giddy, almost, even though he's not necessarily the man he appeared to be from afar. I'm getting the sense that he's somewhat shy—not at all the strong, confident personality I imagined. He's better looking up close than he seemed from a distance, though—deep brown eyes, full lips, more salt than pepper in his hair. And, judging by the way he's leaning toward me, he is way more interested in me than he's let on so far.

"You could say so," I admit. "You'd have to read it to find out."

"Oh, you can bet I will. Thrillers with murder investigations are my favorite kind of stories."

"Do you read a lot, then?"

"I do, yes."

"Have you read any—" I'm interrupted by the sound of my cell phone ringing. I smile apologetically to Jack as I wiggle in my seat, trying to pull the phone out of my pocket, and when I see the name on the screen, I simply can't bring myself to ignore it. It's Stacey.

"Hey," I answer in a whisper. "I'm kinda busy right now. Can I call—"

"I just heard from Jonathan Wells," she replies urgently.

Fuck. I put the phone down, turning toward Jack. "I have to take this call," I whisper to him. "I'll be back in a sec."

I sneak out of my seat, and then I rush toward a quieter corner of the coffee shop.

"David?" Stacey is saying by the time I lift the phone up to my ear again. "Are you there?"

"I'm here," I say. "How bad is it?"

"It's bad, dear. But also sort of good. You see, he didn't really—"

"Stacey, just tell me!"

"They've made an offer for your ghostwriting services," she says. "A guaranteed ten thousand dollars in exchange for a thirty-page proposal, plus a forty-sixty split on any payments due from the publisher if they manage to get a book deal. Forty for you, sixty for him, of course. They're bound to place this somewhere quickly, and I can't imagine Corey's memoir being worth anything less than two hundred and fifty thousand dollars."

A million conflicting emotions swirl around inside of me, even as Stacey's voice rings in my ears. Forty percent of two hundred and fifty thousand dollars is...holy fuck. A hundred grand—and that's on the lower end of what the advance could be. If I'm left with no choice but to sell my soul to the devil, at least the money will be good.

"What's the timeline?"

"They want you to start working on the proposal as soon as possible," Stacey says. "Jonathan said it may take a couple one-on-one sessions between you and Corey to iron out the first thirty pages, so they want to schedule a meeting for next week."

"*Next week?*" I ask. "But I'm—"

"I know, darling. You're hard at work on edits. I've already told them you'll need to deliver your revision to Wagner before shifting your focus to this project, and they had no objection to that."

"Okay," I say. "Okay, that's good."

"We'll schedule a Zoom call for the day after your deadline, then."

"Zoom? So it's not gonna be in person?"

"Well…no. Corey's based in Los Angeles, after all, but we could ask if he'd be willing to—"

"No, no, it's perfect," I say quickly. "It'll be better to do virtual meetings."

At least I'll have a way out if Corey asks me any awkward questions, or if he gets too close to the truth. It won't be the same as sitting in front of him at a restaurant, with no escape and no option but to sit through the entire thing uninterrupted. I'll be able to end the call at the press of a button and pretend there was a connection issue. *Oh, I'm sorry*, I'll say afterward. *My Wi-Fi is terrible!*

"All right. We'll do just that."

"But…Stacey?" I ask, lowering my voice a bit more. "Are you sure this is the right thing?"

"I'm certain of it. There's nothing that could go wrong, as long as we keep our mouths shut and don't give Corey the information he wants. I have faith in us, darling. Now more than ever."

"Yeah," I reply. "I have faith in us, too."

We hang up, and I shove my phone back inside my pocket. When I turn around, hoping to head back to the table and resume my conversation with Jack, I find him gone.

It's a shame, but I can't blame him. He must've had somewhere else to be. I'm certain we'll run into each other again sooner rather than later, and that I'll have plenty of other chances to get to know him better. For now, I'm just glad to be past all the uncertainty and have a bit of insight into Corey's next move.

I'm not going to cower. I'm going to face him head-on, write a hell of a good book for him, and cash my checks. And if he wants anything else from me, he'll have to wriggle it out himself, because I won't hand over any answers willingly.

I won't fall for his twisted games.

The apartment feels hot and stuffy on the day of my call with Corey. I swear, I don't remember it being this warm even at the height of summer. The AC is at full blast, but I'm still sweating through my shirt, and when I look in the mirror, my face is as red as if I'd just finished running a marathon.

In the end, my only option to cool down is to stick my head in the freezer. I've barely gotten a few minutes of relief when a ringing sound comes from the desk, alerting me to the fact that Corey is calling.

"Hey!" I say cheerfully to him when I answer. "How's it going?"

"David," he says. He's sitting in a fancy office, wearing his regular suit and tie. "Thank you for agreeing to this."

"Thank you for…asking me to do this." A fresh wave of heat travels up my neck, making me wish I could turn off my video and stick my head inside the freezer for another minute or two.

"Before we begin, I just wanted to let you know—I'm recording this call. I'm assuming you are as well, but I figured I'd make a backup recording just in case."

"Sounds good," I say. "I—I was also planning to record, yeah."

I have the voice memos app open on my phone, all too aware that I'll need to come back to this conversation a lot over the next couple weeks, as I piece together the proposal. The idea that Corey will have a copy of his own makes me a little uncomfortable, though. It makes me worry a little extra about fucking up—because he will have a recorded confession on hand if I say something I'm not meant to.

"Perfect," Corey says. "Let's jump right into it, then. I have some thoughts on what I want and how I want it."

My head on a platter, as soon as possible, I think, looking at his cold blue eyes on the screen.

"Amazing," I say. "What is it you want?"

"I'd like for us to come up with an introductory chapter about Robert's death. We could talk about where I was when I got the news, the circumstances that led to his passing, and all the details I know about the double life he was living. I think it'll ground the reader in my current state of mind, before we look back on my childhood and everything that led to this moment."

"So...chapter two would be a flashback, so to speak? Will we 'go back to the beginning' after talking about Robert's death?"

"Exactly!" he says, shifting in his seat. "That's what I had in mind."

"I like that. It's a good way to start the book."

"You see, this is why I asked you to be my ghostwriter, David," Corey says. "I had a feeling we would get each other."

Oh, I'm sure that's the reason, I wish I could say. *I bet it had absolutely nothing to do with the fact that you discovered me standing in your hotel room on the day your husband died.*

"How do you want to do this?" I ask. "Do you want to just tell me about that day, and I'll put everything in writing?"

I realize how inexperienced I sound even as the words come out of my mouth. At least I made it clear last time that I'm not the right person to write a memoir, and that I've never ghostwritten for anyone before.

"Yes," Corey says. "Let's do it that way. You can send me the pages whenever they're ready, and we'll review them together."

"Sounds good."

He rearranges his tie, looking straight into the camera, and begins his story: "Robert and I used to spend weekends in New

York often—once or twice a month, if not more. He would some-times fly in a few days ahead so he could attend business meetings, and I'd join him whenever I could, depending on the taping sched-ule for my show."

I make notes while he speaks, even though they don't amount to much: *Weekends in New York. Fly in early. Joined whenever he could.* They'll be of absolutely no use for building out the narrative, but they give me something to do with my hands while I listen.

"We always stayed at the Plaza. At one point, we discussed buy-ing an apartment in the city, but I don't think either of us really wanted to, because we must've looked at two dozen properties and never pulled the trigger. On that weekend in May, he flew in on a Wednesday evening, and I was meant to join him on Friday. I arrived early in the morning…but he wasn't there when I walked into our hotel room."

The pen slips out of my hand. It falls to the floor with a loud clank, but I don't make a move to pick it up. I remain frozen, wait-ing for Corey to mention the alleged hotel employee he found inside his suite that day—one who happened to look an awful lot like me.

"I was surprised, but not at all alarmed. I figured he had headed out to work earlier than usual, and I'd meet up with him later. I went to brunch with friends, ran errands around the city, and returned to the hotel—but there was still no word from Robert. When I answered the phone and was told the police wanted to speak with me, I just knew—even before they told me what had happened, my instinct told me Robert was dead. I'm not a very spiritual person or anything, but maybe we could talk about that in the book—how interesting it is that, when you share a deep connection with some-one, your gut seems to know things before your mind does. I'll never understand why that is."

"Yeah," I say, trying to maintain a poker face. "Yeah, that's fascinating."

"There's still so much about that day that doesn't make sense to me, and the police have been less than helpful. That's why I've hired a private investigator—so he can help me understand."

I choke on my own saliva, clutching my chest as I cough incessantly. "A—a what?" I ask, gasping for air.

"A private investigator," Corey repeats. "I'm willing to share his findings with you, of course, so we can include them in the book. I daresay a lot of the content surrounding Robert's death will end up being informed by what he finds."

It's almost like there's a hand wrapped around my heart, squeezing it tight. That man—the one at the coffee shop, sitting at bars, jogging past me in Central Park, waiting on random street corners.

Jack, he said his name was, but now I'm not at all sure that he was telling the truth.

In slow motion, I replay my conversation with him: The nervousness on his face when I asked his name. The fact that he admitted to having seen me before. And then, toward the end of our conversation, the way he asked about my book.

Is there murder in it?

You could say so. You'd have to read it to find out.

Oh, you can bet I will. Thrillers with murder investigations are my favorite kind of stories.

How could I have been so stupid? How could I not have seen it before? And why, oh why, did I have to fuck everything up by suggesting I'm writing about *murder*?

"Does that sound okay to you?" Corey asks, forcing me back to the present.

"Uh...sounds great," I say, still unable to breathe normally. "Yeah, that'll be amazing."

"I know it's a bit impractical, writing the first draft before we get a report back from the private investigator," Corey says. "I'd like to think we can edit later on, depending on what he brings to the table."

"Absolutely. Yeah, we'll rework the pages to include his findings."

I'm fucked. I am *so* fucked.

"For the time being, why don't we focus on the emotional aspect of that day?" Corey says. "I'd love to tell you more about what I experienced, so we can hopefully build a powerful connection with the reader right from the start."

"Yes," I manage to say. "That would be perfect."

Corey clears his throat and continues talking, but I don't listen. I'm too busy thinking about the fact that his private investigator must be good—the best money can buy, probably. He's going to uncover every last detail about what happened that day and quickly close in on his target.

Me.

CHAPTER TWENTY

W ell?" I ask. "Are you finally going to admit it?"

"Um…"

"Come on, Stacey. You know it's true this time."

"I'm not certain we should—"

"Just say it!"

"Fine." She lets out a long sigh. "We're fucked, as you so color-fully like to put it."

A dramatic cry leaves my mouth. Maybe I didn't want her to say it after all. Hearing the words coming from her lips has made it feel more real—and a fresh dose of reality is the *last* thing I need right now.

I rushed here immediately after my call with Corey ended. It's past six p.m., so the office has all but emptied by now, but Stacey and I are still here, dissecting every little thing Corey said to me.

"This private investigator," Stacey says after a while. "How often have you been seeing him?"

"Very often."

"Every day?"

"No, but… most days, for sure."

"Has he seen you do anything he shouldn't have?"

"I've been on my laptop pretty much every time I've run into him, working on my edits."

"Good," Stacey says. "I'm glad you haven't handed him easy answers, at least."

"Well...I may or may not have chatted with him once."

She raises an eyebrow, staring at me with wide eyes. "*Chatted?*" she repeats.

"Like...flirted. But only a little!"

"Oh, for the love of God, David."

"I didn't know he was a private detective!"

"What did you say to him?"

"Not much, I promise! He asked about my book, and all I did was reveal that it's a somewhat murderous thriller. You called me before I could say anything else."

"Very well," Stacey says. "It could be worse, I suppose. It's not the end of the world."

"I mean, he's still got plenty of other places to dig around. Think of how many people saw us with the body! The PI might even have a way of getting his hands on records showing Robert's phone signal was picked up in Times Square *after* the time of death stated on his autopsy report."

"That may be true, darling. But he won't find it easy to get his hands on those things."

"It's his *literal job* to figure out a way to get them. For all we know, he's been in my apartment already, and that was just him getting started."

It all makes so much sense now—it wasn't Corey who broke into my home. It was his private investigator. And if he's crossed the line of breaking and entering already, I don't think there will be many lines he won't be willing to cross.

I'd love to tell myself and Stacey that it's been long enough since that day, that security camera footage will have been erased by now, that witnesses will be impossible to locate, that the phone company will refuse to hand anything over—but I know better. We're nothing but pawns in Corey's twisted schemes. What his endgame is, well... we'll find out sooner rather than later.

"What will you do about the memoir proposal?" Stacey asks me with none of her usual buoyancy.

"What else is there for me to do? I will write it," I answer. "Why? Do you have any better ideas?"

"It's just... given what we know now, I can't imagine Corey's memoir ever hitting shelves—or at least not your version of it. He could always hire a different ghostwriter once he's dealt with us, but..."

"What's your point?"

"I'm debating, darling, whether we'd be better off distancing ourselves from Corey while we still can. I could call Jonathan Wells and tell him you're no longer available to write the memoir."

"What happened to 'Keep your friends close and your enemies closer'?"

"For that saying to apply, your enemy has to be someone who isn't holding a gun to your temple, ready to pull the trigger at any moment. Since that seems to be precisely who we're up against... well, we might find comfort in a little distance, wouldn't you say?"

I fidget with my hands, thinking quickly.

"No."

Stacey's eyebrows shoot up. "No?"

I nod. "I won't give him the satisfaction of watching us cower."

"David, I don't—"

"We're fucked either way. No matter what we do at this point, he likely has most of what he needs to take us down. And if I walk away from writing his memoir now, he'll get the sense something is wrong, that we've been spooked. He might even put his plans into motion sooner than he otherwise would have."

Silence falls across Stacey's office—a silence so heavy it brings pressure to my ears, as if we were underwater. This is what it's come down to—it's me and Stacey against the world. We are alone in this, and no one is coming to help us.

"I didn't think it would happen this way," Stacey says sadly after a few minutes.

"What?"

"My downfall. I've come close before—closer than I'd like to admit. When my dear husband Harold tragically slipped and fell down the stairs, a forensics team swabbed my entire home. I spent days terrified that they would find oil, or soap, or *something* at the top of the stairs and blame me for his awful accident."

"Stacey, did you actually—?"

"And poor Bradford. Oh, good old Bradford. No one ever did figure out how or why he vanished from the yacht overnight while we were in the middle of the Atlantic, but I certainly feared the police were going to pin it on me."

"Are you saying you—?"

"I'd fooled myself into thinking I was invincible, somehow. I never thought we'd go down for something like this, but here we are." She shakes her head gently. "This is truly the end of the road for us, it would seem."

Okay, I fully want to take it back now—I want Stacey to stop being realistic and resume being her usual, chipper self. If the stress about Corey's plans doesn't kill me, seeing Stacey like this undoubtedly will.

"Maybe—maybe we still have a way out," I mumble, fully aware of how weird it is to be comforting Stacey, when it's always been the other way around.

"Making a run for it, you mean?" she asks, staring at me with a deep frown on her face. "I wouldn't be entirely opposed to the idea, David, but I don't know. It can't be easy to start over in a new country with a new identity—not at my age, at least."

"That's . . . not what I had in mind, no."

"What, then? Murdering Corey before he has a chance to expose us?" Stacey holds her chin thoughtfully. "Again, I'm not against it, but it's risky. It would only add time to our prison sentence if we get caught."

"We're not murdering anyone!"

"Fair enough. Perhaps Corey will, though. If we're lucky, he'll kill us both and put us out of our misery. God knows I'd prefer a quick death over a lengthy prison sentence."

"No! I don't want Corey to *murder* us! There's . . . there's gotta be a different way to put an end to all this."

Silence falls again, and the pressure in my ears is stronger this time. Even as the minutes pass, neither of us makes a move to speak, neither of us comes up with any brilliant ideas.

"I don't think there is, David," Stacey says finally, her voice low and heavy, as if she were speaking at a funeral.

I know she's right. I know, deep down, that there's no way out, but I still feel responsible for the two of us—responsible for finding a silver lining and lifting our spirits, because that's what Stacey would do for me if she were thinking straight.

In the end, I can't find anything to do or say. Nothing except for, "Should we have a drink?"

Stacey's expression shifts slowly, going from despair to curiosity. "Yes," she replies in a whisper. A moment later, she clears her throat. "Yes, I'd say that's exactly what we need."

She pushes her chair back and reaches for her purse.

"Let's get out of here, darling. First round is on me."

———

After five or six rounds of drinks, I'm not sure our despair has faded in the slightest, but our sense of self-awareness most certainly has.

We're sitting at a swanky bar just off Park Avenue, elbows resting on the table as we stare thoughtfully into nothingness. There's soft piano music playing in the background and hardly anyone around— except for a middle-aged couple that's getting handsy in a corner and the well-dressed bartender, who keeps looking our way, waiting for either Stacey or me to signal another round.

"If we get away with this," Stacey says suddenly, slurring her words, "I'm going to live life to the fullest, dear. What I have left of it, anyway."

"You've got plenty of life left," I slur back. "You're gonna live longer than the queen of England did."

"That's what I fear," she says. "That I'll be celebrating my hundredth birthday in a prison cell."

I kind of envy her, but I don't say it. At least she got the chance to live past sixty before any of this happened. Having my life destroyed at twenty-eight just seems cruel.

"What will you do, exactly?" I ask.

"Huh?"

"If we get away with it. What does living life to the fullest mean to you?"

She takes a long sip of her drink—so long that she empties the glass, and makes a gesture at the bartender to bring her another. "I suppose…I'd worry less," she says. "About publishing drama. And men. And the idea of dying alone. I'd buy a nice house somewhere warm and spend the winters there."

"That sounds nice."

"I'd also retire, probably. Hand off my stake in the agency to someone else."

"Now you're just talking nonsense."

"It may be the alcohol talking, darling, but…I think I mean it," she says. "I'd much rather leave on my own terms—before the industry itself forces me out."

The piano in the background stops suddenly, and in the couple of seconds it takes for the next song to start, a dark shadow seems to fall over our table.

"They tell you it doesn't matter what you look like or how old you get to succeed in the book world, but it's all a lie, isn't it?" Stacey adds. "At least when you're in film, or television, or music, you know from the start that everyone expects you to stay young and beautiful forever. Publishing won't tell you that—but it is every bit as obsessed with hot, fresh talent, and it's not afraid to push you aside if it must."

Slowly, I nod to myself. I may not fully understand what Stacey has gone through as a woman her age, but some of what she's saying sounds all too familiar—the way publishing can discard you when you're no longer what it wants you to be. The way everybody can turn their back on you from one day to the next.

"But you're still here," I say. "You haven't let anyone else win. If anything, you've proven you'll always have everything it takes to succeed in this industry."

"I'm still here, yes. But what do I have, really? A network that may seem enviable to some, a list of bestselling books written by authors I no longer represent, and not much else. Perhaps, if we manage to evade prison, it would be time to start living for something other than work."

"You can't leave me. I couldn't survive in publishing without you."

"I'd make sure you're left in good hands. And I wouldn't retire right away, dear. I'd wait for your third book to come out—have one final success before I bow out."

"Assuming it does become a success and doesn't flop like *Walking Home* did."

"It will be huge, David. If it ends up getting published, it'll be your biggest book yet."

If it ends up getting published. When it comes down to it, that's what I'm most terrified of. Every one of my other fears seems to pale in comparison: the idea of being a convicted felon, the notion of being cast aside by my family and the rest of society, the possibility that Jeremy would refuse to be associated with me ever again if he found out what I did. What truly destroys me is the thought that my dreams and my career could come to such an unceremonious end. That I'll be so tarnished by this experience that no one will ever publish me again, no matter how many books I may write.

The bartender comes to our table and sets down two fresh drinks in front of us—one for Stacey and one for me, even though the glass I'm holding is still more than half full.

"How about you?" Stacey asks as he returns behind the bar. "What would you do if we got away with this?"

"I'd write," I say simply. "I'd write book after book, and hopefully publish them all. And...I guess I'd try to be less afraid. Less hard on myself. Happier."

"Cheers to that, then," she says, lifting her glass. "To the lives we would have lived."

"To the lives we might still get to live."

We clink our glasses together, and as I stare into Stacey's eyes, I could swear I've never been more grateful to have her than I am in this moment. Because our lives may be going to shit, but if there is one thing that will always be true, it's that drinking is always better with friends—and even better among best friends.

The first thing I become aware of when I wake up is that there's an alarm chiming in my ears. Or is it a phone ringing? Either way, it is too loud for my liking.

The second thing is that I'm not lying on a bed. The ground

beneath my cheek is flat—wooden, most likely, because it's giving off a faint, expensive smell.

The third thing is how heavy my head feels. What happened last night? Where did I go, what did I drink, what did I do?

Before I can even try to figure out the answers to those questions, the alarm goes off again, louder this time.

"Stop," I mumble into the cold, hard floor. "Just...make it stop."

I reach out a hand helplessly, although there's no point. The alarm isn't close enough for me to snooze it, and I don't think I'd be strong enough to prop myself up and go find its source. But then, unexpectedly, a voice comes.

"I'm trying, darling."

I let out a moan in response. Someone might as well be drilling against the side of my head.

"You wouldn't know where my phone is, by any chance, would you?"

"No," I try to say, but all that comes out is another moan.

Finally, gloriously, the alarm stops, and Stacey's voice echoes loudly against the walls of wherever we are.

"Hello?"

For a moment, there's blissful silence, as whoever is calling speaks into the phone. When Stacey's reaction comes, however, adrenaline shoots through my veins.

"Jackie! I'm so pleased to hear that."

I lift my head, blinking slowly in the bright light. I'm lying in the middle of a classy living room. There's a plush leather sofa on my right, tall windows to my left, and a crystal coffee table littered with glasses and empty bottles right in front of me.

I have no idea how or why we decided to come to Stacey's town house. If I close my eyes, though, I can almost hear a voice and see a man's stern face staring back at me.

My apologies. We're about to close for the night.

Oh, no, please don't close! Can we at least get one last round?

I'm afraid I can't do that, sir.

It's all right, David. We'll go to mine. There's endless alcohol there and no closing time!

"Absolutely!" Stacey says into the phone. "I'm certain he'd be more than willing to do it."

Judging by her tone, Stacey has gotten good news from Jackie—and that may not be enough to make my hangover go away, but it certainly helps.

I push myself off the ground and stumble toward the couch, leaning my heavy head back while Stacey paces around the living room.

"Well, isn't that lovely? Yes, we really do."

I try my best to meet her eyes, eager to ask what's going on, but she's acting as if I wasn't even here.

"Of course! I'll let him know right away. No, no, I know. You as well, love. Bye, now."

She freezes immediately after lowering the phone. She's facing away from me, toward the windows, so I can't read her expression, but I suddenly have a feeling that things are not as good as she was making them sound.

"What did she say?" I ask.

Slowly, Stacey turns to look at me. She looks awful—smudged makeup, disheveled hair—which makes me wonder just how terrible *I* look right now.

"She read your revision."

"And?"

"She loved it."

"That's great," I say, allowing my head to relax deeper into the couch. "It *is* great, isn't it?"

"It is, yes. She also said they're getting ready to announce the book...and they want to do it in a big way."

This is music to my ears. I swear, my headache has disappeared, my skin has cleared, my hair has cleansed itself. Book announcements typically happen on industry websites only. Media placements are rare, except for big books—celebrity authors, new installments in highly popular series, or novels with film deals already attached to them. If Wagner wants to do a big announcement for my third book, it must mean they're really getting behind it. They really believe it'll be a success.

"Well? What do they have planned?"

Stacey purses her lips. "They've secured a brief segment on *The Breakfast Show*."

I would scream, if only I had a bit of strength in me. *The Breakfast Show* is one of the news programs I appeared on back when I was doing promo for *The Millers*—back when everyone loved me, when I was the bestselling author of one of the most critically acclaimed books of the year. I never thought I'd have the chance to be on it again, that I'd have another opportunity like this.

"Maybe we should turn it down," Stacey says.

"*What?* Are you crazy?"

"Think of all the attention, David! All the eager eyes watching, all the people who will no doubt turn against you the second our showdown with Corey Donovan becomes public."

"Our showdown with Corey will be *very* public no matter what. Have you forgotten who he is?"

"He'll get us canceled either way, yes. But if you go on national television and promote a book about a guy who finds a dead body in his bed—and then people find out it was inspired by what happened to *Corey Donovan's husband*—well, it'll be disastrous!"

"What if the opposite happens, though? What if it brings

enough attention to my book that Wagner decides to go ahead and publish it despite the controversy? If there's a chance I can still make something of this novel—if there's a way I can make it succeed, even if I'm in prison by the time it comes out—I just...have to do it."

Stacey stares at me for a long moment. She doesn't seem convinced, but she's not going to argue. *I can't tell you what to do, darling*, I can almost hear her in my mind. *As your agent, I can only give you my best advice.*

I'm not sure how long we remain here, staring into the other's eyes, but after a while, the temperature seems to lower. The light outside the window shifts, and Stacey's expression finally softens.

"Come on, then," she says suddenly.

"Where are we going?"

"I'm making us breakfast. Aren't you hungry?"

I shake my head. "I don't think I can eat right now."

She makes a move toward the couch and sits down next to me. "You want to know what I really think, David?" she asks, and I nod quickly. "I think we must live our lives while we still can. So...yes, you should take that spot on *The Breakfast Show*, if that's what you really want. It may all be over for us before long, and we'll be left wishing we had done more with the time we had left."

"Yeah," I say, looking down at my lap. "I guess you're right."

Stacey sighs. "Until Corey Donovan chooses to enact his revenge, we have only one option."

"What is that?"

"What else, darling, but to carry on?"

CHAPTER TWENTY-ONE

Over the next few days, I spend a lot of time thinking about *Walking Home.*

When I started working on it, I wanted to tell a story about loneliness. The book is about a recent college grad who appears to have everything—looks, talent, personality. He's the life of the party, everyone's favorite companion, so many people's "best and most intimate friend." But as he finds himself in difficult situations throughout the novel, people start dropping him, one by one—his family, his boyfriend, all his so-called friends.

The title comes from one of the last chapters, where the main character realizes he's in a cycle of loneliness that he can't break, and it's eating him up inside. *No matter what I may do, or how hard I may try, the reality is this: at the end of each night, I will always find myself in these same old shoes, walking home alone.*

I remember writing that sentence in the dim light of the living room, back in the apartment I used to share with Jeremy. He was asleep, so I was trying hard not to make any noise, but I just couldn't stop crying after I typed those words. As I tried to suppress my sobs, I kept thinking about this imaginary kid—only twenty-two years old, and already feeling so separate from the rest of the world. Barely at the start of his life and looking ahead at nothing but a road of isolation. It's weird now to think about the fact that, when I wrote that, I was still with Jeremy, and I still had a bright future to look forward to.

Maybe I jinxed it. Maybe I set myself up for failure by slipping into the mindset of that character. Or maybe I could sense something deep down, even then—something that told me my main character's reality was all too possible for me if I wasn't careful. Perhaps all I did was foresee what was ahead for me.

And now, here I am, at the end of my life as I know it, and there's no one to turn to. No one except for Stacey, but it's not like I can be by her side all day every day—no matter how badly I wish I could. I keep playing around with the idea of calling Jeremy, but I have nothing to say. We've continued playing our little game of sending the money back and forth, but it's been over a week since I last sent it to him, and he hasn't transferred it back yet. There's also my dad, with whom I'd love to be able to have an honest conversation for once, but I'm afraid of what his reaction would be if I told him how I've ended up in this situation. As a last resort, I consider reaching out to some of my old friends from college, but it feels like such a waste to restart those friendships when they're destined to come to a bitter end soon.

I spend my days alone instead, leaving my apartment only to pick up coffee from the deli or go for evening walks around Central Park. No matter how much I wish I could enjoy the change of the leaves or the crisp, cool air that has taken over the city, I simply can't find a way to relax. I keep looking around out of fear I'll run into Corey's private investigator, and even though I haven't spotted him in a while, I *feel* his eyes watching me at all times.

What's worse is that I'm forced to listen to the recording of my last conversation with Corey for hours on end, making notes and trying to come up with a narrative for a memoir that will most likely never see the light of day. I promised I would send him a full chapter by mid-October, but I barely manage six pages before giving up altogether.

Hi Corey, I write in an email on the day of the deadline. I figured I'd send this shorter sample so you can give me your feedback— that way, we'll be able to sort out the voice and narrative style before I keep going. Let me know what you think!

There—an excuse he'll find easy enough to believe. I hit Send and close my laptop, hoping against hope that I'll never hear from him again.

Thanks for sending, David, he says in his reply, which comes about two hours later. I will read as soon as possible and reach out once I'm ready to discuss.

Take your time! Don't feel at all rushed to ruin my life, I almost write back, but obviously don't.

Before I know it, the official countdown to my *The Breakfast Show* interview has begun, so I prepare obsessively in the days leading up to it. My publicist sent me a short list of questions that the interviewer will ask and some keywords to convey about my upcoming book: *provocative, raw, relatable, twisty, jaw-dropping*. I'll get less than four minutes on air, so I'm not sure how much of this I'll be able to sneak into my answers, but at least I try my best to remember it all.

The day before the interview, I wake up feeling strangely nauseous, almost as if my body knew something bad is about to happen. Trying my best to push the feeling away, I get dressed and head out of the apartment, convinced that a cup of coffee will be the exact remedy I need.

I'm waiting in line at the deli, thinking I'll keep practicing my answers as soon as I return home, when I hear a commotion happening somewhere behind me.

I turn around to find a man standing nearby, surrounded by

dozens of bags of chips that must've fallen off a shelf. He leans over to pick them up, and as he puts them back in their place, he sneaks a worried glance over his shoulder.

It's him. The person I've been terrified of running into again: Jack, or whatever the fuck his real name is. He might actually be the worst private detective in the world—the exact opposite of stealthy. Then again, I can't help but wonder if he's been given instructions to make himself known—if this is all part of Corey's strategy. He could very well be trying to get me to crack under the pressure.

I step out of the line and head for the door, certain I need to get as far away from here as possible. My legs start carrying me toward my building, toward the safety of home, but I'm not even halfway there when I look back and see him right behind me.

He has followed me out of the deli.

I freeze on the spot, right in the middle of the sidewalk, even as every one of my instincts tells me to run, to scream, to seek shelter. The issue is, I have no idea where to go. I shouldn't lead him to my apartment—that much I'm certain of, even if he *has* been there before—but I can't think of any other place that feels safe. And so, even as the seconds pass and he keeps getting closer, I have no choice but to stand still, staring right at him.

He stares back unflinchingly, not slowing his pace, not shying away from me. He bumps into people here and there as he makes his way down the street, but he doesn't apologize, doesn't even flinch, and that tells me everything I need to know: he's a man on a mission. All intention of keeping a low profile is long forgotten, and now he's merely executing whatever instructions he's been given. Has Corey lost patience? Decided to take the eye-for-an-eye approach, enact his own form of justice? Told his thug to apprehend me, interrogate me, hide my body in a random hotel room like I did Robert's?

Perhaps this guy's not only a private investigator—he could be a murderer for hire, too, depending on what service you sign up for. And, knowing Corey, he probably went for the full package.

It's that thought that makes my legs start working again, that makes me start running for my life. I'm not sure where I'm going, but I seem to be headed in the direction of Central Park. Sneaking a quick glance over my shoulder, I see that the private investigator has broken into a run as well, closing in on me no matter how fast I move.

By the time I reach the corner of 90th and Central Park West, I am entirely breathless. My heart is beating fast against my chest, begging me to take a break, but I have no time to waste. I need to make a quick decision: head into the park, or turn right and keep running down the street.

I go for the latter, figuring the park would be riskier—I wouldn't want us to find ourselves in a quiet spot that would allow him to kill and bury me in one go—but the short moment it takes me to make the decision is enough for the private investigator to get within a few feet of me.

"Aaaaahhh!" An unwitting yell escapes my mouth as I will my legs to move faster. I sprint down the street, set on putting some distance between me and him, very aware of the fact that we're in broad daylight. There are people watching us, but no one questions what we're doing, no one comes to my aid. I should've expected nothing less of New Yorkers. They probably think we're practicing a stunt for a movie, or something.

As soon as I get to the 86th Street subway station, I rush down the stairs, push past the turnstile swiftly, and don't stop until I've reached the Downtown platform. No sooner have I stepped onto it than a train enters the station at full speed. My heart pounds and my lungs gasp for air while I wait for the train to come to a stop and open its doors, keeping a watchful eye on the stairs behind me to make sure Jack hasn't followed me here.

I step into a car alongside a small crowd, allowing myself to breathe a sigh of relief. But when I turn around, I see him running down the stairs. He seems confused for a second, trying to figure out where I've gone, until he spots me standing there helplessly, and—

"Stand clear of the closing doors, please."

He lunges, his hungry eyes set on me. He's only a few feet away, and I'm afraid he might just make it in time, but then the doors slide tightly shut.

The train starts moving, and we lock eyes through the window. His face is red, his gaze intense, yet there's nothing he can do anymore. The train moves into the tunnel, and darkness starts flashing past the windows.

I have no fucking clue what that was all about, no idea what he intended to do. Was he actually going to hurt me, or was he only trying to make sure I *felt* threatened? Trying to break me mentally, push the limits of my tolerance for stress? Whatever the answer, I couldn't be more relieved to have gotten away. The train is nearly empty, so I stumble toward a seat and watch the stations go by, vaguely wondering where I should go next.

The adrenaline starts leaving my body little by little, and then exhaustion hits me all at once. I really need to get coffee somewhere, now more than ever, but that somewhere has got to be safe, private, impenetrable—a place where Corey and his henchman won't be able to find me.

When we get to Penn Station, I hop off the train instinctively and push my way through the crowds, entirely uncertain of why I decided to come here. Perhaps my legs know where I need to go better than my mind does, because all of a sudden, I find myself staring up at a New Jersey Transit screen displaying train schedules.

I have no reason to go home. But maybe I just need to escape from the city, if only for a short while. I need a little room to breathe, to think, to simply exist without the pressure of Corey's goon following me around.

So I hop on a train. I watch the Manhattan skyline become smaller and smaller through a window, and I rest my head back, telling myself that it'll be a good idea to see Pa one last time before my entire life crumbles—to repair burned bridges, to have a final goodbye, to create a single good memory to hold on to over the next several years, while I waste away in a jail cell.

It isn't until I'm walking across the front lawn that I realize it's the middle of the day on a Wednesday. My dad might not be home until much later, but it's just as well. Perhaps Sheila will let me in and allow me to spend some time alone inside my old house. I could use some hours of reminiscing, of searching for whatever traces of my mom are still inside this place.

"David?" Sheila says when she opens the door.

I try my best to give her a smile, shoving my hands in my pockets. "Hi, Sheila."

"What are you doing here? Christmas is two months away."

"I know."

"And it's not Father's Day."

"No, but I—"

"Oh, David, don't tell me you're under the influence of drugs!"

"No! I don't need to be on drugs to make the decision to come over. I'm just...here to see my dad."

"Mmmm." Sheila gives me a careful up-and-down assessment, as if looking for signs of imbalance, red eyes, or enlarged pupils. When she finds none, she smacks her lips. "Your father's not here."

"Could I wait for him to come back?"

"He won't be home for hours."

"I won't get in your way. I'll just…"

"Listen, David, I would let you come in, but I'll be heading out soon to run some errands, and I don't feel comfortable leaving you alone in the house."

"Why?"

She hunches her shoulders, not meeting my gaze. "Well…we do own nice things, and you're not quite—"

"Sheila, I'm not going to rob you!"

She takes a step backward, making the gap between the door and the frame smaller.

"Still, I'm sure you understand."

"I…don't, actually. I'm not struggling with money anymore, if that's what this is about. The first payment for my new book came through."

"Did it?" she says, lifting an eyebrow. "How interesting. Yet you still haven't repaid the money I lent you, have you?"

"I'm sorry. I literally just…forgot. I'll transfer you tonight."

Sheila presses her lips together. I swear, I'll never understand how she manages to fit so much into a single smile—contempt, reproach, annoyance, and a dash of something that might just be mistaken for genuine kindness.

"Wait here," she says, retreating into the house.

"Where are you going?"

"I'm giving your father a call."

"Wait, Sheila—"

The front door slams shut, and I'm left standing on the doorstep with my hands in my pockets.

I don't know why I thought coming to New Jersey would be a good idea. This place has rarely ever brought me anything other than pain, and anxiety, and rejection.

Despite that, I'm not ready to return to New York. I'm not ready to go back home, back to the fear of running into Corey's private investigator or the stress of tomorrow's interview. I lower myself to sit on the front steps and hug my legs, staring out at the quiet street and thinking of a different time—one when Sheila wasn't yet in the picture and I could still call this house my own. One when I would play out here until my mom came out to get me because it was time for dinner. One when I still had a place in the world where I unmistakably and absolutely belonged.

The longer I sit here, the tighter my throat becomes. My eyes keep searching for something along the street, but I have no idea what I'm trying to find—that is, until my dad appears, walking hurriedly up the front lawn, and I realize this is exactly what I'd been hoping for.

"David," he says. To my surprise, there is no suspicion in his voice, no exasperation. Instead, there's something that sounds a lot like concern.

I lift up a hand to shield my eyes from the sun. He's wearing his work clothes—khakis and a polo shirt—and he looks thinner still than the last time I saw him.

"What are you doing out here?" he asks. "Let's go inside."

I make a move to get up, but I can't find the strength to actually do it. The truth is, I don't want to go into the house anymore. That place is fucking haunted—haunted with the presence of Sheila, haunted with memories of my mom, haunted with the ghost of the person I would've become if she hadn't died.

"All right, then," Pa says, grunting a little as he sits down next to me. "We'll stay out here. Beautiful day, isn't it?"

I nod vaguely, even as a light autumn breeze passes by, rattling the leaves of the trees along the street.

"What is it, David? Why did you come here?"

I open my mouth to answer, but the words don't come out.

"Is it money again?" Pa asks.

I shake my head.

"So...your book? Has your publisher canceled publication?"

The thought of that happening makes my stomach turn, but again, I shake my head.

"Are you on drugs?"

"No!" I answer, finally able to find my voice. "And I'd love it if people would stop assuming that I am."

"What, then?"

"It's nothing," I say. "I just...wanted to talk."

"Talk?" Pa's eyebrows shoot up. Of all the reasons I may have given him for being here, this may just be the one that terrifies him the most. God forbid a son should simply want to spend time with his father and share a normal bond for once.

"Yeah."

My father clears his throat loudly. "What do you want to talk about?"

Another breeze passes by—a stronger one this time, which makes the branches of the trees bend with a loud crunch. A car drives by the street, a dog barks somewhere in the distance, and still, I have no idea what I want to say to him.

Maybe I want to tell Pa about Jeremy, and how we're in touch again—if you can call our money transfer contest "being in touch." Or perhaps I should tell him about my interview on *The Breakfast Show*, so he'll tune in and watch it tomorrow. I may even want to brag about how Wagner is getting behind my next book in a big way, and how I might be back on track with my writing career.

But then I'd also have to tell him about Robert, Corey, and the private investigator. I'd have to say that for every step forward, I've been forced to take two steps back. I'd have to tell him that I'm terrified of what's gonna happen next, and that the true reason for my visit was so we could say our goodbyes.

So instead, I say, "Do you ever think about what life would've been like?"

Pa turns toward me with a slight frown on his face. I have a feeling he knows exactly what I'm talking about, but I don't resist the urge to fill the silence with an explanation.

"If she hadn't died. If the car had been going just a bit slower. If she'd taken a different road. If she had only—"

"David."

"Do you?" I ask. "Think about it?"

Pa looks down at his feet, nodding slowly. "Every day, mijo."

"You see, I wish I could say the same. I wish I could sit here and talk about how I think of Ma every single day, and how I like to imagine what would've happened if she hadn't died, and how I still feel her here, but…it's not true." I shake my head to myself. "I only ever think about her when life goes to shit. Isn't that fucked up? That the only time I reach for the memory of my mom is when I'm at my worst?"

"David, please don't curse," my dad says, flinching.

"There's no other way to say it, though. It *is* fucked up."

"It is not *messed* up," Pa corrects me. "It's normal, I'd say. I also miss her a little extra when things aren't going my way. That's when it's most natural to wonder if things would've been different if she hadn't, you know…"

I nod, letting out a deep breath.

"Most of what is good about me comes from her."

"You're right about that, yes."

"I hate thinking of who I could've become if she hadn't died— if I'd had someone to hold me together instead of allowing me to break into pieces. If I'd had a parent who actually cared about me, and protected me from harm, and made sure I didn't feel so fucking alone growing up."

This time, Pa doesn't have an answer. He turns away from me, staring off into the distance. I didn't come here to blame or confront him, but he must know it's true. He must realize all the ways he's willfully broken me, even without needing to hear it from me. He must be aware that he's always put his own happiness above mine, prioritized Sheila over me, and shoved me to the side whenever it was convenient for him.

"I know I haven't been the best father to you, David," he says finally. "But you've also been—"

"What?" I ask, my voice barely louder than a whisper. "Uncontrollable? Unbalanced? Unhinged?"

"Unwilling, I was going to say—to work with me, not against me."

"I was just a kid back then. It wasn't my responsibility to meet you halfway."

"I know. There are many things I'd do differently if I could go back. I wish I could've given you the same kind of warmth that your mother used to, but none of it was easy. I was merely trying to—"

"Survive without her. I know. But I was trying to survive, too, and you left me with no choice but to do it alone."

A feeling of lightness comes suddenly—to my head, to my chest, to my hands. The kind of lightness you can only get from speaking words that have been weighing you down for far too long.

"I was left...broken. With no one to turn to, with nothing to give me comfort except writing. I should've been spending that time with my family. Or hanging out with friends after school. Or finding a community that would've made it easier for me to come out. Instead, I shut out the world and wrote story after story, and now... I have nothing else to hold on to."

My father bends over slightly, placing a hand on his stomach. I would feel bad for transferring all this weight onto him, but I can't find it in me to feel sorry right now.

"I am sorry, mijo," he says weakly. "You deserved better. I just couldn't..."

"What?"

"I couldn't be the person you needed me to be. And maybe I never will be, no matter how desperately I wish I could."

I have no answer to that. We sit in silence for a long time, until a faint banging sound starts coming from inside the house, which makes me think Sheila must be working on her ugly sculptures again. I doubt she ever had errands to run—she just didn't want to be in the house with me while my dad was still at work.

"What is it, David?" Pa asks suddenly, turning toward me with a gleam in his eyes. "The reason you were thinking of your mom today?"

I stare back at him unblinkingly, unable to speak.

"You said you only ever think of her when things go wrong. So...what's wrong?"

Nothing, I nearly answer. No good has ever come from being vulnerable with my dad. "Everything," I say instead.

He nods slowly, as if that was all the explanation he needed. As if that single word was enough to make him understand all the ways I've fucked up my life.

"We all make mistakes, David," Pa says. "Myself included. All we can do is learn from them and move on."

"There's no moving on this time." I swallow hard, trying to hold back tears. "It feels like the only thing I know how to do is disappoint people. Everyone is always expecting more from me than I can give them, and all I do is let them down, again and again. And now...I've really gone and fucked everything up. I did something bad—something no one is ever gonna forgive. Or forget."

"What did you do?"

"I can't tell you."

277

"Did you steal?"

"No, I didn't—"

"Did you plagiarize?"

"Of course not. I'd never—"

"Did you murder someone?"

I pause. "No." *Not technically*, is the real answer. *But I did move a dead body out of my apartment, wrote a book about it, and then entered a business relationship with the husband of the man whose body I mistreated.*

"Well, whatever it is, I'm sure there's a solution," Pa says. "If there's anything I can do to help you find it, all you need to do is ask."

"Thanks, Pa. That's—"

"And, for the record," he interrupts me, and I stop moving, stop blinking, stop breathing, "I'm proud of you, David. It would do you well to stop believing the lies you tell yourself...because the only person in this house who thinks you're a disappointment is you."

And Sheila, I almost say. *And you, Pa, most of the time.*

But then, as we settle into a comfortable silence, I begin to wonder if he's right—if there are lies I've been telling myself this whole time. If I've been too quick to blame him for seeing only the worst in me, when I'm also guilty of seeing the worst in myself. If our relationship over the past few years would not have been as strained if I hadn't gotten into the habit of fretting my visits to New Jersey, or if I'd been a little less wary of him.

"We should go inside," he says, nodding in the direction of the front door. "I haven't had lunch yet. Have you?"

"N-no," I answer. "But I can't stay. I have to—"

"You *can* stay, David," he says firmly. "You know you can."

I do know. And maybe there'll come a day when I will want to, but it's not today.

I shake my head. "I have a big interview tomorrow, and I still have some prep work to do."

"An interview?" my father asks, tilting his head sideways.

"Yeah. On *The Breakfast Show*, actually."

"Oh. Nothing to be too anxious about, I'm sure—it's not like it'll be your first time on television."

I know he means it as a compliment—I know he's trying to reiterate that he's proud of me, and that he's well aware of all the things I accomplished with *The Millers*—but his words don't have the intended effect.

"No," I say, feeling very hot all of a sudden. "It won't be my first time." But it may very well be the last. And I need to make it count.

My dad gets up from the front steps, and I do the same. For a moment, we stand awkwardly in front of each other, and I can just tell his arms are twitching. I think it's gonna happen—he's gonna go in for a hug, or at least try to. I loosen up my shoulders, preparing to hug him back, but then—

"Did I hear you say *The Breakfast Show*?"

Pa and I turn around to find Sheila standing in the doorway. She's wearing a stained apron and rubber gloves, and there's something that looks a lot like clay smeared across her forehead.

"That's right, my love," Pa replies. "David will be on it tomorrow."

"Oh, wow, David!" she says, stepping forward. "I watch it every single morning! Do you know who'll be interviewing you?"

"I'm not entirely sure. They're—"

"Well, if it's Mitchell Spencer, I would just *faint* from excitement." I've never seen her look like this—face slightly flushed, eyes bulging out of her head. This must be Sheila in fangirl mode, and it's a sight to behold. "David, you don't assume you could...bring a guest to the studio, do you?"

I'm sure I could ask. I know Stacey and my publicist, Emma,

will both be there, so I don't see why we wouldn't be able to bring one more person to the set. But then I think about the fact that she left me waiting out here for over an hour. I think about the Krispy Kreme donuts, and all the things she said during dinner on Father's Day.

"Nope. No guests allowed," I say sharply. "Hope you enjoy watching, though!"

"David, could you at least—"

"Sorry! Got a train to catch," I say, already making my way down the front lawn. "Thanks for the chat, Pa. I'll talk to you soon."

"Talk soon, mijo!" he says from the front steps of the house, where he's squeezing Sheila's hand tightly as if telling her not to press further, taking my side for once in his life.

I haven't even called an Uber yet, but it doesn't matter. I'll call it once I've reached the corner, or I might even try to walk the whole way to the station. For now, all I want is to put as much distance between myself and this house as possible.

Right before I turn onto the street, however, I can't help but sneak a final glance at it. I wonder what life will be like by the time I come back here again—or if I ever will. I slow down, trying to take a mental picture of this place to hold on to, for better or for worse, and then I start walking fast in the direction of the train station.

CHAPTER TWENTY-TWO

The studio lights are so bright that they're blinding. I don't remember it being like this a few years ago, when I was last here. Maybe they've upgraded their lightbulbs. Or perhaps they got a new lighting guy who decided the brighter, the better.

This is what I think about as I look over at a countdown flashing with big red numbers: *forty-nine seconds, forty-eight, forty-seven...*

I'm wearing a thick layer of makeup. So thick, in fact, that I hardly felt like myself when I looked in the mirror inside the tiny dressing room the producers assigned to me. *It'll look natural once you're out there*, I was assured, but sitting here with my hands resting neatly on my lap, I can't help but wonder whether that's true, or whether the bright lights actually make me look like more of a clown than I did backstage.

Thirty-six, thirty-five, thirty-four...

Piper Gunn, the woman who will be interviewing me, is also wearing lots of makeup, I notice as she sits down on a beige couch in front of me—even more than I am, I'd say.

"How are you feeling?" she asks, flashing a bright smile at me.

"Excited," I answer, trying my best to return the smile.

I made a big mistake earlier this morning. I decided to google her. It felt like a smart thing to do, especially since I didn't know much about her, but now I wish I hadn't. I wish I'd remained blissfully unaware that she knows Corey Donovan—as in, they're actual besties.

Reunited with this handsome fella, she captioned an Instagram post from January, in which she and Corey are cozied up at some event in the Rainbow Room at Rockefeller Center.

Happiest of birthdays to this classy lady, Corey himself wrote along with a photo on his own profile back in April. Your talent, determination, and friendship are always a source of inspiration to me.

And then there was a *Vanity Fair* interview Corey did a couple of years ago. When asked which personalities in the industry he admires, his answer was: *I have so much respect for Piper Gunn. Her journalistic work is absolutely stellar—and she has become a dear friend. Someone I can always go to for advice.*

A rush of heat travels up my face as I wonder how much they have spoken to each other since Robert's death. Has Corey told Piper about his plan to take me down? Was it a coincidence that she was assigned to do this segment, or did she specifically ask the producers if she could do it, eager for the opportunity to interrogate me on live television?

Thirteen, twelve, eleven…

"Ten seconds to air!" someone yells in the background.

I never should've agreed to this interview. Stacey was right. I may doubt her at times, but in the end, Stacey is *always* right. She's standing in a corner with deep concern on her face. I've never taken her for a religious woman, but she seems to be murmuring something to herself—a prayer, maybe.

Nine, eight, seven…

This interview will go viral, won't it? *Disgraced author makes shocking confession on live TV!*

Six, five, four…

All the things I'd hoped to achieve by doing this—promoting

the new book, talking about the inspiration behind it on my own terms, giving my writing career a fighting chance...no one will care about any of those things. Not if Corey and Piper have their way.

Three, two, one...

A sign with the words ON AIR lights up in red, and Piper turns toward the teleprompter.

"We're back with David Alvarez, the bestselling author whose debut novel, *The Millers*, took the world by storm back in 2021, and who is now here to share details about his new book. David, good morning."

"Good morning, Piper."

"There are so many things we want to know about your latest project, but first...can you give us a taste of what it's about?"

"Of course." I swallow hard. "The book is titled *I'm in Deep Trouble*, and it'll be out next summer. It...it follows the story of Daniel, a twenty-eight-year-old writer who finds himself in a pretty tough situation when he wakes up next to a dead man—and he has no idea who the man is or how he ended up there. The book is mostly about him trying to figure out those answers."

"Wow, that sounds fascinating," Piper says, shifting in her seat. "Now, for those of us who are fans of your previous work, what can we expect from *I'm in Deep Trouble*?"

"You can expect to be surprised, for sure," I answer. "It's very different from my previous books, but...this one is extra special, I think."

"Special how?"

"It's raw, and twisty, and provocative," I say, trying to stick to the script I spent the last few days practicing. "It's also relatable, in a way. I think it asks questions many of us have asked ourselves at one point or another."

Piper smiles gently at me. *You're doing well*, her expression seems to say, which is not at all what I expected. Where's the confrontation? Where are the hard-hitting questions? Where is the moment when she tricks me into confessing what I did with Robert's body and ridicules me in front of the millions of people who are watching?

"Questions about what we would do if we found ourselves in certain situations," I continue. "About where we draw the line between complicity and victimization. About how willing we are to take responsibility for our mistakes—or how far we'll go to bury them."

"Very interesting," Piper chimes in, with the grace and confidence only a professional TV presenter could muster. "We'd all be very curious to know: What was your inspiration for this novel?"

"I think..." I remember this being on the list of questions my publicist sent me. I know I prepared an answer for it. I just can't recall what I was supposed to say. My hands start feeling sweaty, the studio lights seem to brighten, and still, I'm unable to come up with the answer I'd practiced. Something about wanting to break away from my previous novels and try something new—or was that meant to be the answer to a different question?

I have no idea how much time has passed since we went on air, but I do know the segment must be nearly over. Someone behind the camera is lifting up a hand, and when I look over to see what they're signaling, I spot someone from the corner of my eye—a tall man with grayish hair.

He's standing in a shadowy corner of the studio, not far from Stacey. Everything before my eyes has taken on a hazy quality—probably an effect of the blinding lights—so I can't tell who this man is or what his face looks like, but the outline of his shoulders looks an awful lot like the private investigator's.

Is it him? Has he managed to sneak into the studio? Has Corey sent him to scare me, to make sure I'd screw up my interview with Piper? Or have I truly started to lose it, seeing things that aren't there?

He stands directly in my line of sight, resolutely still, before turning around and disappearing into the shadows. That's when I realize that I've been quiet for too long, that I need to come up with something to say.

"I guess...I was thinking back on my own mistakes." Yes, this is good—leaning on my previous answer, I tell myself as I try not to panic, try not to bolt out of my chair. "I felt like...like I wanted to look at myself through a different lens. To reflect on certain things I've done, and the things I *would* do if I could go back. That's how the character of Daniel came to be."

"If we weren't already intrigued by the sound of this book, we most certainly are now." Piper turns to face the camera directly. "Unfortunately for all of us, *I'm in Deep Trouble* won't hit shelves until next June, but we will have David join us again closer to publication so he can tell us more about his explosive new novel. David, thank you so much for being here today."

"Thank you for having me."

"All right, Mitchell, over to you!"

It's over. The entire four minutes have passed, the cameras are no longer pointed at me, and my mic has been turned off. More importantly, Piper didn't make any attempts to expose me as some kind of dead-body trafficker. I didn't say anything I shouldn't have said, and now I get to just sit back and enjoy the benefits that will surely come from doing this interview.

I can just imagine people scrambling to add the book to their to-read lists, marking the publication date on their calendars, rushing online to find preorder links. And, for the first time in what feels like forever, I am able to draw in a long breath and actually feel joyful when I let the air out.

———

"You did such a good job, David," Emma says to me once we're backstage again.

285

"Do you actually think that, or are you just saying it?"

"You seemed a tad nervous," Emma admits. "But it doesn't even matter, cause you did great overall. I truly think that."

"Did I say all the things I needed to say?"

"Absolutely. You hit all the most important points and more."

We both turn toward Stacey, who's been watching us silently with her arms crossed.

She lifts her chin slightly. "You certainly said things, yes."

Emma gives me a quick look—one that seems to say, *What could she possibly be upset about?*

I shrug in response, saying, *Just Stacey being Stacey.*

"I need to have a quick chat with one of the producers," Emma says. "We can head out right after. Sound good?"

"Sounds great."

She throws one more smile at me, a wary nod at Stacey, and then walks off quickly, the bang of her heels echoing loudly against the walls of the hallway.

The dressing room feels tinier than ever in Emma's absence. I was worried about a potential run-in with Corey's PI as we made our way back here, but no one tried to ambush me after I got off the stage, thankfully. Now, to be honest, I'm more afraid of Stacey. She hasn't uncrossed her arms, hasn't unclenched her jaw.

"What?" I ask, even as I sneak a glance at the mirror. I most definitely look like a clown in this fucking makeup. "Stacey, just say something."

She draws in a deep breath. "A book about *how willing we are to take responsibility for our mistakes—or how far we'll go to bury them.*"

As she repeats my own words back to me, my stomach squeezes tighter and tighter, until I bend over, collapsing under the weight of my own stupidity. Holy fuck. *What have I done?*

"You may not have confessed in the eyes of the world, darling," Stacey says to me gravely. "But in the eyes of Corey..."

Fuck, fuck, fuck.

"What do we do?"

"There's nothing *to* do," she answers. "Perhaps we should simply enjoy this moment—celebrate the bump in preorders the interview will inevitably bring. How about breakfast, dear? My treat."

I haven't had anything but coffee since I woke up at five a.m. to come down to the studio, but eating breakfast is the last thing I feel like doing right now. I want to scream, I want to run, I want to get far, far away from here.

My phone pings suddenly with the sound of a new email. I must've forgotten to silence it before the interview, so I'm lucky it didn't chime while I was on live television. I wiggle it out of my pocket, turn it over to look at the screen, and I swear to God, I have to stop myself from throwing up all over the floor of the dressing room. Corey Donovan's name is flashing before my eyes.

"What is it?" Stacey asks, surely able to read the look on my face.

"An email from *him*."

"Him?"

"Corey."

"Well, open it!"

Hi, David, the email says. I've had a chance to review the pages and would love to discuss. I'll be in New York this weekend, staying at the Plaza. How about you come to the hotel so we can have a chat?

"This can't be a coincidence," Stacey says, looking at the screen from over my shoulder.

"You think he watched the interview?"

"I don't think it—he *had* to have seen it."

"What do I reply to him?"

Stacey steps away from me and sits down on the small couch that's pushed against the wall.

"Stacey?"

"Reply with whatever feels right, dear," she says. "I won't steer you in either direction this time around. If the whole thing turns into a bloodbath, I'd rather live without the guilt of having pushed you to go meet him."

A bloodbath? I hope Stacey is joking, but I don't have the energy to ask. The truth is, that could very well be what Corey is envisioning. He must have a reason to ask for this last-minute meeting in person and in private, a plan to put an end to this once and for all.

Maybe his henchman will be there, waiting to beat me to a pulp until I blurt out everything I know about Robert's death. Or perhaps this is an ambush—perhaps Corey is already cooperating with the police, and they'll be there waiting to arrest me.

If I agree to go, I'd be walking right into the lion's den. But if I refuse...wouldn't that just be delaying the inevitable? Wouldn't it be better to face my fate and get it over with?

Letting out a long sigh, I realize I'd almost be grateful if this turned out to be Corey's way of putting all his cards on the table. At least it would put an end to all this anxiety, all this waiting around, which may just be the things that kill me if I'm forced to deal with them much longer.

Hi Corey, I write in my response. Sounds great. Let me know when would be the best time to meet.

I've barely lowered my phone before it pings again with his response: Tomorrow. Noon.

"He wants to meet tomorrow," I announce to Stacey, but she shows no sign of having heard me.

Perfect, I type. See you then!

My finger hovers over the Send button for a few seconds. When I finally hit it, I feel as though I've just signed my own death sentence.

CHAPTER TWENTY-THREE

The interior of the Plaza has never looked grimmer than it does now. The sparkling chandelier in the lobby seems to have dimmed, the chatter of people eating and drinking in the Palm Court muted. Even the red carpet appears to have become a few shades darker, so that it looks dull and maroonish—the color of spilled blood.

As I make my way to the elevators, my mind is filled with images from the night I met Robert: The back of his suit as he walked confidently through this same lobby. City streets flashing past tinted windows. Lips pressing together hungrily on the dance floor.

I try my best to hold on to those memories. They may not be things I want to remember, but they're far better than the other images that are attempting to take over: Robert lying still as a statue in bed next to me. His feet banging loudly as Stacey and I carried him down the stairs. His head lolling in the Uber while we sped down Central Park West. His body lying in the middle of Stacey's office, looking like a life-sized doll.

Corey's suite is on the sixteenth floor. As I approach the door that has the room number he provided, it hits me: this is the same suite he and Robert stayed in last May. Corey must've requested it specifically, wanting his revenge journey to come to an end in the same place it started—the room where Corey and I first met. The one where Robert and I formed what felt like a real bond. The one where all our lives collided.

It's almost poetic, so I'll give him points for that. I'm wearing khakis and a nice shirt, and I made sure to tame my hair before I left home. If Corey's plan culminates with me being led out of the hotel in handcuffs, I at least want to look good for the reporters who will surely be waiting outside.

I straighten my collar and run a hand through my hair one last time before knocking on the door.

"David," Corey says when he opens it. "You're right on time."

The room is perfectly clean when I walk in. It looks nothing like it did the last time I was here, when the evidence of my wild night with Robert was still scattered all over the place. But then, as I approach the living room, I notice a few things that aren't quite as they should be. There's a bunch of towels lying in a pile right next to the couch. Sneaking a glance sideways into the bedroom, I spot a lump of plastic that looks a lot like a folded body bag, and on the center table in the living room is a long, shiny knife.

Holy fuck. He's going to kill me.

God knows I'd prefer a quick death over a lengthy prison sentence, Stacey's voice rings inside my mind. Perhaps she was right. Perhaps, of all the possible outcomes that this debacle might've had, death is actually the most preferable—better than facing financial and reputational ruin, better than the public scrutiny I'd have to face if I went to trial, better than spending the rest of my days withering in a dark cell.

"I don't think I've ever asked you where you live in the city," Corey says, staring over at me.

"No, you haven't," I reply. *But your private investigator must've surely shared my address with you by now.* "I live on the Upper West Side."

"Ah, fair enough. I hope it was easy enough to get here, then?"

"Yeah. It sure was."

Maybe he's planning to bring my dead body back to my apartment after he murders me. I wouldn't be surprised if he intends to do with me what I did with Robert—parade me around the city for a few hours before dropping me off at my final resting place.

"Can I offer you something to drink?" he asks, moving toward the bar while I stand still in the middle of the living room. "Some champagne, maybe?"

"Ch-champagne?" My heart leaps as he lifts a bottle that looks strangely familiar—the greenish tint on the glass, the golden label. It's the exact type of champagne Robert offered me when we met. "Why would we drink champagne?"

"To celebrate," Corey replies. "Our new business partnership is worth popping a bottle over, don't you think?"

"Yes," I say, nodding a little too quickly. "Yes, that makes sense."

The sound of the cork releasing sounds almost like a gun. If I didn't already know what Corey's weapon of choice will be, I could just imagine him shooting me and then sneaking his head out the door once someone came to investigate. *Oh, that noise? No, no, it wasn't a gunshot. I just popped open a bottle of champagne. See?*

He steps away from the bar and joins me in the living room, holding two glasses.

"Sit," he says. It sounds more like a command than an invitation, so I obey him. He sits on the opposite end of the couch, and then he offers me one of the glasses. "To our new partnership. May it always be guided by respect, creativity, and honesty."

"Cheers," I say, staring into his cold blue eyes.

He takes a sip, but I hesitate before doing the same. I didn't get a good look at him as he was pouring the glasses—he wouldn't have slipped any kind of poison or sleeping pills into my champagne... would he?

Then again, if he did, it would probably be for the best. The alternative—death by stabbing—sounds pretty painful. I take a swig and empty half the glass in a single go.

"Lovely champagne, isn't it?" he asks, studying me with renewed interest. "Have you ever had it before?"

"No!" I say in a near-shout. "I—I mean...no, I haven't."

How could he possibly know? I ask myself, but then I realize Corey must've seen the hotel bill from the night before Robert died. He must've guessed Robert didn't have that bottle by himself, and he must already know it was me who drank the other half.

Clutching my glass tightly, I turn toward the window. Central Park is gleaming with the colors of autumn. The treetops blend together into a canvas of green, yellow, orange, and red, and the sky above is a deep shade of blue. I long for the feeling of the crisp air on my skin, for the glimmer of sunlight sneaking through the branches of trees, and the joy of reading a good book while the leaves fall around me. When I realize I may have already experienced all those things for the very last time, I swallow back tears, because there's no chance I'll be getting out of this alive.

"This view really is something, isn't it?" Corey asks when he notices me staring out the window.

"Yeah," I say. "It is."

"This used to be my favorite hotel. Not just in New York, but in the world, really. The Ritz in London is a close second—and the Four Seasons in Maui may just take the third spot. But I've always thought there's a certain magic about the Plaza that is impossible to find anywhere else. Or I *used* to think that, anyway. I haven't been able to feel the same way since Robert died."

"Oh."

"I somewhat envy anyone who's still able to find that magic

here." Corey takes his gaze off the window to stare directly at me. "Tell me, David, have you ever been in the Plaza before?"

"No."

"No?"

"I mean, I've had drinks downstairs a couple times. Also... brunch once, I think. But I've never been in one of the rooms."

Corey's grip tightens around his champagne glass. "Really?"

"Mm-hmm," I squeak in response.

"That's funny," he says with raised eyebrows. "Because you look an awful lot like someone I met back in May—in this exact same suite, actually."

I stare at him for a long moment. And then my whole body deflates, part by part—first my lungs, then my arms, and finally my legs—until I'm nothing but a collapsed balloon on the couch.

I feel so stupid all of a sudden, as I think back on everything Stacey and I did to try to get away with this, to hold on to the idea of the futures we might've gotten to live. It was pointless, I realize now. This was always going to happen in the end—no matter what we did, Corey was always going to win.

The words leave my mouth before I've even made up my mind about speaking them. "It's time, isn't it?"

Meeting Corey's resentful gaze, I have a near-absolute certainty that he knows exactly what I meant. Time to quit the bullshit. Time to tell the truth.

But then he says, "No."

"I don't under—"

"This is not the *right time* to come clean about what you did to my husband," he says in a chilling whisper. "The time should've been the same day it all happened. Or on the day you and I met for lunch. Instead...look what you made me do. You left me with

293

no choice but to play a stupid game of cat and mouse, hoping you'd come clean sooner rather than later. But telling the truth was never part of your plans, was it?"

"I...I didn't mean to—"

"Of course you meant to lie!" Corey's shout booms against the walls of the suite. In a swift movement, he gets on his feet and starts pacing dangerously around the living room. "Do you have any idea what you put me through? What it was like to learn that Robert had been found dead in a random hotel room with no explanation? That drugs were involved? To hear from the police that their investigation was closed, and there was nothing they could do because his *cocaine-induced stroke* was deemed *accidental*? Do you have a clue of how many nights I spent lying awake, racking my brain for answers, wishing I knew what really happened, wondering how Robert's body ended up at a *Hilton*, of all places?"

I don't have a way to respond. I may as well have forgotten how to speak. In the back of my mind, I can't help but think of the Corey I thought I knew—the calm, collected man who reports the news on television. The one who's as strong and cold as an iceberg, who never lets his emotions shine through. Because the man standing in front of me now is not him—not even close. His face is red, his eyes are bulging out of his head. This is someone who might just have the nerve to reach for the knife on the table and sink it into my heart.

I shrink away in my seat, looking down at the gleaming blade. When I lift my gaze again, Corey is towering over me threateningly, waiting for me to speak.

I have no idea how to begin. I don't know how I'm meant to explain everything that happened between me and Robert when I can barely even breathe, so I start with the one thing I can say with absolute honesty.

"I'm sorry."

Corey's face crumples into a frown. He doesn't move, doesn't even blink, but the hunger in his eyes reveals to me just how long he's been waiting for this moment.

"I never meant for any of it to be this way. I promise. I never—"

"When did you and Robert meet?" he interrupts me, his voice nothing but a hoarse murmur that sounds, if possible, even more dangerous than his yelling.

"The night before he died." My voice is the exact opposite of his—shrill, whiny, desperate. "We started chatting on an app, and he invited me to come over."

"So you lied. You *have* been here before."

"I—I have, yes."

Slowly, he moves to sit on the couch next to me, but he isn't as poised as he was earlier. He grips the armrest tightly, his knuckles turning white as his eyes dig into mine.

"What else have you lied about?" he asks.

Again, I'm at a loss for words. How can I even begin to explain all the things I've been dishonest about? I have no way to list them, no way to justify any of the shit I've done, so I choose to tell him the whole story instead.

"It was meant to be only about sex. I came up to his room, and we hooked up, but then...he asked if I wanted to go out for a drink. Just like that, we were running around town, going from one bar to another. We got really drunk, and we...we somehow ended up in my apartment."

"You didn't *only* get drunk," Corey says firmly. "Not according to the autopsy. Was it you who supplied the cocaine that killed him?"

"No! And I didn't do drugs with him, either, if that's what you're implying. He kept disappearing to go to the bathroom—I can only assume he was snorting cocaine every chance he got."

295

"What about the Xanax?" he asks. "This wouldn't be the first time I've heard of Robert indulging in cocaine, but prescription drugs weren't usually his style."

"It was mine. The Xanax, I mean. Robert said he had a headache when we made it back to my place. I—I gave him some pills to help him feel better, only I…grabbed the wrong bottle."

The silence that follows is haunting, but it thankfully doesn't last too long.

"What happened after he took the pills?"

"We went to sleep. When I woke up the next morning, he was dead."

Corey's eye twitches. "Was he really? Or are you lying to me again?"

"It's the truth. I swear."

"But you didn't call 911."

"I was going to. I fully intended to make the call, but then…I started thinking."

"Thinking?"

"About what would happen if the police came to my apartment. About the things people would say about me on the news. About what this whole thing would do to my career, and I panicked. I was exhausted, and hungover, and so fucking confused. I was worried that I was gonna be blamed for his death, that the Xanax might have had something to do with it, so—" It all sounds so stupid now. None of this should've ever happened, but I have no one to blame but myself. "I figured, if I could bring his body back to his hotel room, then everything would be okay. All I wanted was to lay him to rest in his own bed. I never intended to—"

"Why were you in here that morning?"

"I came to scope out the room. I wanted to make sure it was

empty so I could bring Robert up, but then I ran into you, and I knew I could no longer go through with the original plan."

Corey clenches his jaw, his eyes flicking ever so briefly in the direction of the knife, and a deep dread settles over me. I'm all too aware that the only thing standing between me and death is the self-restraint of the man sitting in front of me—and that the more I hand over the answers he's after, the closer I get to the end.

He clears his throat. "How did Robert end up at the Hilton?"

"I brought him there," I answer, careful not to say *we*. I shouldn't place any blame on Stacey. Not if I can help it. "I—I found a key card for the Hilton in Robert's wallet. I realized he had two hotel rooms in the city, so I dug around for his room number, and then I just...left him there."

"And your new book? The one you so proudly talked about on *The Breakfast Show* yesterday?"

"I never intended to write it," I say. "I just...needed to process everything. That's what I do—I write about things that happen to me, things I need to understand better, so I started telling this story without ever thinking anyone would read it. It was so stupid of me to send it to my agent, but I was desperate to pay the bills, and I just...fucked up."

It happens in slow motion—the way a flush of red travels up his neck, reaching his face and rendering him completely unrecognizable. His hand wraps around the armrest tighter, so that his veins pop out, and his expression becomes chaotic—something between sadness, hurt, and pure fury.

I draw in a deep breath. I'm trying to stop myself from crying, but I just can't help it. As I release the air through my mouth, the tears start pouring uncontrollably. "I really am sorry, you know? I've fucked *everything* up, and I just...don't even know how or why."

I wipe my eyes with the back of my hand, but the tears keep coming. "I fucked things up with my family by writing a book about them. I ruined my relationship with the only man who's ever truly loved and believed in me. I pushed away every single one of my friends—the few ones I had to begin with, anyway. I fucked up my career without even realizing it, and now...I've really gone and done it. The moment I decided to move Robert's body, I destroyed my entire life, and I just...I wish I could understand it. I wish I could understand how a single person could fuck up so many times, and still manage to go and fuck up again. Like...what the fuck is wrong with me?"

I'm half expecting Corey to answer. I'm expecting him to tell me he has no idea how anyone could be so unbalanced, that he wishes our paths had never crossed and that I hadn't come into his life. Instead, he remains eerily silent.

"I was thinking a couple of days ago," I continue, not even bothering to wipe my tears at this point, "about what my life would've been like if certain things had been different from the start. If I'd had two supportive parents. Or if I hadn't had to play a character all through my school years so the other kids wouldn't know I was gay. Or if I hadn't been left with no choice but to rely on my writing to feel complete. I've been wondering what it would've been like to grow up without that brokenness. I mean...does anyone even get to have that? Cause if they do, then fuck them. Fuck them and their unfair advantage."

More blank stares, more silence, and still, I'm unable to stop crying. I hate myself for breaking down in front of Corey. There's just an impulse telling me to speak while I can. To make my last words count, since the only way I'll be leaving this hotel room is in a body bag.

"I'm not trying to blame anyone," I say once I feel like my tears have finally run dry. "It's not anyone else's fault that I did what I did to your husband's body. So...I'm ready now. To face the consequences, I mean. Do whatever you have to do." I stare over at the knife, which is gleaming in the bright light coming from the window. "Just...just do it."

I close my eyes, ready for the pain to come. A gash along my neck. A stab in my abdomen. A hole in my heart. But even as the seconds pass, I don't feel any of those things.

After a while, I start wondering if I'm dead already. Maybe it's true what people say: that death is faster and easier than falling asleep. It's possible that I simply didn't notice Corey sinking the knife into my body.

I sneak a peek out of one eye, almost expecting to see a long tunnel and a bright light, but there's only the gorgeous suite and Corey's cold gaze staring back at me. I close my eyes again, squeezing them tightly, hoping he'll make up his mind already. I just want him to get it over with.

"David," he says suddenly, "what the hell are you doing?"

"I'm...waiting for you to kill me?"

"*What?*" he asks. "Don't be ridiculous."

"So...you're *not* going to kill me?"

I look over at the knife once again. The light outside the window is shifting, but there's still a twinkle of sunshine reflecting off the blade.

Corey lets out an annoyed sigh. "Killing you was never my intention. Even if it was, I wouldn't do it with a knife. It's too messy."

"Why is the knife there, then?"

"I ordered room service when I got in last night," he answers stiffly. "The steak knife slipped off the tray. I put it on the center table so they'll remember to pick it up when they return later."

"How about the body bag?"

"Body bag?"

"The one in the bedroom."

"David, that's a suit bag. I unpacked my clothes this morning."

"And the towels?"

He rolls his eyes. "What about the towels?"

"You're...not gonna use them to wipe up my blood?"

He lets out another sigh—this one louder than the last. "I took a shower earlier and forgot to bring the towels back to the bathroom. Are you satisfied now?"

"I...guess?" I say, shifting in my seat. "I just wish you'd tell me already—what's it gonna be? If you're not going to kill me, what will you do? Are you gonna call the cops and have me sent to jail? Or...call up everyone you know in media to make sure I never publish another book again? Or—" I gasp loudly—"are you saying *you're* not going to kill me, but *someone else* will? Honestly, I'd rather just know. The anticipation is too much—"

"I have three questions for you," Corey interrupts me. "What I choose to do next will depend on your answers."

I swallow hard, feeling a drop of cold sweat travel down my neck. Suddenly, I feel as though I'm on a demented game show, where Corey is the host and I'm a helpless contestant putting his life on the line for the opportunity to win a big prize.

"Okay," I say. "What's the first question?"

"Who initiated the conversation on Grindr?"

"He did. He messaged me first. There—there was no public photo on his profile, but he sent me a face pic in a private message, and that was when we started talking."

Corey moves forward slightly on the couch, pressing the palms of his hands together. Whether I gave the right or wrong answer, he doesn't say. He jumps straight to the second question: "Did you know about me? While you were having sex, or hopping from one bar to the next—did you know he was my husband?"

"I had no idea he was married. I didn't even know who you were. I—I mean, no offense, but I'd never watched your show." I look down at my lap, taking small breaths through my mouth. "Robert wasn't wearing a wedding band, and every single thing he said implied he was single. That he wanted...a *future* with someone."

Corey's face turns slightly redder. "A *future?*"

"Yeah," I say, feeling myself flushing as well. "He told me all the things I wanted to hear, I guess. He—he made me feel special... and I was too stupid to see that he was only trying to get into my pants. I mean, he even—"

Corey lifts an eyebrow, which feels like a cue for me to stop talking.

"Last question," he says, and everything in the room seems brighter as I wait for him to speak. I can almost feel an imaginary audience holding their breaths as they wait to find out whether I'll win the prize or not. "Why did you agree to write my memoir?"

"I was scared," I admit in a small voice. "Scared that if I didn't agree, you would hire someone else—someone who might've found out the truth and exposed me for what I'd done. I figured that, if it was me writing it, at least I'd be able to have my say in the narrative about Robert's death. At one point, I even believed you and I could be a great team—you know, if it wasn't for the way we came into each other's lives. I guess...there won't be a memoir after all, will there?"

"Of course, there won't be. Not one written by you, anyway."

"So, I was right? You were only using it as an excuse to get closer to me?"

Corey presses his lips together. "Your version of what happened that day was the only piece of the puzzle I was missing. I've been gathering evidence for months—my private investigator got the security camera footage from the Hilton, where you and your *agent*

301

are seen dragging Robert's body across the lobby, with him dressed like a fucking idiot. We spoke to a taxi driver who said he picked you up at the Plaza and dropped you off at an office building on Sixth Avenue, and to eyewitnesses who told us just how unabashed you were, lugging a seemingly lifeless man around. Even this conversation is being recorded—every single word you've said is on tape."

I nod once. I should've thought of that before I went and spilled the whole truth, but I suppose it doesn't matter either way—not if he already has all the other evidence Stacey and I had feared he would find.

"I knew from the start that the police didn't have the whole story—but the only lead I had was the memory of meeting you that day. I knew you looked familiar, but I couldn't place your face... until I remembered. I own one of your books."

I hold my breath, remembering he told me it was Robert who convinced him to read *The Millers* in the first place.

"I went to the police, of course. Told them I'd figured out the identity of the person who broke into my room the day Robert was found dead, but they were useless. His cause of death had already been established, so they refused to reopen the case. That's when I decided to take matters into my own hands.

"I got in touch with a literary agent and told him I wanted to write a memoir—and that you had to be the ghostwriter. All I wanted was a chance to talk to you, to give you an opportunity to come clean about what had happened between you and Robert— but when you refused to hand over the answers, I had to take things up a notch."

"That's why you hired that private investigator, then? To bully me?"

"Not initially, no. I hired him because I genuinely wanted

answers. But the more evidence he collected, the clearer it became— you were the only one who could give me the explanation I needed. And that was when I realized breaking you was the only way to get you to hand it over."

He has done it. He has broken me. I feel absolutely, irrevocably defeated, and all I can do is hope that he doesn't intend to break me any further. I don't think I'd be able to take it.

"I've spent much of the last few months daydreaming about what I would do to you," Corey says. "At first, I was convinced that I was going to turn everything over to the police—send you to prison for what you did to my husband's body, at the very least, but it didn't feel right. I didn't like the idea of you locked away someplace where I wouldn't be able to witness your suffering."

He turns to look out the window, frowning slightly as he gets lost in thought.

"I'd be lying if I said I haven't enjoyed tormenting you through my private investigator. After a while, I started wondering if having him hurt you would bring me any sense of peace—but the thought of a couple broken legs and some bruising didn't quite cut it."

I shiver involuntarily as I think about two days ago, when his detective chased me down the street. Is that how it would've ended if I hadn't gotten away? With me in the hospital with broken bones?

"Then again, there was the possibility of ruining your career. Watching the whole world turn its back on you, your reputation ruined, everything you've built for yourself canceled and discarded." The corner of his lip twists into a wicked smile. "Or even better—a mix of all three. That might've left me feeling satisfied, wouldn't you think?"

I'm not sure if he's actually expecting me to respond, but I doubt I could get any words out through the knot that has formed in my throat.

"However," he adds, and I inch forward slightly, a voice in my mind blaring like an alarm: *There's a however!* "The person I spent all that time daydreaming about ruining is not quite the person sitting in front of me right now."

"Wh-what do you mean?"

"The version of you I had in my mind was cold and calculating, trying to outsmart me. He was someone who knowingly had an affair with my husband—certainly not this sorry, wretched kid that you are." He lets out a snort. "I allowed myself to get carried away so much in my fantasies that I'd even convinced myself that you might've actually killed him, even though that was the only thing the police were able to confirm with any degree of certainty—that Robert died of a stroke."

"It's true. I…I swear, I didn't kill him."

"That leaves me in an interesting position, doesn't it? To enact revenge against the person I thought you were…or deal differently with the person I know you to be now."

This time, I'm the one who remains motionless. I don't want to nod, or blink, or do anything that might sway his decision in a way that would be unfavorable to me. I may not like the thought of him turning me over to the police and ruining my career, but I can't say I like the sound of being "dealt with differently" much more.

"I suppose…" Corey begins, turning back toward the window, "the reason I started this is because I wanted the truth. I *needed* to know what happened that day." He swallows, his eyes gleaming in the soft light. I never thought he'd be capable of displaying emotion like this. I never imagined him as someone who could allow himself to be vulnerable, but Corey has done nothing if not surprise me today.

"And?" I ask, trying to fill the silence.

"And…hearing the truth from you hasn't changed anything for

me. I still lost my husband. I lost the person I thought he was, and nothing will ever change that, no matter what I do to you." Corey lets out his breath in a trembling sigh. "What you did was awful. I will never understand how anyone could have the gall to treat a dead body like that. And your lack of honesty has caused me many sleepless nights. But...I don't think that ruining your life would help me sleep any better. And it won't make me any happier."

"It...won't?"

"No."

"Are you...sure?"

I almost want to kick myself after asking that last question, but I can't help it. I need to know for a fact that Corey is being honest, that this isn't another part of his twisted games, because I don't think I'd be able to cope with this going on any longer. I need for all this to be over, regardless of how it must end.

Corey seems to have finished saying his piece, because he doesn't answer my question. He continues staring out at the park thoughtfully, not giving any indication that he intends to say anything else.

When he does speak up again, his face and voice are back to normal—firm, strong, emotionless. "You will not go near Piper Gunn or any of my friends ever again," he says, his eyes finding mine once more.

My mind works fast as I think of what that will mean—turning down the follow-up interview on *The Breakfast Show*, always checking to see if a journalist or news anchor has any connection to Corey before agreeing to be interviewed by them, burning bridges with people in the world of media without ever giving them an explanation.

"I can do that," I say. "I promise."

"I don't ever want to see or hear from you again."

"You won't."

"And you will send a copy of your new book to my lawyer. He will read it and decide whether we're okay with it being published or not."

My heart aches. I know exactly what the most likely outcome of this will be—*I'm in Deep Trouble* will probably never see the light of day. I'll have to cancel the contract with Wagner, give back the money they've already paid me, and face the resentment of Jackie and the entire team. I will go back to the beginning, back to being a failed author, back to having no money to pay the bills and no ways to save my publishing dreams.

"Of course."

"Now, get out."

"You mean—"

"Exactly what I said. Out. Now."

I jump from the couch and start moving my heavy legs toward the door. The room feels long all of a sudden—longer than I remember it ever being before. And as I try to close the impossibly large distance between me and the exit, I think of myself in this exact same room, staring at the sparkling lights of the Upper East Side through the window.

I think of Robert's firm hands on me and the look on his face as he said, *You're really something, aren't you?*

I think of the pounding in my chest when I heard a beeping outside the door the next morning, the coldness in Corey's eyes when we first came face-to-face with each other, and the moment I realized Robert wasn't the person he said he was.

And then I think of myself sitting on the couch, barely a few minutes ago, thinking my life was about to end. But it didn't. It won't. Not today, at least. Not now.

The instant my hand closes around the doorknob, a deep sense of relief appears inside my chest, spreading to every corner of my body. I take the elevator down to the lobby and walk quickly by the reception desk, past the sparkling chandelier, and toward the main entrance of the hotel.

I push my way through the revolving doors and stop for a moment on the front steps, feeling the warm sunshine on my skin and breathing in the brisk autumn air.

"Excuse me," a bellboy says to me as he comes up the steps carrying a set of heavy bags, and so I move to the side, searching for my phone inside my pocket.

Stacey answers on the first ring. I imagine she must've been waiting anxiously by the phone, wondering when she would hear from me—or if she ever would.

"David," she says. "Talk to me, darling. What happened?"

"It's okay. It'll all be okay," I say, my voice trembling. "It's finally over."

CHAPTER TWENTY-FOUR

Autumn fades into winter. Winter recedes, spring skips by, and before I know it, I'm waking up on the first Tuesday in June to the feeling of a warm summer breeze sneaking in through an open gap at my window.

It's weird now to look back on the past eight months and feel as though they flew by, because I certainly didn't feel that way when I was living them. Time does that sometimes, I suppose—it's slow until it isn't.

I've spent all these months fearing that today would never come—the release day of *I'm in Deep Trouble*. Even yesterday, I was calling Stacey every few hours, asking if she'd heard anything, whether there were any last-minute roadblocks, and she assured me about a million times that everything was proceeding as planned.

I throw the covers off and reach for my phone. It's barely past eight, but there are already over a hundred notifications waiting on the screen—people congratulating me, or tagging me in photos on Instagram, or posting videos about the book on TikTok.

I don't look at any of it. I'll need to like all the posts and thank all the people who are showing their support, but now is not the time. I plant my feet on the ground and head straight for the closet to get dressed.

The sun is shining today. It's one of those perfect early summer days, where the sky is a deep blue and the temperature is just right. I pick up a coffee from the deli and head straight to Central Park, sipping on my cup, twisting and turning with the paths, and while I do, I think about last fall, when I was working on the manuscript.

I can't help but miss those days. It's illogical, really, because I don't miss the stress or the anxiety of Corey closing in on me. I do, however, miss those long evenings of sitting on park benches with a notebook or my laptop balanced on my legs. I miss the days I spent holed up inside my apartment, writing tirelessly, and I miss the comfort that this story gave me when I needed it the most. I wish it could've remained mine and mine alone. I wish I could've protected it, nourished it, and kept it close to my heart, but I suppose there's no use in telling a story if there's no one there to listen to it. And as of today, it no longer belongs to me. It belongs to anyone who reads it.

I walk all the way down to the lower end of the park and exit at Central Park South. This is when my day truly begins. I have a list of bookshops around the city that I want to go to before five p.m., which is when I'll need to head back home to get ready for my launch event tonight.

As I make my way into the first shop—the Barnes & Noble at the corner of Fifth Avenue and 46th Street—I'm reminded of the day *The Millers* came out, when there was a stack of copies adorning one of the store windows. I also think about the day *Walking Home* was released, before I knew just how bad the reviews and how terrible the sales numbers would be, when I stepped into this same store to find an entire table devoted to me and my books.

This time around, there's none of that, but there is something better: a deep sense of peace as I walk around the store, trying to find the new releases section. I'm not nervous about sales numbers, or reviews, or praise. All I want is to see it on shelves and enjoy this one day, because the simple fact that my third novel is out in the world feels like my wildest dream come true—one I spent the last two years worrying wouldn't happen.

When I find a stack of my new book neatly placed on a shelf, among all the other new releases for the week, I nearly start crying. The cover is bold and pink, and it shows the main character looking at us over his shoulder. He looks innocent yet anxious, and there's a bone-chilling gleam in his eyes that suggests he's keeping secrets. A perfect cover, if you ask me.

"Hi," I say to a bookseller—Amy, according to a tag on her shirt. "I—I wrote this book, and I'd love to sign the stock."

She smiles immediately. "Amazing!" she says. "Hold on. Let me get you a Sharpie."

"No need," I reply. "I brought a few of my own."

Amy helps me as I sign all the copies, and before I leave the store, she thanks me a million times for stopping by. I thank her a million times in return, and then I'm on my way to the next bookshop.

I keep an eye on my phone the whole day—not just because it keeps lighting up with new notifications, but also because there's still a slight fear in the back of my mind that Corey Donovan might try to sabotage the release somehow. I never heard back from him, even though I sent his lawyer a copy of the manuscript, exactly as he asked me to. I wonder if he chose his own peace—if he chose to erase me from his memory and pretend I don't even exist—or if he was somehow able to see the book for what it is: a story that's not truly about Robert, but about me trying to make sense of myself and all the mistakes I've made.

It isn't until I'm making my way to one last store, exhausted after running around the city the whole day, that I look down at my phone and see a notification that makes my legs stop working. A text—not from Corey, not from his lawyer, and not from anyone in the publishing world.

It's from Jeremy.

Hey. Congratulations on the new book. I came across this
yesterday.

A photo pops up a second later—one of the promo posters my
publisher made, which shows all the details for the launch party
tonight.

I'd love to come, Jeremy says. But first I wanted to check if you'd
be okay with that.

I'm in the heart of SoHo. There are people moving all around
me and cars driving down the street, and the noise and movement
are starting to feel like too much.

I wish I could shut it all out—quiet my brain for a moment so I
can think clearly. *What do I say? Do I even want Jeremy there? Would
his presence make me feel supported or distracted?*

The answer comes to me suddenly. Yes, I write back with shaking hands. I'd love to see you there.

Amazing, he replies. Can't wait to celebrate you and your book.

I remain frozen on the sidewalk for the longest time, rereading
his texts. At some point, I look down at the time and realize I'll
need to head home soon.

I turn around and start making my way toward the subway. I'll
go to all the bookstores left on my list later this week, but for now,
I need to shower, change, and fix myself up. I need to get ready for
my event, and now I have a reason to make sure I look extra good
for it.

The bookstore is packed. All the chairs are taken, and a few people are still trickling in through the door in the back, searching for
places to stand along the edges of the room.

Granted, it's a small bookstore—nothing like the huge event

spaces I used to fill up when I was promoting my first book—but this is everything I'd hoped for and more. The mere thought that all these people took time out of their Tuesday evening to come hear me speak is enough to bring tears to my eyes—tears that I have to swallow back, because the event is about to start.

"Welcome, everyone," the bookstore manager says into a microphone, and the chatter of the crowd dies down. "I'm so happy to introduce to you David Alvarez, who is here tonight to present his latest book. Also joining us is bestselling author Oliver Baumann, who will be leading the conversation today. Oliver, please take it away."

Oliver is an old author friend who debuted the same year as I did. Unlike me, he hasn't had any of his books flop, and his career has been on an upward trajectory from the start. Most recently, he announced a big movie deal for his latest novel, which came out only a couple of months ago. Still, when I asked him if he'd be willing to join me on stage for my book launch, he was kind enough to agree.

"Thank you very much," he says. He has a strong, deep voice, and sleek blond hair that makes him look more like a model than an author. Some people really are God's favorites, aren't they? "David, it's such a pleasure to be here with you tonight. How do you feel?"

I look out at the crowd as I consider my answer. Stacey is in the front row, sitting right beside Jackie, Emma, and other folks from my publishing team. There are several faces I recognize—readers, librarians, and booksellers who were there when my first two books came out and who have somehow decided to give me another chance. My dad is sitting somewhere in the middle next to Sheila, and several fellow authors came to show their support. There is no sign of Jeremy—not that I can see, at least.

"I feel good," I say. "Really good, actually."

Oliver's first few questions are easy enough to answer—the inspiration behind the book, some of the most important themes, my favorite scene. But then he asks about Daniel, the main character, and all of a sudden my heart is beating fast.

"I found it somewhat funny—Daniel, David. They're similar enough names," Oliver says. "Was that intentional? Did you set out to write a character who was similar to you?"

"Well...yes," I answer. From the corner of my eye, I see the door of the bookstore swing open, and I look up to see Jeremy stepping inside. He must've come straight from work, because he's wearing his suit and tie, and he looks slightly embarrassed to be late as he takes a spot among all the other onlookers. "Every single main character I write is a reflection of me, in one way or another. But this one was different."

"How so?"

"There are things about Daniel that I unconsciously put on the page. It was only recently, when I was rereading the final version of the manuscript, that I realized just how similar his life is to mine. And how much our journeys intersect."

Oliver uncrosses his legs. "What do you mean, exactly?"

"Well...in the book, Daniel is the product of a world that has never allowed him to be complete in the first place. Some of it has to do with the fact that he's gay—so many gay people grow up pretending to be versions of themselves that don't really exist, which leaves us struggling to figure out who we really are later down the line. But some of it has to do with other circumstances—growing up without an adequate support system, without access to positive role models. So...once he reaches his twenties, he doesn't know how to move through the world, except by pretending to be someone he's not. Every first date he goes on, every new friend he makes, every friendly encounter at a bar he has, he's forced to play the role of someone confident, someone fun, someone who's not in crisis."

I look out at the crowd. Everyone is attentive, patiently listening to me.

"At the start of the story, Daniel is aware of his brokenness, but he doesn't understand it. Once he finds himself in a life-and-death situation, though, he has to peel back all the layers and figure out who he is and what actually matters to him. And…my life over the past few months has been about all that. In some ways, this character saved me."

For the longest time, there's silence. It could simply be that Oliver is waiting to see if I want to add final thoughts to my answer, but he doesn't reach for his microphone, doesn't make a move to speak.

"This is meant to be a fun night, though," I say, and a few people let out small laughs.

Oliver smiles. "It is, indeed," he says, shifting in his chair. "So, David, in the interest of fun, why don't we move on to some questions from the audience?"

This is my favorite part of any event. Slowly but surely, people start raising their hands, asking questions about the story, the characters, and my writing process. And while I answer, I feel happier than I have in months—or years, maybe—because this connection, between me and readers who understand what I'm trying to say in my books, is real.

This is one of the few relationships in my life where I can truly come as myself, where I feel seen and understood, and the one that matters most.

"You've done it, darling. You were brilliant," Stacey says to me once we're standing in a corner of the bookshop, finally getting a moment to ourselves.

People have been coming up to me nonstop to offer their congratulations, to ask questions they didn't get to ask during the

Q&A, or to get their copies signed. The whole while, I've kept an eye on three people: my dad, who snuck away with Sheila a while ago, saying they needed to head back to New Jersey before it got too late; Stacey, who's been smiling proudly at me all night; and Jeremy, who's been keeping a careful distance while he waits for his own chance to come talk to me.

"What did you think about the turnout?" I ask.

"Solid enough. I told you people would show up, didn't I?" Stacey throws a glance at the back of the store. "I heard the manager say they've sold nearly two hundred copies today alone. I'm not saying we should be hopeful for bestseller lists, but . . . who knows, dear. Maybe we'll have something to celebrate next week."

"I'd almost prefer not hitting the lists."

"Really?" She narrows her eyes at me. "Why is that?"

"You said it to me back then—that you wanted one final success before you retired. Maybe, if this book doesn't take off in the way we hoped, you'll have a reason to stick around a bit longer."

"David," Stacey says, leaning closer to me, "I may have spoken too soon when I said those things."

My heart skips a beat. "You're not gonna retire, then?"

"I will, one day. But there are many stories yet to be discovered, don't you think? Many books yet to be published."

She smiles at me, and I smile back. Somehow, the news that she won't be leaving the industry is the best thing that has happened today. I haven't fully settled on a concept for my fourth novel— let's just say the romance idea died after the whole private detective debacle—but knowing Stacey will be there to help me bring it into the world is all the inspiration I need to start working on it.

"It seems as though someone has been eager to talk to you," Stacey says, sneaking a glance over at Jeremy, who's still standing in a corner holding an empty wineglass in one hand and a copy of the book in the other. "I won't take up any more of your time. But why don't we do dinner later this week?"

"Sounds good."

She makes a move to walk away, but before she has a chance to go too far, I pull her in for a hug. Her arms remain very stiff for a second, but then she places them gently on my back.

"Thank you, Stacey," I whisper in her ear. "I couldn't have done any of this without you."

"You could have, darling. Though perhaps it would've been a bit less of an adventure."

When my eyes fall on Jeremy again, he's looking right at me. And by the time Stacey steps away, he's already halfway across the store, making his move before anyone else has a chance to steal my attention.

"Hi," he says.

"Hi," I say.

"Sorry I was late. I tried to—"

"It's okay. I'm glad you made it."

"Congratulations, David."

"Thank you."

We stand in front of each other for a minute, looking into the other's eyes while an uncertainty of what to do or say next floats around us. After waiting for me for over an hour, I thought he'd have planned what he wanted to say, but it doesn't seem like he did at all.

"Can I, uh...get my copy signed?" he asks, lifting up the book he's holding.

"Of course," I say, a smile spreading effortlessly across my face. "Who should I make it out to?"

It's my attempt at a joke, at relieving the tension, and it miraculously works. Jeremy laughs.

"The name's Jeremy," he says, his eyes sparkling in the soft light.

I sign his book, and as he takes it back from me, our hands brush gently.

"How is—"

"Listen, I was thinking," he says. "Would you want to go grab dinner? Or drinks? I just...wanted to celebrate with you, unless you have other—"

"I have no plans," I answer quickly. "But...won't that be weird? I mean, did you tell Julián that you were—"

"We're no longer seeing each other."

"Oh."

"Yeah. We...broke things off a few months ago. I thought I'd mentioned it to you, but...I guess I hadn't."

"No. You hadn't." I'm certain of it. We haven't talked at all lately, and our game of transferring the money back and forth fizzled out a while ago. I forget whose account it ended up in. It may have been mine.

"So?" he asks, raising an eyebrow. "Dinner?"

"Sure. Let me just go say goodbye to some people."

The restaurant Jeremy picks is on the Upper West Side, not far from my apartment. It's a tiny, intimate spot with small tables and dim lighting—more the kind of place you'd go to on a date, rather than a book release celebration.

"Get whatever you want," he says while we're looking through the menu. "This one's on me."

"We can split the bill. I'm good for money now." More than good, actually. I received the second payment months ago, when Jackie accepted the final draft of the book, and the last payment is due on publication, which means the rest of the money should be in my account within the next few days.

The waiter comes, we order, and then we're silent again—but

317

this silence feels very different from the one we shared back at the bookstore. There's no nervousness, no wariness, no hesitation. It's the kind of silence that feels easy, comforting—the kind that only two people who know and love each other can share.

"I'm proud of you," Jeremy says. "I wish I could make you see just how much."

I smile at him. "Thank you."

"Hearing you speak back there was just...amazing. I mean that. I'm so happy to see how far you've come."

"Thanks. It hasn't been easy."

"I know it hasn't been. And, David...I wasn't sure how to bring this up, but I've been thinking about it all night. I owe you an apology."

I frown. "For what?"

"For not being there for you as I should have been. For giving up on us. I hate the fact that I hurt you, and I am so—"

"Jeremy," I say softly. "You don't have to be sorry."

"But I do. It's—"

"You were trying your best. You did what you had to do to survive. I could never blame you for that." I take a deep breath. "Besides, it's been two years since the breakup. I'd like to think we're different people now."

"Yeah," he says, nodding. "I think we are."

My heart soars as I think about what that could mean—that we may just be stronger now, and better, and willing to try again. That despite all the time and the distance, we have found our way back to each other, just as I always hoped we would.

"I want to hear about you," I say. "I mean, I know tonight is technically about me, but..."

"What do you want to hear?"

"Anything."

He leans forward, setting his hands over the table. "Life's going well," he says. "Work's been good lately. I spoke with a different firm last week, and they made an offer—same title, more money— but I think I'm going to say no."

"Why?"

"I'm happy where I am," he says, shrugging a little. "My new apartment is great. Been seeing my family a lot. I've even made some new friends. The only thing I've been missing is, well..."

I hold my breath, waiting for him to finish his sentence, hoping he'll say: *you.*

"Someone to be with," he says instead. "You know?"

"Yeah. I get that," I reply, not staring directly at him. An instant later, though, my stomach lurches in a way that reveals to me I'm not being entirely honest. I clear my throat and try again: "Or, actually...I'm not sure I do."

Jeremy tilts his head slightly. "You don't?"

I press my lips together, staring into his warm blue eyes. There's sadness in them all of a sudden, and I wish more than anything that I could make it go away, but I don't know how. I don't know what I'm meant to do, other than tell the truth.

"I haven't been thinking about relationships lately—not really."

"How come?"

"I'm not sure. I guess there have been other things on my mind."

I've spent the last eight months thinking about Corey Donovan, yes, and whether he or his lawyer were ever going to contact me again. But mostly, I've been dreaming about this day—about walking into stores to find my book on shelves, about sharing this story with readers, about sitting on a stage and talking about my craft.

"It's all gonna be very different with this new book," I say. "It won't be like before, when *The Millers* or *Walking Home* came out, and I felt like the fear of failure was...like a shadow, threatening to swallow me whole."

Jeremy's brow wrinkles slightly. His eyes glaze over, and I can tell he's remembering, remembering, remembering—the way I shattered under the pressure back then, the way I became someone who was completely unrecognizable from the guy he'd fallen in love with, the way I was burning at both ends.

"That's good," he says in a small voice. "I can tell you're happier now."

We sit in silence for a while, breathing calmly. Some of the hope from earlier is still lingering in the air. Perhaps the new versions of us who are sitting here tonight really are a better fit for each other. Perhaps this is truly the beginning of something. Perhaps Jeremy will reach for my hand, and I will reach for his, and we'll realize that we're finally ready to give it another try, and never let go of each other again.

But then, when Jeremy lets out his breath in a trembling sigh, all of that seems to vanish, leaving behind nothing but the soft hum of other people eating and talking around us.

"You're not ready, are you?"

I look down at the tablecloth. I know exactly what he's asking—whether I'm in a place that would allow me to refocus my energy toward rebuilding what we once had. Whether I'd be able to put all of me into our relationship the way he would want me to. Whether I could hand over all the trust and hope I've spent the last two years trying to recover.

"I'm not sure," I say in a mere whisper.

Something protests inside my chest—it's as if my heart is trying to break free from its cage, scolding me for not taking this opportunity, trying to remind me of how many nights I've spent desperately wishing to get back together with Jeremy.

"What does that mean?" he asks.

"It's just…" I begin, but my voice loses its strength before I finish my sentence. Without meeting his eyes, I make another attempt: "There are things I need to focus on first."

"Like what?"

"I don't know if I can explain it."

"Try," he says. "Please. Just … try."

I remain silent for a moment, searching for the right words. When they don't come, I draw in a deep breath and do exactly what he asked: I try.

"Over the past few months, I've learned a lot about myself," I begin. "And, I guess … one of the things I've realized is that people are … well, like houses, almost."

Jeremy frowns. "Houses?" For a moment, I fear I've lost him. He looks concerned, wary, almost as if he suspected me of being drunk.

"Yes, houses," I reply. "We need foundations. We need … a solid platform, on top of which we can build. One you can return to if everything else goes to shit. I mean, just think about your family."

He nods slowly. He's one of the lucky ones—one of those people who gets to have a tight-knit, supportive family. He lost his dad a few years ago, but he still has his mom, and his brothers, and his nephews—people who will always be there for him. People who will forever be willing to put him before anything else.

"Or think about your friends," I say, and a second flash of recognition crosses Jeremy's face. He's also one of the lucky ones in that sense. Having remained in the same city his whole life, except for a few years in college, he's had the opportunity to build lasting connections. On any given weekend, he has the option of hanging out with different groups—his childhood friends, his Yale friends, or his work friends, many of whom came close to becoming my own friends while we were dating.

"For me, my foundation is writing. It's the place I run to. Whether I like it or not, it's what makes me feel safe, and without it, I'm…lost, really. I think that's why everything went wrong after *Walking Home* came out. That part of my life was crumbling, and it's taken me a long time to rebuild it."

"Well, have you?" Jeremy asks, lifting his chin slightly. "Rebuilt it?"

"For the most part," I say. "But that's the thing…it's all very fresh still. After *Walking Home* came out, and you and I broke up, I had no one and nothing to turn to. Not even my own stories. And I don't ever want to be in that position again. Maybe I need to spend more time with myself, and understand how different pieces of my life fit together, and make sure everything is stable enough before I let anyone else in. And I know maybe none of this makes sense to you, but I—"

"It does," he says softly. "You're forgetting that I know you better than anyone, David. Or I used to, anyway. I *know* how important your writing is to you, but I just wish…"

"What?"

"I wish you'd allow *me* to be there for you. Maybe that's what the problem was before—when things weren't working out with your publishing dreams, you wouldn't let me lift you back up. You wouldn't let me become your foundation."

He's not wrong. *It would do you well to stop believing the lies you tell yourself,* my father said, and I've spent the last eight months trying to listen to him—asking myself why I've spent so much time feeling alone, when I've also been guilty of pushing people away. Trying to understand why I've let myself believe romance wasn't meant for me, even though it was me who couldn't fully let in the one person who went out of his way to love me. Perhaps that's why I need time. Time to grow, time to understand, time to become someone new—someone better than I was.

"Will there ever be space for me?" Jeremy asks. "In your life, in your mind—will there ever be room for me again?"

"That's what I want," I answer. "More than anything."

I wish that I could give him more than this—that I could assure Jeremy that I will always make room for him. I wish I could convince him that the relationship between my writing and my publishing dreams is going to be much healthier from now on, and that I will never again let anything get in the way of me and him. I just can't bring myself to make any promises to him out loud.

"One day, I'll be able to let you in again. I know it for a fact," I say. "But it might not be tonight. It might not be tomorrow, or even next month."

Jeremy nods, his eyes catching the reflection of one of the lights overhead. "Maybe one day, then."

We allow those words to float between us. *Maybe one day.* And God, do I want that day to come. But until it does, we'll have this moment to hold on to—the coziness of the restaurant, the feeling of our legs brushing under the table, and the possibility that the life we long for by each other's side is possible and will become a reality. One day.

The air is warm when we step out of the restaurant. The sky is dark, but the street is glowing in the soft, yellowish light of windows and streetlamps.

"Congratulations again, David," Jeremy says, turning toward me.

"Thanks."

We stand in front of each other, our arms hanging limply by our sides. There doesn't seem to be anything left to say, anything left to do except close the distance between us and hug.

His arms around me feel warm, familiar, and safe. Somewhere in the back of my mind, I realize how badly I wish I could remain here forever, but when he takes a step back, I do the same. A deep sadness floods my chest as the moment ends, but then he leans forward and presses his lips against mine.

We kiss gently, tenderly, the way we used to when one of us was feeling down, or when we were cuddled under a blanket on the couch during cold winter nights, or when we were so exhausted that a good night kiss was all we could offer each other. And just like that, everything makes sense again: The person I was, the person I want to be. The good things I can't wait to get back, and the bad things I want to leave behind. The darkness that I'm trying so hard to move on from, and the sweetness that I know I'm capable of finding in the world around me.

It is there, with his lips still on mine, that I start to cry. I don't want him to notice, so I remove my mouth from his and hug him instead, big, hot tears dripping onto his shirt as I try not to make a sound. Breathing in the scent of his cologne, I wonder if I should take it all back. I want to tell him that all we have is today, that we shouldn't waste any more time before giving this thing another try, that I will go to the ends of the earth to give him what he needs.

But I don't. I only keep hugging him, trying to etch this moment into my memory.

"I love you, David," he whispers in my ear. "I always have."

"I love you, too," I say. "I always will."

We let go of each other, and Jeremy throws me one last smile, wiping a single tear from my cheek before turning around and walking away, in the direction of the park. I remain frozen on the spot until he rounds a corner and disappears from view, and then I start walking home.

We must've been in the restaurant longer than I thought. It's nearing midnight, and the streets are deserted. The tears have stopped, but there's still something hurting deep inside of me. There are unspoken words in my chest weighing me down, long sentences I wish I had said, millions of feelings I should have translated into language. A tinge of regret appears in the bottom of my stomach as I sneak a glance over my shoulder at the empty street behind me, but then I start thinking about getting home, sitting at my desk, and writing down all these emotions. I start thinking of all the pages I'm going to fill, the things I'm going to do, and the stories I'm going to tell, and everything starts to feel okay again.

As for *this* story, well…I guess this is as far as it goes. If you've been with me this whole time, I'm sorry I couldn't give you a happier ending. I'm sorry I couldn't be the person you may have thought I should be—one who's cute, and wholesome, and wise, and who never fucks up.

I'm sorry to disappoint, but that's not me. This is me: imperfect, and hopeful, and anxious, and insecure, and trying his best to be happy, but sometimes not.

And that's okay.

I'm okay.

Are *you* okay? Because I definitely am. I promise.

ACKNOWLEDGMENTS

Working on this book has been one of the most joyful, fulfilling experiences of my writing career so far—which was somewhat unexpected, since the initial inspiration for the story came from feelings of loneliness and disappointment. *I Might Be in Trouble* has served as a much-needed reminder for myself that amazing things can come out of less-than-ideal ones, if only we're willing to look at life through a different lens.

First, I must thank you (yes, you! The person reading this!). It is because of your willingness to pick up this book that I get to do what I love most in the world, so I am eternally indebted to you. And if you've ever felt isolated or left behind in any way, I hope David's story has helped you feel just a little less alone.

I'm incredibly grateful to my literary agent, Pete Knapp, whose initial response after reading this novel was an enthusiastic, resounding: "Yes!" I still can't believe how fortunate I am to be working with one of the best agents in the industry, and I'm so excited for us to keep bringing books to the world together. Thank you to Jerome Murphy for your sharp editorial eye, and to Stuti Telidevara for all the assistance you've provided. To everyone else at Park & Fine: You're all a classy bunch. Thanks for everything you do.

My wonderful editor, Rachael Kelly, believed in me and David from the moment the manuscript landed on her desk. Rachael, I

ACKNOWLEDGMENTS

couldn't be more thankful for all the enthusiasm, passion, and care you've shown for this story. To Ben Sevier, Karen Kosztolnyik, Andy Dodds, Theresa DeLucci, Kamrun Nesa, Leena Oropez, Anjuli Johnson, Albert Tang, Maddie Caldwell, and all the other amazing folks at Grand Central Publishing who have helped bring this book into the world: thank you, thank you, thank you.

Claire Wilson, my literary agent in the UK, I am so grateful for everything you have done to champion this story. Thank you also to Safae El-Ouahabi and the team at RCW.

To my incredible film agent, Mary Pender-Coplan, and the entire team at UTA: I feel so lucky to have you in my corner.

I'd love to pretend that I wrote this novel in a single, happy burst of inspiration, and that the process was as smooth as can be, but the truth is that I couldn't have done it without the support of Conor McDermott. Thank you for being there to provide encouragement and reassurance when I needed it, and for your unwavering belief in this book.

To my friends (you know who you are): thank you for making life fun. Jacky Carrasco and Paulina Reynoso, I know there's debate about who has actually been my friend the longest, so I'll refer to you both as my "oldest friends": thank you for being there through the years and decades. Growing older is so much more joyful knowing you're by my side.

Finally, I have to express the most heartfelt gratitude to the people who have shown enthusiasm for my first two books. If you have read, reviewed, or shared *Indivisible* or *Brighter Than the Sun*, and you've chosen to come with me on the wild ride that is *I Might Be in Trouble*, please know your support means everything to me. I promise to continue creating stories for you.

ABOUT THE AUTHOR

Daniel Aleman is the award-winning author of *Indivisible* (Little, Brown Books for Young Readers), which received starred reviews from *Booklist* and *Publishers Weekly*, was a winner of the Tomás Rivera Book Award, was selected as a "Top 10 First Novels for Youth 2021" by ALA Booklist, was named one of the Best Books of 2021 by the Chicago Public Library, and was called "deeply moving" by Jodi Picoult. His second YA novel, *Brighter Than the Sun*, was also published with Little, Brown Books for Young Readers in March 2023. Aleman was born and raised in Mexico City. A graduate of McGill University, he is passionate about books, coffee, and Mexican food.